# THE
# LONG
## OF
# LONE
# WOLVES

# THE
# LONGING
## OF
# LONE
# WOLVES

### A FAE GUARDIANS NOVEL

# LANA PECHERCZYK

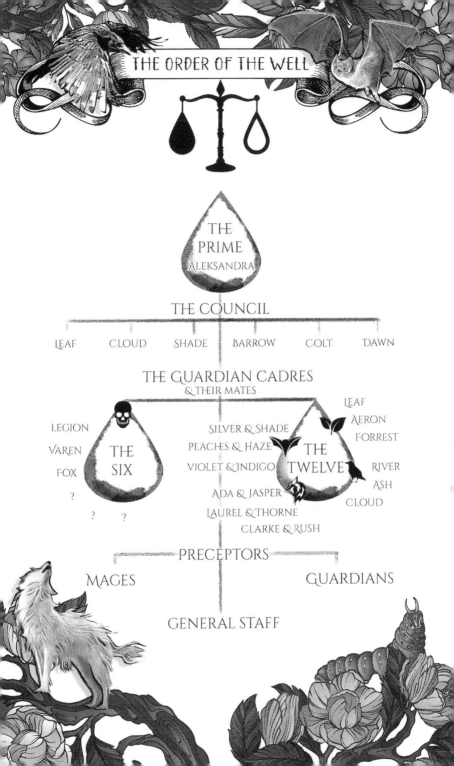

# THE ORDER OF THE WELL

## THE PRIME
ALEKSANDRA

## THE COUNCIL

LEAF    CLOUD    SHADE    BARROW    COLT    DAWN

## THE GUARDIAN CADRES
& THEIR MATES

LEGION
VAREN
FOX
?

### THE SIX

?    ?

SILVER & SHADE
PEACHES & HAZE
VIOLET & INDIGO
ADA & JASPER
LAUREL & THORNE
CLARKE & RUSH

### THE TWELVE

LEAF
AERON
FORREST
RIVER
ASH
CLOUD

## PRECEPTORS

MAGES          GUARDIANS

## GENERAL STAFF

Clarke O'Leary woke up yawning. Then the tang of sulfur burned her nose and she sneezed, jolting with a splash.

A splash?

She opened her eyes and blinked until everything came into focus. She lay in shallow warm water. Icy air bit her nose. Tall snow-tipped fir trees crowded her on one side, and on the other, clear blue sky. *Blue* sky. The shock of it slammed through her.

*Where the hell am I?*

Because it wasn't Vegas. At least not the one she knew with the scorched sky and nuclear winter. *That* Vegas had been quarantined, half-underground and isolated in the futile hope of avoiding radiation drifting across the continent.

Clarke jackknifed up and grasped her head at the giddy

onslaught. Her stomach revolted and she leaned to the side to vomit something thick, dark and sluggish. *Gross.* Moving her eyes hurt. God, everything hurt.

Shifting away from her mess, her fingers hit something rough underwater. Smooth and curved. She pulled out an oxidized Coke can. The letter "C" had been carved into the aluminum. It was just like the can she had drunk from last night... but old. And in water. In the middle of nowhere.

A growing sense of doom settled in her stomach. She noticed more odd things. The metal on her watch had deteriorated and a network of rust covered her bracelet's brittle charms. She fumbled about the shore, searching for more evidence of... of what, she wasn't sure... but all she came across was more mud, more strange sulfur smelling water, and more throat-tightening panic.

Where was she?

Why was she there?

She jammed the heels of her palms into her eye sockets.

*Calm down, Clarke. Think.*

Scrambling back in time, she tried to conjure the last thing she remembered—the long sleep, waking in water—but her brain was as sluggish as the surrounding lake. Tiny warm waves lapped against her legs in a soothing way, as if to say, "It's okay. Don't stress. You are where you're meant to be."

*Think.*

She had to reach further back than that. Back to *before* the sleep. To yesterday. To the end of the world.

She had been in a one room apartment, watching apocalyptic news on a tiny television, drinking soda with two girlfriends—Ada and Laurel—wondering if it would be her last. *Knowing* it would be her last. The memory solidified in her mind. Laurel wouldn't stop switching channels, looking for more up-to-date news. Ada had paced beside the couch. And Clarke had scratched her initials into the Coke can. But that was yesterday... wasn't it?

Chilly air brushed her face and nipped at her skin. This wasn't her apartment. And she wasn't in war-torn Vegas. But she was alive.

Clarke checked down the shore. The lake stretched for miles. She glimpsed a cabin hiding in the snow-capped fir trees some distance away. Smoke curled from the chimney until it disappeared in a lazy dance. It looked like something out of a fairytale.

But this was real. Down in the water, her reflection still belonged to the same freckle-faced redheaded grifter. Flushed cheeks. Fever-bright blue eyes. Purple lips and chattering teeth despite the warm water. It was her, Clarke O'Leary, petty thief. Sometimes psychic, sometimes fake. Always a dreamer.

*Think, Clarke. Breathe.* Remember.

The world had gone crazy. She'd just come home from the casino. With her precognition skills, she could usually feel out when the cards would play her way. Usually. But this particular night, she'd gone home early. The casino had been closed.

*Why had the casino been closed?*

Because of the war. They'd thought they were safe, that the bombs hadn't hit Vegas, but it was the fallout they should have worried about. The war came for everyone, and for those it missed, the scorched sky took care of them. Weather patterns changed. Crops wouldn't grow. Nuclear plants went into meltdown. Around the world tectonic plate movements tore buildings down as the land shifted. They'd tried to continue with normal life for as long as possible, hoping they'd be safe. Until they weren't.

A wave drew back from her legs like a blanket, exposing threadbare jeans and previously white tennis shoes, now brown and full of holes. She tapped her watch. Dead. Her rusty charm bracelet tinkled, and the matching earrings rocked at her ears. Her father had given her the jewelry. A gift for every important event in her life. A candle charm for her sweet sixteenth. An ice-cream charm for her graduation. The watch when her mother walked out on them. Her father had died just before her eighteenth birthday. Heart attack.

But that was years ago. She shook off the memories and picked at her disintegrating clothes. If this was the outfit she wore yesterday, then why was it falling apart? Why was her bracelet so rusted? And the weird vomit...

Something landed on her lashes and she blinked. Another thing got in her eye. She pushed wet hair from her cheek and trapped it around her ear. The unmistakable flurry of snow floated down to dust her face. Wonder warmed her, and then the memory hit.

She'd stepped outside the apartment because it had been snowing. In Vegas. That was the last thing she remembered.

# TWO

F ifty years of hunting rogue humans had brought Rush to this—peeping at a woman while she bathed in the hot springs of a lake. *His* lake. He scrubbed his face at the absurdity and stepped out of the forest to see better, but couldn't keep the scorn from his mind. Him, an ex-Guardian, leering like a teenager.

"What do you think," he grumbled to the gray wolf next to him. "Does she look good enough to eat?"

For much of the past decade, the scrappy old wolf had been Rush's constant companion. Him and his pack of snow wolves currently hunting in the surrounding forest. Even though Rush had not shifted into wolf form for decades, the locals still scented him as a kindred spirit and bowed to his energy.

Rush winced. He may not be with the original Nightstalk family, but he'd made a new family. A new pack.

Gray growled and licked his teeth, eyes never leaving the woman, his prize. *Their* prize. Rush's curse forbade him to touch another living being, but the wolf at his side was free. The pack helped Rush hunt wayward humans roving into their territory. They were how Rush continued to keep the realm of Elphyne safe, even if his job as a Guardian was finished.

The woman had overlong russet hair. Pale, creamy skin. A delicate neck that drew the eye down to plump breasts stretching her top. She was a beauty like no other, but she would forever be out of reach for someone like him. He tugged at the neck of his fur-lined cape. Despite the snow surrounding him, he cooked.

"Possibly a nymph, playing in the water?" he murmured.

Gray snorted.

Maybe.

She couldn't see Rush. No one could. The curse took care of that too. So he studied her openly.

She wore strange tattered clothes in a fashion he'd not seen before. Rush had traveled all over Elphyne, even beyond into the forbidden Crystal City where humans killed fae on sight... if they'd been able to see him. But this woman, her clothes were strange. She tugged at her shoes.

A snarl ripped from his throat as a shard of light hit his eyes.

"Metal," he hissed to Gray. "She's wearing metal on her wrist."

His hand moved to his belt and hovered over the bone knife, still bloody from his recent hunt. The knife almost sang as his palm hit the hilt. It wanted out again, and when the woman tucked long red hair behind a small round ear, Rush gave the knife what it wanted. He pulled it out.

*She's human.*

Through clenched teeth, he ordered Gray, "Go back to the pack. Wait for the word."

Gray snuffled in protest.

Damn it. He should have brought his sword *Starcleaver*. At least with that, he'd have less of a chance at touching her and triggering the pain that came with the curse. Another order was on the tip of his tongue, and then movement near the lake caught his attention. Multiple bodies crept toward the woman from the sides. Two, three... six. Six fae. And—Rush sniffed the air with a throaty snarl—someone he hated more than anything in the world. Thaddeus. His uncle. And now alpha of the Crescent Hollow wolf-shifter pack.

CHAPTER

# THREE

T he howl of a wolf snapped Clarke's attention to the shadows of the woods. The hairs on her arms lifted. She crawled out further onto the bank, leaving the warm water behind. A feeling wrapped around her chest. The familiar buzzing of premonition. And then... *caution*. Someone or something watched from the darkness of the woods. The sense of it creeped up her spine and then *she knew*. Something was hunting her. It was the same as all her premonitions. Good or bad, the sensation she felt in the square of her chest predicted her own future when she saw everyone else's in full color motion pictures.

Another howl.

Breath caught in her throat, her pulse picked up speed, and she squinted to scan the area for the source of danger.

She found it.

But not in the woods as she'd thought. Crouching, hostile shadows closed in on her. Two, maybe three from each side. To the right, muscular men with long, white hair crept toward her. Others encroached from the left. The buzzing in her chest grated with slick bad vibes, just like it had every time Clarke had been around an evil person in her past. These men fit the mold. All of them held weapons —swords, axes, hammers. None were metal, but still looked dangerously fierce. Wooden handles with creamy white blades. She swallowed. Bone. They were made from bone.

Run.

*Run!*

The only escape was the forest ahead. Ignoring the protest of her stiff body, she bolted. Her feet flew across the sodden shore. Hair whipped behind her, and the wind whispered in its place. *"Run faster. They're coming for you. They'll eat you alive. Run."*

And then she heard it.

Thudding footsteps behind her. Every step, every clouded breath, was echoed by a deeper, heavier one. Guttural. Powerful. Getting closer. Closer. Almost... Terror filled her, gushing from within. Something brushed against her back, causing her to stagger. She let out a scream. Her cry shook the trees and echoed across the water. Birds took to the air in fright.

A hit between her shoulder blades blasted air from her lungs. She launched forward onto hard snow, only inches from the forest's edge. Hidden sharp things dug into her cold palms as she slid across the ground like she was on a sled. Her hands hit something smooth under the snow and she tried to grasp it, but couldn't gain purchase. When she stopped, what she saw beneath the snow didn't make sense. The familiar pattern printed on shiny perspex didn't belong here. Red. Yellow. Blue. White. It couldn't be. But it was. One second, that's all it took, and then her brain clicked. She'd fallen on the *Welcome to Las Vegas Sign*, cracked and deteriorated.

Old.

Ancient.

Something heavy landed on her back and jarred her out of her shock. It pressed down with a beastly warning snarl that breathed heat on her neck. Her face squashed into the sign until her nose hurt. She whimpered, struggling and bucking frantically, but the thing on her back was too heavy, too strong. And then she felt it snuffling into her wet hair, breathing her scent in. Clarke froze, petrified. *What the hell?*

Something soft yet rough explored the ridge of her curved ear, running from top to bottom. Outraged, she pushed the last of her stamina into her limbs, but she only convulsed beneath the immense pressure. She hit her chin. Dizziness blurred her vision.

A deep male voice bloomed hot in her ear. "Don't move, filthy human."

*A man. Not a monster. Men were made of flesh and blood,*

*not beings of terror and dreams.* Men could be fought. Men could be defeated.

"I should kill you right now," he said and pressed something cold and hard against her neck. It was a knife. She was sure of it. "But I think my soldiers are hungry."

A chorus of male snickering and boots crunching announced more attackers. The hungry he spoke of wasn't food. She could almost feel their hostile energy surround her like a living thing. Every instinct in her body screamed that they would hurt her, claim her, destroy her.

*Never.*

She'd never let Bishop's boss take her. And she wouldn't let these men. Clarke gritted her teeth, kicked out and scrambled forward, clawing at the edge of the forest, grasping the dirt and leafy debris for something to hold. Just a little further. Just an inch.

Find a rock. A stone. A piece of the sign.

The male behind her cursed, gripped her ankles and dragged her back with a grunt. She dug into the ground, gouging for purchase, but it was no use. He was strong, and when he flipped her body so she was on her back, she knew why. Her nightmare was real.

A man loomed over her, almost seven foot high. Fur-lined cape. Long silver-white hair tied at the nape. A puckered scar across the hollow of his cheek. He looked to be in his mid-thirties, but the menace in his eyes told another story. It was full of age-old cruelty, and when he sneered with salacious knowing, her skin crawled.

"What have we got here?" he drawled.

Shadows pressed in around her. Stag horns protruded from the head of a stocky man with a longbow strapped over his shoulders. Two men had ram horns curling in their dark, oily hair. They also had cloven feet. And when her gaze shifted back to her captor, she realized one thing linked them all.

Pointed ears.

Tipped with a light dusting of fur.

Was this a costume party? Some kind of weird anime cosplay convention? Even though it was illogical, some part of her mind still tried to send her back to Vegas, to any excuse that made this a dream. But the sign beneath her body told another story. The old can in the lake. Her rusted jewelry...

The scarred one's ears flattened. He bared vicious teeth that belonged on a wild animal.

Clarke's fingers curled around snowy dirt, and she threw it in his eyes.

He dodged with a smile that never hit his cold eyes.

The stag-man, sucked his teeth loudly. "I don't think you should let 'er get away with that, Faddeus."

"It's Thaddeus, you imbecile. Th-th-*th*. Crimson, save me." Her captor rolled his eyes, but then his mood changed in an instant. He was on her, flattening her with his powerful body, gripping her chin painfully, forcing her lips to squish like a fish. He made her look into his yellow gaze. "You'll pay for that, human wench."

Then his weight was off her. He barked to his men, "String her up."

Hands of steel gripped her from all sides and carried her toward a tree. They pushed her back against it and tied her wrists to the tree.

"Get off me, you pointy-eared beasts!" She kicked out.

But they only laughed and dodged. Excitement rolled off them as much as fear convoluted inside Clarke. One of them struck her across the cheek until her eyes blurred. Pain numbed her mind and she retched, nauseated.

More cruel laughter.

Thaddeus, seemingly their leader, stalked up to her with a curious glint in his eye. His bone sword dragged lazily in the snow behind him. He used its tip to lift the tattered hem of her shirt and dipped his gaze to take a cheeky look beneath. Then the sword lifted, shredding her shirt in two, exposing her dirty bra.

That bone was sharp. It would cut deep.

Whistles of encouragement spurred Thaddeus on and he puffed out his chest. He grazed the sword tip up to her chin, then gently pushed her hair out of the way to inspect her ear again. For a moment, his eyes narrowed and turned thoughtful.

"Red hair," he murmured softly. "Red wasn't on the list. That means you're mine."

The point of his blade caught on her earring, and he ripped it from her lobe. Agony exploded. Gulping, she repeated a mantra in her head. *Don't show weakness. You are not a victim. You are a survivor.*

At her lack of reaction, he gave a disappointed sigh. "And to think I was going to keep you for my own pleasure. With your face, I almost mistook you for an elf. Almost. Oh well. I guess all that is left to do with your kind is use you for sport." He leaned in close, his stale breath on her cheek. "My crew have been hunting for days. We're not allowed to play with the other humans we found, but you're not on the list. It means you're mine."

Clarke spat in his face.

A backhand to her cheek sent her face careening to the side. The rope tugged sharply at her wrists, keeping her upright.

But then something odd happened. Through blurred eyes, she saw a tall, well-built stranger casually wander into the group and lean against a tree. One of them, but... not. Where the others triggered sickly vibrations in her chest, this one provoked good tingles. Fluttering. There was no other way to explain it. All the pain, fear, and terror in her body emptied as she locked eyes with the golden-eyed man. No... not man. Male. Like the others, he was the male of some new species. Silver shoulder-length hair was pulled back to reveal fur-tipped and pointed ears. A short beard peppered a sharp jaw. Unbridled curiosity played across his handsome face. The fact he took no part in her ridicule showed he had nothing to prove. He was already aware of his own strength.

Just as tall as Thaddeus, just as muscular, but a world apart in sophistication.

"Help," she croaked.

Dark brows lifted, and he checked over his shoulder, as if she spoke to someone else.

Her attackers continued to paw at her. The forced removal of her shoe demanded her attention, but she refused to accept what it meant. Already she felt her consciousness try to leave the physical constraints of her body, to distance herself from what was about to happen, but she wouldn't take her eyes from the golden-eyed stranger. He pushed off the tree and prowled toward her, wending through those watching the show, intense eyes always on Clarke. No one else saw him, but they shifted out of the way as though they felt the wind and parted for the storm.

There was power in that man. It licked against her skin.

The others made no move to suggest they knew of his presence. They continued to rib and pat each other on the back for their delicious find, a bonus considering they weren't allowed to play with their earlier hunt.

"You can see me," the stranger stated, voice deep like rolling thunder.

"Am I not supposed to?"

Another shoe came off. More raucous male laughter. And then a ram-horned man came up with a lascivious look on his face. His thick, stubby fingers dug into her jeans and tugged down. He had hair on his knuckles.

Clarke let out a cry of resistance and kicked out. But they liked that. Another took hold of an ankle, and a third took the other. Someone sucked her toe. There were too many hands. Too many faces. Four, five of them? Thaddeus watched from a few paces back, enjoying every moment as he picked his nails with a knife.

"Come on!" Tears burned Clarke's eyes as she turned to the stranger. Why wouldn't he help? "Don't be an ass. Do something."

"Oh yes, you'll beg," Thaddeus laughed. "You'll beg right up until the end. Humans always do." He turned to his crew, rested a boot on a rock, and then leaned on his knee. "Isn't that right? Humans and their disgusting *mana*-less lives. You'd think they'd love to end their pitiful existence sooner, but they always want to be spared. And for what?"

His men stopped pawing her to grumble, scrunching their faces in confusion.

"Humans have nothing," Thaddeus elaborated. "It's why they want *our* land. The land we earned through blood, sweat and tears. The land we fostered back to life, now so full of plenty and magic. While they live between cold walls, we have this!" He gestured at the greenery bursting from beneath the snow.

Clarke looked too. Truth be told, it was greener than she'd expected wildlife to be in a cold territory. When the nuclear winter had settled, Vegas heat made way for ice.

All plant-life had suffered. Nothing much grew as boun-tiful as it did here.

The men shouted their agreement to something Thad-deus had declared. Clarke tuned into the tail end of it.

"... it's why I'm the alpha of Crescent Hollow. Your Lord. I'm the only Nightstalk who can protect you from both fae *and* human threats. I'm the only one who can play both sides of the game and win. I'm the only Nightstalk who will reward you like this." He gestured at Clarke, to the three touching and groping her.

They cheered.

A look of disgust ghosted the stranger's features. He met Clarke's eyes coolly.

"I'll help you."

"Thank you," she murmured.

Thaddeus laughed. "Thank you? Are you insane? Never say thank you to a fae. It means you are in our debt."

Clarke slid her eyes back to the stranger. Was this true?

He gave a curt nod. "I need something in return. A bargain."

*Are you fucking kidding me?* "Fine. Whatever. I'll do whatever you want."

Her attackers broke out into glee-filled laughter.

"Hear that? Line up, fae," one of them said. "No need to turn into heathens. We can share."

A long, peaked tongue ran up the side of her face and she shuddered in revulsion. Another wet tongue hit the skin of her stomach.

"What," she whispered. "What do you need me to say?"

"Say you want more, wench," one of her attackers said and then laughed.

She gritted her teeth. Why couldn't they see the stranger? Or hear him?

The stranger tossed one side of his cape over a shoulder and then rolled up his sleeve to reveal a corded forearm covered in blue glowing glyphs.

"You can be heard when I cannot," he explained. "So you will be my voice where I cannot speak. You will be my hands, where I cannot touch. Do you understand?"

"Yes. For crying out loud," she shouted at him. "Just do it already." Whatever he was about to do. *Do it now.*

The men surrounding her started to look oddly at each other.

"Never had a willing participant before, boss," noted a ram-horned one.

Thaddeus, still picking his nails with the tip of a small bone knife, only shrugged. "You learn something new every day."

Clarke scowled at the handsome stranger.

"I need you to do these things for me," he added. "Do you accept?"

"I already said yes."

"Just making sure." His lips curved in a slow, wicked smile. Clarke's heart skipped a beat, and for a moment, she thought the good vibrations she'd picked up from him were wrong, but he slammed his palm onto hers. A deep electric shock made her fingers spasm and shot heat down her arm.

His eyes widened. "I can touch you."

So intimately close, his lashes lowered on her with awe. A strange blue teardrop tattoo glittered under his eye. Clarke had no time to wonder what it meant, and then the electricity intensified at their joined hands. Energy and light rippled between their touch, casting the area into blue relief.

"Then we are bound," he rasped, letting go.

The light flared only for a moment, just long enough for Clarke's attackers to jump back with shock.

"Witch," someone shouted.

Thaddeus answered calmly, "Impossible. She's human. She's forsaken by the Well."

"Hurry!" Clarke shouted at her supposed savior. The idiot still stared at his palm, proud as punch.

Snapping out of his daze, he winked at her—*the bastard winked!*—and then let loose a shrill whistle. Wincing, Clarke shut her eyes and turned to the side, waiting for something to happen. Nothing.

She opened her eyes to see her attackers gathering themselves. They hadn't heard the whistle. Not one of them. Maybe this was all a dream, a delusion. Maybe she still lay in the frozen yard in Vegas, and she'd seen that sign before she'd passed out. It made better sense than the evidence she'd been presented with... that she had awoken in a time long since past hers.

But then the first haunting howl of a wolf sounded in the distance.

And then another.

And another.

Each time, the sound grew louder.

"*Damn it*," spat Thaddeus. He pointed his knife to the stag-antlered man. "Take the left." He pointed at the rams. "To the right." Then to the remaining men, "You wolves with me."

Wolves? They looked like normal men with unusual ears. Clarke glanced at her savior. His ears perked as though he'd caught the mouse, and then he flashed her a grin. He had the kind of smile that transformed a face. It created double brackets next to his mouth, crinkles besides his eyes and infectious mirth in Clarke's own body. Words vacated her mind.

Only for an instant.

Then shock slammed everything out as a pack of snarling wolves emerged from the trees. One by one, the wild animals prowled closer, baring teeth beneath trembling lips. A gray wolf locked onto Thaddeus with single-minded focus.

Thaddeus strode into the center of the small clearing and tossed a placating look at his crew. Something like, *I got this.* And then he crouched into an attack stance and snarled back at the gray wolf.

Energy burst in the clearing. It made Clarke feel like she should turn tail and run for the trees, but the gray wolf wouldn't back down. It stepped toward Thaddeus, strengthening the power of its snarl.

Shocked, and a little confused, Thaddeus blinked. He gave a short, impotent laugh, and then seemed to gather himself. Cracking his neck, he refocused on the wolf and shook out his fists. This time when he snarled, it transformed his body. Energy rippled from him. Claws protruded from his fingers. His nose elongated. His canines lengthened over his bottom lip, and the deep alpha snarl that came from the base of his throat froze every movement within Clarke's body. He was more wolf than man. Every inclination within wanted her to lie on the floor and submit.

The gray wolf paused. It stopped snarling and whined. It too felt the driving force of the alpha's growl.

With a smug toothy smile, Thaddeus advanced.

"Gray," her savior warned.

But the wolf rolled to show its belly.

A curse ripped out of her savior's mouth. He tossed a concerned glance at Clarke, clearly grappling with a decision he didn't want to make. Then he refocused on the wolves.

"Attack," he ordered, voice as gravelly as Thaddeus's had been during the change. Power exploded from him. Clarke could feel it against her skin as though she'd come too close to a fire.

The pack of wolves changed. Submission gave way to dominance. They launched at Clarke's attackers, ferociously biting down on whatever piece of skin they could find. The stench of fresh blood filled the air, and she swooned. Memories from her past hit her squarely between the eyes. Stumbling into an alley to find Bishop and his men executing someone. A gunshot. Blood. Brains. The blurry video of a man watching it all from a smart phone. The sour burn of a Tequila Sunrise as it regurgitated up her throat.

A wave of dizziness drove Clarke to the side to puke. Something like mud came out again. She groaned. So gross. Heat and sweat prickled her skin. She only had time to register Thaddeus give the order to retreat when blackness crowded her vision.

Everything went fuzzy. No.

*No no no.*

Not now. Don't—

# FOUR

Thrashing in sleep, Clarke's dreams took her back to her past.

She shivered as she ducked inside the Bellagio lobby. She lifted her chin and pretended she had the right to be there, despite the rain drenched outfit she wore. Squelching along the tiled lobby, she headed straight toward the casino. The electronic pings and ca-chings covered her grumbling stomach. Those sounds meant food. They meant survival.

Armed security eyed her as she entered, but she pushed past as though she had somewhere to be. For all they knew, she was on her way through the casino, to the hotel access on the other side. This was the third casino she'd tried today. Each time security had strongly encouraged her to leave. Word must be getting around about her card reading skills. Still... a girl had to eat.

Knowing her face was most likely on a watchlist wall somewhere, Clarke decided today she would try her luck at the slot machines. She squeezed water from her ponytail and wiped her face as she trolled the slot machine aisles, listening to that little feeling in her chest that fluttered when she neared a lucky machine. It took a few laps. When an old man wearing a Baker Boy cap vacated a quarter slot machine, she took his place.

The seat was still warm.

He sat down next to her with a frown cast her way. Probably wasn't a polite thing to do when he'd been working the machine for hours. But she was hungry. She put a quarter in, and pulled the lever. Tension rode her body as she waited for the slots to line up. Two stars and a cherry. Not this time. She popped another quarter in, and held her breath as she pulled the lever. It shouldn't be long now. The fluttering was worse.

The slots whirled in a dizzying blur of motion. Then slowly... each slot stopped with a blip.

Cherry.

Cherry.

*Cherry*.

The alarm bell went off and money poured from the collection tray. Shit, she'd forgotten to get a cup. Next to her, the old man pulled his cap off and handed it to her. "Got more luck than me, girl."

Her heart tugged. "Thank you."

She collected the coins, took out enough for a meal,

and then handed the cap back to the man with a smile. "You warmed the machine up for me," she said.

His mouth opened in protest, but she didn't stick around. She turned and left. Just as she approached the exit, she bumped face-first into a security guard. The big beefy guy glared at her and then at the coins in her hands.

"I know you did something to fix the machine."

She lifted her chin. "You can't prove anything."

"We've been watching you, red. Give the coins back, or you're done in this town."

Begrudgingly, she handed him the money she was going to use for dinner. There was no way to prove she'd cheated, but she didn't want to draw attention. Not if she wanted to keep using this town as her paycheck. She'd have to lay low for a while until her face came down from the watchlist.

Cold and shivering, she trumped out of the casino and went to stand before the fountain. The jets burst and danced to a Celine Dion tune. She wanted to hate it, but couldn't. Vegas was home.

A man sidled up next to her.

"Beat it," she snapped. "I got no money."

"Neat trick you did in there," he replied.

Fuck. She groaned and turned, but it wasn't security. It was a man in his thirties, smiling at her all charming and winsome as the breeze lifted his short brown hair.

"I don't know what you mean." She looked away.

"Sure you do." He held out his hand. "The name's Bishop."

"As if I care."

His laugh was hearty and infectious. "You might if you hear what I have to say."

"What?"

"My boss will pay top dollar for someone like you. Come work with me and I'll show you how to use that gift to earn more than a few quarters. I'll make sure you're never taken for granted again."

His hand still hovered between them. She eyed it warily.

And she wasn't sure why she did it. Maybe Celine Dion knew how to serenade. Maybe it was his smile. Maybe she was sick of living day to day. It certainly wasn't the fluttering in her chest because that had made way for the harsh buzzing premonition of dread. But when she put her hand in his, she found she didn't care.

He took her hand and, thinking about her hungry stomach, she let him. But it wasn't a restaurant he took her to. It was through a void.

The dream became a nightmare.


FIRE AND DEATH SURROUNDED HER. Wails and screams compounded in her ears. Thunder shook the ground and she thought she might fall through.

Smoke.

Blood.

Brimstone.

*Was this hell?*

No.

This was the end.

CLARKE SCREAMED AWAKE. Her eyes stung with the remnants of the nightmare still making her heart gallop. *The fire. The terror.* She cried out again, but her voice lost power as it carried away.

Breathing deep lungfuls of air, it took her a moment to get the charred smell out, but eventually the scent of cedar and bergamot filled her nose. Calmer, she shut her eyes. *The nightmares were back.* Strangely, hope flared in her chest. Maybe it was all a dream—the lake, the pointed-eared men who attacked her, the other wolfish man who'd saved her—she opened her eyes.

"Nope. Not a dream," she groaned.

No longer near the woods, she was inside a one-room log cabin. A cozy wood fire blazed in the hearth opposite her. To her right, a window, and on the left, a long kitchen counter. Over it hung a collection of utensils, ceramic pots, and wooden crockery. An unusually large potted plant was in the corner, its leaves weaving up a spindly trunk to branch out like an umbrella near the roof. The foliage fanned halfway across the ceiling. She'd never seen that kind of plant before. Its leaves seemed almost blue. It gave the illusion of living under a forest canopy.

Pinned to the walls on all sides of the cabin were remnants of someone's life. Knick-knacks, papers with sketches, and little glass jars filled with odd biological samples. Stones. Leaves. Wooden carvings of little wolves and people. Nothing looked valuable. Nothing worth selling or stealing for later use.

Shelves overflowed with old books. A chest of drawers and trunk stood at the end of the bed she lay in. An old leather battle jacket with segmented pauldrons hung limp on a hook behind the door. Faded blue and black, the jacket belonged in a medieval war zone.

A flurry of white drew Clarke's attention to the window. Through it was a winter wonderland of towering trees around a small, semi-frozen lake. She wasn't far from where she woke up. Nerves bundled in her stomach. She tried to sit for a better look, but bindings halted her. Her hands were tied to the wooden bed frame on either side of her body. The woolen blanket previously pulled up to her neck had fallen to her lap. Split down the middle, her shredded top showed her bra. The grazes on her hands were cleaned.

"What the hell?"

The restraints wouldn't budge. Clarke twisted and pulled until, exhausted, her heavy head fell back on the pillow. A musky, male scent bloomed. She tensed. It smelled good. Homey. Comforting. She turned and inhaled, eyes fluttering closed. God, it was so good. She missed the smell of a man in her bed. There was nothing like two powerful arms surrounding her to chase the nightmares away. That and a good round of physical, muscle-aching love-making was the perfect recipe for a peaceful night's sleep. But she hadn't had a man for at least half a year, about the same time the war had started. The same time she'd realized the depth of Bishop's insanity.

Six months.

That's all it had taken for things to go too far, for panic to grip humanity, for the weather to change and then for the inevitable chaos and death that followed. She bit her lip and wondered what had happened to her friends. Laurel and Ada had helped Clarke leave Bishop and his manipulating ways.

Thumping on the porch warned her before the door opened. In came the tall and broad-shouldered stranger, still as imposing as the first moment she'd laid eyes on him. That restrained strength. That silver-white hair. That dangerous expression. She gulped.

This must be his home.

This must be his bed.

She had smelled him. And *liked* it.

Disgusted with herself, she blurted, "We had a bargain. Let me go."

He dominated the open doorway. Fingers twitched at his side, but he didn't falter. He just stared at her as though she were made of something foreign. Then he kicked his boots on the doorframe to shake the snow and stepped inside. He removed his cape and hung it next to the battle uniform on the hook. Try as she might, she couldn't stop staring. The breadth of his shoulders, flat stomach, and aura of strength, completely captured her attention. He was simply magnetic.

Maybe it was just her brain trying to force this all into being a dream again. She'd been blinded by the charm of a man once, but she'd never do it again. Pity she would have to pull one over this guy and escape. Once Clarke shifted her mindset into grifter mode, she could be callous with her mark's feelings. It was that or live on the streets. She'd chosen her own survival.

Clarke forced her feelings back to the clear and present danger—her captor who was taking a moment to trace a reverent finger down the leather jacket's collar. He tossed a frown Clarke's way, and then reached outside to collect a small, skinned carcass. Maybe a squirrel. He waved in a scruffy looking wolf and then kicked the door closed. It slammed shut with a finality that unnerved her more than she wanted to admit.

That was the same wolf who'd led the pack that ripped into her attackers. And now it padded to a mat before the fire to watch her with golden eyes... the same kind of eyes as her captor. Who looked similar to the man who had turned into a half-wolf. Did that mean her captor was capable of the same terror?

He dumped his catch on the kitchen bench and unhooked a pot. After placing it on the counter, he pushed back the sleeves of his sweater to bare forearms covered with strange blue glowing marks. Clarke stared at his hands for way too long, trying to gauge how much strength was in that grip. How much power would she need to get out of it?

A lot.

Better to use her wit, mind and clever knack for reading people. Plus, she could always shiv him when he wasn't looking. She just needed to find a shiv.

Knowing she stared, he turned the full force of his glower her way. She sunk a little lower on the bed and then realized she was still half naked.

"Are you going to leave me like this?" she muttered. "It's humiliating."

"You *were* covered."

"So this predicament is my fault?" She raised a brow. "Untie me."

"The bargain"—he planted his hands on the bench and leaned toward her—"was for you to be my voice and hands. I never agreed to anything about your *predicament*."

Clarke gasped.

He continued to slice, unperturbed. The fire crackled in their silence. Vegetables tinkled as they hit the pan.

"Hey!" Clarke shouted, irritation heating her neck.

His knife paused mid-slice, but then he continued to work.

This was insane.

What happened to the cheeky, mischievous attitude she'd seen before in the woods? That wild and reckless grin he'd tossed her way before whistling for his wolves. Forget about trying to swindle him. She was getting downright pissed off.

"If you don't untie me, give me some decent clothes and... well if you don't, then you're no better than the men you saved me from."

His face darkened. He growled in warning.

At the fire, the gray wolf's ears perked up.

"I am nothing like that bastard."

"So prove it."

He slammed the knife down and came over. It took all of Clarke's resolve not to cower, but he only tugged the blanket up to her chin and then strode back.

"Oh yeah," Clarke said. "Real mature. I'm still tied up."

"You're a human in fae territory. You don't have rights," he grumbled, and then carried on with his work.

Clarke swallowed a retort because another part of her mind was shouting at her to pay attention to his words. *Fae territory.*

She narrowed her eyes. Didn't the scarred man say something about fae as well? What was his name... Thaddeus?

For the millionth time, she wondered how the hell she'd found herself in the future. Only one possibility kept circling her mind. Could she have been frozen and slept for so long that the world had changed? Evolved into something else? So why the hell wasn't she freaking out?

It was that fluttering *knowing* lodged between her breasts. She explored the premonition further. It was stronger than the fancies her mother hated her having.

"*Mind your fancies today, Clarke. We don't want the congregation thinking you're a nit-wit.*"

Her mother had left because she was afraid of Clarke's premonitions. As a child, Clarke had told her on more than one occasion that the world would end, and when some of Clarke's smaller predictions rang true, her mother walked out. But not before calling her the devil's spawn.

Clarke cleared her throat and sent her awareness around her body, thought about the large fae now stirring a pot at the hearth, of how he'd saved her from being attacked—at his own leisure and gain—and of how she was tied to his bed. He was definitely linked to the fluttering in her chest.

She should be freaked out, but she wasn't. For Christ's sake, she swooned at his scent on the pillow.

Over by the fire, he whittled with a bone knife, turning the wood with aggravated care. Clarke thought the irritation was aimed at her, but when she saw the carving more clearly, she recognized a man with the face of a wolf, like Thaddeus. He was carving memories.

He stared long and hard at the figurehead and then ditched it into the fire. Sparks caught. Shadows moved in the flames, almost making them come alive. Tense and concentrating, he went back to the pot like it held the world's answers. He refused to acknowledge her, but every so often when she looked his way, he must have sensed it. His wolfish ears flattened.

And then it came to her—*he* was the one freaking out. He'd tied her not only to stop her escaping, but because she confused him as much as he did her.

# CHAPTER FIVE

Damned woman.

Crackling flames warmed Rush's face as he stirred stew in the pot. Two fire sprites watched in avid fascination from a log. But Rush's attention was elsewhere. Despite the hum of awareness down his body, he refused to look at the female in his bed, or think about the night she'd spent there. The *human* female, he reminded himself.

He could smell her from where he sat.

The next time he slept, her scent would be in his sheets, invading his space with her sweet musk, reminding him of what a selfish asshole he was because he'd put her there for that very reason. A part of him wanted that smell. He'd come home with her unconscious in his arms. Her soft, fragile body curled into his... and he'd felt so big. He'd felt needed. She'd just been attacked, and all he could think was that he didn't want that feeling to go.

Lock her up and never let her leave.

The wolf inside him agreed. It was tired of being caged. It wanted out, and it wanted to be useful again. The rescue had sparked something deep within Rush, and for a moment, he'd forgotten his place.

He shut his eyes, inhaled, held his breath and let it out slowly.

Decades.

It had been decades since he'd touched... *anyone* without suffering. Usually, upon a touch, his curse made them disoriented and forgetful while he became violently ill. It prevented him from communicating by clamping down on his intentions. Small animals had a lesser effect, and like Gray, he got away with the occasional pat of affection before feeling sick.

But with her, no sickness had come. At all.

It would do Rush well to remember that she was the enemy. It was against the law for his kind to mix with hers. They had zero affinity with magic of the Well —*mana*—and held zero capacity for storing mana within. Their love affair with metals and plastics had taken care of that. Mana refused to exist where those resources were present.

He'd taken both plastic items and metal from her body when he'd found her. The wrist item had proved most curious, and he would be sure to ask her about it later. It was

like nothing he'd seen in the human city. Their craftsman-
ship was not so advanced. Not anymore.

None of that mattered anyway. Regaining control of
the pack used up much of his mana reserves. One more
burst of power, or one shift to wolf, and there would be
nothing left to hold the curse at bay. Soon he would look
and feel the one hundred and seventy-eight years he'd
lived. He would die within minutes.

Unless he found a Well-blessed mate.

May as well get *Starcleaver* and hunt down the myth-
ical dual tusk el'fant. He scoffed. A mate was hard enough
to find in this violent and cruel world, but a Well-blessed
mate, someone with whom the cosmic divine spirit of the
planet deemed worthy enough to share his power.
Someone whose magic called to his own. What a fucking
joke. There hadn't been a Well-blessed union in centuries.
No one expected Rush to break his curse. They never had.
And a union between a human and a fae? Impossible. She
had no magic.

When the Prime from The Order of the Well had cursed
him, she expected him to die a long, lonely death, suffering
for the recklessness of unsanctioned breeding in a finite
world like theirs.

Shifting awkwardly, Rush tried to ignore the sense that
she watched him. She had more demands than a princess.
But that wasn't the only thing odd about the woman. He'd
not seen a human this far east on their own, let alone a
female in tattered clothes. Everyone knew the dangers of

being in the Elphyne wilderness without protection. The humans knew. Thaddeus's hunting party was tame compared to the creatures and monsters further inland. Even fae rarely dared leave the safety of numbers for what lived in the wild.

A tingle in Rush's palm reminded him of the cost of the bond he'd made with the woman. A blue glowing glyph had appeared right there, a symbol that his time was ending. Soon all his skin would be covered, and all his mana would be gone. The amount he'd spent today to control the pack had been borderline brainless.

*It will be worth it.*

He'd failed to help his sister Kyra in Crescent Hollow. He'd failed to protect the female who'd borne his child, and he'd failed to protect that child. But with this human to help him, he wouldn't go to his deathbed without speaking to his son Thorne for the very first time.

Afterwards, he'd have to kill the human.

*To protect the Well, our eternal souls, and the future of our planet.*

He shut his eyes at The Order's mantra and reminded himself what they taught the young Guardians during training. At the first sign of rot, a plant must be pruned swiftly and without mercy to stop the infection from spreading. One human this far into Elphyne signified more would come, perhaps try to reclaim the land they destroyed. The woman in his bed might be the harbinger of war, and Rush owed it to the Order to let them know.

"You built this house," she declared.

He tensed. "What?"

"It feels like you've built it yourself. Am I right?"

His breath hitched at her white irises. The blue had washed out. He'd only ever seen that color in the eyes of a Mage of the Well—one blessed with foresight. A Seer. Then the white dissolved to color and the human scowled at him.

"Not that I should give you advice for the way you've treated me, but you shouldn't stand so close to the fire," she quipped. "It might spark and catch you in the eye."

A rumble of dissent vibrated in his throat, and he turned back to the fire. But when he glanced at the sprites dancing, toying with a charred whittled piece of wood, unease tickled his gut. The sprite couple had moved in recently. They kept the place heated and warm while he was out, and he gave them somewhere to live on this frozen, Well-forsaken mountain. But they were irresponsible, wild, and needed to be tamed. There had been accidents on more than one occasion.

Rush rubbed his beard.

The human's eyes had been white.

Like a Seer.

He removed the pot from the flames early. It was ready, anyhow. Time to dish up and see to feeding her. The moment he crossed to the kitchen, the fire sparked, and an ember shot out. Wide-eyed, he watched it arc high into the air, and then descend to smolder on his wooden floor.

A tittering of laughter filtered out from the fire.

He bared his teeth at the flames, and the laughter stopped. Gray joined in, his lip curling with warning.

"Get out." Rush waved at the sprites. Enough. "Shoo."

He strode to the door, opened it wide and stood there waiting with a crinkled forehead aimed at the hearth. Frigid air rushed in, but he wanted those little cretins to know he meant business.

A high-pitched whine shot back at him.

"I told you if you set fire to my house, you're out," Rush ground out.

The male squeaked a challenge, but a piece of fire in the shape of a woman broke loose, jumped to the floor and picked up the smoldering ember before returning to the flames. An almost inaudible voice piped up.

Rush put his hand to his ear. His hearing was excellent, but he wanted to prove a point.

"What was that?" he prompted.

"See? All fixed," the female sprite squeaked.

"Don't do it again." He booted the door shut and then rounded on the human in his bed. "How did you know that would happen?"

"I didn't," she mumbled. "I mean... what the hell? Did you see those things? They were real, right?" She squeezed her eyes shut. "Honestly, if this is a dream, it's the best one I've had."

"I can assure you, it's not a dream, and I'm very real. Now, answer my question."

"Lucky guess, I suppose."

He wasn't convinced.

But how could a human use mana? Could they somehow steal it from a fae and use the power for themselves? Even though they held no capacity for holding it?

None of these questions seemed logical, but in his unseen trips into Crystal City, he'd seen things that defied logic. Giant metal machines billowing smoke and soot. Boxes that carried humans inside and moved on their own accord through the streets. But in all his trips, he'd not once seen any evidence of mana being used. He'd only seen their filthy war machines.

A coldness ran through him at the memory. One day, the humans would use them on the fae, and there would be no turning back for this planet.

He rubbed his jaw again. "But the cabin. How did you know I built it? Have you been spying on me?"

"I only just got here!" Her eyes flew wide.

He filled a bowl with stew and walked over to the bed. Sitting down next to her, he braced himself for the contact-sickness. Old habits died hard. Even though there had been no evidence of it with her, he had to be wary.

He held a spoonful near her mouth, but she clamped those plump lips shut.

"Eat," he ordered, ears twitching.

"I'd rather you untie me so I can feed myself."

A surge of irritation boiled under his skin. Infuriating woman. He was doing her a favor. She'd *thanked* him. She owed him a boon for saving her from assault, mutilation, and who-knew-what by his uncle.

Thaddeus.

The name beat against his mind with unfurling hatred. The bastard uncle. Him being so close to Rush's home was disconcerting, and with a hunting party no less.

*I'm the only Nightstalk who can protect you,* Rush mocked in his mind.

Thaddeus couldn't protect his crew from the wind.

"I refuse to be treated like a prisoner," she insisted. "We made a deal."

"Fine," he shouted. "Don't eat. Starve." He stood up so fast, hot liquid sloshed out of the bowl and landed on her arm.

She hissed in pain.

Damn it. This was too much.

He strode back to the kitchen and tossed the bowl on the bench. More liquid spilled, but he couldn't care less. With his hands braced on the counter, his knuckles white, he barked over his shoulder, "Well I'd rather not have a filthy Well-damned human in my house, but here we are."

"If I'm human, what does that make you?"

# SIX

T he human's gumption astounded Rush. Could she not see who was in charge here? How could she not know? Maybe she didn't. Some humans in Crystal City had been ignorant to what went on beyond their walls.

He faced her with slitted eyes. "I'm fae. Or as you Untouched like to call us, a Changeling."

"A fae changeling," she laughed. "Like when the fairies would swap human babies with a cursed one of their own?"

"Have your people been locked away in your Crystal City so long that you've forgotten?"

"I'm still not following." The mirth in her eyes died, and she bit her bottom lip and then took a deep breath. "I'm sorry if this is rude, but okay, here goes. Why do you have pointed ears? Can you do what that other... fae did?

Make your face extend like a werewolf and have claws come out of your hand?"

A werewolf? The wolf in him howled indignantly at the insult. He was a full-blooded shifter, not some mythological creature that only half-turned on a full moon. He was more than that. Before his curse, his mana capacity allowed him to transform five times the size of a normal shifter. That's what being a Guardian of the Well gave him. Being the alpha heir apparent to the Crescent Hollow pack also gave him a great capacity to hold mana, and an even faster rate of replenishing from the cosmic mana that existed in nature.

If the curse hadn't blocked him from refilling his internal mana stores, he'd never have needed to rely on the pack to take Thaddeus down. He would have done it on his own. And none of them would be left standing.

But Rush was cursed. And he couldn't replenish his mana stores. His wolf was a part of him, the darker, more primal part, but still him. Even though he didn't have enough mana to shift, it still howled inside his heart, yearning to be let out.

"Okay," she continued. "Untouched by what? Changed by what?"

Had the humans forgotten their conjoined history?

"Untouched by the magic of the Well," he confirmed. "I'm changed from what you puritans called the superior race. All fae descended from both human and animal. I'm fire-fae. I shift into a wolf through the grace of the magic of the Well. Being connected to the animal species gives us a greater appreciation for the land that feeds us. It is why we are blessed with this glorious power. It gives us the means to defend the land from monsters like you."

"I take offense to being called a monster."

"I don't care. The magic of the Well doesn't care."

"Magic. Shyeah, right." She snorted. "And I'm Mrs. Claus."

"All right, Mrs. Claus." At least they were getting somewhere.

She grimaced. "It was a joke. That's not my name. My name is Clarke."

*Clarke.* He tested the word in his mind. It rolled off the tongue nicely.

"This is where you tell me your name," she prompted. "Or should I call you Wolfie?"

"I don't have a name." Gritting his teeth, he collected the bowl and went back to the bed. The moment they had cursed him, he lost his Guardian name, D'arn Rush. Then the moment he rose from the ceremonial lake to initiate into the Order, he'd lost the name he was born with, Kaden Nightstalk. As far as his loved ones were concerned, he was a ghost.

A brief image of his proud sister and her long white braid tucked over her shoulder, came to mind.

"Eat," he grumbled and shoved a spoonful toward Clarke's mouth.

She would either have to part her lips, or deal with a

disaster down her front, which was already becoming bare with each movement she made. That damned blanket kept sliding down, giving him a tantalizing peek at her odd, but not entirely unwelcome undergarment.

She opened her mouth, took the spoon inside and seemed to melt from the pleasure of it. A little husky moan of appreciation escaped her lips.

"*Crimson*, woman. When was the last time you ate?"

She made an incomprehensible sound and then begged for more, eyes bright and glued to the bowl. He gave her another mouthful, which she devoured with equal relish. Rush's mouth dried and he couldn't take his eyes from the wetness as she licked every morsel from her lips.

"Mm," she moaned. "Goddamn, the fae can cook. Could use a touch more salt."

He raised a brow. "Any more demands, princess?"

She mashed her lips to hold a smile.

It took him a long, pained minute before he could ladle another spoonful of stew and feed her again. This time, she took it silently, watching him watching her. Something primal reared up inside him at the action of feeding her. It was the wolf's longing. Its nature. Provide. Feed. Protect.

Or maybe it was his own.

Seeing her devour something he'd hunted, made, and now hand fed... it wound everything tight.

This was torture.

This was a sacred act reserved for loved ones.

By the time he scraped the bowl clean, and she gave her last feminine moan of appreciation, a very uncomfortable stiffness grew between his legs. He went back to the kitchen bench and ladled himself some stew. With his back to her, he ate it until the evidence of his inconvenient arousal was gone.

*Crimson.*

She didn't know how she sounded. How she looked. That blanket had fallen too far down her front, and he'd ignored it knowing that it was there. Maybe he had spent too much time watching humans. His body responded as if it didn't care. Heat flushed up his neck, hitting his ears.

Time to get out of this house. He cleared his throat and collected his cape from the hook on the door. He tossed it on the bed, along with a linen tunic he'd pulled from his clothing trunk.

"You'll put those on," he demanded, then found a pair of boots and added them to the heap. "Those too."

"Why?"

"Because you'll perish out there in the cold if you wear improper clothing. You're worth more to me alive than dead."

He untied her and waited for an attack or an attempt at escape, but nothing. She only stood tall and proud, chest and chin out. Not a care in the world for the state of her underclothes. None that she let him see, anyway. She made no move for the tunic splayed on the bed, so Rush picked it up and tugged it over her head. A frustrated sound came from beneath the linen, and she wrested it out of his hands.

"You'll pull all my hair out if you continue doing that," she huffed, and stuck her head through the neck hole. "Plus my old shirt needs to go first."

Not wanting to seem indecent, he averted his gaze and folded his arms. He stared out the window as if it were about to move.

"They're too big," she announced. "Whatever your name is."

Too big?

Unsure of the state he'd find her, Rush gingerly looked over his shoulder and relaxed. The tunic was on, and she held a big boot in her hand.

"Then you can walk barefoot," he replied. "Through the snow."

Her jaw flexed, but after darting a look outside, she fitted them on.

He gathered the rope to retie around her wrists. His bargain would control her movements, but his curse could keep her invisible, like him—only if he touched her, or her by extension.

Rush took Clarke's wrists. The heat of her touch sparked. Her eyes clashed with his, as though she'd felt the jolt too. A moment of blissful connection coursed through his starved emotions, bringing to life urges he'd long since denied. For a long forgotten minute, she wasn't the enemy.

She was just a female with startling blue eyes. Touching him.

He reached into his pocket to grasp the strange object he'd found on the lake shore while she'd slept in his bed. Made of two strips of plastic, and one square piece of glass, he'd sensed that it belonged to her. That it might be important. But like the metal jewelry he'd removed from her body, it was just more proof of her blasphemy. And it helped him to stamp down the wicked hope flaring in his chest. He bared his teeth in distaste at the realization a human was the first person to see him in decades.

It could have been a pix, an orc, or even a royal. Hell, he'd take a manticore. But a human?

He looked to the lake through the window. There were two ways a fae could replenish his personal stores of mana. One was to let it seep back into his body from the cosmic mana present in the world around him. Depending on the strength of the fae, this replenishment could take a night, or a week... or a few hours for a Guardian. The other option was to find a source of power, like the hot springs in his lake. It was rife with rejuvenating mana. When he'd built the cabin, he'd liked the idea that if he could break his curse, he'd be able to simply walk into the warm waters and replenish his stores fast. Then he could shift and run in the woods with the pack.

If he had a red coin for every fantasy he'd had while cursed, he'd be a rich man.

He tugged the rope tight, ignoring Clarke's wince.

Leaving a long length so he could use it as a lead, he pulled until she staggered out the door and onto the porch where he secured her to a patio pole. Like an obedient soldier, Gray watched her while he went back into the cabin.

The morning air was still cold, but the temperature further down the mountain would be warmer. Rush had given his only cape to Clarke, and he couldn't shift to keep warm because he saved the last of his mana for emergencies. He had no other option than to use his old Guardian uniform.

An errant thrill tripped in his stomach.

With trembling fingers, he lifted the Kingfisher blue and black garment from the hook and shook it out. Blooms of dust clouded the air, and somehow the blue seemed brighter. He slipped it on, flexing his fists as they emerged, as though coming alive for the first time in decades. Perhaps he was. The jacket fit him like a painful embrace. The last time he'd worn it, they had stripped him of his ability to replenish from the Well. He'd not run on four paws since.

That was half a century ago.

As if sensing his yearning, Gray whined from outside.

Rush smoothed his touch down the front bone buttons as he did them up. Next was his sword, Starcleaver. He collected it from beneath his bed and inched the beast from its sheath. Spanning four feet, the steel blade was always clean, as was the edge sharp. No other fae in the realm could use metal and still access their mana. No other fae, but Guardians. The Well had blessed him through a life-threatening initiation. But having this dual ability—to use the very item the rest were forbidden to touch—it was priceless, especially when eradicating magic born monsters. Metal nullified magic.

Two thousand years ago, the humans destroyed the planet. The fae rebuilt it, but at a cost. Magic had an inky side, just like the darkest depths of the ocean, it harbored things and creatures no one had predicted. Every so often, one of these things emerged, ravenous for anything that held mana in its body. Born out of necessity, a Guardian's job was to protect the realm from such creatures, and to preserve the integrity of the Well. Without magic, fae would become mortal like the humans, and they wouldn't be able to foster the frigid land back to life.

Tempted to draw Starcleaver and get reacquainted, he gritted his teeth and resisted, settling for admiring the Elven glyphs on the exposed pommel. He shoved it back into the scabbard and strapped it to rest between his shoulder blades as though it had never left. The sword would provide an additional level of protection through the Whispering Woods.

After he packed, he strode to the hearth and kicked ash over the flames until nothing was left but the two sprites.

"Light this while I'm gone," he warned, "and you'll have nowhere to live when I get back. Understood?"

The female sat on the smoldering log and rested her head in her hands. Her male partner flared blue with rage, but a stern squeak from his female set him straight. He joined her on the log and lifted his glowing hands in surrender.

Good.

Rush slung the rucksack over a shoulder, locked up and joined Clarke on the porch.

He waited for her to comment, to tremble in fear from the sight of the blue, to piss her pants or faint in a swoon. It was often said in omen, if you happened across the flight of the Kingfisher, it would be the last thing you'd see. But the woman watched him with curious eyes, taking in everything from the pommel peeking over his shoulders, to the logo stamped on his breast pocket—a set of scales with a drop of water on each side. No sour scent of fear bloomed in the air, only her infallible sweetness that had confounded him from the moment he'd captured her.

He exhaled sharply through his nose to get her scent out.

"Let's go," he growled and untied her from the pole, then tugged her down the steps and through the shallow snow. She'd better pick up the pace. He wanted to be down the mountain before dark, and it was at least a four day walk to Crescent Hollow.

To his surprise, after a few minutes, she trotted up and overtook him until she walked as far ahead as the lead allowed. Suddenly, she became the one dragging him.

He almost smiled at her tenacity.

Once again, the oddness of her behavior struck him. If

she truly knew what he was, she'd never have let him walk behind her. In all his time as a Guardian, he'd never come across a prisoner who'd run headfirst into their doom.

Fear of Guardians kept the humans locked behind their crystal wall.

Not knowing what else to do, Rush examined her from behind as they walked. Scratching his beard, he looked first to the round shell of her ear. He'd have to cover that before they got to Crescent Hollow. The law said a fae must either have their ears visible or be prepared to show them on request on pain of incarceration. With his mana stores so low, and without access to the Well, he couldn't cast a glamour to make her ears look pointed. He'd have to keep the hood of the cape up and hope no one stopped her.

As if she felt his gaze, she tossed a glance over her shoulder. Their eyes met, and that jolt of awareness speared him again. Growling and yanking on the lead, he glared until she remembered her place and returned her attention to the front. The set of her narrow shoulders tensed. She kept walking, but slowed down.

"Tell me more about this place," she said. "I mean, if I'm to help you, I need to know about it."

"Where are you from?" he asked.

"Vegas."

He gave a sound of acknowledgment, as though he knew where this human city was, but he didn't. There was only one human city. One.

"It's been a long time since any human ventured this far from the Crystal City fortress," he added.

"Oh? How long?"

"Since... you don't know?"

She gave an exasperated sigh. "Let's just assume that I know nothing about this world. Remind me of everything."

"Since the fae killed your queen and the brief trade routes were closed."

"Oh. Yeah, that sounds like that would do it."

He narrowed his eyes.

She skipped a rock. "Tell me more."

"You next. Where is Vegas?" He didn't expect her to answer.

"In Nevada. America."

He halted, jerking her to a stop. Gray yipped behind him.

*America.*

He'd not heard that word since he was a pup. History told of the ancient custodians of this world. No matter the continent they lived, they'd pillaged it for minerals and treated every living thing with disrespect, infecting its surface with metal and plastic, ensuring magic from the earth could not flourish. And then they destroyed it all with their war machines. It was a story all fae children learned from the moment they understood speech. Of course, like cockroaches, some ancient humans had survived. They'd hidden themselves underground, quarantined from the change that blended human DNA with animal until centuries later, they emerged and took their place in the new world.

Greedy humans were never happily contained on their insignificant piece of desecrated land. No. They wanted more. They wanted to harvest the abundant life growing anew—the life the fae had fostered in harmony with the Well. These humans—the Untouched—they were long past reasoning with. Their queen had ordered the invasion of Elphyne, but the fae wouldn't stand for it. After the fae executed their queen, humans used reviled steel, iron and filthy metals to slaughter thousands of fae in retaliation. Decimation continued on both sides until the humans had run out of weapons and retreated behind the high walls of their city like the filthy sacrilegious cowards they were.

The queen's death was centuries ago, before Rush was cursed, before he was exiled from the Order, before... he forced the painful thought from his mind and focused on the human and what she represented.

The Order of the Well would pay dearly to have one such as her in their grasp. Maybe even enough to lift his curse, maybe even enough to reinstate him as a Guardian. And if they didn't, then he had her as his voice. Yes, he could use the woman.

# CHAPTER
# SEVEN

The trek down the mountain had taken hours. Clarke's captor only allowed her to stop for a quick toilet break behind a bush, still linked to the lead. She'd tried cajoling him into removing the shackles, but no dice. The fae was rock solid with his decree to keep her tied.

His wolf trotted behind Clarke's heels, yipping when she slowed too much. Her initial drive to lead the way had waned with each passing mile they walked. It would have been laughable if she weren't feeling a little afraid. And tired.

The snow-capped mountain range they descended separated fae territory from human, but all Clarke saw was the lush green forest down the side they walked on. Eventually they wound down to a plateau that showed a one-eighty view from both sides of the mountain, and it was true, on the other side was nothing but white wasteland.

Her captor forced her to stop. Her grateful feet sighed in relief. He pulled out a waterskin from his rucksack and fiddled with the ceramic nozzle while he watched her with intense eyes.

*Whatever.*

Sometimes working a mark took time. You had to get them in your confidence and trick them into complacency. At least she was alive, fed, and relatively unharmed. The fae hadn't once made a move to assault her the way the others had, in fact, he'd attempted to keep her dignity intact. He wasn't truly bad, he just needed her for something, and as soon as she found out what it was, she could use it to weasel her way out of his bargain.

And then she'd take his jeweled bone knife. Or better yet, his sword. Either would go a long way to help her protect herself. The jewels on that knife would fetch a price... wherever things were sold in this world.

Clarke walked to the edge of the natural viewing platform and shielded her eyes with bound hands. Wind rushed up to greet her. It smelled fresh. Unpolluted. So unlike the air that had been in Vegas at the end. That had been dusty and dank. This was amazing, pure and restorative. To one side was the vast tundra. Not much grew there. Turning, she took in the other side of the mountain where a lush forest thrived.

*Magnificent.*

Anticipation thrummed when she faced in the forest's direction. She pointed. "So what's down there? That's where we're headed, right?"

The fae studied her while playing with his waterskin.

When he didn't answer, she pursed her lips. "Fine. I'll guess it on my own."

His cocky snort of disbelief made Clarke want to prove him wrong. She drew on the gift that had served her well over her life. It surged to the surface, as though waiting for her call. The longer she spent in this time, the stronger her instinct got. It responded to her call like a living thing. Unnervingly, she could *feel* it growing inside her.

She focused on the unknown land and let the *fancies* come. Images of golden people, laughing and dancing swam before her eyes. "I think that way is... well, down south a little further is a kingdom where the sun shines more than the shadows hide, and beings come from far and wide to bask in the warmth. I can see them sunbathing on the stone near the water. They dance. They have parties. And a queen—no, a king—with golden hair crowned with glass rules over them all. He's beautiful. But... something is wrong in his mind." She slid her captor a glance. "How did I do?"

His handsome, rugged face had turned to stone.

"Your eyes went white again," he eventually noted.

"What?" She touched her lashes. "What do you mean?"

"Your irises turned white when you spoke those words."

63

"That's weird."

He barked a laugh. "No. It's a sign of magic flowing through you."

She enjoyed seeing his smile. He frowned too much. Then what he said sank in. It was her turn to laugh. "Again with the magic. Right."

But the instant the words came out, she felt in her gut that he was right. How else could she explain her premonitions? She'd always been psychic and, since waking, it had become stronger. Had her years of lying hidden in the earth exposed her to this cosmic mana that he'd proclaimed existed, or was it something else?

A profound sense of home settled in her bones. It was as if her entire life she'd been waiting to be here, to come to this world where her idiosyncrasies weren't exploited. Where she wasn't forced to use her gift to cheat for others, but where her gift was accepted and lauded.

If only she weren't tied and bound. But she was working on that.

"Was I right?" she prompted, a smile forming on her own lips.

He gave a stiff nod and pointed far south-east. "The Summer Court is a new addition to our realm. The thaw in Elphyne only began a few centuries ago. Until then, life had survived as best it could in this harsh, icy realm. Whether Seelie or Unseelie, all fae races existed in the Winter Court. But then Summer came. Summer is an unfamiliar concept to us all, and it's a drug to many." His gaze turned wistful. "It's like our bodies remember what was once here in this world, even after all this time."

"And how much time is that?" Clarke asked warily.

An eyebrow shot up. "Two thousand years, give or take. No one knows for sure. Maybe the humans with their record keeping, but out here, we only began tracking the passage of time when Jackson Crimson discovered the link between the magic of the Well and the treatment of the land. No magic flows where metals and plastics are used."

Her fingers moved to touch the watch on her wrist and found it was gone. She missed being able to tell the time. And the convenience of having a smart watch. She'd have called a cab already.

Clarke had worn metal her entire life. If what the fae said was true, then it could have been blocking her from reaching her true psychic potential. It could be the reason she felt it moving inside her now.

"Tell me more about the summer kingdom," she said.

The frown smoothed from his brow as he gazed out at the land. "I remember first hearing the story of when King Mithras broke from the winter lands and created the glass throne in the sun. After he did that, the Spring elves broke away and started the Spring Court, and the Autumn Court followed. I was only young, and the Summer King was a wolf—just like me. There had been a sense of pride amongst my entire pack because it was one of our kind who had created the magnificent glass palace. But I was more interested in joining the

Guardians." He tapped to the logo of scales over his breast pocket.

When he was young? Didn't he just say the thaw began centuries ago?

"How old are you?" she blurted.

"One-seventy-eight."

"Years." She blanched. Surely she heard him wrong.

He nodded. "I was only a child when the Seelie Court was made."

"Seelie?"

"Fae races are divided into two. Those that prefer to live in the light—the Seelie—and those that like the dark —the Unseelie."

"Got it."

"Before the Seelie Court existed, there was only one kingdom in the winter lands, and all manner of fae, whether Seelie or Unseelie were under its rule. But the pull of the sun proved too much for many, and it split in two. Then it split into four. The Spring and Summer Courts are part of the Seelie Kingdom, and the Autumn and Winter are part of the Unseelie."

"Sounds incredible. I'd love to visit one day."

It was the wrong thing to say. Her captor narrowed his eyes on her. "I've spoken too much."

She shrugged. "What am I going to do with that information? Look at me. I'm tied up and dragged around by you. I'm surprised you haven't gagged me."

"Now that's an interesting idea."

His laughter turned her scowl into a smile. It couldn't be helped. It was those lips of his. The double brackets and mirth twinkling in his eyes. The way it lit up his otherwise downcast face. And she'd helped put it there.

But he was the mark. She was being friendly to get under his skin. She had to remember that.

He thought for a long time, then said, "Why are you using magic? How?"

Clarke shifted her gaze back to the summer kingdom. "I guess I've always had a bit in me. Since before this time."

"What do you mean, before this time?"

*Here goes.* "I think I've been frozen beneath the ice since my kind went to war what seems like many, many years ago."

"But you're human. And you use magic."

"If you call this magic, then I guess not all of us were lost to it. I can feel it growing inside me."

He grunted, deep in thought and murmured, almost to himself, "Now that I have removed the metals from your body."

She lifted her fingers to her ears. One was still raw from where Thaddeus had ripped the ring out. The other was bare.

"So... Vegas is gone?" she added.

"Your America is gone. This land you see to either side is all that is left. But it's not the same. The earth has shifted. Where there are hills, there might have been valleys. Some ruins remain."

Clarke's throat tightened. Tears burned her eyes. It was stupid. She'd *known* the truth, deep down inside, but still she hoped for this all to be a dream. It wasn't. Maybe she was the last of her kind. From a time long forgotten. That part of her life was gone.

As if the turn of her thoughts brought it on, dread gripped her throat and spread through her body. Panic engulfed her. She knew this feeling. It was the one she woke up with after nightmares. But it was the middle of the day... darkness crowded her vision and she dropped to the ground.

"No no no," she muttered.

"What's wrong?" The fae's voice came at her from a distance.

"I can't stop it. It's happening."

"What..."

"The nightmare."

Laurel's scream rent the air.

"Stop!" Clarke tugged at the ties binding her to a chair. "Just leave her alone. She's done nothing to you."

But the mercenary who had Clarke's friend under his grip, cared little. He took Laurel's bloody hand, caught the only intact nail in a pair of pliers, and cast Clarke a warning look. "Last chance, Clarke. Give us the numbers."

Laurel's short black bob was plastered to her face. Her

light-brown skin had paled. She looked about to pass out, but she refused to show defeat to the shadowed face on the cell phone video. The Void, Clarke had named him because she'd never seen his face, just a shadow that seemed to suck the life out of everyone. He was Bishop's boss.

Bishop stood to the side, arms folded. Clarke was the one tied to a chair, yet he glared at her as though *she* embarrassed *him*. "Just tell them, Clarke."

"Fuck you," Laurel spat.

"Move to her teeth next," said the Void.

*No!*

"Fine," Clarke cried.

"No," Laurel blurted. "They want it this bad, Clarke. It's not good."

"She's right," said the Void. "The numbers are the nuclear codes. I need them to stop the war."

"He's telling the truth, Clarke," Bishop added.

*They're lying.* Clarke knew because of the sensation buzzing in her chest. It grated like nails down a blackboard. Panic engulfed her. Tears burned her eyes. She couldn't let her friend suffer.

Laurel's scream shattered the dream.

Clarke whirled away... out of her memory and into another. This time, she was the voyeur in a room, listening to a group of faceless people talking. But one voice she recognized. The Void. Only this time he wasn't so faceless. Tall. Dark. Grayed streaks at his temples. Clearer, but still far away, still emanating the sickly dark vibes. She had to strain to hear what he said.

Leaning over a map, the Void pointed at a spot. "There," he said. "That's where we find the copper deposit." He pointed at another spot. "And there is the tungsten."

"It's too deep into their territory," replied his companion. The mercenary.

"So we bleed it out."

Clarke only had enough time to look at the map and register a familiar word. Elphyne. She gasped. And then the Void looked up. His eyes clashed with Clarke's.

She was booted out of the vision and into never ending inky water.

She couldn't breathe.

She was drowning.

*Elphyne.*

Whirling in darkness, she repeated the word, as if she could return there like Dorothy in Oz. Elphyne. Her new home. Maybe if she repeated it enough, she'd leave this nightmare.

*Elphyne.*

The darkness gave way to light, and she found herself soaring over the magnificent green forests of Elphyne. A spark of red caught her eye, and she dived. The closer she got, the larger the spark grew until it became a campfire.

Clarke saw smiling faces of men... not men, fae. Males of different fae species, all surrounding a campfire, laughing with shared camaraderie. Warmth flooded through her. They were enjoying themselves. A drink or two, a clap on the back.

Every male was made from thick muscle and broad strength. Ruthless eyes, scarred hands. Swords leaning by their sides. Bows. Axes. Other strange weapons she'd not seen before. Every single one wore a blue coat. Kingfisher blue.

Guardians.

Safe. Somehow she knew she was safe with them.

One by one, their pointed ears pricked up. Each male turned their face in the same direction, toward the darkness Clarke's sight couldn't pierce, and then the incredible roar of an explosion decimated her eardrums.

Fire. Destruction.

The land of Elphyne was burning. Water wasn't safe. Ice wasn't safe.

All gone.

In a heartbeat.

And then....

A mocking laughter echoed in the dark.

Emptiness. A Void.

# EIGHT

Clarke came out of her vision, throat raw and eyes burning. She looked into the face of the fae, his brow crimped with worry. Her head rested on his lap, and his warm hands steadied her face. The wolf whined at their side.

"Are you well?" he asked.

And it was that small act of concern that broke the banks of her emotion.

"He's coming," she whispered, silently sobbing.

"Who's coming?"

But she couldn't voice it. Not yet. For long moments they stared at each other. In his golden reflection, she saw herself. Not the woman she used to be, but a new one. The person she wanted to be. None of her past transgressions were a part of this world, nothing was stopping her from being a different person... one who used her gift for good, not selfish gain. She could take control of her life. She could be stronger.

The gift in her body surged, as though in agreement.

And then she remembered the first part of her nightmare. Those "lotto numbers" weren't lotto numbers at all. They were the nuclear codes that started the destruction of the world.

Oh, God, she felt sick.

"What's wrong. What did you see?" He seemed to stare right through her facade and into the tragic truth wrapping itself around her heart.

She twisted off him and landed on her hands and knees. Nausea rolled in her gut. Guilt. Bone crushing guilt.

"I can't breathe," she wheezed, and tried to loosen the cape's neck tie with trembling fingers. The war was her fault. When she'd used her gift to feel out the numbers of the codes, she'd known what they were for. He said he was going to stop a war. But he created it.

*Her fault.*

All because she'd failed to listen to herself.

She squeezed her eyes shut. She'd always had a choice on some level. Behind her eyelids, the sins of the past flashed and morphed with the images from her vision. The Void was pointing at a map of Elphyne. But that was in *this* time. At first she'd thought it was a repeat of what happened in her time, but... that other vision. With the fire and explosions. Those were fae she'd seen.

Unless she did something about it.

A darkness clouded Rush's expression as he grasped her shoulders. "What did you see?"

"Doesn't matter."

"You're lying."

His wolf snarled at her. She clamped her lips shut. How could she make a difference if people saw her as evil? She was already battling against a preconceived notion that humans were the enemy.

"*Tell me*," he ordered.

This time, the fae's words seemed to reach within her body, grip her voice box and demand it work. A tingling force compelled her to move her lips. She blurted her shame before she could stop. "I saw my past. I saw the moment I helped them uncover the nuclear codes that armed weapons that ended the world. And I saw the same fiery destruction in this time."

A darkness like she'd never seen before washed over the fae. Every muscle in his body tensed. Nostrils flared. Jaw clenched. "You are the one responsible for annihilating the old world? *Tell me.*"

Alarm skated up her spine. As before, the words blurted out in an uncontrollable flood. "Yes. But he made me do it."

As if that excused her. The end of the world came. Laurel died anyway.

He stilled. "Someone forced you?"

"Yes." Fingers going to her throat, she tried to stop her words with actions. What the hell was happening?

"Who forced you? Who used you?"

"My boyfriend. His boss. Another mercenary called Bones." Fear clogged her throat. "What are you doing to me?"

"I'm compelling you through our bargain."

"You're *making* me speak?"

"I can make you move, too."

The horror of it hit her. This whole time he'd lulled her into a pretense of complacency. The bindings were a ruse. He could *make* her do anything.

"You asshole." She jerked out of his hold. "You had no right to force that out of me."

"It's a good thing that I did. I had no idea the woman I'd captured."

"I had no idea the jerk I'd bargained with to save my life."

"Tell me about this person who forced you."

"And are you going to tell me about your deepest, darkest shame? Those blue glyphs are there for a reason. One you don't like. I've seen you glaring at them. You're not perfect."

He folded his arms, pushing out his biceps and returned her glare. "Do I have to compel you?"

She sighed, suddenly feeling exhausted. What was the point in trying to hide things? She stared out into the forests of Elphyne.

"You ever heard the story of the boy who cried wolf?" she asked.

His lip twitched, but he shook his head.

"It's about a child who used to shepherd his family's flock of sheep. He found it so boring on his own, that he would pretend a wolf hunted in the paddock and run screaming for his parents to come and have a look. Every time they went down to check, there was nothing there but the boy laughing. One day, an actual wolf wandered into his paddock, but when he called for help, no one came. The boy got eaten."

Clarke turned to the wasteland side of the mountain and took in the lack of life.

"My entire life I had these visions," she said. "Some turned into reality, but many didn't. As a child, I had no way of telling which dreams were real and which weren't. My mother's answer was to walk out. She couldn't handle a daughter with issues. My father was there for me. He helped me as much as he could, but he never believed me.

"I saw his death. I saw that it was from his unhealthy lifestyle, but he didn't believe me, all because I'd grown up telling many lies with the truths. My psychic powers weren't always reliable, and sometimes I made things up for attention."

She wiped her eyes. "One person always believed me. He turned my small little quirks into an empire. And then he sold my skills to someone worse. By the time I had the nerve, or the support to get out of there, it was too late. The damage had been done."

If it weren't for Ada and Laurel, and their friendship, Clarke would never have left Bishop. She depended on him. Thinking of her two friends sent an ache through her body. She missed them. So much.

The big fae at her side squinted into the distance, zeroing in on something.

She'd not noticed it before, but could now see a structure reaching into the sky. It looked faded and purple from the haze that separated them, but it was an unmistakable city. Tall skyscrapers in the middle, and a dull wall of crystal surrounding them.

"Is that..." But she knew. The rightness of her next words just made them come out. "It's the human city."

He nodded.

"But"—she focused harder—"what is that over the top of the tall buildings, something strung between?"

"It's barbed wire. It prevents winged fae from entering the city from above. Or rather, if they get in, it stops them from flying out."

"So... they use the wire to cut winged fae down?"

He nodded grimly. "And by electrocuting them, then keeping and dissecting their bodies for research."

She frowned. "But that would also harm any winged creature who dropped into the city, right?"

A meeting of their eyes said it all. Yes, all animals were harmed, and yes, she understood how vile humans could be. She was one of them, and yet, it was a hard pill to swallow.

She might not be one, but she knew good people. Her friends Laurel and Ada were good. Ada rescued abused animals and rehabilitated them for the wild. Laurel ran a fitness empire and donated self-defense lessons to victims of domestic abuse. It still baffled Clarke that the two of them wanted to be her friend.

"There are good people out there," she declared. Surely some still existed.

"And there are bad," Rush answered. "But the Well cares not. This land cares not. It only wants to survive and flourish. We don't choose the rules of life, but if we don't follow them, we're destined for nothing."

His words were an echo of the emptiness in her nightmare. They shattered her nerves. There was nothing left to say. They went back to staring at Crystal City in the distance until some time had passed, and he began talking.

"Apart from myself, only one fae escaped that city intact. A crow shifter. He'd been a curious thief in his teens who'd flown down on a dare. He'd been in crow form when he'd dropped through the gaps in the barbed wire. The fool didn't realize the same wire made it impossible for him to fly out, and because that place is desecrated land, you cannot draw from the Well there. They've tampered too much with the natural order of things. For all we know he'd depleted his personal mana stores and was trapped there as a crow for all that time, unable to shift."

"And if he'd had some left?"

"Then he might have had one or two shifts in him."

"You don't know?"

"One day he reappeared in Elphyne as a crow. It took

78

him a while to shift back, and it took him even longer to think and speak coherently again. He never spoke of the horrors he endured... if he could remember them at all. When he got out, he joined the Guardians. He's one of the most ruthless we've ever had."

"I'm sorry."

"What for?" he asked, surprised.

"I guess for everything."

"We don't need your pity." He reached into his pocket and gripped something. His face hardened, and then he took hold of the lead. "Let's go."

For the rest of the journey down the mountain, Clarke forced herself to come to terms with her new reality. She wasn't near Vegas. Vegas was gone. She was in the future. In an unfamiliar world where magic desperately wanted to bloom, but the withering greed of humans still wanted to reign. But not all humans were evil. Many, in fact, were not. She'd pick-pocketed and conned people, but that was to survive. She'd never stolen from people she didn't get bad vibes from. She never considered herself an amoral person.

But was she good?

A good person wouldn't use their powers of premonition to steal at all. A good person would try to stop the evil of her dreams from eventuating, no matter the cost. She'd been given a second chance at life. This world had been given a second chance. She had to at least try to make it worth it.

All she knew for sure was that this fae holding her captive knew her darkest shame, and yet he wasn't looking at her with disgust. Perhaps his darkest shame was worse than hers.

⚖

As Clarke wended down rocky terrain, the snow melted and revealed fresh dirt and abundant nature. The more they descended, the grumpier she got. Something shifted inside when she saw how the world had changed because of the way she'd lived her old life. Death had been on one side of the mountain and life on the other. Even though she'd had a part, she didn't want to be lumped in with humans who'd intentionally destroyed the world.

The fae's words came back to her. *"We don't choose the rules of life, but if we don't follow them, we're destined for nothing."*

"You know," she said as she dodged a divot in the path. "We've been walking for hours and you still haven't told me your name."

She was also tired, itchy, and hungry.

The fae nudged her between the shoulder blades. She almost lost her footing.

He may have a giant sword, scary mother-fucking teeth, and a powerful body she was sure could snap her in two, but her instinct just wasn't feeling the fear. He had the ability to control her words and her actions, yet he'd only just used the power. She rounded on him.

"Take these off me," she demanded. "Free me."

He looked down his nose and flicked his gaze to the restraints. Her breath stuck in her throat and, for a moment, she thought her instincts needed a serious talking to. But then he moved toward her. *Fast.*

With a speed that left her breathless, and a flick of his powerful hand, his bone knife sliced through her restraints. Clarke's fists dropped to her sides.

He leaned forward, his menacing presence only inches from her face. And then he sniffed, nostrils flaring as he trailed his nose along her cheek, jaw and neck. Where he stayed. Hot air puffed out as he exhaled, and goosebumps erupted over her flesh. The tattoo under his eye flared, casting an eerie blue glow as he bared sharp teeth and bit the air, snapping with an audible click.

Clarke squeaked. A tremble of fear skated up her spine.

He raised a brow. "It matters not if you are free. You will not run."

"And why not? Because you'll compel me to stay?"

"Because, woman," he growled, mouth curving into a wild, wicked grin, "I am the reason for those goosebumps on your skin. I am the reason children have nightmares, and in there"—he pointed into the shadowed woods only a few hundred feet away—"there are far worse things than nightmares. I am the reason you will live to breathe another day."

LANA PECHERCZYK

"So I need a monster to fight a monster, is that it?"

*Stupid woman. Stop provoking the beast.*

His eyes narrowed and held her gaze.

An unearthly howl came from deep within the woods. At least, Clarke thought it was a howl. It could be any manner of creature in this foreign place. His pet wolf stiffened and raised his hackles.

Watching the woods, the fae stilled in a way that was wholly inhuman. He reached for his sword. Fingers locked tight around the hilt. Knuckles whitened. His ears pricked up straight.

Leaves rustled and trees whispered that night was falling. Then the tension left his shoulders and he let go of the sword. He tossed a self-righteous look at her, and then swaggered away, continuing toward the very forest that had caused him concern only moments before.

*Goddamn it.* She wanted to stomp her feet.

Smug, smug bastard.

She should leave just to spite him. But where would she go? To the human city that brutalized fae and animals through a barbed wire ceiling? The one the source of her dread came from? No thanks. She had to face facts. She was in a strange place and on her own. There were dangers out there in the night, and her gut said to go with the fae. He had the upper hand.

She hurried to catch up, for she knew something he didn't. She could make friends with nightmares. She'd had practice.

# CHAPTER
## NINE

Clarke thudded along the path behind the fae. He continued toward the darkening woods as if it didn't scare him, as if the gnarled trees didn't cause every bone in his body to quake. He stopped at where the trees grew thickest and looked at the darkening sky.

"We'll camp here for the night," he announced and dropped his heavy rucksack.

He shuffled debris, stones and leaves out of a ten-foot diameter area, and then busied himself with pulling out six yardsticks from his pack.

Her stomach rumbled. Her skin itched. Her boots rubbed. She could use a good bath. *I'm so over this.*

With a sigh, she said, "Can you *please* tell me your name? I'll stop asking only when you tell me."

She had to get him to trust her and first names were everything.

The uncertainty in his eyes gave her a chill. There was more to this than he let on. It made her think, perhaps, he could be on the run from the law, if there were such a thing in this place. He'd called himself a Guardian, but maybe that logo on his jacket wasn't from a friendly place.

She ducked her head to where he faced. He couldn't avoid her, or the question.

He gave an annoyed grunt. "Like I said, I have no name. I am a ghost."

He continued to stake each yardstick into the dirt until he made the shape of a circle.

*A Ghost.*

Okay. They'd made progress. But it still wasn't enough.

"And what does that mean? You look pretty real to me."

He stabbed the last yardstick and rounded on her. "None of your Well-damn business."

"Shall I guess it?" Why not? Her guesses had been right lately. She didn't need some sort of compulsion on her side. She already had an inbuilt lie detector.

Something like fear flashed in his eyes, and then he clamped down hard. "Fine. Call me Rush."

She tried to hide her smile, but failed. *Finally.*

Her smile threw him off. He did a double-take, paused long enough for her to know she'd caused discomfort, and then kneeled. Looking into his wolf's eyes, he calmly said,

"You should go back. I need you to protect the cabin and your pack needs you."

The wolf whined, but Rush gave it an affectionate scrub between the ears, stood and made a shooing motion. The wolf trotted back the way they had come, gave one last look over his shoulder at Rush, and then kept going.

Clarke didn't miss the way Rush winced after the wolf had gone. Once the wolf was out of earshot, he mumbled to himself, "These woods aren't suitable for an old wolf like him. He's better off on his own."

He finished checking the perimeter of stakes and then sat toward the center of the secure circle and pulled out a wrapped package of dried meat and nuts. He took his fill, and then begrudgingly handed her a few morsels. While Clarke ate, he shoved his rucksack behind his head and sprawled his long legs out. Without a word, he closed his eyes, shimmied to get comfortable, and then relaxed.

Seriously?

After a minute or two, when she was sure he'd think she'd just given up and gone to sleep, she chewed loudly and asked, "What are those sticks for?"

Silence.

She asked again. "You know, the sticks around us?"

He gave a grunt and rolled away from her.

"Rush."

The tension in his shoulders revealed he regretted telling her his name.

An incredible urge to get a rise out of him washed

through her, but she used the self-control of a god, and kept it inside. She ended up resting her elbows on her legs, head in hands, and leaned forward. Staring.

If he fell asleep, she might be able to rifle through the rucksack. Find some money. Something to help her when she managed to get away from him. With each breath he took, his chest moved and the knife at his belt tilted, catching the dying light of the sun. Jewels were embedded in the pommel. Jewels were as good as cash in any time.

It didn't take long for him to open an eye. Then another. His attention dipped to her chest and lingered long enough to let her know her shirt must be gaping. The tunic he'd given her was too big. That heated linger caused her nipples to contract.

He lifted his gaze to her lips, then her eyes where they locked and heated with a sensual challenge. A dark eyebrow lifted. The message was clear. *"I'm game if you are."*

She'd never used her femininity to get what she wanted, but couldn't deny it was useful. Regardless of whether she was human or fae, he was attracted to her, and that gave her a little power.

The memory of the two sides of the mountain came back to her. One dead. One living. She'd sworn this time, she'd do things differently. No more manipulating, sneaking, or lying. Her darkest truth was out there, and the world hadn't crumbled. This fae hadn't looked at her with bone deep scorn, and if she did this... use her body to get what she wanted... then she was back to old tricks.

For a single insane moment, she wished she could see her own future, then she would know exactly what was in store between her and the fae. But as usual, nothing stronger than a flutter or buzz vibes influenced her own life. Warnings. That was all. And she got nothing where he was concerned. That should be a good thing, she supposed.

He thought she was his enemy, but he wasn't hers.

"I want to know about the stakes," she pushed, and gestured to the sticks.

Tension diffused, he closed his eyes again. "You seem to know it all. Guess."

She glanced around. Okay. A test. Maybe she wanted the same thing. So she took a deep breath and focused on the sticks. They had stones wrapped to the tops with a leather cord. She'd not noticed in the light, but now the sun had dipped beyond the horizon, the stones resonated with luminescence.

"Solar powered lights?" she asked, but the moment the words came out, she knew they were wrong. Like a light-ning strike that turned her thoughts to dreams and dreams into reality, she knew the answer. "No. They're more than that. They're for protection. From what?"

He opened one eye and then closed it. "Get some rest, human. The nights are brief in this part of the woods." He paused, his breath evening out as he slipped deeper into relaxation. Just before she thought he was asleep, he mumbled, "And don't listen to the wind."

"Why not?"

"It listens back."

Shit. She cast a wary glance into the darkness beyond the bracket of trees. Things seemed to stare back at her. Things she couldn't see, only sense. Shivering, she wrapped his borrowed cape around her shoulders and laid down in the cramped space provided by the luminescent stakes. She tried to ignore the buzzing bugs in the air, and the phantom itches up her sleeves and legs. But no matter how hard she tried, she couldn't shake the feeling of being watched, and when the wind whispered inaudible words, she shuffled closer to her sleeping captor, irritated that he knew this would happen and that's why he'd cut the binds on her hands. She needed his protection. Even knowing all this, she was fast becoming accustomed to the notion he wasn't the monster he made himself out to be.

She shuffled closer.

# CHAPTER TEN

A snuffling and scratching to Clarke's right made her snap awake. The silhouette of a man back-lit by dawn hovered over her. She blinked and recognized Rush's face, inches from hers. Was he coming in for a morning cuddle? Her languid body didn't object to that, even if some still waking part of her mind did. He smelled good. Like comfort. She held her breath and smiled tentatively. But then...

Amusement flashed in his eyes. "I'd love to play, princess, but a warada is about to eat you."

He kept moving. She held up her hands for protection, but he sailed right over her body and stabbed something to her right. A shrill squawking filled the air, grinding her nerves.

*Oh, my God. What is that?*

Scrubbing her face, she blinked and then felt sick when she saw what squirmed beneath Rush's sword. His biceps bulged through his jacket, straining to pin a hog-like beast to the ground. The wild, writhing animal was only a foot from where Clarke had lain. With sharp teeth, mandibles and leathery black skin, the animal was a cross between a boar and an insect. It had a barrel chest, sharp claws and six legs. If that thing had gotten to her...

Rush had saved her life.

The creature still writhed and screamed beneath Rush's sword. Its cries grated down Clarke's bones. Rush twisted his sword to anchor it to the ground. She tried not to look at the ominous stain blooming beneath the beast. If she closed her eyes, it sounded like a normal animal in pain. Maybe it was.

"Hold this." Rush shoved a glass container into her hands. "Catch the manabeeze when they release. Get as many as you can."

"The what?" she gasped, still hazy and disorientated.

"The manabeeze." He snatched the glass cylinder from her hands and twisted it at the halfway mark. It opened. He then showed a sweeping motion, as if he were catching air. Then he closed the container.

"I'm not stupid," Clarke groused. "I know how to close a container."

His lip curled in a one-sided smirk. "Someone isn't a morning person."

She couldn't say the same for him. He'd woken looking just as handsome as he did going to sleep. Hair brushed back as though he'd run his hands through it. Beard looking a touch thicker but not messy. Laughing eyes watching her. Her body hummed in the most delicious way and she remembered her first thought when seeing him upon wakening. She'd liked the idea of a morning cuddle. It was stupid. She shouldn't even be thinking about that, but she was half asleep. Her guard was down. And she was lonely.

She didn't want to be thousands of years from anyone she'd ever known. She didn't want the nightmares to be her only friend. She blurted, "Yeah, well, you wouldn't be a morning person either if you were always dreaming about fire and death."

*Liar.* Her dreams last night had been nightmare free. That only happened when she was around someone she felt safe with.

"You are a confusing woman, Clarke." He used his knife to gesture urgently at the glass container in her hands. "Use it to catch the manabeeze."

She opened her mouth to explain, again, that she knew nothing about manabeeze, but shut it when he gripped the creature's head and held it to make the neck taut. Every line in his body tensed and strained as though it hurt to touch the little beastie. "You ready?"

"I—"

He lowered his voice and closed his eyes, muttering a prayer of respect. He sliced the neck, killing it, and then said, "Now."

She jolted, and then the strangest thing happened. Little white balls of light buzzed out of the animal's body and hovered in a swarm.

"Catch them!" Rush barked. He retrieved another container from his rucksack.

Jumping to her feet, Clarke opened the glass container and tried to scoop as many balls of light—*manabeeze*—as she could. Restless energy rippled through her body. She released a yip of excitement. It was like catching fireflies. She chased the damned things around the circle as they swarmed in lazy patterns, getting faster and flying higher with each lap around her. One brushed her face, tickling like an electric caress. She giggled. There was something so pure about the light.

Twirling around like a school girl in a yard, grinning from ear to ear. She stopped just in time to see a single manabee buzz drunkenly and come straight for her.

Rush saw it at the same time. "Don't let—"

It hit her sternum and soaked into her being, spreading warmth.

"—it go through you." Rush's shoulders slumped.

Clarke felt woozy. Who moved the ground? Stumbling, she barely held upright and tumbled into Rush's arms. "Wha... What's wrong with me?"

He shook his head and set her straight. "You shouldn't have let it go through you. Now you will pay."

"Do you accept Visa?" She giggled then clapped her hand over her mouth. Why was she laughing? Because it was funny! She felt funny too. The world around her became hyper-focused and yet soft at the same time.

Rush rescued the glowing glass canister filled with buzzing manabeeze from her hands. Her knees buckled, and she landed hard on her butt, blinking lazily at the sky swirling pink and yellow with a new day. But she felt... a fizzing through her body. From the tip of her toes to the end of her hair. Which was totally weird. Hair had no feelings.

She laughed again.

"I feel great." She shot him a goofy grin.

He stowed his prize. "You're lucky it was only one, and it was from a warada."

"A warada?"

"Doesn't matter. Point is this stuff is potent. If you ingested mana from a stronger being, you'd be hallucinating the memories of their life right now... among other things."

She blinked. Wow. "So this... this stuff is like a drug."

"This *stuff* is sacred. It's the last remaining mana left in one's body before you die. It has many uses, all of which are lucrative."

"What happens if you just leave it?"

"It rejoins the Well—the cosmic mana of the planet."

Clarke sighed. "That sounds so nice. Cosmic. Say it again and let me watch your lips move. Coz-mik."

He rolled his eyes, but couldn't hide his humor. "Here we go."

"Hey, you know you're pretty cool, right? You're not nearly as scary as you pretend to be."

His smile dropped and he raised a brow. "Cool."

"Yeah, I mean," she continued, "I once dated this guy who used to make me tell him the lotto numbers every week. And then he sold me to this scary dude who pulled my friend's fingernails out so I'd tell him those other numbers." Her voice turned soft. "Can't believe I dated him."

Rush stared at her. "He sounds like a floater."

"Don't know what that means, but don't worry, he got what he deserved." That man, along with everyone else she knew, had died with her old world. His greed had given him nothing in the end.

A shiver ran up her spine when she remembered that she'd seen two of them pouring over a map of Elphyne. Maybe he wasn't dead.

"No." She shook her head. "Only good vibes, please."

Rush looked at her long and hard, then went to the warada and lifted it to inspect the spiky tail. Even with the permanent grimace, he was much nicer to think about than jerk-face Bishop. Or his evil friends. Enough with those floaters.

She giggled. What a weird phrase.

But Rush. If it weren't for the fact he was trying to use her, she might have liked him.

"You're also pretty cute when you frown." She rested her chin on her hand. "If you stop forcing me to do things, we could be friends, you know."

# ELEVEN

**R**ush froze at Clarke's words.

*We could be friends.*

The problem was, he'd been holding the warada when he froze, and the contact sickness hit. Like a jolt of anti-adrenaline, the curse dragged his energy down, just like it always did when he touched another creature. *Stupid.* He knew he'd felt off when he'd sliced its throat but ignored the warning, just like he did when he gave Gray a scratch or tickle. It was stupid to get distracted, but her talk of a man who extorted her powers made him angry and he'd neglected to pay attention to the sickness creeping up on him. He knew better.

His hand snapped open and the carcass fell to the ground as the nausea hit. The second wave of the curse was always worse. It took all his restraint to hold the pain in, hoping Clarke wouldn't notice in her state of disarray.

Sweat itched beneath his beard and above his brow. Taking deep, even breaths, he concentrated on the thing that triggered his curse.

The warada was reckless to come so close to the perimeter stakes. Usually the magic stone deterrent was enough to send all creatures skittering away, even the larger monsters. They were only at the start of the woods. It would be a few more days until they got through. Perhaps something spooked the creature and made it desperate.

Biting through the waning pain, Rush reminded himself that he had to be watchful. A cursed reaction from an animal the warada's size was bearable. A bigger creature, not so much.

He looked at the forest and groaned inwardly. If they were attacked, he'd better be careful not to touch, or he would be incapacitated in hostile territory for Crimson-knew how long.

Damned curse. He was over it. Fifty damned years and he was completely over it. The sooner they got through the Whispering Woods, the sooner they got to Crescent Hollow, and the sooner they found a portal stone to take them to the Order. Without a stone, the journey would take weeks on foot.

Rush removed Starcleaver from the beast, wiped the blade on the body, and then sheathed it over his shoulder.

A glance at Clarke showed she'd already forgotten

about him and studied the way her hand looked before the sky. But her words still rattled in his mind.

*If you stop forcing me…*

He tapped his thigh, deep in thought. The woman had been forced to do a despicable thing. He was under no illusion that she was perfect, that she deserved his pity, but he also wasn't the kind of male who forced a woman to bend to his will… not like the way his uncle did. He was nothing like Thaddeus, and the fact that Rush had to use magic to compel Clarke didn't sit well with him.

He turned to face her, ready to corral the town drunk, but found she studied him.

"What?" he demanded.

Her still-glazed eyes dropped to his right ear. With a sway and pout of plump lips, she said, "I want to touch them."

"Oh no. No, you don't." Rush backed up, but she advanced on him. Two pale hands outstretched and grasped air, aiming for his head.

"Woman." He dodged and weaved out of her reach. Putting his back to her and shaking his head, he finished packing away the canisters. "The manabee effect will wear off soon. Just sit down and don't hurt yourself."

He shouldn't have assumed. She came up behind him and touched.

Every aching bone in his body stiffened, expecting the sickness to hit again. Shutting his eyes, he tensed, but the only pain was bittersweet. A woman's touch. A tender sweep of fingers over the arch of his ears. A slide of blissful agony as she pressed under the lobe. And a stroke over the furred tips, then back down again.

Every nerve in his body sang at the connection. Ears were erogenous for fae. A tremble wracked through him. His eyes fluttered. His limbs loosened. The bastard he was, he pushed into her hand, nudging his head into her touch like a bleedin' scrappy pup.

*Touch there.*

"Feels so good," she murmured, dusting the furred tip of his second ear. "It tingles my skin."

A wave of need washed down him. Arousal became a tight, hot weight beneath his skin and he remembered how she'd looked when she leaned toward him the night before, all feminine curves and temptation. He rounded on her. "Stop," he croaked.

Wide, naïve eyes met his. "Why?"

Rush's response lodged in his throat.

*Because I want to tear off your clothes and feel you from the inside.*

She had no idea how long he'd waited to sink into the tight, wet center of a female, and he was afraid of the lines he'd cross to make it happen. But he wasn't the deviant his uncle had made him out to be. Even if his family would never know, *he'd* know.

Why indeed. "We have to keep moving."

Disappointed, she dropped her hands to her sides. "I need a drink."

"Anything else, princess?" He handed her the waterskin.

She flattened her lips. "If we're being honest, I'd like my watch back."

"Your watch?"

"The thing you took from my wrist. It tells the time." She pouted. "I hate not knowing what the time is. I feel as though, if I do, then I'll know where I am. It's stupid."

She shook her head.

Rush wasn't giving her the plastic and metal watch. He put the protection stakes away and willed his body to forget the way she'd made him feel. Less isolated. Less forgotten. And less in control of his urges. He wasn't wrong when he'd called her a confusing woman. Shouldn't he hate her for who she was?

But he knew as well as anyone, that one thoughtless act made in the heat of the moment could have dire consequences.

Growling in frustration, he collected his rucksack and stalked into the woods where the thickest trees thinned suddenly from a wending path between. The trees bowed toward him and shifted in the wind, their leaves rustling in greeting or warning. He could never decide.

While he waited for her to follow, he willed his arousal away, but his hormones didn't care if she was human. They didn't care if his time on this earth was coming to an end. They didn't even care that he was about to enter a dangerous place. He'd screw her anywhere if he could.

*Fuck.*

He scrubbed his face.

No, he wouldn't.

From the sound of her thudding feet, she followed. So he set off.

# CHAPTER
# TWELVE

Another two days of endless walking passed.

Rush set an unforgiving pace. He was used to it, even though Clarke wasn't. In Elphyne, they had no moving metal boxes, like the human city had. They had to walk, or use portals. Since he had no access to the Well, he couldn't create one. He had to find a mana-imbued stone instead. Crescent Hollow was the nearest market he could find a portal stone.

Each day they made camp when the sun set, and rose with the dawn. Determined not to put himself in a position of arousal again, he kept his distance, and refused to engage in conversation, despite her babbling and questions about Elphyne.

Every night, she shuffled closer when she thought he was asleep. And every night she made these little sounds of feminine exhaustion. Sighs and moans that reminded him of fantasies he'd dreamed in his loneliest moments. In the middle of the night, he'd caught himself reaching for her. He woke each morning with hard steel between his legs, and the wolf inside him closer to the surface, howling for a taste of her.

Damned woman.

Until she'd come along, he didn't think he would miss the quiet solitude of his curse. His words came less frequently when no one talked back. Being cut off from the Well meant the past few years had been blessedly silent. Until her.

She got under his skin in a way he wasn't entirely certain he wanted to end. An itch at his palm—at their bargain site—punctuated the thought. He shook out his fist and concentrated on the path ahead.

The last time he'd visited Crescent Hollow was just after his son, Thorne, had been shipped off to the Order at the tender age of twelve. That was forty years ago. Destiny was a cruel, hungry beast that kept devouring long after death. It ate Rush's father, it ate Rush, and it still went for his son. It was for his son that Rush needed to lift the curse. Rage rose swiftly in him at the memory, at the panic riding his system when the alpha, his uncle Thaddeus, had announced Rush's son would be the pack's yearly tribute to the Order.

Thorne needed to know that he didn't need to live the life of a Guardian, despite being forced into it.

Rush should have been the alpha. He should never

have messed up his father's life by wanting to join the Order, but he could never say he'd regretted becoming a Guardian. Only what came before and after because of it.

"So, like, where are we headed again?" Clarke asked.

Rush bared his teeth and snapped at her. Should have known the blessed silence wouldn't last.

She should have been afraid. Should have jumped back. But she only blinked at Rush, waiting. Must be losing his touch.

With a grunt, he trudged onward, ignoring her and the wind whispering sweet things into his ears. *Stay awhile, Rush.* He shut out the voices until nothing but the dirt leaf-littered path and the occasional earth sprite skittering behind the trees held his attention. He found them more reliable for news of danger than the wind. If the sprites weren't bothered, then the road was clear.

Onward he plodded. The light from the sun waned. It was only mid-morning, but the woods were thickening and the grim life held inside seemed to stretch its shadowy touch across everything. As though walking through a barrier to another world, the greenery and chittering birds turned to death and eerie silence. The temperature dropped.

They were here. The last leg of their journey. If they took this route, they'd be in Crescent Hollow by nightfall. He withdrew Starcleaver. Just ahead was a fork in the path. Down one, the limbs of trees bent to connect with the other side to create a gloomy tunnel. Reaching into the rucksack, he retrieved a jar of manabeeze, still buzzing and giving off light.

He handed it to Clarke. "Hold that."

Her eyes darted between the two paths, clearly seeing that the one with the most light wasn't the direction they were headed.

"No." She shook her head and pointed down the dark path. "We're not going down there."

"We have to. It will only take a few hours. The alternative route will take days."

Clamping her lips, she shook her head again. "No. There's something bad down there. I can feel it."

Crimson save him. It was times like these he truly missed the ability to shift. All he used to do was shred his human skin, let the beast out, and the very air would quake with fear.

"Woman." He clenched his jaw. "I will keep us from harm."

He couldn't say the same for when they arrived at the Order, though. But as long as he got to his son, whatever happened to her after that wasn't his concern.

A tightness constricted his chest, and he frowned at his own callousness. When had he become so cruel as to discard the safety of a female? Even a human one. The rogue humans he'd hunted over the years were all men, all scouts from Crystal City. It was easy to kill them. They were as monstrous as the magic-warped creatures he exterminated when he worked for the Order.

"I'm not sure you can," she said. "No offense."

He planted Starcleaver's tip into the ground and leaned on it with a sigh. "If you had any idea what a Guardian is, you wouldn't be saying that."

"So tell me."

Rush raised a brow. She was serious.

"And then tell me why you are no longer one," she added.

He had a mind to not tell her anything. They had to keep moving. A sitting duck was dinner in these parts.

"A Guardian has gone through a special initiation where their hearts and courage are tested by the Well. When they emerge, if they emerge, they have a deeper capacity for holding mana within their bodies. They can also draw from the Well at any location, as long as they are connected with the land in some way. Most others can only replenish slowly over time, or from a location of power. Like the lake you woke up in. When I shift into wolf form, I'm larger than most other wolves. If I concentrate, I can control the elements too."

He preferred to use his mana to shift. Elements were unstable and the domain of Mages or elves who lacked the ability to shift.

She swallowed. "What happens during the initiation?"

Flashes of Rush's hit him, as fresh as the day it happened. Drowning. Water. Suffocating. Sinking to the bottom, then, just as his lungs were bursting for air...

"Rush?"

He met her eyes. "You don't need to know. Only that the strong survive, and those weak in heart and courage drown in their own fear."

His father had not made it. He'd not intended to enter the ceremonial lake. He'd thought Rush had, and went to rescue him. The thing was, his father was an alpha, the strongest Nightstalk that had lived in centuries. He was neither weak-willed nor a coward, yet the Well hadn't chosen him. It had spit him out until his bloated body floated on the surface for all to see his shame.

Rush still remembered the day Thaddeus told him that his father had died because he'd thought Rush had snuck off to the lake. The shame and the guilt in his youthful mind had been all consuming. And so, at twelve, the official age allowed for initiation, Rush followed his father. He didn't expect to come out of the lake a Guardian. Not when his father, the fae he'd looked up to, had been rejected. Floated.

Before that, Rush had an unhealthy obsession with the powerful Guardians in Kingfisher blue. Every time they came through his village, most sneered in disgust. Many only saw the tax they paid for the protection the Guardians provided, but Rush knew their job went beyond prohibition of metals and plastic. They fought monsters. They bled to keep chaos out and harmony in. They gave their lives to preserve the integrity of the Well. For the future of fae kind.

"Every year," he began, "There is a mass offering from

around the realm to the Order. When Guardians die, only Guardians can replace them. Metal is needed to kill magical monsters, and only Guardians can use metal without diluting their mana. When fae realized the initiation ceremony lost more than it approved, they stopped wanting to become Guardians. So once a year tributes have to be made." He ground his teeth. "And sometimes they are taken from the age of twelve."

*The terror on Thorne's young face, his eyes squeezed shut as they pushed him toward that jetty edge. Rush had tried to stop it. He'd stabbed a few fae with Starcleaver, but soon they caught onto what happened. Rush couldn't get to Thorne without touching anyone and then the sickness took over.*

"Old enough to remember, but young enough to be molded." Her touch on Rush's arm shook him out of his thoughts. "I'm so sorry."

"How do you keep doing that?" he whispered, searching her attentive eyes. Did she see all the way into his heart? Into the black pit of guilt. His father. His lover. His son... Rush couldn't protect any of them.

"I just know things." She tapped between her breasts. "In here. It's worse now than before. Or better, I suppose, if you want to look at it that way." Her eyes turned wistful. "I don't suppose I can convince you to take the lighter path?"

"No."

Her brows lowered. "I just finished telling you I *know* things, and you're ignoring me. Why?"

Infernal woman. "I should just kill you and be done with you."

She gasped and took a step back. Fear was an acrid scent in the air.

Rush growled, "But I need you. I need you as payment for lifting my curse. I'm tired of being a ghost. I want people to see me again. And not only are you human, but you have magic, and seeing as you're related to how this world came to be in its state, you're also important. Now you know how desperate I am, and you know there is no escape for you. Unless you want me to force you…" He pointed his sword at her neck despite the bitter taste his words left. "Move."

"No." She planted her feet. "I refuse to be the person no one listens to. My nightmares are real. I saw things. Elphyne is in danger, and I refuse to be the person who does nothing to stop them. Not this time."

The fire in her eyes was admirable.

"You say you're a Guardian. You wear the coat. But you're a coward, Rush."

"You're walking on shaky ground, human."

"Yeah that's right. I'm human. The most despicable creature you can think of in your world and guess what? I'm the only one trying to save it. So, go figure. You know what? I don't care. Kill me then. Be done with it. At least I'll know I went down swinging."

"Go float yourself, Clarke," he snapped.

"I would if I knew what that meant!"

"It means you're not worthy of the Well. If you'd gone through the initiation, you would have been rejected, floated and bloated."

She gasped. "You, sir, are the one who can go float himself!"

With a frustrated, drawn out grumble, he gripped her wrist and yanked her down the path. It took him a good few strides before the truth of her words hit him in the chest. All this time he'd been consumed with the selfish need to have his curse lifted and see his son, but he'd failed to remember what had drawn him to become a Guardian in the first place.

He wanted to protect.

Instead of floating during initiation, against all odds, he'd sunk and been blessed by the Well. He'd emerged more powerful than before and blessed with the responsibility of being able to hold metal and mana at the same time. The Well chose him to be its protector. And it took a human to remind him of that.

# CHAPTER
# THIRTEEN

Clarke clutched the jar of manabeeze to her chest as though it could protect her from the unnamed terror she felt coming. Like the imprint of a future memory, the psychic backlash already affected her. But without seeing it, she had nothing to tell Rush, and the stubborn fae refused to acknowledge she was right. His mood had soured with every mile they traipsed.

Onward they walked. Every so often a skittering and scuttling sounded from deep within the darkness behind the branches.

She flinched.

He didn't. Calm as the center of the storm, he strode.

*Goddamn you, Rush.*

But when she thought about it, Clarke was more angry

at herself than him. Why should she expect this fae to be any different to the man who'd manipulated her most of her adult life? Right before she'd taken Bishop's hand that day at the Bellagio fountains, she'd felt his bad intentions. But then the bad vibes had disappeared. It took her a long time to realize it was because Bishop's fate had been entwined with hers, and she couldn't see her own future, so how could she see the parts of his overlapping hers? Maybe that was why she sensed nothing from Rush that went beyond the initial fluttering when he was around. His fate was linked with hers.

He could be just as bad as the worst, and she had no idea. He could be taking her to her doom. Glancing down at his knife again, she reminded herself to be vigilant. First moment she had, she'd take it and escape.

A sound to her right didn't belong. Clarke stopped, heart pounding in her throat, and listened.

A heartbeat echoed hers.

*Thud-thud. Thud-thud.*

She swallowed and hugged the jar. The area darkened from the cover of her hands. She forced herself to relax and let more light through her fingers.

Rush's gaze collided with hers. "What is it?"

"Did you hear that?"

He cocked his head, ears pricked.

*Thud-thud. Thud-thud.*

"I hear nothing," he said.

"But it's there. It's another heartbeat. I swear."

"Unless you have the hearing of a wolf, I'm right."

"But—" Something was watching them.

"Hurry up."

That feeling of ominous dread wouldn't leave. It tightened her skin. Clarke quickened her pace, trotting to catch up to Rush.

Every step she made, she heard an echo. Every breath, another just behind her. Every heartbeat, it reflected.

After another hour of walking at a brisk pace, the ground grew soft and wet. It squelched underfoot. The sound of her own, and a shadow's.

She blurted, "How can you not hear that?"

"It's probably still a side effect of the manabee going through you." Frowning, he stopped and focused on her and lowered his voice with serious intent. "I would hear anything that tried to get close to us."

"Would you? What about something masked with magic? That can happen, right?"

He paused.

"I want a knife," she added.

"No."

Screw him. She reached and made a grab for the one at his belt. He caught her hand.

"Why can't you just admit that I might be right?" she hissed.

"Because—" His words bit off.

A woman's keening wail cut through the air. Clarke jumped closer to Rush. His nostrils flared, and he turned in a three-sixty rotation until he sourced the direction it came from and then scented the air. He peered into the darkness, eyes scanning for danger.

After a breath, he murmured, "Let's go."

He pulled her by the wrist. His long legs ate up the muddy floor. Clarke jogged, splashing brown mess out with every step.

"Almost there," he said, breathing hard. "Just another few minutes."

But that hollow wail echoed through the trees like a siren's song. And that heartbeat. It followed. It quickened in time with Clarke's.

*Thud-thud. Thud-thud.*

They broke out of the tunnel and into a clearing where the sun failed to break through thick bracken overhead. Gray mist hung low over a muddy bog separating them from the safety of the path on the other side where green willow trees grew. It was either head back down the gloomy tunnel of trees, or wade through the mud. Trees without leaves looked like dead spindly limbs weaving in and out of the bog. Stress gripped Clarke's heart. She wasn't sure how much of this she could take. That woman's cry wouldn't stop.

"Well, this is new." Rush rubbed his beard.

"What do you mean?"

"Never used to be a bog here, but I guess it's been a while since I've passed this way."

"We have to keep going," she said, glancing back over her shoulder with a shiver.

During the walk, Starcleaver had never left Rush's hand, but now he sheathed it in the scabbard between his shoulder blades. He tested the strength of a long thin branch jutting out of the ground. It snapped off. He used the length to test the depth of the mud.

"About a yard," he noted. "That's not bad."

"Here, but what about in the middle?" she replied.

"Then we go around the perimeter."

The eerie feminine wail turned soft, like a song. Like she was cooing and coaxing. But what? Who? Coaxing them, or someone else? The obvious answer knocked at the edges of her mind, but she refused to let it in.

"Hurry," Clarke said.

"Don't let your fear take hold of you," he added, retrieving the manabeeze from her. "No one can see me, so I won't be the target. As long as you ignore the White Woman's song, you'll be safe. And if you get caught in her web, I'll be here to drag you out. Just follow me and do what I say."

*The White Woman? Web?* "That makes me feel so much better."

He pursed his lips at her sarcasm and then repacked the glowing jar before adjusting his rucksack over his shoulder. The fae moved as though this was a regular occurrence for him—the surprise danger—with swift and efficient actions. If she wasn't so shit-scared, she might be impressed with his confidence. He made sure the knife at his hip released and then sized up which side of the bog was easiest for them to traverse.

The eerie song picked up speed and intensity, and suddenly Clarke knew what the danger was. Her voice... it was like a drug. Soft chords melting her insides, and making her want to get closer to hear more. She shook her head.

"That's right," Rush said. "Don't listen. Ignore it."

"Why doesn't it bother you?"

"I've had training."

Clarke tried to move forward, but she couldn't. Terror had taken control of her senses.

"This way," he said and gestured for her to hold his hand. "If it makes you feel safer, hold my hand. I won't let go."

His unwavering confidence gave her the strength to take his hand and move forward under his guidance. The moment her feet hit mud, she sank to calf-high, but his hold kept her from lowering too far. The cape behind her lifted and floated. It stank. It stuck.

"Dear God, I will need a bath after this," she murmured.

"Your God doesn't exist anymore. I would pray to the Well for guidance instead."

"And where has that gotten you?"

A sharp look made her blanch. Fine. Whatever.

"Dear Well," she started. "Please find me a bath after this."

He snorted in a half-laugh but continued without breaking his pace.

"With lavender soap," she added, to keep her mind occupied. "And a nice hot fire."

Her voice trailed off as she concentrated. They got half-way around the bog when the woman's song became too hard to ignore. Clarke needed a distraction.

"Tell me what happened to my world," she said. Maybe if they talked, she wouldn't hear the woman.

A breathy grunt. "Not sure you should hear that."

"I know about the war. The sky being scorched. The nuclear winter... but is everything gone? Across the oceans too?"

Rush's grip tightened around her hand, but he continued to drive them through the mud. "I think nothing survived. Our Seers have seen no evidence of life beyond Elphyne. This is the last remaining pocket of life on the planet."

Sadness filled Clarke. "And I'm the first to wake up from my time?"

"You're the only I've heard of."

But she wasn't the only one.

"And my watch... there's no hope of getting that back I suppose?" Not that it would work.

"It was metal. It's been destroyed."

"It was a gift from my father."

Silence. "That is unfortunate."

She bumped into his broad back. He'd stopped.

"What is it?" she whispered, but his gaze locked on the center of the bog.

A beautiful woman was perilously stuck, flailing. She hadn't been there a moment ago. The area around her seemed less viscous, like a brown lake. Little dark streaks slashed across her pale skin. Muddy water glued her white dress indecently to her skin, giving them both unrestricted view of her naked breasts. Black hair floated behind her and dragged on the surface. Two large brown eyes implored them.

"Help me," she breathed. "Please."

Clarke frowned. This was too... convenient. And she wore white.

This thing was the source of her dread. The moment she understood, the woman's appearance shattered like a broken reflection. Gone was the stunning female, and in its place stood a humanoid bug-like creature. Enormous brown eyes that belonged on a praying mantis blinked at Clarke, as though she were its prey. It cocked its triangular head. Its frothing mouth ticked. Black hair fell from its head in stringy streaks. Folded forelegs pawed at the mud as though it drowned.

Gross.

"You are *so* not drowning," Clarke said and shook her head.

*Focus, Clarke. Ignore her.*

It was surely a her. The breasts were real. The white tattered dress was real. But the rest... it was a warped mess of human and insect. A monster, like the ones Rush said he fought. Clarke turned her attention back to the task at hand, getting around the bog. But Rush's gaze was fixed on the creature.

"I have to help her," he said. He let go of her hand and waded out.

"No!" Clarke reached out. "Stop!"

But it was too late. She missed him by a hair. He only had eyes for the thing.

"Rush!" Clarke's eyes burned. Panic gripped her throat. "It's not real. It's not the woman. It's a monster!"

He paused and glanced at Clarke.

The cooing and singing picked up in strength and speed. It may not see Rush, but maybe its magic did. It focused on Clarke, but Rush was caught in the snare of its magic web.

"Don't you see?" she shouted. "It can't see you, but its spell can affect you. If you continue, it will catch you anyway. Come back!"

He didn't. He kept wading toward the monster's pawing forelegs. The further he went, the deeper he got. The muddy water came up to his armpits. Any second, the creature's arms would hit him and then it wouldn't matter if Rush's curse kept him invisible. It would *feel* him.

A rising sensation took control of her body. Panic.

Desperation. The need to help him. Her instinct moved inside her, bubbled up her throat, and she let it out with a tremendous scream. All that buzzing and fluttering in her chest pushed out with her emotion.

*"You need to see the truth!"* she shouted.

The power of her voice pushed air from her body. It was more than her voice. It was power... magic. Waves rippled, branches rustled. And Rush stopped wading. Slowly, both beings turned to each other, seeing the truth for the first time.

Rush saw the monster.

The monster saw him.

Understanding scorched through both of them. A breath. That's all it took. And then they attacked.

The monster's mandibles screeched wide. It dragged itself out of the muddy water to reach for him.

"Good God," Clarke murmured. The body hidden in the water was half human, half bug. Four legs, two arms. Six limbs. All splashing and thrashing. It was like something from a horror movie, a science experiment gone wrong. It paralyzed her, but Rush... he exploded into action.

He withdrew his sword and swung, aiming for the monster's head. It dodged with otherworldly speed, but it wasn't fast enough. Rush's blade lodged in the space between the monster's shoulder and neck. Rush strained, his muscles extending, veins in his temples popping. He pushed the blade down and down.

Bones cracked.

An almighty screech rent the air.

Clarke covered her ears and winced. When she looked, Rush waded back to her with a grim look on his face and the blade was back in its scabbard. Behind him, the monster sank.

# FOURTEEN

Rush had let his guard down, and it was unforgivable. How the White Woman had caught him in her web, he couldn't say, but he knew with absolute certainty that the woman he waded back to had broken the spell. Unlike any human he'd ever seen, this one had the capacity for magic. And she knew little about how to use it.

She was a recipe for disaster.

He could deny it no longer. This changed everything.

She reached out and helped draw him close. He searched her blue eyes. The only way to know how powerful she was would be to test her at the Order.

She jutted out her chin and straightened her shoulders, but the contrary tremble of hands told Rush she barely held it together. This would all seem strange to her.

"How did you do that?" he asked cautiously.

"What?"

"You know what I'm talking about. Peeling back the glamour the creature had cast. That was you."

"I meant, what, no thanks? No—oh, hey Clarke. You saved my life. Awesome." Her lips flattened. She let go of his hand.

He raised a cocky eyebrow. "Were you the one in there with the sword?"

"You're incredible. And I don't mean that as a compliment."

"And you're avoiding the question. How did you break the spell?"

"I, um..." She looked to the center of the bog where the monster had disappeared. Thick viscous bubbles popped on the surface. Clarke's delicate neck bobbed with a swallow as she dragged her gaze back to him. "I don't know. One minute, she was this woman in need of help, but then I saw through it. I saw the truth, but you couldn't. And then I wanted you to see it. I didn't want you to die. Something broke out of me... and..." Her eyes glistened. "What's happening to me?"

He wasn't sure, so gestured in the direction they were headed. "We need to keep going."

The hairs on Rush's arms lifted. His ears pricked. Ice slid down his spine.

Something was wrong.

The monster burst out of the muddy water, its sharp

forelegs aiming for Clarke, snagging her cape. It happened so quickly. She was there, and then she wasn't.

*"Clarke!"*

He dove into the bog, aiming for where she'd submerged. *The bargain's bond.* He concentrated on it. Like the red string of fate, it bound his hand to hers. All he had to do was follow it through the thick, viscous mud. She couldn't be far. His fingers grazed something.

Soft skin.

The monster's had been rough and segmented.

He grasped. He yanked.

Her scream rose with bubbles and he hoped he hadn't ripped her arm from its socket, but she broke free. They hit the surface, gasping for air. Both covered in mud and sludge and bits of forest debris.

"Go." He pushed her.

Spluttering, crying, she didn't think twice. She used her arms to windmill through the swamp, but the cape was caught. The monster. He used his dagger to cut the neck tie and then free her. He shoved her toward the shallows.

"Get to the edge and out of the bog."

With his eyes still on her, something hit his right arm, tearing through his jacket. Fury unleashed, and he twisted, dagger in hand, aiming for its eye.

But it had touched him. The sickness triggered. His arm became heavy, his weapon weighted. The dagger should have gone through its socket, right to the brain. It didn't. It lodged halfway to the hilt. That's when he saw it—blue glittering glyphs on the side of the creature's neck. It was cursed, just like him.

But who would track down a White Woman and curse her? For what purpose?

There was no time to unsheathe Starcleaver. Gritting his teeth, fighting the blurriness dragging him under, he yanked the knife and stabbed again. Two things happened at once. His knife entered the creature's throat, sinking to his fist, spurting fiery blood over his hand. And a burning slice of pain clamped his shoulder as a mandible chomped down. His energy waned. He only had time for one more blow. It had better be good.

But the knife hilt got stuck on the collarbone. With his fist still lodged inside its body, his other hand held its pincers at bay. Defeat battered at the edge of his will, waiting for him to falter.

The voice of his uncle rose to the surface, as clear as it had been the day he'd been cursed. *You can't even protect yourself.*

Fuck you, Thaddeus.

*One more push.*

He could draw on the last of his mana.

He could ask Clarke for help.

He could force her.

*No.*

Instead, he clenched his teeth and took a chance. He released the dagger, let go of the pincer clamping onto his shoulder with the force of a hunting trap, and gripped either side of the monster's head. Agony screamed down from its bite. If this didn't work...

He twisted. Heard a crack. And exhaled.

The monster was dead, floating on its back. The muddy water slowly reclaimed its body, but he gripped onto it, refusing to let it go. Those curse marks needed to be investigated.

Too late.

With no energy left in his body, he slipped. He searched through his haze for the shock of red hair that signaled Clarke. He found her. Near the exit path lined with Willows. She crouched on solid ground, watching him with a furrowed brow.

"Clarke," he rasped, reaching.

Why was she just watching him?

She stood up and shook her head, resignation in her eyes. "When I was in peril, instead of helping me, you made a bargain that put me in your servitude. Then you kept me tied up and forced me to reveal my darkest shame."

His eyes fluttered. His consciousness drifted. But he wouldn't release her from their bargain. He needed her to act as his proxy. He gritted his teeth and shook his head.

"Then why don't you compel me to save you?"

Body going limp, floppy, the mud enveloped his shoulders.

Maybe this was how it ended. After all that.

The gray around his vision turned black, and the last

thing he remembered was a muttered, "Stubborn bastard," before his face dropped into the bog.

*Rush walked* along the dirt path that led to his old clan compound at Crescent Hollow. The fortress was nestled between the foot of a mountain range and the Whispering Woods. Only fools would try to invade based on location alone. But despite this, the buildings were made from thick stone. A high wall ran around the outside to protect the ten-thousand-plus residents inside.

A heavy pat on Rush's back jolted him forward. He turned to the grinning face of his Guardian comrade, D'arn Jasper. A tall and athletic black-wolf of the Mithras line, Jasper had shoulder-length brown hair tipped in black, and a pretty-boy face he hated being known for. It was the same as the king's. To combat the similarities, the wolf had tattooed his body, but it wasn't enough. His pretty face was something no Guardian let him live down.

But there was a darker reason Jasper had joined the Guardians. Whilst he'd never spoken about it, they all knew he needed to escape the rumored culling of Mithras descendants by the Seelie King. For centuries King Mithras had ruled the glass palace. Hell, he'd built it. He was The King. The High King of the Seelie, including both Summer and Spring Courts. But with each offspring he bore, more paranoia crept into his mind, and when a powerful Seer foretold that one of his own would dethrone him, he executed them all.

"Good to be back, yeah?" Jasper said, black brows quirking. "Even if we're covered in monster guts."

Rush looked down at the black gunk covering him from head to toe. Jasper was the same, yet he somehow still looked presentable. That stiff royal spine was always present, no matter how much he tried to deny it. Rush growled low. "You know I hate this place."

"Hate. Love. Same thing." Jasper clapped him on the back. "Last time you were here was what, nigh on a year ago?"

Rush flicked monster brain from his shoulder. "Bit less than that."

He preferred not to take jobs there, but when he had to, he did his duty and then spent the rest of time at the tavern, usually balls deep in some nameless female until he forgot about the haunting memories around every Crescent Hollow corner. The sound of his sister's feminine war cry still echoed in his mind as she chased him through the fox-tail fields. And then there were their dares to get as close to the Whispering Woods as possible without caving to the call of the forest.

"And so how much tax are we to ask for again?" Jasper asked.

A heavy weight descended on Rush's shoulders. He hated this kind of call out. "Shouldn't you know this? You're the senior Guardian."

"I may be older in age, but younger at heart." He shot Rush an incorrigible grin.

*Damned joker.*

"It's two red coin," Rush said.

"Balls," Jasper muttered. "I hate these."

"The law is the law."

"Yeah, yeah." Jasper waved him down. "We exterminate the magical monsters. They pay for their gratitude. Pity none of them actually give a shit."

Rush gave a casual shrug. "When the monsters eat the children, they will."

"Maybe that's where we've gone wrong. Should let a few of them get taken first." Jasper broke off a piece of jerky he'd retrieved from his pocket and handed some to Rush. "Want some?"

Rush screwed up his face. "After it's been in your monster gut filled pocket? No thanks."

"Suit yourself." Jasper popped it into his mouth with a wink. "All I know is that I'll need the energy if I see that tavern wench again."

"It's been months. What makes you think she'll remember you."

Jasper blinked. "Everyone remembers this face."

With a snort, Rush turned back to the Crescent Hollow compound. Just outside the gate, a pregnant female was tied to a pole, strung up, and treated like a criminal all because a child grew in her belly. She must be in labor. Two midwives stood by, ready to take the child after she expelled it.

Rush's gaze darkened at the sight.

Jasper spat out a masticated mess, then straightened his Kingfisher blue coat. "Looks like an unsanctioned breeding."

The two of them strode forward. With every heavy step Rush took, tension increased in his body. He knew the captive female. Intimately. Long silver hair, cherry cheekbones, round face.

One night of passion, many moons ago.

A glance down at her protracted belly was all the clue he needed to know the child was his. The timing fit, and he could sense it in her shifting scent. She smelled like kin. The rightness of it hummed across his skin. The child was his. Alarmed, he checked to see if his fellow Guardian recognized her, but he didn't. Jasper just looked as undignified as the female most likely felt. No Guardian enjoyed seeing this kind of punishment, but with resources scarce, population had to remain in check. Well, that's what the king told them.

It had never sat right on Rush's shoulders, but...

"Not magic. Not our problem," Jasper mumbled under his breath.

Jasper didn't recognize the female. He had been with Rush at the Laughing Den when they'd met, but he'd been upstairs, face between another female's thighs at the time. Rush couldn't even remember her name, he realized with shame.

The two midwives sneered at the Guardians as they neared.

"Relax," Jasper drawled. "We're not here for you."

A stout female wearing a scarf around her neck folded her arms and gave him the side-eye. "But you're here to take our coin, no doubt."

Jasper shrugged, and Rush saw how callous it was for the

*first time. It was all callous. He looked at his hands, at his jacket... what was he doing with his life to be part of a system that brushed away a pregnant female's plight like this.*

*Why?*

*Because the Prime said their resources were already spread thin. Because the magic of the Well was more important than caring about the affairs of the every day fae.*

*The stout midwife gave the captive female a worried glance and then tugged her friend. "Let's leave. The pup won't come yet. We have time." She gave the captive a gentle pat on the shoulder. "We'll be back. Don't worry, love."*

*Then the midwives scurried away.*

*Rush's ex-lover lifted her weary gaze and widened her eyes.*

*"Find the alpha," Rush ordered Jasper.*

*Sensing something was off, Jasper's ears twitched, but he nodded. The moment Jasper moved out of earshot, Rush turned on the female.*

*"Why?" he asked. "Why didn't you tell me?"*

*He could have helped her. Could have done something!*

*Guilt splashed over her face. "Because you would have told me to get rid of him."*

*Darkness unfolded within Rush. No he wouldn't have. Then a single word in her sentence stood out.*

*"It's a boy?" Rush's throat clogged.*

*She nodded grimly.*

*After joining the Guardians—a group of fae who rarely mated—Rush had given up on ever having his own family.*

*"But you and I..."*

"*Véda,*" she offered with a small, defeated smile. "*My name is Véda. Although I'm not even sure we exchanged those. I've always known where to find you but thought I could get away with saying I was... forced.*"

Blood drained from Rush's face. "*But I never.*"

"*Not by you. Just someone I never saw. I thought they would let me go. I didn't want you to know.*" She squeezed her eyes shut as a contraction came over her. A keening cry of pain ripped from her lips. Rush tried to hold her upright, so she didn't pull too much on her bindings.

When it was done, she kept her eyes closed as she spoke. "*It was my decision to keep the child. And I needed to know that if I was found out, at least one of his parents would be around to care for him. If no one knew it was you, then a Guardian would be the perfect protector—*"

"*So the father is revealed.*"

Rush whirled to see his uncle, Thaddeus.

Jasper stood by with a shocked, but stoic look on his face. He knew what this meant, what he'd have to do to both Rush and Véda. There was no way Thaddeus would let this go.

A slow, slithering smile curved up Thaddeus's mouth. "*You can't even protect yourself, let alone this wench.*"

Rush turned to Jasper who only flinched and said, "*The law is the law.*"

"Wake up."

A slap on Rush's face drew him out of the past.

He blinked until his vision cleared. But the pain of his curse still crippled him. He could barely lift his head from the soil as air dragged in and out of his lungs.

Clarke crouched before him, beautiful face crumpled with worry.

A wash of emotions hit him—surprise, relief, disbelief.

"You saved me," he croaked. "Why?"

Was it the bond? But he never compelled her.

So why help him?

"I've been asking myself the same thing," she admitted. "The thought crossed my mind to steal your belongings and continue on by myself, but I didn't. And the only reason I can come up with is that despite what happened to this world because of a mistake I made, I'm not a killer. I'm not a cruel person. Unlike you, I can't stand by idly and watch another person suffer. You saved my life, and instead of forcing me to save yours through your despicable bargain, you didn't. So I saved you anyway. I'm making the choice to be a better person."

Her words cut straight to the core of his guilt. His inability to do anything when Véda had died but watch her suffer. The way she'd accepted her fate was the bravest thing he'd ever seen. All for the life she grew inside of her. And Rush? He'd been a coward.

This human was worth more than him.

She stood, checked one direction of the path they were on, then the other. She dusted her hands and tugged her shredded shirt closed. And then she clenched her jaw with determination before locking eyes with him.

"Why are you cursed, Rush?" He wished her away, but she kept talking. "I could guess, I suppose. You think I haven't noticed that touching other things hurts you, but I have. You were surprised that first time we touched. You wince in reflex, as though you think it will hurt. And you looked in pain with the warada, and here you are in pain again."

He said nothing.

"Fine. Don't share. I mean, I'll get close enough to the truth eventually, but once again, I'm not like you. I'll never force someone's darkest shame out without their consent. I'd rather you share it with me yourself."

"I saved your life three times," he breathed.

She sneered. "It's all a currency in this world, isn't it? Say thank you, and you're in debt. Do a good deed, get one back. Doesn't anyone do anything because it's the right thing?"

He had no answer to that. She was right.

"See you around, Rush."

His bones were heavier than iron. All he could do was watch her walk away and know that this was what he deserved. He couldn't save Véda. He couldn't protect his son. And Clarke? She was the one who'd forced him to see the truth.

He closed his eyes. Letting his guard down wasn't so bad. It was keeping it up that hurt.

CHAPTER
# FIFTEEN

Clarke strode with determination down the path leading from the bog.

It was fine that she left Rush there. Completely fine. She'd pulled him out. She'd stopped him from drowning. She didn't even steal his belongings. She didn't need him.

Surely she could get by in this new world without him. How different could it be? The urge to stay must be wrong because it was simply cruel to side with a fae who cared little about her dignity and more about whatever secret drove his need to hold her to their bargain.

But he let her walk away.

"There's work to do, damn it." Her voice rang clear and lonely on the path ahead. "I have work to do."

Lives to save. Evil was coming. No. It was already in this world. Memory of the Void was a constant companion,

138

pushing her forward. The certainty of it filled her mind. *This* was her purpose. Save this small scrap of habitable earth from annihilation. It wouldn't make up for what had happened to her world, but it would help this one.

So why did that ache in her chest get worse with each passing step? Why did her mind keep traveling back to the nice things Rush had done? Feeding her. Clothing her. Letting her explore those incredible ears even though it caused him great discomfort. Holding her hand to cross the bog. Diving headfirst into murky water to rescue her.

He could have forced her to save him. But he didn't.

Her whole life she'd been forced to use her powers for other people's gain. Bishop couldn't have cared less if he'd forced her to save himself. In fact, he'd done it frequently.

*"Tell me my future, babe."*

*"You're going to die."*

*Bishop laughed. "Then tell me how to cheat death."*

Leaving Bishop before the world froze didn't feel like this. Leaving Rush hurt like her soul was being ripped in two, and half was back with him. Why?

Clarke stopped. She clenched her fists and rubbed them over her sternum. And then she screamed her frustration, letting the sky and the air know how she felt. With every fiber of her being, she told the world, *This isn't fair.*

For once, she would like just a little free will. Just a little.

Those days grifting in the casino, only worrying about her next meal, were looking like a dream.

The last note of her cry left her breathing hard and her stomach stinging. With a wince, Clarke glanced down. Red welts ran down her front. She poked around but saw no worrying damage. The monster's claws had just scraped the first layer of flesh. She'd been lucky.

She wanted to hate Rush. He was a grade-A stubborn fae. But he needed her, even if he wouldn't admit it. One of them had to be mature about this. If she ignored her intuition, then she was no better than him, no better than the fools who ignored her warnings and destroyed her world.

She used to think her ex was the fool. By the time she'd caught on to his greed and callousness, he was already knee deep in messing with all the wrong people. The Void and the man who did his dirty work for him. His name was Bones. A mercenary with sharp angles.

She heard an echo of Laurel's scream as Bones pulled her nails out.

*"These numbers will only bring death and destruction,"* she'd warned Bones.

Clarke slammed the heel of her palms into her eye sockets, hoping to shove the memories away. But they were as sharp as the day she'd made them. She should have done more. She should have done *something* instead of walking away, but all she could think of was that she'd not expected them to actually release Clarke and Laurel. And when they had, they didn't look back. If they had, the Void might have changed his mind.

But was it worth it?

Was Laurel's life worth it?

She dropped her palms and lifted her gaze to stare at the sky through the branches. And what was she doing right now? Walking away from the tug of destiny. Her instincts weren't telling her to run forward, they were telling her to go back.

Spinning on her heels, she stomped back to the bog.

And found Rush on the ground, still as the dead under the branches of a willow tree. Hatred fled, leaving her cold and empty. This was the result of saving her. Like a crocodile in a death roll, that monster had dragged her down, but Rush had fearlessly come after her. There weren't men like him in her time. None that she'd known anyway.

Rush had known touching the monster would make him sick, yet he'd done it. He was just too stubborn to admit it. She refused to believe it was because of some bargain he'd made with her when he wouldn't even use the bargain to ensure his survival. His pride may have stopped him from reneging on their deal, but this... there must be more to his story.

He remained unmoving, face pale and pinched.

Clarke went to him and landed on her knees. She touched his hot skin and then felt for a pulse at his neck. He jerked, gold eyes opening to lock on her with turbulence. Fury and hurt and shame shone back at her. She could see it in every line of his strained face.

"Get away," he growled and tried to shift his big, linebacker body but he managed nothing more than an inch, a drag in the dirt.

"No," she replied.

An anguished frown scored his forehead.

"Why?" he whispered.

*Why did she come back?*

Firming her lips, she squeezed his hand. His reason must be strong enough to think he didn't deserve to live. Clarke knew that feeling. A single tear ran down her cheek, and he looked away.

"Rush," she whispered and smoothed hair from his face. "I don't know how this is happening to me. I keep coming back to you and I can't think of why, only that maybe I've been brought to this time for a reason, and you're part of it. Your god, your Well of Life, or whatever you want to call it, put me on your doorstep. It thawed me in your lake. I guess together we are stronger. Alone, we are nothing."

Denial flashed in his eyes, and he looked away.

She bit her lip. "I hate the way you forced me into your bargain, but I can't deny the pull between us. You feel it too. I know it."

The breath that left him was shaky. He gathered enough strength to push himself to sitting. "When they cursed me, they made me invisible to everyone that mattered to me. And when no one can see you, they forget. You... disappear. I lost my purpose."

"Now you have a new one."

"What, to protect you on some divine mission to save the world?"

"That sarcasm is uncalled for. You're a Guardian. You tell me. What about me seems normal?"

He scrutinized her. "You have magic."

"I know."

"But you're human."

"I know."

"I'm supposed to kill your kind."

"Again... I know."

Was this his way of apology? She couldn't say his prejudice against her kind was unfounded, but she wouldn't mind a little regret.

"You made me see the White Woman's true appearance, simply by willing it."

"I think you should call her evil bug-woman, but..." Her breath caught on a sigh. "Yeah. I think I did. For the record, this is just as disturbing for me as it is for you. Trusting someone is hard when I've been used before. But I'm trying. By the way, that was a good segue for you to apologize for using me."

"Fae don't apologize."

"You don't apologize. You don't say thanks." She rolled her eyes. "What else don't you do?"

"Lie." And then closed his eyes with a wince.

Her eyes widened. They couldn't lie?

But they could withhold the truth. Maybe if she could force the monster to see the truth, she could force him to speak it. But that would make her as bad as him. She would never do it. Not unless survival was on the line.

She bit her lip. The wind picked up and gusted her hair. She turned and hugged her knees, staring at the trodden leaves and sticks on the floor. An insect that reminded her of a dung beetle crawled up the base of a branch opposite her. She fixated on it, grateful for something familiar in this place because this power inside her was frighteningly foreign. The visions were getting stronger, and the new ability—she'd *seen* the evidence of her energy explode outward from her body. It still moved and rolled inside her, waiting for the next time she needed it.

The touch of his hand hit between her shoulder blades. She scrunched her burning eyes closed.

"Learning to trust is new for me too, but... I'll keep you safe. Fae don't lie." The baritone of his deep voice rumbled through her like rolling thunder. Bit by bit, she relaxed. It wasn't just his words, it was the *knowing* inside. Her chest fluttered. He told the truth.

"As to your purpose here?" he continued. "Only the Order can confirm that."

"And that's where we're going?"

He nodded.

"What if they think I'm lying? I'm human, right? I can lie."

"After what I've seen, I find that hard to believe. It's clear you have the magic of the Well running through your veins." He rubbed his bottom lip, eyes shrewd on her. "I don't know how, or why, but the Order will know."

"So what now?"

"I believe I owe you a bath."

A laugh barked out of her. "I *believe* I prayed to God for that, not you."

He lifted a haughty shoulder, more energized. "Your god is a being with magical powers. So... same thing."

"Right."

They shared a smile. It was good to see the light back in his eyes, even for a moment. But already his expression turned somber as he angled toward the bog. "That thing should never have caught me in its spell. The White Woman is a malevolent member of the Unseelie Court, yet she shouldn't even be this far south. It's either the thaw, or..."

"Or what?"

He pushed to his knees. "I think I can stand now."

She lifted him by the elbow, and helped him get to his feet.

Out of breath, he waited a moment with his hands on his hips before unbuckling the baldric keeping his sword strapped on. "You can't go into town with that torn shirt."

"What are you doing?" She kept a cautious eye on him as he removed his outer layer.

"Giving you something to wear." He handed her the mud-covered jacket and reached over his neck with a wince to draw his shirt off.

"You're injured. You need it." An angry slash scored his neck.

"No one can see me. And I've had worse. When we get there, I will find us fresh clothes while you clean up at the inn."

With his shirt removed, blue light flashed and Clarke squinted at the piercing glow. Shimmering glyphs covered his entire frame, sparkling like the tiny tear drop under his eye. Her cheeks flamed as she scanned his sculpted abs and perfect torso, his muscular physique flexing and rolling. Thoughts fled. She'd never be able to unsee it. He wasn't so animal after all. He was pure, hot blooded male.

"Get a good look," he said. "Once the curse ends, I'll be shriveled and old."

Bitterness laced his joke. And she didn't care. Her hand was on him in an instant, tracing the shape of the glyphs, fascinated and wondering what they meant. He took a sharp breath, but she couldn't stop. With every turn of her touch, glimpses in her mind's eye showed someone painting them, and then watching the glyphs sink into his flesh.

"They weren't always like this," she murmured.

"The more that appear, the closer I am to the end." His voice was dark honey near her ear.

The markings tingled against her palm. Every time she shifted her touch, a slow burn built inside her, making every feminine instinct aware of his state of undress. She lost her clinical demeanor and enjoyed the heat of his touch. She watched, enthralled, as his skin went taut in response to the press of her fingers. A stillness came over him, as though he held his breath.

He watched her.

She knew.

Co-awareness bounced between them. Lifting her lashes, she met his gaze. An eternity passed as they stared into each other's eyes. She wanted—needed—to know more about him. Everything. Starting with his body.

Why that jagged scar from beneath his rib cage to his hip? Why the wolf tattoo over his pec? It was dark and liquid, throwing colors as though oil spilled in water. Maybe it wasn't even a tattoo. Shifting her touch, her thumb grazed his Adam's apple. It bobbed on a swallow. She stroked his beard... along to his pointed ears.

"You need to stop now," he rasped.

"Why?"

"Because you're turning me on, and it's been"—he licked his lips, a sight that had her stifling a moan—"it's been a long time. Fae can be... relentless in their lovemaking. You are a fragile human."

"But I'm not that human, am I?"

"You won't like me when I lose control."

"So make me stop."

He didn't. Her brazen fingers glided back down his front, bumping over abdominals, aiming for the top of his breeches. She couldn't stop. Desire took control of her function. He'd said *lovemaking* and *relentless,* and now she couldn't get it out of her mind. Two sweaty bodies, naked and tangled with primal need. A mindless craving pushed her every action. Her fingers dipped into the private space beneath his waistband, teasing the coarse hair there. His skin was so hot. She moaned, low and hoarse. He halted her movement with a hand. A warning growl escaped his throat.

"I find I cannot stop," she murmured, eyes lowering to watch her hands, still alive with sensation. Veins popped on the flesh of his hard lower belly. His heady scent called to her, and it was everything she wanted. Right there. Right then. She needed to see more and... she licked her lips. "Let me—"

"Stop touching me." His words compelled her, and her hands snapped to her side, forced by the bargain binding them.

Agape, she stood back.

He stared as though a tempest raged in his mind, as though he wanted to devour her and fought hard not to. As though he hated himself for wanting her. He ran trembling fingers through his silver hair, downcast eyes on her.

God, moving like that, lifting his arms and popping biceps... he made it worse. Clarke shivered. Her cool hands flew to pat her hot cheeks. "I'm so sorry. I don't know what's come over me."

It was a desire like she'd never felt before. It wracked her body and hummed along her skin. His hot gaze dipped to her lips, lowered to her bra, and then went to where the need was strongest. Nostrils flared as though he could scent her arousal. His attention caressed her body, lighting her up.

In two quick strides, he was in her space, bringing her lips to his. But then he paused. Hesitated. Their breaths mingled. Was that her heart beating, or his... or...

She didn't care. She needed it. Wanted it. Expected it.

*Mine*, her mind growled possessively. But he didn't ravage her like she wanted, like he'd promised. He lowered his lips and touched hers with tenderness. The softness of pillowed skin. The scratch of his beard. Then the gentle, shy push of his tongue requesting access. He nibbled her bottom lip, savoring a moment before thrusting through her parted lips and devouring with a guttural growl of need.

Heady. Salty. His taste smashed right through her restraint. She gripped his neck and pulled him flush against her body. The feel of his long drawn-out moan against her chest turned her liquid. They kissed and licked and tongued. God, she needed him.

It was only when her spine hit the spindly trunk of a tree did she realize he'd pushed her backward. Pressed hard against the bark, he took her mouth as though she was his. Lost in his arms, his taste, and his complete devotion, Clarke sank into the moment. No inner alarm screamed for her to run the other way. It was all him. His hard body, his warmth, his roving mouth.

She pushed his hand down to her breast and arched into him. "Rush, touch me."

He jumped back, chest heaving with ragged breath.

"Clarke." He shook his head, a pained look in his eyes. "I can't."

She blinked and hugged herself. What just happened?

"You sure look like you can." Was it really this human versus fae thing? "Never mind. I get it."

His brows lifted in the middle. "I let desire cloud my judgement once, and someone died for it. I can't..."

Someone had died?

"I understand."

She removed the torn tunic and replaced it with his shirt. The muddy and wet thing came down to her thighs, but it was whole.

He put on his jacket and left it unbuttoned as if he were too hot to close it. A flush had ruddied his complexion too. He retrieved his rucksack and then finally buttoned the jacket before putting the baldric and sword back on.

Everything had shifted between them, and yet nothing had. He'd not reneged on his bargain. He wasn't ready to let go of his prejudices, but his perception was changing. For the first time since waking in this strange version of her world, she was on the right track.

That kiss had felt good, damn it. She wanted him. Not because her powers told her to, or this mystical Well, but because he was hot, sexy, desirable. He made her want.

And he made her feel safe. Knowing it, and taking ownership of it made her feel good.

Clearing her throat, she gave him a smile that said they weren't done yet and moved, but he got in her way. A solid wall of fae blocked her. She met his gaze and saw something different. No more hate. No. This darkness was more like the need she felt. Like the want. Her chest warmed with hope.

"Clarke." His velvet-storm voice slid over her in a wave. She held her breath, waiting, wishing. But he only tugged her muddy hair over her ears. "Keep your ears hidden."

# CHAPTER SIXTEEN

They emerged from the Whispering Woods into a field painted gold by the setting sun. Rush's original plan had been to make a quick trip beyond the border walls of Crescent Hollow and steal a portal stone from the markets. Back then, he couldn't give a fee-lion's whiskers about her state of dress. Now he wouldn't let her stay covered in mud. He owed her that act of kindness. Plus, with the late hour, it might take some time to locate a portal stone. Without one, the journey to the Order involved a trip across the Seelie Sea, or further up river via Cornucopia, the trade city.

So to an inn it was.

The thought of sharing a room with Clarke sent a tug straight to his balls. Rush didn't trust himself alone with her, not with the way she looked at him, and not with the way she'd kissed him. After all these years, she was a temptation he couldn't succumb to, especially since she wasn't his Well-blessed mate, and more so because he was beginning to not care.

He still remembered the look of disappointment on his sister's face when she found out he was an unsanctioned breeder. It was one thing to dip your wick, but they expected you to take proper precautions. The elves brewed a certain elixir for these exact purposes. But Rush had not planned. It was a mistake that ended in death for an innocent woman.

He was a disgrace to his father's legacy. Not only had their father died trying to save Rush from drowning in a ritual he'd yet to take, but his mother had followed his father into death not long after. Kyra had lasted as long as she could in Crescent Hollow. She'd cared for Thorne, but after he was the tribute to the Well, she'd had nothing left for her at the Hollow. Thaddeus was cruel to her, so she left.

He should have found a way to help Kyra more. He'd followed her around for a few months, making sure she settled into her job at Cornucopia. He'd found a way to drop coin to help her finances, but in the end, it wasn't enough. It was never enough.

But they were here. At Crescent Hollow. Rush had Clarke to speak for him. There was something he could do now. Maybe if he couldn't get to Thorne, he'd get to Kyra. At least then he'd know what to say.

With Thorne... he was at a loss for words.

"I'm thirsty," Clarke said.

"Yes, princess."

The compound came into sight and they regrouped. Rush handed Clarke a last swig from the waterskin. She took a mouthful and then sprayed it out when her eyes caught on the walls of his old town, just across the field. "*That's* where you grew up?"

He nodded. "Not much to look at, but it kept us safe."

Clarke wiped her mouth. "Um. I'm pretty sure the word you're looking for is castle. Or fortress. With a village inside the walls."

He forced himself to look at it as though for the first time. It was no castle. Village, yes. A small community of about ten thousand.

"More like a fort," he agreed.

"What's on those banners flying over the gate?"

"The Nightstalk Crest." He tapped his chest, where his own family crest had been tattooed on. "You've seen the emblem on my skin."

"And you were the heir?" She returned the waterskin.

"Alpha heir apparent."

"What does that mean?"

"It means I'm strong enough take over the leadership of the pack from my father without being challenged. We wolves call him the alpha, but the king calls him a lord. Lord Nightstalk."

She raised a dark eyebrow. "And you gave that up to join the Guardians?"

He narrowed his eyes at her. "I didn't give it up. More so encouraged to do so after my father died."

Her plump bottom lip disappeared between her teeth. "That sucks."

He shrugged, eyes stuck on those lips of hers.

"If you had the chance, would you want it back?"

He rubbed his chest. No one had asked him that before. Even if he did somehow break his curse, the Order would have to let him go. He'd have to be accepted back into the Nightstalk pack. Then he'd have to challenge Thaddeus.

"Even if I had a future there," he replied. "I'm a Guardian."

"But they cursed you."

"They own me. Even if I get them to lift my curse."

"That... well, that sucks."

He shrugged. "Giving your life over to the service of the Well for enhanced abilities isn't something you can take back. Come on. It's getting dark."

The dirt and grass they were on turned into a red gravel path that crunched when they walked. On either side of them stretched fields of dandelions and fox-tail weeds. They'd only walked half a mile when something lying in the middle of the path caught their attention. Little fee-lions hopped about, prancing and playing. The mischievous creatures were often a sign of irreverence.

"Are those cats?" Clarke asked, shielding her eyes from the sunset.

"They're pests."

"Oh, come on. They can't be that bad. Look at how cute their faces are, all smooshy and those tails swishing about, all agitated. Wait. What are they doing?"

The little beasts lifted their heads. One sniff of his inner wolf and they scampered off with a chitter.

"Don't." He put a palm to her chest, holding her back. He caught a scent on the wind. Sour, rotting flesh. "It's a body."

Which in itself wasn't that unusual. Between the different fae racial clans, a dead body frequently turned up. Guardians didn't solve squabbles between clans or courts. They were better than that. The kings and queens that ruled Elphyne had their own military to keep their subjects in line, but there was often a gap. The poor and smaller races could be overlooked.

"I'll check it out," he warned. With a glance her way, he found her unworried, just curious. "Stay there."

She nodded but tried to see around his body. "Something's not right."

Rush strode toward the dead fae and strained his senses. No heartbeat. Definitely putrefying flesh. It was a satyr. Part man, part goat, the fae's horns had been shorn off. The puncture marks in its neck signaled a vampire's bite, but the corpse wasn't exsanguinated. Perhaps one of the Unseelie had gotten a little rough while eating, a little too far from their territory. But to dump the body here in full view of a Seelie compound. Something smelled off.

It wasn't the first time on this journey something had smelled wrong. The White Woman was far from her usual northern haunt. And she had been cursed, perhaps forced into moving south. That made two Unseelie causing inexplicable harm in Seelie territory.

He went to wave Clarke onward, but she was already behind him.

"What happened?" she asked.

"Vamp got overzealous."

"Why am I not surprised you have vampires?" She frowned down at the body. "Shouldn't he look a little less, I don't know, full of blood?"

"Vamps don't drain to feed. They like to relish one meal over days and usually their meals walk away." Rush took another look at the satyr. His tanned cheeks were rather plump. The hooves sticking out from beneath his nicely creased trousers were shoed with precious stone. So he was well-off, perhaps one of the Seelie gentry. Rush kneeled down and touched the face with the back of his hand. His curse didn't work on dead things.

The satyr had warm skin.

"Recently dead," he murmured. "And vamps rarely travel during the day."

Not unless they had been conditioned, like those in the Order.

"Something about it just doesn't feel right," Clarke added.

Rush agreed. He met her eyes. "You *seeing* something?"

"No. But... maybe..." She patted her sternum and scanned the body. "Maybe check under his shirt."

He lifted it. The lightly fuzzed torso had scorch marks consistent with a mana related attack. Except the pattern was wrong. Instead of a darker ring on the inside with an explosion of striations, the marking was uniform. Not a direct hit to the middle and the visual effect of the blow. This was more like a water stain. Or a mana stain. As though the magical life-force had been ripped from his body, not thrust into it or allowed to naturally escape upon death. He sniffed again and caught a slight metallic scent coming from the body, but when he checked the pockets, there was no metal to be found. Could someone have forcibly taken the mana while he was alive? Rush dropped the shirt and took Clarke's elbow.

"Let's keep moving."

"Why?" She jogged along next to him, hurrying to keep his pace.

"Because someone used magic to kill that fae, and they tried to make it look like a vampire did it." He flexed his jaw with the understanding. "Vampires are Unseelie, yet we are in Seelie territory. With the White Woman far out from her home, it looks like the precarious peace between the two kingdoms is about to break."

"Shit, that's not good."

"Dead bodies are never good. But it's not my business."

It was best they stay out of it and stay on course. The last thing he needed was for Clarke to get caught up in something like this. "We should get into the inn and be out tomorrow as early as we can."

# CHAPTER
# SEVENTEEN

Clarke tugged the hair covering her ears. Coming up to the gate of the compound, it was clear the two sentinels standing beneath the stone portcullis could only see her and not the big brooding fae stalking next to her. He wasn't happy coming back to this place, and it had little to do with the two heavyset guards wearing dirty white uniforms, strapped with weapons. A longbow flashed over their broad shoulders and the scarred faces and broken noses gave her no reason to believe she'd ever be able to escape if they deemed her a threat. Not to mention the lethal wolven fangs pressing into their bottom lips.

*No turning back now.*

Still fifty feet away, she forced each step closer to remain steady and tried not to look at the strange vines

160

hanging over the walls of the compound. She tried to ignore the way they swayed and shifted, or how tendrils unfurled with predatory focus when a butterfly got too close. But she couldn't ignore the suspended wooden cage on each side of the gate. In one was a wolf. In the other, a petite female fae with prismatic dragonfly wings. Short disheveled, blue hair stuck to her face. Pearlescent tear tracks smeared down her dirty cheeks. She slept, or was passed out, on the base of the cage. A dainty hand dangled through the bars as though she'd tried to reach the wolf on the other side.

Clarke looked at Rush.

"Eyes forward," he reminded.

"Sorry." She did as was told and continued walking.

"They're being punished," Rush explained. "By raising a fae from the ground, it cuts them from the source of the Well. Not being able to replenish your spent mana is akin to a hangover you can't escape from. It's torture. And of course, it stops you from shifting as the shift expends a lot of mana. They have trapped the shifter in his animal form until they lower him to the ground."

"You say that like you've experienced it."

He lifted a shoulder. "They tried it on me once. That's when they learned even metal bars can't keep a Guardian from accessing the mana in the earth. It's why they had to resort to a curse." His gaze darted to the female. "My guess is the pix already belonged to a harem, and the lord in

161

charge here has dispensed local reprimands to avoid starting political unrest with the pix clan."

"Harem," she mumbled under her breath. How horrible. "She's being forced into being a sex slave?"

Rush laughed wryly. "So you don't know everything."

She clenched her fists and spoke through her teeth. "Why are you laughing?"

"Because, naïve little princess, for each pixie female, there are at least three male partners and protectors. I've seen some harems reach up to twelve males for one female. She's not being forced into anything. They treat their females like queens."

Clarke's jaw dropped to the ground. "Three men weren't enough for her?"

"Well, you know what they say." He gave her a salacious, toothy grin. "Once you go pack, you never go back."

She blanked. Then got it. "Oh, you're real hilarious, Wolfie."

Pure male smugness rolled off him. "It's not a joke."

"Whatever." Her mood darkened. "It's still wrong to dictate who you can and cannot fall in love with."

She must have hit a sore spot because he gave her a dark sideways glance and compelled her. "*Stop talking.*"

Her lips clamped shut on their own accord. Irritation hit just before the two sentinels hailed her down.

"You. Female." A brutish fae broke away from his friend and stepped toward her. His bruiser face accentuated a stocky body. Bushy eyebrows and hair gave him an unhinged vibe. "State your business."

"Tell them you're just here to get cleaned up after a lengthy journey and that you'll be on your way in the morning."

Before Clarke processed Rush's words, they tumbled from her mouth. Alarm pricked through her. She couldn't stop them. Rush's demand was her compulsion.

The words of the deal came back to haunt her. *You will be my voice where I cannot speak. You will be my hands, where I cannot touch.*

Goddamn him. She had thought they were past this. Pain burned hotly from her nails digging into her palms.

The guard leered at her. "I knock off in five minutes. There's plenty of room at my place. If you need a hand cleaning up... well, I'm real good at using my tongue." He licked his lips.

Ew.

The other guard snickered. From the corner of Clarke's eyes, Rush reddened with fury.

"No thanks," she said of her own accord.

The guard looked her up and down. He lifted his nose and flared his nostrils. "You're not a wolf. What manner of fae are you?"

"Say you're Elven," Rush ordered.

"I'm Elven." She smiled weakly.

"Far away for an elf." The guard still under the shadows of the gate stepped forward, eyes narrowing. He held a drumstick of some animal in one hand, complete with blue and purple feathers still sporadically attached.

Rush nodded to the cage. "The pix is far away too. Is that a crime?"

Clarke was compelled to repeat his words. The two guards looked at her, and then the stocky one laughed.

"The pix's crime is that she fornicated outside her clan."

"Nah," said the other with a chortle. "She's there because she denied Lord Nightstalk."

"If Thaddeus hears you talking like that, you'll be next."

Clarke's blood turned to ice. Thaddeus?

Rush grumbled something under his breath. Unwilling to look at him, Clarke had to assume he knew well that Thaddeus was here. And from memory, Rush said something about an alpha running this place. Which meant only one thing. Clarke was about to step into the territory ruled by the fae who'd tried to assault her.

The guard sniffed and wiped his nose, then motioned for Clarke to enter the compound.

Still fuming at herself for failing to see Thaddeus's connection to this place, and Rush's inability to tell her the truth, she stormed inside a good few feet before taking in the place.

She stopped and gaped. Cobblestone roads. Townhouses with terracotta tiled roofs. Ivy over archways. Moss and lichen painted a patina across the limestone steps and walls. It was quaint, inviting, and it smelled like mouthwatering cooked onions, garlic, and something else she couldn't place. But it was delicious.

Many fae bustled down the streets. From those who looked virtually human, to others with wings or horns. There were no modern amenities... at least none that she saw. From her point of view, it looked like she'd stepped through a looking glass and into the Middle Ages. No cars. No electric lights.

The wonder must have shown on her face because Rush leaned toward her to say, "Wait until you see Cornucopia. That place has fae from all over Elphyne. Or even better, wait until you see the Summer or Winter Court. One castle is made from glass, the other from obsidian. The Spring and Autumn Courts aren't bad either. The summer solstice festival is one you won't want to miss, at any of the Courts."

His words stole her breath, and then she remembered she was furious with him. Her brows slammed down, and she strode forward into the unknown. Following the scent of cooked onions seemed a marvelous idea.

Rush jogged to catch up. "I should have told you Thaddeus was the lord here."

"You think that's the only reason I'm angry?" she replied, then smiled at a gray-haired woman with jaw tusks who looked at her strange for speaking to the air.

"Why else?"

Typical. Males of any species were all the same. "You forced me to speak for you. Again."

He put his hands in his pockets. His expression turned distant, then he nodded up ahead. "Next right. The Laughing Den is where we can stay."

He put something cold in her hand. She looked down and opened her fingers to see two coins made from red glass. Light hit an embellished letter M suspended in the middle of each coin. She lifted it to the sky and turned to marvel at the intricate refractions inside.

"M," she murmured.

"For King Mithras. Good in the Seelie Kingdom and the neutral ground of Cornucopia. That will pay for a room, food and a meal," said Rush. "It's also enough that they'll look the other way."

She desperately needed to bathe, so strode onward until she came to the small narrow street he motioned to turn down. It wasn't so much as a street, but a set of higgledy piggledy stone steps leading upward to a mezzanine with a wooden door and a sign dangling overhead. A laughing wolf carved into the wood meant she was at the right place. Stomping up the steps, she considered asking whether he would force her to speak for him again, or if she was safe to do so herself.

The door burst open and a bodybuilder type came barreling out. Stag horns protruding from his head knocked on a support beam and he jimmied his head a few times to get loose.

Clarke tugged on her hair to hide her face. The stag was from Thaddeus's hunting party. And he was drunk. Rush bared his teeth and pulled Clarke to his side. She narrowly missed the stag as he tumbled down the steps, belching disgustingly. She stood frozen until he made it to the bottom and tracked out of sight.

Rush stared after him. Clarke had to tug him back to attention. Fiery eyes clashed with hers. He'd been close to chasing after the stag.

"What's wrong with you?" she whispered.

He bared lethal fangs. "The wolf in me wants out."

*Christ.* That's just what she needed. "Keep it in your pants. You can't chase him. You'll get sick, and I don't have time to wait on you. I need a bath, a meal, and a nap."

The primal fire in his eyes turned soft when he dragged his gaze down to her. He gave a curt nod.

She tugged open the door and went in.

The foyer filtered into a raucous tavern. The smell of onion was stronger. Her stomach rumbled.

"I'm going to order everything on the menu," she joked.

"Make that two."

"Done."

His lip curved, and he waved toward the back of the tavern. "Take the coin to the bar."

Clarke paid no attention to the curiosity thrown her way by tavern patrons. She knew she must look a sight with mud in her hair, on her face and all over her clothes. Rush looked worse. With his fierce gaze roaming the room, and the battered Guardian jacket barely holding his pumped muscles, she knew many patrons would run the other direction if they could see him. Not to mention the enormous sword angled over his shoulder.

Dodging the sweaty males and occasional scantily clad female, Clarke wondered if the inn was just a magnet for testosterone, or if all drinking establishments were the same, no matter what the era. A female sitting on the lap of a ruddy cheeked male giggled. He moaned. The jimmy of her hand under the table made Clarke blush.

Just exactly what kind of inn was this place?

Finally getting to the bar, Clarke hailed down the barmaid, grateful she seemed normal and not some madame who might wrangle service from her. The brunette had larger than normal arched ears and smooth chocolate skin. A bead dangled down her cheek from a leather headband. It bobbed every time she moved. Black coal rimmed her eyes in a fifties cats-eye fashion. On second glance, the black rims appeared part of the barmaid's physiology, perhaps part of the animal she evolved from. Dusted black, the tip of her nose scrunched as she approached Clarke.

"What," she snapped. "Do I have something on my face?"

Movement low behind the barmaid drew Clarke's attention. Wow. She had a bushy wolf's tail sticking out of her pants. Clarke opened her mouth to speak, but nothing came out.

Rush compelled her to talk.

"I need a room with a bath drawn," she said.

"Put the coin on the bench," Rush instructed.

Her hand whipped out jerkily and slammed money onto the wooden surface. It was as though she were a puppet, and Rush the master.

"Now ask her for two steins of the house ale, cheese, bread and some beef and gravy to be brought up to the room."

The request blurted out of Clarke's mouth.

The barmaid wiped her palms down her black apron and eyed the money. "That's a lot of red coin for those things."

"Throw in some lavender soap," she replied on Rush's command. "And then I want to be left alone."

"Fair enough." The barmaid swiped the coin and put them in the front pocket of her apron. "Two of everything? You expecting someone?"

"I'm hungry."

"Right. Well, I'll put you in the room with the big bed. Just in case." She winked at Clarke. "I'll get the boy onto getting a room and bath prepared."

Rush touched his mouth and then arched his hand low and out. "Repeat that action as a sign of gratitude."

She copied him, touching her fingers to her lips and then out. It was like she blew a kiss but without the blow.

169

She nodded and then reached under the bench and withdrew a key, which she placed in Clarke's palm. "The name's Anise. You need anything. You come see me."

Clarke nodded, was about to say thank you and then clamped her lips shut. She did the action.

Anise tipped her chin toward the far right of the bar. "Up those steps and second door to the left. Give us ten to get the room and meal ready, and then head up." Anise grabbed Clarke's wrist and lowered her voice. "Make sure you bolt the door before you retire for the night."

Another small nod, and then Clarke went with Rush to wait in the shadows at the base of the stairs. The floor was sticky with spilled ale. Every step met resistance beneath her boots. God, she hoped it was ale.

This bath couldn't come sooner. Honestly. When she got into that water, she wasn't coming out until it was cold. At the stairs, she faced the tavern and ignored the fae at her side.

"Clarke," he whispered, remorse lacing his voice.

She held up her palm.

He'd taken control of her body as if it were his own, and to be frank, she felt violated. She couldn't speak with him now. Not with a room full of drunk and disorderly fae who may or may not include members of Thaddeus's hunting party. The stag hadn't recognized her, but someone else might. Being alert and focused on her ability might be the only thing keeping them safe. She also needed to know more about this world if she wanted to survive here.

Clarke let her gaze wander the room and tried to relax, to let her instincts talk to her. Most of the patrons seemed to be wolf shifters. Except that guy. Her eyes roved toward a table near the blazing hearth where one of the biggest fae she'd ever seen sat, joking loudly with his companions. Even sitting at the table, his head towered over the others. He was hard to miss with the big mop of shaggy hair, beard and horns coming down from either side of his forehead to bow outward near his pink-tinged cheeks. Jovial eyes danced as he listened intently to a hooded figure she couldn't identify. Must be a story. Within seconds, a roaring laugh came out of him and he thumped the table, sending every stein and jug soaring half a foot into the air before crashing back down.

"Again!" he shouted to the cowled figure.

A small smile echoed on Clarke's lips.

"He's a muskox shifter," Rush murmured. "Turns into a bull."

Clarke folded her arms. She didn't want to talk to Rush, but who else would translate this place? "Tell me about this village."

He sighed heavily. She didn't know what he was brooding about. He was the one using her as a puppet. He should be fine.

"My uncle is the alpha, or the lord, as the rest of Elphyne call him. Mainly snow wolves live here. We're at the edge of Elphyne, so not much west except the human wasteland." He lifted his shoulders half-heartedly. "Most people here want to get as far away from society as they can. Not sure what else you want to know."

"Do you have family here?"

He stilled. "Mother and father are dead. Sister is... not here."

"I'm sorry to hear about your parents." When she looked at him, he appeared lost. "Have you seen your sister since they cursed you?"

"Not for many years."

"Do you want to?"

"I owe her gratitude."

A male dressed like the soldiers at the gate, and a female in a sheer flowing skirt, bustled passed. No top on. Her breasts bounced far too close to Clarke, and she had to duck out of the way as the soldier chased her up the stairs. The female squealed when he grabbed her rear. He trapped her against the wall, halfway up and gave her an open mouthed kiss.

"Was there no better inn than this?" Clarke murmured.

"This is nothing compared to Cornucopia. It's also the only inn which won't question a female traveling alone." He lowered his lashes, amused. "And I wouldn't go pulling that face on the professional females. They sacrificed their wombs to work here. And they make good coin for it."

She gaped. "Sacrificed their wombs?"

"For the prospect of earning a very good living. None of them have been forced."

She supposed she could understand that. It was a

choice, whether in her time or this. But getting rid of your womb. Surely that was extreme.

A gangly youth of about fifteen descended the steps. He stopped halfway, spotted Clarke and said with a breaking voice, "You room six?"

She checked her key and nodded.

"It's ready."

# CHAPTER
# EIGHTEEN

Rush followed Clarke into their small allotted room and placed his rucksack against the wall near the door. He sniffed about and resisted marking his territory. The overwhelming urge had been all-consuming since arriving at the Hollow. Thaddeus's scent was everywhere. The wolf inside Rush wanted to obliterate it with his own. It would be satisfying to know his uncle would smell him all over the village. But he couldn't risk Clarke's safety. Rush's fresh scent would only draw unwanted attention.

He took stock of the room. It was about twenty-five feet across, with a double bed and window overlooking the street. The long red velvet drapes matched the comforter on the bed and the rug on the floor. Extra pillows and a fire blazing on a hearth felt cozy. No sprites. Thank the Well. A long wooden tub had been dragged in and steamed with water heated by mana stones at the base. A small round table for two was the last piece of furniture by the hearth, and it was laden with food. They'd been given the best room red coin could buy. It was clean. It would do.

He could ignore the moaning and thumping coming from the next room across. Sure.

Clarke groaned upon entering. The husky sound was a bolt of heat straight to his groin.

"I don't know what to do first," she sighed. "A four day hike is the longest I've ever been on. This seems like heaven."

Rush broke off some bread and dipped it in gravy. He shoved it in his mouth and then took a chunk of cheese, curiously watching her choose food. She made more tiny feminine sounds of satisfaction when she ate.

Her lips mesmerized him. He could watch her eat in a timeless loop.

It had been so long since he'd been like this with a female, he'd forgotten the minor things that brought him pleasure—the brightness in her eyes, the flush in her cheeks, the relish as she chewed. This was a different kind of intimacy he missed. The kind he'd always longed for with a mate. Small, domestic moments in which they would sit, complacent and content. She could sleep, and he could keep watch, protecting. Doing what he was born to do. But those longings had been pushed to the side the moment he became a ghost.

He was a fool. Guardians rarely mated anyway.

And he had no time for such indulgences. There were things to do before they left. He couldn't do it in his torn jacket. Since it was easier to leave it than to carry it around while he sourced clean clothes, he unbuttoned his baldric and removed his sword. Then he did the same for his jacket and tossed it against the back of a chair. He took a swig of ale and then another mouthful of cheese.

Clarke flinched and hesitated.

"What's wrong?" he asked.

"Oh nothing," she cooed with a hint of sarcasm, then she narrowed her eyes. "Nothing beyond waiting to see if you'll compel me to strip, or something equally humiliating."

He almost spat out his cheese. "You think I'd command you to..." His voice trailed off as he took in the tub, the bed, and his discarded jacket. She also grumbled about the type of establishment it was. He swallowed the painful lump and then strode to her with a growl. "Never put me in the same category as Thaddeus and his men. I'm leaving the jacket because I can't carry it around with me. It's torn and dirty, but it is a crime to leave it in public as someone could steal it and impersonate a Guardian."

"I thought it was invisible." She lifted her chin.

"Only when I touch it."

A contrite blush tinted her cheeks, but challenge danced in her eyes. He didn't think she realized what that did to a wolf like him. It made him want to dominate her.

To take her. He tossed the rest of his cheese on the platter and headed to the door.

"Where are you going?" she demanded.

"I'm leaving you to your privacy. Bolt the door and don't go anywhere." He opened the door and slammed it behind him, shoulders pressed against the wood until he heard the satisfying thud of the bolt falling into place. If she refused to let him back in, he could either use the window or compel her. Until then, he had work to do.

There was only one place he could use to clean himself up. The abandoned family home passed down to Thorne. Hopefully, it might still hold some items of clothing. Kyra hadn't been back to the family home since Thorne's initiation to the Order.

A FEW HOURS LATER, Rush returned to the inn, bathed, cleaned and in borrowed buckskin breeches and a woolen sweater. Before he entered the Den, he stood outside on the street, and let the fresh night air cool his skin.

The family home had been clean, but clearly not visited in years. Thorne had probably only taken the apartment because it was the one thing that had been left for him after Rush's sentence. Thaddeus had run Kyra out of town, but the Order of the Well had power over the Crown and its lords. They wouldn't have let the house be taken from a Guardian.

Rush had sat too long in the house, wondering what his son thought of him, wondering what he would say to him if they ever got to meet. It was always the same questions running through his mind, but since Thorne had been forced to join the Guardians, Rush had seen little of him. Going back to the Order had been too painful.

Thorne was the same size as Rush, albeit a little smaller in the chest, so finding something to wear had been no issue. Clarke's clothes, on the other hand, Rush had to break into the neighbor's house and pilfer from the closet. He now had a pair of leather pants, a blouse, a thick-waisted belt, and a pair of lace-up boots that might actually fit her.

He dropped some coin to pay for the clothes. Long ago Rush had learned that if he accidentally dropped coin, the curse didn't think he was trying to communicate. The loophole had served him well when he'd helped his sister establish herself in Cornucopia after her exodus from the Hollow.

But he still needed to locate a portal stone. He figured he would drop the outfit off and then head out again. Better than letting Clarke sit on the bed naked.

Heat crept up his neck at the thought, and his mind kept returning to the kiss they had shared in the woods. Her lips were so soft it maddened him. At the time, he'd lost all sense of logic. He'd reasoned that if he let himself have that one moment, he could use it to... he didn't know what... take the edge off his loneliness? Something like that. And the tortured bastard he was, he let himself replay the scene over in his head, relishing in the touch and feel of her against him. That scent of hers... It had only made things worse. He couldn't stop thinking of her. His mind stalled when he got to the part where she'd taken his hand and demanded he touch her.

He went to tug his collar and realized he had none. The jacket wasn't on, and the sweater had a low V-neck. Crimson save him. Tonight would be difficult. Maybe he'd take the floor... or even sleep in the drained tub. Maybe he could sleep outside in the hall and just hope no one tripped over him.

Time to go in.

He strode into the tavern, took his time going up the stairs, and then got to their room and knocked.

A shuffle came from within.

A scraping sound came when the bolt lifted. Not sure what state to expect her in, he cleared his throat and froze when the door swung open. He almost forgot his purpose for being there. She was... beautiful. Red hair, cleaned and brightened to match the flames in the hearth. Milky white skin glowed and smelled like the lavender soap he'd compelled her to order. The one she'd fantasized about having when she rambled while they'd crossed the bog. Now he fantasized about that lavender on her body.

Bright blue eyes flashed defiantly, and for a moment, he failed to understand why. Then his gaze dropped to her cover. His Guardian jacket. Washed clean, virtually dried, and with the rip at the shoulder mended. Too big and heavy for her, it hung off one shoulder, giving him a tantalizing taste of décolletage.

Had she mended the jacket? For him?

A swollen sense of pride hummed at the sight. A Guardian let no one wear his jacket. Ever. But on her... it was perfect. *Both belong to me.* The thought came out of nowhere, but once it had, the wolf inside him howled. *Mine.*

His fingers clenched so tight on the package in his hands that he feared he'd rip the items in two.

She stepped aside to allow him entry. "You took your sweet-ass time."

He couldn't move. His stillness was the only thing keeping his raw instincts from reaching out and claiming her, biting, and marking her as his. His tongue thickened and dried. His chest heaved with ragged breath. And he couldn't stop staring at the rosy bottom lip caught between her teeth.

This was insane.

She was human. He, a cursed fae. This would never work.

"What?" Her brows puckered. "I cleaned and fixed it before I put it on. There was a small sewing kit in a drawer. My jeans were ruined, and your tunic was too cold."

He shoved the package into her arms. It gave him the excuse to get close, drop his nose to her hair, and inhale deeply. He lived for that moment. Would battle a horde for

180

that moment. But when it was done, he left the room and slammed the door closed behind him. He leaned back on the wood. Again. This was the second time he'd found himself speechless and leaning against this door. Curse him again.

His wolf wanted her with a savage intensity he'd not felt in all his years. It claimed her as his. What did this mean?

Mind whirling in confusion, he took the stairs two at a time until he burst through the exit. He broke into a jog, heading for the markets and hoped he crossed paths with that stag… or any of his uncle's hunting party. But if he didn't, he'd find a way to release this pressure of need inside him, even if that meant he was crippled with pain afterwards because the truth battering his defenses was too difficult to accept.

That he'd found a mate.

But not one blessed by the Well, or they would have instantly received an identical blue mana-marking along their arms, a mirror of the other. The marking signaled the Well—nature—approved. It would link them in mind and spirit.

But if they weren't blessed, then the curse wouldn't be broken.

What cruel world would taunt him with happiness so close to his death?

# NINETEEN

Clarke had to burn her bra and jeans due to severe deterioration and disgustingness, but was pleased with the outfit Rush had brought her. It could have been worse. It could have been one of the stuffy medieval type dresses some ladies had worn in the streets. Or one of the flimsy sheer skirts and strips of fabric covering the working women downstairs. Instead, she ended up in soft brown leather pants, a gray linen blouse, and a thick belt that went around her middle, almost like a corset. With the blouse tucked, the folds gathered around her roving breasts, holding them in place.

Did Rush know how this would look on her when he chose the outfit? Curves accentuated, bust amplified... She touched her lips at the memory of their kiss. He'd left so suddenly after giving her the clothes. He'd looked nervous.

In the black glass mirror behind the door, her reflection

showed no evidence of the person she used to be. Clarke smoothed her hands down her hips. Everything fit, even the calf-high boots. Rush had purposefully sourced an outfit similar to what she had already worn. Knowing the big brooding fae had been thinking about her made her stomach do a little flip. She tried to suppress the flutter by putting her hand to her stomach. Her dreams were still filled with nightmares, but more often than not, her instincts kept veering toward Rush. She realized he used to be an honorable fae. His past and curse had changed him, but she didn't believe that part of him was completely gone. Still, it wouldn't hurt Clarke to start thinking about a plan B. Trusting a man had steered Clarke down dark paths before. Trusting herself was a better option.

The woman staring back at her was someone she didn't recognize. A different person. Something about Rush empowered her to speak her mind. To stand her ground. He was a big bad wolf, yet she'd snapped at him, shouted at him, and even saved his life. And that part had been hard. Dragging his heavy body out of the swamp. There had been a moment or two when she'd thought it was too much, but she did it.

Purpose and resolve hardened within her. She would find a way to warn the right person about what she'd seen in her nightmare. Maybe it was the king. Maybe it was someone else. If Rush would not help her, then she'd find someone who would.

Either way, she was learning that making her own

decisions felt a hell of a lot better than having someone make them for her.

The memory of the barmaid's pretty face came to mind. Clarke would go down to the tavern, have a drink at the bar, and speak with her. Barmaids in any time would be useful sources of information, and Clarke was good at talking.

Clarke fluffed her hair to ensure her ears were well and truly covered, and then on second thought, tore off a strip from the bottom of Rush's old tunic. She wrapped it around her head to keep her ears from sticking out. Once satisfied her look was solid, she rustled around in the rucksack for more coin. She found a collection of different colored glass discs in a bag. Red, blue, yellow and clear. From the way the barmaid had reacted, the red was worth more. But to be safe, she took a variety of each and pocketed them. Rush wouldn't miss them, and if he did, she didn't care.

She also found a curious little wooden carving, just like at Rush's cabin. Picking it up, she let the figurine roll in her fingers. It was a wolf. Deciding she liked it, she shoved it in her pocket next to the coins.

Feeling more upbeat already, Clarke paused at the open door and pushed out with her senses to feel for any bad vibes filtering back from the tavern downstairs. Biting her lip, she concentrated hard on her instincts. After a moment, nothing echoed back but continual joy and merriment. A smile tickled her lips. Perfect.

Down in the tavern, the place had become crowded. The line at the bar went two people thick, and new bartenders fielded the drinks. Disappointment swamped Clarke, but then an urge pulled her gaze to the right. On a small table near the fireplace, Anise sat sharing a meal with the largely muscled muskox fae she'd noticed earlier. As though sensing her attention, Anise looked up and met Clarke's eyes. Her lips curved, she leaned toward the fae at her side and spoke. His gaze flicked Clarke's way, and then he grinned. An enormous hand lifted into the air, high over others' heads, and waved for Clarke to come over.

This could be the opportunity she'd been waiting for, and the wherewithal to proceed on her own in this world. If Rush continued to push her to uncomfortable limits with this bargain of his, then it mattered not if she thought he was honorable. She needed a better escape plan.

She straightened her blouse, smoothed her hands over her hips and strode forward as though she belonged there. She had to sidestep an energetic arm wrestle by two rotund looking fae, but she made it otherwise intact.

"Hi," she said upon arrival and smiled.

"Take a seat." The big fae's voice was a deep, slurred rumble. If he'd been drinking since she'd arrived, he'd be quite drunk. He pulled a stool out for her to sit and then hit his chest with a fist. "I'm Caraway."

"Nice to meet you, Caraway. I'm Clarke." She held out her hand over the chipped table for a shake.

He looked at her hovered hand and chuckled heartily. "What do I do with that?"

"Sorry." Probably not a custom observed in this time. She wiped her palm on her pants. "It's something we elves do."

Clarke sat down in a rush and noticed Caraway had a blue teardrop tattoo under his eye.

"You're a Guardian!" she exclaimed, excited that she knew something of worth.

He stiffened. Anise looked at her with shrewd eyes. "That's not a problem, is it?"

"No." Clarke held up her palms. "I meant no offense."

"Well, I'm off duty," Caraway mumbled.

She sensed anguish lacing the big mountain-man's soul. It was the same suppressed melancholy she'd felt in Rush. Something in the way he laughed, but it didn't quite hit his eyes. Maybe all Guardians had it. Their jobs were brutal, unforgiving, and often went unappreciated. When Anise's tail swished in agitation, Clarke realized she was staring.

"Elf, hey?" Anise asked as she tore into the cooked leg of an animal. "What brings you this far west?"

"Oh. Um." Shit. What had Rush said? Nothing? Clarke scrambled with her instincts, looking for something to say, but Anise saved her from embarrassment.

"It's the secret beau, right?" She gave Clarke a wink.

"Uh. Yeah. Sorry, I didn't want to mention before."

"Thought so." Anise turned to Caraway. "Pay up, big boy."

His cheeks pinked, and he pulled a clear coin from his pocket. After giving him a smug once over, Anise shifted her stein toward Clarke. "You want it? I have to get back to the bar in a minute."

Clarke lifted the stein to her lips. The ale tasted like sour cherries.

"This is good," she declared.

"Probably not the same quality as you're used to, but I make it myself." Anise's eyes lit up with a sudden thought. "If you're wanting something a little more up your alley, I have a few Elven elixirs under the bar."

"Oh? That sounds interesting."

"I'll bring some over after I go back." She waggled her brows. "I'll even bring something you can use later."

Clarke smiled over the lip of her stein as if she knew what Anise meant. "That sounds great."

Caraway and Anise shared a conspiring look that led Clarke to believe the elixir was something either completely disgusting, or very good and perhaps illicit. Either way, if it led the two to trust her, then all the better.

# TWENTY

Sitting across from Clarke on a chipped wooden table, Caraway's cheeks were pink. His eyes sloped down at the sides like a puppy. Anise glanced often at him from beneath her lashes. It was clear the two of them were hyper-aware of the other's presence.

"So, Caraway," Clarke started. "Do you mind if I ask you a question?"

"I'm all ears." His low muskox ears twitched out. And then he boomed a belly laugh at his own joke.

She smiled. "If I wanted an appointment with someone important at the Order of the Well, how would I go about getting one?"

He looked at her strangely, and Clarke knew this must be a very obvious answer to all fae.

Caraway scratched his beard. His deep voice rumbled, "You mean like the Prime? Or one of the Council?"

She nodded. Sure. That would do.

A loud burst of male voices cut through the room, and then a hush followed as the front door opened. In came three tall, haughty fae. All wore red embroidered coats and had jeweled bone-weapons strapped to their bodies.

"What are they doing here?" Anise grumbled.

"Don't know. Don't care." Caraway lifted his stein and drank.

"You might not have to serve the king, but I do."

Caraway turned ruminative and something unsaid passed between Anise and he. A lick of tension sizzled, and Clarke didn't need to be psychic to know this was a bone of contention between the two. Anise looked at him. Her lips pressed together as though she was holding in a tirade of words.

Clarke slid her gaze over to the serving bar to see most people in the tavern had given the guards a wide berth. And it was exactly what they liked. She didn't get the sense they were soldiers. They looked too pretty and too clean. From the polished, filed finger nails to the trimmed facial hair.

"They look like they're insta-famous assholes," Clarke said under her breath.

"Like what?" Anise asked.

"Oh." Heat hit Clarke's cheeks. She kept forgetting no one here knew a thing about Instagram, Facebook, or anything technically advanced. "Nothing."

Anise just rolled her eyes. "They look like they were born in a bed of red coin, that's what."

"They wouldn't know how to use those swords if they fell on them," Caraway grumbled.

"So why do you let them run around and cause so much trouble when they're here?"

"Because it's none of my business. Not magic, not my problem."

*Oh. Here we go.* This was the source of their contention.

Anise's eyes lit up with anger. "You keep spouting that bullshit, and I swear I'll—" She bit her words off.

Caraway's brows lowered. His voice rumbled. "You'll what?"

They stared at each other. And then Anise answered. "Being a Guardian is your job, Caraway. Not your life." Anise stood and shook herself from head to toe. "I'd better go before my pay gets docked. I'll bring back some of that elixir," she added to Clarke, and then strode off.

Caraway's droopy doe-eyes watched her rear the entire way, and from the extra swagger in Anise's step, she knew it. Clarke hid her smile behind the stein and pretended not to notice.

Caraway turned back to Clarke with a brooding scowl. "She's wrong. Being a Guardian is my life. And sticking my nose into local politics isn't in my job description." He slammed his fist on the table. "Right. Where were we?"

Clarke jolted with the sudden turn of conversation.

"You were about to tell me how to get an audience with the Prime."

"Yes. Good." He rubbed his thick beard. "Helps if you know a Guardian or a Mage of the Order, and it just so happens, you're in luck." He tapped the tattoo under his eye. "I know both."

"You're both Mage and Guardian?"

A booming belly laugh came out of him. Clarke wanted to join in.

"No," he replied. "I'm barely one. But I know plenty. When you get there, ask for Thorne and tell him Caraway sent you—he's an honorable Nightstalk wolf. Or if you want a fellow elf, ask for Leaf. He can be a right warada's tail sometimes, but he's on the council. Stay away from Cloud."

"Right. Thorne—wolf. Leaf—elf. Er, stay away from Cloud. Got it. Th—" She took another a sip of ale to hide her thanks. Damn it. She needed to watch that. The last thing she needed was to be in debt to another Guardian. She remembered the action Rush had taught her. She touched her fingers to her lips and pushed out.

"Don't mention it," Caraway chuckled.

A burst of mocking laughter drew Caraway's attention to the bar. His expression darkened, his shoulders tensed, and his gaze moved as though following someone. Anise headed back their way. Her ears drooped and her bottom lip disappeared between her teeth as though she were trying to stop it trembling.

She put the two steins of cherry ale on the table and stood there, fingers clenched around the handles, eyes squeezed shut. "I hate those floaters."

Caraway's eyes softened. His hand moved to cover hers. "Neese..."

"Don't," she snapped and took her hand away. Water pooled at the black rims of her eyes. "You don't get to give sympathy when you refuse to do something about those cretins."

He drew his hand back, and for the first time, Clarke saw a flash of the lethal Guardian flickering beneath his casual demeanor. Those horns spilling from his head suddenly seemed extra pointy and hard.

"What did they want?"

"Nothing," she mumbled. "Some drivel about a dead body outside the gates. Apparently a vamp is hunting in the area."

"That's... odd." Caraway frowned, but then shrugged. "Guess it got overzealous."

Anise dipped her hand into her apron pocket and pulled out two little vials of glowing liquid. She placed them on the table before Clarke.

Caraway stiffened and glanced around. His gaze went specifically toward the red-coated guards loitering at the bar. "You know I don't like you dealing that shit in public, Neese."

Anise rolled her eyes at him. "Fuck them. They're not

193

even looking. Besides, I like to know at least someone will get slippy tonight."

From Caraway's blush, Clarke guessed "get slippy" meant sex. And then Clarke blushed.

Anise sat down and pointed to the blue bottle. Her husky voice came out rushed. "This will give you and your beau stamina to last the night long." She pointed to the diluted pink water. "This will ensure you avoid an execution warrant."

Yep. Definitely sex. Wait. Clarke blinked. "Execution?"

"Unsanctioned breeding," Anise elaborated with a "duh" tone to her voice. "If you ask me, the law is archaic. They sit in their castle with mountains of food enough to feed Elphyne ten times over, yet they still insist on keeping control of who can have children and how many."

Caraway grumbled something under his breath.

"Yeah I get it," Anise snapped at him. "None of your business. But what if it was someone you knew or cared about? Oh, sorry. I forgot. You lot don't care about anyone but yourself."

"Low shot, Anise."

She raised her brows in challenge but said nothing.

Caraway took the bait anyway. "Need I remind you that Thorne's parents were both on the receiving end of that law. I know exactly how it affects the lives of those left behind."

"So why don't you do something about it?"

"The law is the law."

"The Guardians are above the law."

"Not that one."

"Ugh," Anise groused and turned her back on Caraway to face Clarke. "I'm over Guardians."

"Shh." Caraway cast a wary eye at the people surrounding them and waved her down. "Enough."

Anise lifted her eyes to the ceiling and took a breath, then refocused on Clarke. "Okay, well, because of that stupid law, don't use the blue one for a good time unless you're using the first elixir. Pink generally works within a few hours. Blue works in a few minutes. I'm not sure how the elves dose it in Delphinium, but don't take more than one drop of the blue, otherwise neither of you will be able to sit down for days, if you know what I mean." She winked mischievously.

Clarke sat there for a moment letting Anise's explanation sink in. One elixir was an aphrodisiac and one was contraception.

"So crude," Caraway said into his stein, but the brightness in his eyes told another story. He was into it. Perhaps had even tried the aphrodisiac. Maybe even with Anise.

"How much do I owe you?" Clarke asked, not wanting to be rude and turn it away.

"Nothing," Anise replied. "The two red coin you gave for the room will still cover it."

Caraway spurted ale out and then tried to wipe his front. "*Two* red coin? What on earth do you do for a living?"

Clarke decided something closest to the truth would be best. "I'm a Seer."

He raised a dark eyebrow. "Must be good if you earn red coin."

She shrugged. "I do okay."

"Do me." He waved a hand her way. "Read my fortune."

"Okay," Clarke laughed. "But nothing comes free."

"What do you want?"

"Information," she replied.

"Already done."

"Ooh, you drive a hard bargain." Clarke smiled. "But maybe you can give me a little more?"

He nodded. "Double done."

She did this sort of thing all the time back in Vegas. Before Bishop. Usually it was a bunch of fumbled guesses based on a combination of vibes she sensed, body language, and her vague instincts. But she managed well enough to score a quick buck and to feed herself. Sometimes she even swiped a watch from the wrist of a customer. Caraway had no valuables in easy reach, and she was trying to turn a new leaf, damn it.

*Stop thinking about stealing.*

Clarke took his hand and tipped it palm up. Making a show of smoothing his calloused fingers until he relaxed, she sent Anise a quick sideways glance to see if she watched. She did. Avidly.

*Interesting.*

She cleared her throat and concentrated on the Guardian's palm. "Very curious," she murmured.

"What?" He shuffled in his seat.

"See this line here? It's the life line. Very long and unbroken. That's good."

He snorted. "That's not unusual. Fae live long."

"But this line." She traced down another wrinkle on his palm. "This is the fate line. It twists and turns and links into your life and love line. Looks like you'll find your love from a pool of people you've spent much of your life with and will continue to do so."

"You mean I'll find a mate?" He blinked. "But I'm a Guardian."

She shrugged. "I can only tell you what your lines show. And there's a powerful link between them. Also this bit here." She pointed to a crease in his little finger. "This means you look excellent in buckskin breeches."

He blanked.

So did Anise.

Then the two of them burst out laughing. Clarke's own smile warmed her face, and she hoped she'd planted a few seeds to give the two of them a push in the right direction. Anyone who argued like they did, and stole glances at each other the way they did, must harbor hidden romantic feelings. Sometimes they just needed a nudge to get there.

She squeezed Caraway's hand, intending to let go, but a sudden spark of electricity zapped into Clarke's palm and she jolted. As the tingling intensified, her sight darkened around the edges. The sounds of the tavern filtered away to be replaced by a nightjar calling as a vision took hold of her.

Sun shone brightly in her eyes, and she lifted her hand to shield. When she took her hand away, it wasn't the sun, but a bright ring sparking with lightning and warping the vision inside. Through the ring, three dark human sized silhouettes formed. It was like she stared at something from a fantasy movie. A portal. Silhouettes stepped through. A shudder ran through Clarke's body when she recognized Thaddeus. Her vision swung to the side and landed on the stout soldier from the gate. He made a disgruntled face before he threw his feathered drumstick down.

Then Clarke was back in the tavern, blinking at both Caraway and Anise, who in turn looked at her with wary surprise.

"Your eyes went white," Anise murmured. "You truly are a Seer."

"It was a true-dream, wasn't it?" Caraway added, eyes dark and stern. "What did you see?"

"Um. I think the Lord of Crescent Hollow has returned. I should go." She shoved the blue vial his way. "Here. It's a gift. For when you meet that longtime friend."

His complete mortification took Clarke by surprise. Caraway darted a glance to Anise and then made a hasty exit with his stein. He didn't even say goodbye. He rejoined his ragtag group of male fae, still arm wrestling, and belched loud enough to cover the laughter. Then he made some crude comment. They all raucously cheered and lifted their steins.

Clarke looked to Anise. "What did I do wrong?"

She only laughed until tears glistened in her eyes. "You insulted his masculinity, you numb-nuts. Elves might be a bit liberal with their use of elixirs, but it's still a secret stimulant everywhere else... or maybe a private agreement. Also some use it when they're having trouble between the sheets, if you know what I mean. It's not exactly encouraged considering the laws about breeding."

"Oh." This conversation wasn't going so well.

Anise's humor dropped. "I'd keep the blue vial out of view if I were you. He wasn't wrong with not wanting to do this in public. If word gets around to the alpha that I'm dealing under the bar..." She bit her lip. "But with the taxes here, a wolf has to do what a wolf has to do."

"Say no more." Clarke swiped the tiny vials and tucked them down her blouse and wedged them under the pressure of the belt. She would find a way to get rid of them later... well, her cheeks heated, maybe she would keep the contraception elixir. That unsanctioned breeding law was savage.

Clarke looked at Caraway with a frown. "He left before giving me that extra information."

Anise collected an empty stein and wiped the wooden table with a rag. "What do you need? Maybe I can help."

"I think I've *Seen* something." Once again, a side of the

truth was always the best lie. "I think it could endanger everyone and I'm not sure who to go to with it. Caraway gave me a few names from the Order, but now..." Clarke fumbled with a tie on her belt.

"You think they won't stick their noses into business that isn't theirs?" Anise finished for her.

Clarke nodded.

"Well," Anise continued. "If what you saw has to do with magic, then they'll help, no doubt about it. If not..." Anise glanced back to the bar where the red-coats still made trouble. "I don't know who else to suggest. I'm sorry. How will you get there?"

"To the Order? I guess I'll walk."

"It's a long way. Seems you could afford a decent portal stone."

A portal. Of course. "And where do I get one of those at this hour?"

"Just so happens I have a friend who sells them. Ask for Peytr at the markets. His stall is the one with the blue pix on the sign. If he's closed, just go around the back. He lives behind."

Clarke made the "thank you" hand sign just as someone shouted Anise's name from the bar.

"I need to go," she said. "Nice to meet you, Clarke."

"You too, Anise."

It was time for Clarke to leave. The vision she'd had worried her. It was hard to tell from the vision, but the soldier had been the same one she'd seen at the gate.

Thaddeus was either in town, or he would be soon. And then he'd probably find her at the inn. She needed to track Rush down and alert him, or better yet, secure herself a portal stone. If it did what the name suggested, then it could be her ticket out of there and to safety.

# CHAPTER TWENTY-ONE

Rush whittled the finishing touches on a small carving as he stood quietly in a corner of a room at the barracks, watching a clandestine meeting take place. The meditative act of his hands cast his mind into the past, and the changes he'd gone through since his curse.

It had taken him most of his life to realize the benefit of understatement. From a young age he'd been enraptured with the power of the Guardians, the strength of his father, the alpha, or the glitz and glamour of the Seelie King in his castle of glass. To a young wolf, this attention and power had meant dominance. Worth. Righteousness. But it wasn't until Rush's identity was stripped from him did he realize the magic of being overlooked. No pressure to perform. No heightened ridicule. No gilded cage of expectation. For the first time, he'd been free.

The joy of it had lasted only a short while, and then he'd started learning things. Secrets. Lies. Manipulations. He'd seen the true colors of the fae he'd dedicated his life to protecting, and not all of it was pretty. He'd learned how much stock the castle kept in their cellars. Money, food, health elixirs. Enough to feed an army and more. Enough to supply their entire realm. The Winter Queen—the High Queen of the Unseelie—hoarded in the same way. The irony wasn't lost on him. Fae believed they were the better race because they had survived the ravaged world the original humans had left behind. But the thing was, fae were descended from humans. They'd inherited the same intrinsic desire for war and that driving urge to be on top of the food chain, no matter what the cost. Greed ran in the veins of both races.

So what made one better than the other?

Nothing.

Rush had to become a ghost to learn the fact. He'd seen inside the human city, how they acted and followed their leaders... exactly the same way fae did in Elphyne. Shadow copies of each other. Fae weren't the better race. They were the lucky race. Through no fault of their own did fae evolve from mixed human and animal DNA. It was a freak skip in evolution, possibly brought about through the nuclear cataclysm that saw the extinction of most other beings. But it also involved the magic of the Well. The planet didn't want to die, and it needed someone to fight for it, so the fae were born, and they were given magic. And now they thrived. An undercurrent ran in the collective minds of complacent fae: they were the real gods. They were on top of the food chain. And they deserved to say who lived, who died, and how they went about doing it.

They talked a lot of shit.

It wasn't until Clarke came along that Rush was reminded not all were the reflection of their label. That he didn't have to stay indoctrinated to the beliefs forced onto him. That he could think for himself.

And right now, he was staring at a mislabeled mistake, thinking some terrible things. Thaddeus. Supposedly the town's protector, their alpha... their wannabe lord. Bullshit. Here he was having secret talks with three other underhanded fae: the Captain of King Mithras's Royal Guard; a dishonored Dark Mage of the Order; and a vampire of the Unseelie gentry. From what Rush gathered, they waited on a human.

Here were the most depraved beings on this land he could conjure, and that included the monsters he fought in the wild. Rush couldn't even say he was surprised by their collusion.

It made sense they'd picked this location. Crescent Hollow was the last fae settlement this far west, and it sat isolated between a mountain range and a dangerous forest. The barracks were near the gate. No one came down to these dank and shoddy stone buildings except for the sentinels and Nightstalk militia.

"I'm not willing to stake my reputation on the promises of a human who can't even turn up on time," the vampire said, folding his wiry arms across his chest.

"What reputation?" Rush scoffed aloud. "You can't even keep your shirt free from meal stains, let alone keep your colony safe."

This was the only part of his curse he enjoyed. He could mouth off to anyone, to their face, and they knew nothing. As a Guardian, he'd had to hold his peace on more than one occasion, especially when it involved opinions of kings and queens.

Rush snorted and gave the vamp a scathing once over. From his luxurious clothing, the vampire was clearly a lord of some kind. The vampires in the Order were brutal and lethal, but this one... he smelled weak willed. He looked entitled. He was nothing but a sleep-feeder, preying on the helpless and docile for his sustenance.

If Clarke were there, she'd probably tell him she had bad vibes about the fae.

A slight smile lifted Rush's lips when he thought of Clarke in his Guardian jacket, and how she'd mended it. For him.

He scrubbed his hand over his face. His world was turning upside down, and the worst part was that he was finally in a position to be smart enough to know which things needed changing, and that maybe Clarke was right, and he did want to do something about it, but his time was running out. Soon he wouldn't be changing anything, and the world he was leaving for his son was on the same path of destruction as the one that was destroyed millennia ago.

Casting his gaze around the small barracks room, Rush tried to commit their appearances to memory. This illicit meeting clearly had undertones of subterfuge. Every single person in this tiny room was a traitor to the Well, and potentially to the Elphyne as a whole.

Next to the vampire stood the Dark Mage. Once a member of the Order, he was now banished and exiled for using mana in twisted and unnatural ways. Like a drug, mana could take hold of one's logic and convince them their underhanded ways were acceptable. The wings peeking from beneath the Mage's long robe were skeletal-thin, just like his body. If there had been feathers there once, there weren't now. Rush would be surprised if those wings flew at all. Mana-addiction had a tendency to drain the body of all other nutrition, and the user often forgot to sustain themself. It's why the monsters they hunted were so ferocious. Many of them hunted to eat mana and nothing else. Malnutrition gave the Mage's long hook nose a more sinister appearance. He was probably striking once.

Shifting his gaze to the right, Rush surveyed the other two fae. A red-coated captain of the Seelie Royal Guard, and Thaddeus looking smug and content with his arms folded as he leaned against a small desk.

"I agree," the captain said, his one ear twitching. "I

don't enjoy waiting, Thaddeus. You said this human would be here, and he's not."

"Relax," Thaddeus replied. He flicked a piece of lint from his navy woolen coat. "We didn't go to the effort of staging a murder just to get you out here for a game of three-stroke cards. He's on his way."

Rush's ears pricked up. So he had been right. The murdered satyr was a pretense for subterfuge.

"And the rest?" the captain asked.

"We've deployed a handful of monsters around this realm. Soon word will get out that the Winter Queen is encouraging her subjects to take up residence in Seelie land. King Mithras will take the bait."

"Good."

Disgust simmered beneath Rush's skin. He'd always known Thaddeus was underhanded, but he'd never believed he would commit treason. And to hear he was the reason for the White Woman. Clarke had almost died. Again. Everything about this situation was off.

Including, he realized with a start, that he cared whether Clarke lived or died. But once his mind had gone there, the feeling lodged with certainty in his gut. No. He wasn't prepared to put her in harm's way again. So... where did that leave them?

The door opened. A dark hooded silhouette stood in the threshold, his face hidden within the recess of the cowl.

"Ah," Thaddeus said. "Come in. We've been waiting for you."

The hooded figure walked in. From the breadth of the shoulders and the sheer size of him, Rush knew it was a man. And—he sniffed—the bastard had metal on him, in thick and heavy quantities. Forbidden weapons. War machines.

Two shifters walked in behind the human. Rush recognized them from Thaddeus's hunting party. And then Rush looked ten feet beyond the two fae, to further down the street. A familiar face made his heart stop. Pale skin. Beautiful red hair. Clarke stood in the alley outside the door, looking just as surprised as he. What the hell was she doing here?

No one seemed to notice she was there. He threw his gaze back to Thaddeus who had gone still, like a predator stalking its prey, eyes locked on the distance—outside the open door.

No.

Thaddeus turned to the hooded human. "Did you bring someone with you?"

The hood shook his head.

"Not a female? A woman with red hair?"

"No," came the gruff voice from inside the shadow of the cowl. "I came alone."

"Stay here," Thaddeus ordered his crew, and then flicked his right hand out until claws protracted from his fingers. He gave a low warning snarl. "Out of my way."

208

He moved, shouldering through his two wolf shifters. Rush stood no chance of getting between Thaddeus and Clarke. He pursued all the same. The moment he entered the dark stone cobbled lane, Rush caught a whiff of lavender soap and Clarke's unique musk on the wind. Dread unfurled in his gut. She'd just signed her own death warrant. There would be nowhere she could hide. Not now that Thaddeus had her scent a second time. It was too unique.

"Did you dress up for me?" Thaddeus's voice had a wicked lilt as he prowled toward Clarke.

Her eyes widened. She glanced at Rush helplessly, then spun on her heels and ran. Red hair streamed behind her.

She got a few doors down and then Thaddeus launched, pushing her up against the stone wall of an adjacent building.

"Well-damn it." Rush put on a burst of speed.

Thaddeus's claws went for Clarke's throat, but Rush reached around him and took her wrist. He yanked her body to him and found another piece of bare skin to put his other hand on—her sternum. With Clarke in his arms, Rush backed up cautiously until his own back hit a wall, praying to the Well that his curse would extend to blanket her temporarily as it did all things he touched.

Thaddeus shook his head as if clearing it. He blinked at Clarke, head cocking, eyes flaring. With every breath Thaddeus took, it was clear he fought the curse trying to cloud his mind. Rush wanted to laugh in his scarred face. The very punishment that Thaddeus had called down on Rush was now working against him.

Except the curse wasn't strong enough. Rush's bond with Clarke wasn't strong enough. She was a living thing, not an object.

Thaddeus's hands went to his head. He shook it, and refocused on the woman in Rush's arms with a growl. "I've been hunting your kind for years. You won't get away this time."

Clarke struggled in Rush's arms. "We need to run."

"Trust me," he said, gritting his teeth. "Don't move."

She stilled until it was only her chest heaving beneath his touch.

This would work. It had to. But their connection needed to be stronger. Only one other bond he knew of linked a female and a male so completely—the mating bond. Rush sank his teeth into the tender flesh between Clarke's neck and shoulder, just enough to mark and trigger the mating ritual. Scent glands around his body swelled and released pheromones to coat her, marking her.

The wolf inside him unfurled from its long slumber. It sniffed the air, caught Clarke's scent and battered itself against the cage of Rush's body. *Mine.*

Thaddeus twirled around, dazed. His yellow eyes darted about the street. If the curse worked, he saw an empty street. Most had retired for the night, or were safely ensconced indoors. Rush kept his teeth and grip on Clarke, willing his curse to hold and ignoring the painful urge to complete the mating ritual and take something she hadn't made the choice to give. She must have guessed a little of what he was doing because she leaned back into him and gripped his forearm over her sternum.

A haunting howl of frustration tore out of Thaddeus, and he paced the area before them.

They were standing not five feet away, yet Thaddeus couldn't see them. He couldn't scent them, and he couldn't remember them, but a part of him knew he'd been robbed. Shaking his head with a growl, Thaddeus stalked back to the room near the gate. The fae inside looked out, but Thaddeus only shook his head. He took one look back out at the street and then went in, closing the door behind him.

If the curse did its job properly, none of them would remember.

But now Rush had another problem. With immediate danger gone, his mating instincts were taking over, becoming all consuming. Once triggered they were hard to stop. *Mine.* His jaw tightened, teeth still on Clarke's flesh. He pressed down with the undeniable urge to deepen his mark on her because if he'd done this a long time ago, she'd have never disobeyed him and left the inn. She would have been safe.

Stay.

That's what he'd said.

Stay in the room until he came back for her. Any wolf would bow under the will of an alpha's energy like his. But she was frustratingly not wolf. Not pack. And not the kind who enjoyed submitting. She was a strong-willed woman who would make the perfect mate for an alpha like him. A partner. A matriarch of their own pack. The mindless primal instincts of his inner wolf battled with human logic inside his mind.

*Take her. Make her submit.*

She won't submit. She's loyal. Feisty. Fierce.

*She's everything you want in a mate. Claim her.*

She has a will of her own.

*I like it.*

She is soft beneath your hands. Feminine. Juicy.

*I need it.*

"You're hurting me," she whimpered.

Keeping his lips on her, he unlocked his jaw and smelled fresh blood. He'd broken skin. His musk was all over her. Anyone scenting her now would know she belonged to him, that she was under his protection. This was a wolf village. They'd all know. Pain and regret hit him hard in the chest. He hadn't meant to mark so deep. He shouldn't have gone so far, so irrevocably without conscience, yet he couldn't let go of her, couldn't bring himself to lift his lips from her.

"I'm sorry," he whispered against her skin. "I'm so sorry."

He was sorry because the pain he'd just inflicted on her

flesh was nothing to how she'd feel when his curse broke down and he inevitably died. He'd essentially ruined her chances of mating again. His scent would take months, maybe years to completely come off. No male would want her with the scent of an alpha on her.

A part of him didn't care.

She was his, and he was hers.

He liked it.

He wanted her.

He was a sick, selfish bastard.

No denying it now. There it was, his mark, his bite, glistening under the light of the moon, clear in the night as it would be during the day. His inner wolf couldn't be prouder, even though deep down inside he knew it wasn't the blue marking of a Well-blessed union. That his curse would never lift. That he'd ruined her.

But even as the destructive thoughts hammered against his skull, blood heated in his veins, and desire mounted in his heart. A deep inhale of her intoxicating scent and he forgot where they were. His tongue darted out and lapped her wound. He laved and cared for the injury he'd made, the only one she'd ever suffer by his hands, teeth, or words.

She stiffened. "What are you doing?"

"I'm sorry." *I'm not sorry.* He kept repeating the words against her skin, licking and laving while his hands moved to bind her stomach and pull her against him, to grind the sweet curve of her ass against the aching need between his legs.

"Rush," she protested, squirming. "Let me move. What's going on? We should be out of here."

"No one can see us," he murmured. "You're safe now."

He growled and reversed their positions, flattening the length of his body against hers. Pushed against the wall, she had nowhere to go. And since they were still touching, flesh against flesh, neither of them were visible to any passersby who dared leave their dwellings after dark. Just as well, Rush couldn't take his eyes from the bountiful breasts bound by the tightness of her blouse. Lowering his lashes, he had trouble resisting. If he didn't get her home soon, he would take her against the wall. But she deserved better. He'd give her good memories, not hurried.

"*Touch me*, Clarke," he compelled, blind with desire.

Her hand lifted to his chest, to stroke his pecs through the woolen sweater, and then... she shoved him. Hard. He didn't budge, but it was enough to get his attention, to snap him out of the mating haze gripping his senses. She stomped on his foot.

"Get off me." Her cry came out strangled and thick.

Still inches apart, their gazes clashed. To his horror, he found hers glistening with tears.

"You're my mate." He frowned, as if that explained everything.

"What does that even mean? And..." She pushed again,

but he wouldn't budge. "It doesn't give you the right to come onto me like this... here. To force me... Right after..."

A slap stung Rush's cheek, and he stood back, shocked. Putting his palm to the burning side of his face, he blinked at her.

"And you bit me!" she hissed, hand covering the mark on her neck. Her bottom lip trembled, but she lifted her chin. "Why did you bite me?"

"Shh," he hissed. "People can hear you now."

There was no one around, but wolf shifters had very good hearing. Thaddeus might have forgotten their previous interaction due to the curse, but there was always the possibility of new interactions.

"I don't care," she hissed back, but she lowered her voice. "Why did you bite me?"

"That bite saved your life."

"It's more than that, you arrogant pig." Her nostrils flared as she took him in, and Rush hated it—the look in her eyes—she acted like she didn't know him. "You look like you want to eat me."

His lashes lowered. Yes, he did. He stepped toward her again with a lazy grin curling his lips.

"Stop," she warned, a palm to his chest. "What's gotten into you?"

And oh, how it burned. Her imprint scorched through to his hammering heart, making itself a permanent fixture. His inner wolf howled in frustration. It wanted to claw its way to her. Couldn't she see?

215

"I'll never stop hungering for you, Clarke. Even in my death, I'll be thinking of you."

"Is this what all wolves are like?" The shake in her voice gave him pause. "Is this why you have a law against unsanctioned breeding?"

"What?" Coldness seeped in. The light leached from the night sky.

The fire in her eyes had become twisted. "Unsanctioned breeding. That's what they told me at the tavern. A crime punishable by death. They made it sound like a survival thing, but I'm not so sure anymore. This world is insane. Unsanctioned breeding, my ass. It's just another term for a woman being forced."

His world closed in. His mouth dried. "I didn't. I'm not..."

He backed up.

She's not wolf. She didn't understand. She thought he was as beastly as his uncle. Thaddeus may never have been caught for unsanctioned breeding, but that was because he killed everyone he screwed. Clarke thought Rush was the same, and that's why he was cursed. Clarke, who could see the truth in everyone. This was his heart laid bare, and she believed it was made of the same inky substance as his uncle's.

"If I didn't need to keep you safe," he murmured. "I would never have started the mating process with you."

He realized his mistake the moment her brows lifted.

"Clarke," he held his hand out. "I didn't mean it like that."

"Oh really? I don't know what to believe. Because you've said since the start that I'm a filthy human and you should just kill me and be done with it. How was it Thaddeus put it, humans are only good enough to use for sport, isn't that right?"

"I am *not* my uncle." His fingers balled into fists. "And you need to stop comparing me to him."

"You're not explaining anything! How else am I going to take it?"

"Obviously I want you." He gestured to the still present bulge in his pants. "Regardless of the shape of your ears."

"The shape of my ears?" she scoffed. "Yeah. Real nice. Well, I hope you die from blue balls. You deserve it." She walked away, paused and then turned back to him. "And for the record, I was only coming to find you because I had a vision about Thaddeus being in town. Stupid me for thinking you needed my help."

"Yes, stupid you. I don't need help. No one can see me."

"That's what you said right before the White Woman took you," she said and then continued away.

"Stop." He launched at her, took her wrist and jerked her back to him. He forced her to hold his hand. "I release you from our bargain, Clarke."

A tingling zipped from his palm to his elbow, and then an emptiness haunted his hand. One more sliver of mana had been expended, and another set of blue glyphs appeared. The itch of it crept up his neck. His curse shifted. The veil thinned. Death waited for him, just outside the periphery of his control. But none of it compared to the loss he felt, the ache in his chest when she simply removed her hand from his and glared with disappointed eyes. Then she walked away.

# TWENTY-TWO

Clarke strode two steps, and then spun back with another harsh word on the tip of her tongue. She stopped. Rush was gone. In a blink, he'd blended into the shadows and disappeared in a way she'd not thought possible for one with such bright hair. Her hand went to her neck, to where he'd bitten her. It was tender, but strangely not painful. And she felt... she wasn't sure what she felt, only that she had an inexplicable urge to find him.

She took a few more steps toward where she saw him last. She willed her movements to quieten as she came back to the barracks building Thaddeus had disappeared into. And then she stopped, listened and watched. She ducked beneath a wall of overhanging jasmine and hoped they weren't the same kind of vine that ate butterflies. When nothing reached out and took hold of her, she narrowed her focus on the room to see if she could feel out whether Rush had gone back in, but all she sensed beyond the big wooden door was ill omens. Nothing good existed there.

The buzzing feeling in her chest was the opposite of how Rush made her feel, when he wasn't being a pushy jerk. Even then, her emotions clogged her throat with confusion. Being in this world, in this foreign time, became suddenly overwhelming.

Why did he have to ruin the budding friendship they'd carved out? Was the biting a claiming of some kind? Did it come with proprietary rights to her body? Was that how they did things in this time? The modern woman in her revolted, but then maybe it had nothing to do with modernity. Maybe it was the fact the last time she'd been "claimed" by a man, she'd allowed him to distort her life. All because she was afraid to be alone. Afraid that, like her mother had thought, there was something truly wrong with her.

Her stomach fluttered in confusion. She liked Rush. Was attracted to him. So much. The fae wouldn't get out of her head. But she'd be damned if another man, male, whatever this world had, demanded her body in a way she wasn't ready to give. Maybe it had been stupid to come down to the gate and see for herself if Thaddeus had arrived, but she *had* to see. To make sure it was real, and not a fancy.

Anxiety and yearning tugged a knot in her heart. Both

emotions at once. He'd bitten her—that *hurt*—but then he'd released her from the bargain, and that *relieved*. The glow of his curse creeped up his neck, and that had alarmed her. The moment she'd turned and lost sight of him, her anger had waned. For some reason he'd needed her help so much that he bargained her free will for it. He was ashamed of his behavior. There were things he wasn't telling her, and it was high time he did.

He said fae couldn't lie.

Deciding to confront him, once and for all about his motivations, Clarke crossed to the other side of the street and kept to the shadows as she passed the barracks. With one eye in the direction the bad vibes came from, and one eye ahead, she almost missed the familiar face through the barracks window. She took two steps before it registered. She stopped. Tensed. And cranked her neck back to face the window.

There, through the glass pane and deep in conversation with other fae, was an unforgettable man from her time. A long face and small jaw, he had always reminded her of some kind of bird. She'd made the mistake of dismissing him as unimportant once and lived to regret it. Bones. That man was a sadist for sale. He worked for the Void. And now he was here, in this time, speaking with the vilest fae Clarke had met.

More of a conversation she'd had came back to her. She was sitting in that warehouse room with the nuclear codes before her. Bones was at another chair, holding Laurel's fingers. And Bishop was laughing.

*"Tell me my future, babe," he'd said.*

*"You're going to die."*

*Bishop laughed. "Then tell me how to cheat death."*

The part she'd forgotten was Bones' mumbled, *"We already know."*

Cold ice grew in the pit of her stomach. She'd never forget that face as long as she lived. And there he was, just like her, a thawed remnant of the past. Her nightmare had been a true vision. But if he was there, then Bishop could be there. Worse, the Void could be there. Everyone who had a hand in the apocalypse could be back. And just like her, they could have developed magical abilities.

Jolting into action, Clarke ran, fear nipping at her heels. She had to get back to the inn. She had to tell Rush.

But would he be there when she arrived?

Panic gripped her throat as she charged into the inn. She raced through the tavern, up the stairs and skidded to a halt as she crested the final step. Rush sat with his back against the door, long legs bent, and head in his hands. His gaze lifted, met hers, and held.

"I wasn't sure if you'd still be here," she admitted.

A flash of something washed over his expression, too brief to catch the meaning. His voice came out gravelly. "I can't leave you now, even if I wanted to."

Clarke wanted to say the same thing, but he already knew. She'd tried to leave him. The frustrating fae had kidnapped, tricked, and compelled her to do his bidding, and yet she still couldn't find it in her to walk the other way.

"What's wrong with us?" she whispered. "Why can't we leave each other?"

A look from his eyes to her neck said it all. They were mated. Whatever that meant. Maybe it happened long before he put his mark there. A link had always existed between them. She would find out what it meant, but first...

"There's something I need to tell you." She pulled the key from her pants pocket and nudged him with her boot to move. "Come inside and we'll talk."

He tensed, but didn't move. He stared up at her with a challenge in his eyes as though he spoiled for a fight.

"You're so stubborn, Rush. Just shift aside and let me in."

Eventually, he swallowed and got to his feet until he stood with his hands in his pockets, big body looming next to her.

Clarke opened the door and went inside. Casting the key onto the table near the fire, she noted the bath had been removed while she was out, and a complimentary bottle of liquor, hard cheese and dried fruit was left on the small round table. She put her hands on her hips and began pacing the small length of the opulent room.

"I saw someone from my time. A very *not nice* some-one." She bit her nails. "He's here, thawed, just like me.

And he worked for an awful man. I saw the same awful man in my nightmare that day out on the path."

She expected Rush to take a seat, but he didn't. He bolted the door and dipped his hand in his breeches pocket. He handed something to her.

"It's the portal stone. You should take it and head to the Order. They'll want to know."

She eyed it warily. "You're coming with me. I thought you need me to talk for you."

Although, he still hadn't revealed why.

His jaw clenched and he shook his head. "It doesn't matter anymore."

"And where will you go then?" she demanded.

He only lowered his gaze. "I don't know. Maybe back to the cabin."

"No."

"No?"

"You heard me. I don't think you're leaving. We've both admitted it. Neither of us can deny this thing between us. It was there before you bit me. It's been there from the moment I laid eyes on you in the woods."

He flinched.

"And for the record," she continued, "I'm well aware there is something driving you to behave the way you do, and when I ask, you give me half-truths and avoidance. I want answers. So sit." She pointed at the armchair facing the fire, still glowing with embers warm enough to keep the cool night air at bay.

The fight seemed to leave him, and he went to the chair. Clarke poured both of them a small glass of liquor from the decanter and handed Rush a glass. He swirled the amber liquid and stared while Clarke kept the advantage of height and stayed standing. She tapped her finger on her glass, eyes glued to the harsh lines of the fae's flawless profile as he grappled with words warring in his mind.

"This is where you tell me why you are cursed," she prompted.

With a sigh, he shot back the drink and then sprawled low in the chair, stretching his long legs out toward the fire. He watched the tiny flames dance. Clarke replaced the glass he held with her hand. Just like she had with Caraway, she smoothed the lines made by the passage of time and tried to ease his nerves. Through it all he watched her intently.

They shared an identical pattern on their fate lines. She pressed her smaller palm onto his larger one and marked the difference in size. He was so much bigger than her. Her fingers laced through his and squeezed.

"What is it you're afraid to tell me?" she asked.

He frowned and then pulled away. "It's not that I'm afraid. It's that I'm... ashamed."

Clarke's heart reached out to him. Whatever his secret was, it hurt. Deeply. She took the chair opposite him, next to the fireplace. The only light in the room came from low lit oil lamps in sconces around the room and the dying embers before them. Rush's hard features seemed to soften in the glow. His white hair colored. And his cheeks looked flushed. For a moment, Clarke forgot he was a magical fae, part wolf, and just saw an ordinary man relaxing before a fire.

"I fathered a child."

"Okay."

Maybe he expected something more from her because he glanced at her. She did her best to keep her features schooled to encourage him further.

"I... uh... I didn't know about the pregnancy until it was too late," he said. "I'd long since given up my claim to be a breeding male, and was with the Guardians, at any point. I know I couldn't save the mother, but I still feel as though I failed her."

"Did you know her long? The mother?"

He shrugged. "It was a one time thing. Her name was Véda. She was there and willing when I came in after a hunt. I left the next day and didn't come back until months later when I found her about to give birth, tied to an execution pole."

"*Jesus.*"

"She confessed her plan had been to make it seem like a stranger had forced her. She thought that if I didn't know, then nobody could hunt me down and punish me too. They'd either let her go because she was forced, or one of us would be there to care for the child. I suppose it was a good enough plan."

"What happened?"

"Thaddeus overheard us talking. He called the Royal Guard. The Guardian I was with refused to get involved. The breeding law is something the Courts enforce. It has nothing to do with magic, and so nothing to do with the Order. When Thaddeus called for my head, the Prime had found out, and convinced them that death would be too kind." He pushed back the sleeves of his sweater. Blue lights flashed and glittered in his living tattoo. "She stepped in at the end. Just not the way I wanted."

"But you didn't know about the pregnancy!"

"It didn't matter. I clearly wasn't careful enough to avoid it. Véda had told the entire village for months that she was forced. They all believed it to be true. According to them, because I couldn't keep control of my desire, a woman would lose her life and a child would be born parentless."

"I'm so sorry." Tears stung Clarke's eyes, and she reached out to him, but he tensed. Her hand fisted in the air and came back to her side.

"She gave birth right there outside the gate. Her arms were bound to a pole the entire time." His jaw clenched. He shook his head. "They refused to let me hold the newborn before they took him away. And then the Royal Guard slaughtered her before my eyes. Thaddeus laughed as they took me away. The bastard laughed. I should have ripped his throat out then."

The arms on the chair creaked from the force of his grip and suddenly it all became clear.

"You want to speak with your son," she whispered. "He's at the Order, isn't he?"

He gave a curt nod. "I have no excuses. I just want to speak to him. I don't even know what I would say."

He poured himself another big drink, and chugged it before sitting back down.

"Hey, Thorne," he said to the fire. "It's your dad. Sorry about your mother. But hey... couldn't keep it in my pants. Sorry I wasn't there to stop them from making you the tribute for the Well, but remember about those random acolytes who suddenly fell in the water at your initiation? Yeah that was me poking them with my useless sword."

"You're being too harsh on yourself."

"It's the truth."

For a long while, they both stared into the fire listening to the crackle made by tiny flames. Clarke didn't know what to say. He'd been given a raw deal. But could she forgive him for...

"Tell me about the mating and the marking," she urged.

He sighed. "It was the only way to keep you safe."

"I understand this. And I also understand that I'm very unprepared to live in a world like this. Not yet, anyway. But why did the mating make you behave the way you did? Why did you get so... aggressive and... it was almost like you were lost in a dream."

His fiery gaze snapped to hers. "Because you *are* a dream, Clarke. Never in my wildest imagination did I imagine a female like you coming into my life. Before you came, I'd given up. Even when you saw me at my vilest, you didn't leave. I have been cruel to you, and for that I will never be sorry enough. But you came back." His gaze softened. "The wolf inside me recognized that loyalty before me. You haven't met him, but he knows you. When I marked you as mine, it was all the permission my wolf needed. Nature can make me do things I wouldn't normally do. Sometimes the wolf is closer to the surface than I like to admit."

"Is it going to bite me as well?"

He laughed softly and shook his head. "I forget how human you are sometimes. No. It just wants to know you."

She rubbed between her breasts, hoping to ease the ache, but her fist hit something hard. The two vials Anise had given her were still there. It seemed so long ago now.

"You still haven't answered my question," she continued. "Not fully. I don't understand what mating means?"

"It's the fae version of marriage."

She narrowed her eyes. "We're married."

He had the decency to look repentant. "It's a little more than that."

"What can be more than marriage?"

"When we mate, it's a bond that goes beyond the natural order. My scent on you will make us hard to be around if any other males are interested in you." He scrunched his nose. "A Well-blessed mating lets us sense each other's emotions. For a union like that, a sacred blue light springs from the land to envelope the couple and leaves a visible marking. Then the couple share not only their thoughts and hearts, but their mana. I could borrow from you, and you could borrow from me. Our hearts would be open to each other. If we were blessed. Which we are not."

"You sound disappointed."

"A Well-blessed mating would break my curse."

"Oh." She bit her lip, surprised at the disappointment rising in her chest. "Then if I can't break it, we will make the Order remove the curse," she decreed.

"It's impossible."

"We have to try. It wasn't your fault. You shouldn't be in this situation. It's wrong. I know bad people, and you're not one of them."

Slowly, he lifted his gaze to hers. He stood, shifted his hand to his rear and pulled a small package from his pocket. He held it in his hands and turned the item over, unwrapping the teal patterned cloth to reveal something made from wood. Upon seeing it, Clarke shot to her feet and the two of them met before the fire. She held her breath as she looked down.

"You keep saying you wish you knew the time. So I made you this."

It was a carved sundial.

# CHAPTER
# TWENTY-THREE

Clarke hadn't received a gift like the one in Rush's hands for... she blinked, trying to remember. It hadn't been since her father had given her the charm bracelet and the watch.

He'd carved it himself.

"When did you have time to do this?" she asked.

"To be honest"—he scratched his head—"I started when we were walking here. I just didn't know what it was until earlier tonight."

Her finger traced over the intricate pattern around the dial. Roses and willow branches. "You're very talented."

He touched his fingers to his lips and hand-signed his thanks.

She shifted toward the fire to see the palm sized sundial better, trying hard to hold in her emotion, but her brows knitted together with the effort.

"You don't like it?"

She turned, eyes watering. "I love it. I... I'm speechless. Why?"

A pink tinge stained his cheeks and he dipped his gaze. "I don't know. I think... I think I just wanted to give you something you needed. Something that could help you, even after I'm gone."

His words hit the deepest part of her soul. Never before had anyone thought about her needs before his. Twice now. He'd saved her life at the bog. And now this? Suddenly, she no longer felt like a foreigner in a strange land. She felt like her old life was a dream, and this was her new reality. She crossed the floor, intending to thank him, but he stepped back and lifted his palms out.

"I don't want you to think I did this to manipulate you, or..."

To force her, he meant. The alarm in his eyes hurt to see. It shot straight to her heart and stabbed deep.

"Rush." She swallowed. "But I do like you. You haven't forced me. You've done quite the opposite. You made every attempt to make me hate you, yet... here I am. Wanting you."

His lips parted, eyes wide. He didn't believe her.

She flattened her lips and pulled the vials from beneath her shirt. "Look." She handed them to him, speaking fast and bumbling. "I intended to use these on you, or with you, or whatever. Anise sold them to me. She's the barmaid downstairs. Apparently elves love their elixirs. Do you know what they are?"

His gaze narrowed on the pink and blue vial and then sharpened with recognition. He growled and threw the blue into the fire. Flames burst as though gasoline had been thrown. Still agitated, he braced his hands on the mantle, head bowed. Every muscle in his back rippled with restraint as he took a moment to calm himself.

"Jeeze," she blurted. "You fae are sensitive with your masculinity."

He whipped around, eyes blazing. "I don't need any help being aroused for my mate."

Clarkes eyes dipped to below his belt and saw the evidence tenting there. She had to bite her cheek to hold back a smile. "Nope. No you don't."

Anguish stifled his expression. He turned back to the fire. "You think this is funny?"

He wanted her. Now he knew she wanted him. So why was he avoiding her? Had she not been clear enough? She wasn't ready before. But now she was. Knowledge had been exchanged and the power balance had shifted. She was more than willing. Her gaze ran down his body. God, he was hot. Sexy. Broad shoulders tapered to a small waist, an ass made by the gods, and thick, muscled thighs possibly double the width of hers. She imagined running her hands over his naked skin. The heat. The soft unyielding strength.

Heat speared between her legs. She bit back a groan.

Something was holding him back. Clarke's mind shifted back to his earlier confession and she stepped forward. Maybe this reluctance was more than his curse. Maybe he'd been cut deeper than he admitted. His sexual gratification had ruined lives.

"Rush." She dropped her palm onto his back. He shuddered beneath her touch. "You're not a bad person for wanting this, you know. You shouldn't feel guilty about your desire."

He tensed as if he wished her away, as if he wished his feelings away.

There was only one way to make her position clear. She stepped back until her thighs hit the edge of the bed and then unlaced her belt. Straightening her spine, she rolled up the belt length and threw it at the wall above his head. It bounced and landed on his shoulders.

He turned, confused eyes colliding with hers. But then his attention dipped and studied her from top to toe. With every inch he covered, heat smoldered in his eyes until his gaze snagged upon the motion of her fingers on the top pearl button of her blouse. She fingered it open, daring him with her eyes.

"I want this," she said, voice thick. "You're not forcing me. I've already had a drop of the pink elixir. I'm prepared." It was true. She'd taken some the moment she left the tavern. "No lives will be ruined if you let yourself go tonight."

Her finger plucked the button. He growled in warning.

"It's not bad to want a little comfort in each other's arms." She popped another button. "You chase my nightmares away, Rush."

"Stop."

"I want to feel your body against mine."

"I said, *stop*."

She paused. "Why?"

He licked his lips, eyes still caught on her fingers, and then a yearning so deep and open flashed across his face. His voice dropped low. "Because I want to do it."

Clarke's heart almost soared out of her chest. Slowly, her hands drifted to her side. She lifted her chin, a dare in her eyes. *Come and get me.*

He pushed off the mantle and stalked forward, golden eyes never leaving her face. His arousal pushed against his breeches, giving her a dark outline of his shape. Seeing it only made her pulse thud faster with anticipation. His intensity, his predatory focus, gave her insight to his animal side and she knew that when he finally graced her with his shift, she'd be in awe. His wolf would be majestic.

The toe of his boot hit hers and he stopped, all brooding energy and thunderous scrutiny. Inches away, his eyes were wild, proud, and lit with some savage desire. First, his gaze landed on her breasts, to where her nipples strained against the fabric of her blouse. Then his hand went there, capturing the weight. Her lips parted. The touch rasped against the fabric and sent tingles zipping through her body. He squeezed and kneaded, taking his time in learning her shape, never removing his intense stare from her face as though he cataloged every reaction she gave him.

She closed her eyes, enjoying his simple yet consuming caress melting her from the inside. Two hands now, both toying and rolling each breast with skill and reverence.

"Playing with your food, wolf?" she teased.

He gave a guttural grunt, and then the weight at her front was gone. Her eyes snapped open to find him lifting trembling hands to cup her face. The rough pad of each thumb stroked along her cheeks. Golden eyes heated with a mix of wonder and adoration. It was so open, so raw, that she felt the tug down to her core. She pushed into his touch and smiled. This felt right. This is what her instinct had been trying to tell her. This was where it all pointed. To be in his arms. They were stronger together.

"Clarke..."

"Shut up and kiss me."

His eyes widened, and then he took her mouth in a consuming kiss. No more reservations. Nothing between them. Clarke sank into his heat, into the soft lips and bristle of beard, into the hardness of his chest. His tongue tangled with hers. It was a hot, heady kiss that wrenched a moan from deep in her lungs. She felt wanted. Needed. She couldn't get enough.

"I'm going to put my mouth here next," he murmured and touched her breast again.

"Oh God, yes."

"And then I will show you how I play."

He traced his lips on her jaw, nipped and nibbled and licked his way down her neck, leaving a trail of fire everywhere he touched. One powerful hand splayed on the small of her back, holding her up, the other worked at the buttons on her blouse until she was laid bare to him. Air hit her skin, sending goosebumps pebbling all over. He stepped back, eyes hooded, and then said, "I changed my mind. I want you to take the rest off while I watch."

Clarke lifted her brow. "And what about you?"

Something like amusement mixed with curiosity flashed over his features, and then his expression hardened with intent. He gripped the back of his sweater and dragged it over his head. His hair became disheveled in an altogether come-hither way that almost unraveled her.

"You're taking too long." He gave a pointed look at her pants.

But she didn't care about herself. He'd already unbuttoned his breeches, giving her a taste of the wicked delights beneath. Flexing abdominals, dark gray fuzz dusted with silver, the top of that hard length... and his thumbs were hooked on the waistband, ready to pull down. The blue glyphs covering his body only increased his preternatural physique. She wanted to trace her tongue around every blue line.

Clarke barely registered that she'd sat on the edge of the bed. Maybe she got one or two buttons on her pants open, but then she'd stopped, eyes glued to his undress. He slid those pants over his hips and ass, the arch of his thick thighs, and then completely down. Enraptured, her mouth dried.

Naked, the fae was a study in male beauty. Every minute move he made flexed muscles and tendons she never knew existed. The only time she saw a body like this in her time, was on the cover of a sports magazine. Or one of those calendars you bought to raise money for charity. But in this time, the people had to work to survive. The fact his shape was carved out of necessity made it even more desirable.

He was strong. A protector. A provider.

Her eyes dropped to below his waistline, to his desire jutting eagerly between his legs. An impatient snarl of need burst from her throat. She didn't care if she sounded like an animal. She suddenly knew how he'd felt out there in the alley. She had to have him. Now.

"When you look at me like that…" he murmured.

"Come here."

He wrapped his fingers around his arousal and stepped closer until the tip came before her face. She licked her lips and looked up to find raw anguish in his expression. Holding his gaze, she unwrapped his fingers and replaced them with her own. From his reluctance, he wasn't used to conceding, and even less used to being touched. But she got what she wanted. With long, smooth strokes, she let him see what she could do for him. The immediate defocus of his eyes made every feminine intuition scream with triumph. Locking eyes, she lowered her lips to his blunt tip and teased the sensitive ending with her breath. She intended to hold his gaze, but the moment her tongue darted out and tasted, her eyes fluttered closed with a groan. She took him inside and swirled and flicked with her tongue.

A shaky breath escaped him—a muttered curse as he threaded trembling fingers into her hair and let her take control, never once demanding something she wasn't ready to give. She licked and sucked and loved. She took pleasure with his body until she could feel him going taut, until the veins bulged at his abdomen, until his breath quickened and he twitched, fingers spasming in her hair.

He pulled out suddenly. He gripped her chin and angled it so she stared into his eyes, open with need. She felt like she was falling. Every line on his face was taut with need and the very sight sent hot tingles rippling through her body. No words came out to explain his thoughts, just a dark look of passion that twisted his features into something so breathtaking nothing else existed.

Rush crouched, tugged her pants off, and then his hard body was atop her. Lips landed on her skin and tasted every inch as though a starved man. He kissed and laved the marking on her neck with reverence. He grazed teeth along tendons and caressed with his fingers. It all heated her eagerly, sending her soaring after her fall. Up, up, up. While his mouth was busy, his fingers explored. Over breasts, nipples, stomach... lower... and then he found her wet.

A snarl tore out of him. He used his knee to pry her legs apart and he plunged a finger into the heat of her core. She arched into him greedily, holding his gaze, but he retreated down her body. He widened her thighs for a better view and traced fingers through her center. Then lifted them to his mouth and licked with a throaty growl of satisfaction.

"*This* is playing with my food, princess."

"You're cruel." She arched into him, begging for more, but he held her down.

She threw her head back onto the pillow with frustration.

"Tell me how you like it," he demanded.

"Whatever you want is how I like it."

The tickle of his beard on her thighs was the only warning before a long, torturous lick straight down her center sent her back bowing, and her hips driving into him. She pulled a pillow over her mouth and let loose a long strangled and drawn out moan.

# CHAPTER
# TWENTY-FOUR

The mating need had never left Rush. Not since the moment he'd sunk his teeth into Clarke and coated her with his scent. Before they'd entered the room, he'd smelled himself on her body and it made every instinct within him howl with possessive pride. The way she'd taken him into her mouth... it had made him weak for her touch. And now he had her at his mouth while he feasted and probed and swirled. Her taste was drugging, and the way she responded to his every touch sent his mind spiraling, falling and crashing. He would turn into a beast of need if he couldn't keep her roving hands off him. She pushed him to a new urgent pace. The woman knew what she wanted, and she wasn't afraid to ask for it. Assertively, she took his head and guided the direction of his tongue to where she wanted it. He pulled back with a growl of restraint.

She looked down her body, cheeks flush. "Don't stop."

"You said whatever I want," he reminded.

She nodded.

"So I want to take my time."

A frustrated sound mewled out of her and she dropped her head to the pillow. "I don't know if I can wait that long."

"I've waited decades for this. I won't be rushed." He stroked her thighs. "You will wait."

"So bossy." But she said it with a bright-eyed smile.

She was the elemental divine made flesh. Silken flames flowed around her shoulders. The color also dusted her sex. He never wanted it to end, and she was eager for it to go faster. He wasn't playing. He was avoiding because if he let her have her way, he feared his resolve to make it last.

And it needed to last.

He hadn't been wrong when he told her she was a dream turned real for him. Any time he'd fantasized about being with a female, he'd imagined the flesh, the carnal act, but not the deep satisfaction filling the aching hollow of his chest. This connection went beyond gratification. It was like she'd said, there had been something between them from the start, something waiting for them to acknowledge, and now that they had, it was there to stay. With her, he never felt alone. She saw him. She saw *into* him.

The whisper of her voice floated back, "*You're not a bad person for wanting this.*"

He only wished *this* wasn't so close to the end of his curse.

He shook the thought away. There was no place for that here. Right now he had to make himself last. His eyes tracked again to the torn tunic wrapped around her head.

"Clarke," he said, voice hoarse with an idea. It deepened. "Princess."

She drew her fevered gaze back to his.

"Do you trust me?" he asked.

No hesitation. She nodded. Her complete and utter submission sucked the air from his lungs. She trusted. Knowing this clicked something inside him. He would prove her trust founded. He would give her the best of him.

He gave an affectionate goodbye kiss at the apex of her thighs, just for now, and then prowled up the length of her body. He tugged off the torn strip and enjoyed splaying her red tresses around the pillow. She watched him, eyes dancing with humor. It would get messed up soon, but that wasn't the point. The point was she allowed him the moment to learn another intimate piece of her identity, an act reserved for loved ones. Tonight he would find many more of these brief moments with her.

"Do you have a thing for tying me up?" she teased.

"Only when you test my resolve."

"So this is my fault."

He bared his teeth. "The fault is my lack of restraint at the want of your touch."

She snorted, but gave him her hands.

With one knee on either side of her hips, he gathered her wrists and gently tied them together. As he lifted her bound arms over her head and leaned toward the bedhead, the tip of his cock grazed and tickled her abdomen, sending fire scooting up his spine. He cursed. Tensed. He was so close to the edge. All it took was a trace of her skin and he was almost over. Satisfied she couldn't reach out to him, he came back down to her, surprised to find her eying his member with heat.

He took himself in hand and squeezed. "Do you want this in your mouth again?"

She nodded, licking her lips.

He pumped until the aching need abated a little and then whispered low and rough in her ears. "First, I want to take my time giving you every pleasure I've fantasized about for decades."

"You torture me," she moaned. "I'm going to die."

"You'll die happy."

"Rush," she pleaded.

His lips curved up one side, and then his amusement dropped. "If it's too much, tell me." He eyed the wrist bindings warily. "You tell me. Understand?"

She licked her lip and nodded. "What... what did you fantasize about?"

His gaze lingered on the way her breasts lifted with her quickening breath. Tight, hard and aroused. She was more than his fantasy. He captured a pebbled nipple in his mouth and swirled his tongue, sucking and groaning around the peak. "This," he murmured, and then did the same to the other. "And this." He moved down her center, stopping and studying every inch as though it was his only chance. His last. Because tomorrow he might wake with the last of his mana expended. If Thaddeus came for them in the night, he would use any and every tool in his arsenal to protect Clarke. One more shift into wolf, one more slip of control, and he would be done. He was well aware that he could lose his hold even now. At least he'd have this moment, this small taste of honey. Frowning once again at the direction of his thoughts, he moved down her stomach until he reached the red patch of hair and nuzzled between her legs. He licked. She made little whimpering sounds. Then he opened her wide and blew a jet of air right where it mattered most.

Her writhing cry of abandon brought a smile to his lips.

"You like that?" he asked, then laved and did it again.

She tensed in response, and so he ran his finger around her heat, teasing the outside before finally slipping in. A deep, inarticulate sound came out of him when he found her ready.

"You really want this."

"God, yes." She lifted to him.

He increased his pace, dipping to explore with his tongue, taking more insistent strokes until his own need churned within restlessness. Every mewling sound she made, every bow of her back and small thrust of her hips delighted him to no end. He slid his hand beneath her pelvis and lifted her to him, increasing the pressure of his tongue. Her thighs clenched, coiling her tight. He gave more until her scream of ecstasy filled the room and she went languid beneath him.

Drawing back, he took pleasure in the way she panted to catch her breath, the sated expression on her face, and most importantly, the way she watched him, the way she saw him—with complete carnal belonging—it was the way he felt about her. He untied her hands and gently rubbed her wrists, giving each a reverent kiss on the inside.

"Thank you," he said. "For giving me that pleasure."

She arched a brow. "I think you have it all wrong, baby. It should be the other way around."

"Baby." A short laugh burst out. "Why do you call me a babe?"

She huffed, chagrinned. "It's a term of endearment in my time."

"Did I act like a mewling newborn?"

"No, sir, you most definitely did not."

His gaze darkened. "Maybe I thanked you because I want to be in your debt."

"I'm sure I can arrange something." She shimmied down the bed and hooked her legs around his waist, nudging him closer to her center. Her eyes fluttered closed and he scolded her.

"Keep them open, princess. I want you to see me when I fill you. I want you to always remember it is me bringing you to this bliss."

"God, you say the most arrogant things."

He angled himself at her entrance and in small teasing movements, sheathed himself to the hilt. The shear electric buzz of it curled his toes. She fit him, perfectly. Holding his position until he could function, he lowered his lips to hers and murmured, "You can touch me now."

A wicked gleam flashed in her eyes. "Maybe I'll tie you up."

He circled his hips. She whimpered.

"Nope," she breathed. "I'm... I can't. Oh God, do that again."

He dragged out and in, enjoying the way she went boneless beneath him. He did it again. And again. Each time he watched her reaction, finding something new to revel in. A lick or bite of her lips. A euphoric roll of her eyes. A slight frown of concentration. It was all a reaction to *him*, to the genuine moment they shared. He was alive. He was seen.

Each time she revealed herself, it carved out a little piece of his heart, making space for her to crawl in and occupy. He knew, without a doubt, that no matter what happened next, even if she didn't stay with him, or if these were his last moments, that space would still be there. It would follow him into the next life.

Clarke's breath caught, and then she let out a shuddering moan, bowing her back. His mark on her neck had never been more on display. Desire broke the banks of his control and he kissed her with hunger, swallowing the remnants of her bliss. His movements turned frantic, and it was all she could do to hold on. Tension rode his system. Every bone, muscle and tendon retracted from too much sensation. But he was powerless to stop. He thrust and pounded, kissed and nipped, faster and harder until the headboard crashed against the wall, and sweet heat sizzled up his spine. Until he planted himself and shuddered through his release with a deep, rumbling growl of satisfaction.

He stayed inside her, holding her in his arms. The oil in the lamps was almost spent, and the fire was almost out. Her breathing seemed to even out and he pulled out, jolting her awake.

"We're not done."

"What?" Her eyes flew open.

"We have all night."

She gave him a listless smile. "We have to sleep at some point."

"Yes." He dragged his teeth along her jaw. "At some point."

"I'm kinda hungry too."

Another swell of warmth hit him in the chest. He shifted off the bed and found a cloth at the wash basin to clean her, and then he filled a glass with liquor and broke off a chunk of hard cheese. Through it all, she studied him with one hand propped behind her head.

"You're glowing," she noted. "It's covering more of you now."

He settled on the bed and lifted a piece of cheese to her lips. "It's close to the end," he admitted.

"How much time is left?"

"Maybe a few weeks. Months at most."

She ate and sat up with a frown, chewing. Before she could speak, he lifted the glass of liquor to her lips. She drank, swallowed, but then scowled. "What's with the feeding?"

"I like knowing I'm providing for you." For now. He winced.

Her gaze softened and dropped to the glyphs. "Rush," she whispered, forlorn.

"Don't speak about it. Let's have tonight." He used his thumb to wipe a drop from the corner of her mouth. "And it's only just begun. I have more fantasies for you to fulfill."

# CHAPTER TWENTY-FIVE

Clarke woke from a deep, dreamless sleep and instantly knew the warm weight over her body was Rush's arm and leg. Naked and cocooned in his arms, she didn't want to move and drifted lazily listening to the sounds of the inn waking up below them. Someone emptied water in the alley. Birds tweeted nearby. Banging sounds thudded on the wooden floors elsewhere in the establishment. The smell of fresh-baked bread wafted in and her stomach grumbled.

It was no wonder she was hungry. They'd stayed up half the night enjoying each other's company. Rush wasn't wrong when he'd said he needed no elixir to keep aroused around his mate. Clarke stretched languidly, feeling the pleasant pull of their lovemaking in every aching part of her body. The fae was a machine with endless stamina. Clarke was the one who had called it a night because she simply couldn't keep her eyes open any longer. Rush didn't complain. He'd tucked her smaller body into his larger one and surrounded her until she drifted away.

Not a single nightmare plagued her sleep.

Clarke rolled from her back toward the window to see if she could ascertain the time of day by the amount of light peeking through the cracks in the drapes, but Rush grumbled and placed his teeth on her shoulder in warning. He did that a lot—teeth on the neck or shoulder—to let her know without words what his feelings were. In this instance, it was not to ruin his deep comfort. It was never a sharp bite like it had been the time in the alley, but only a light pressure that eased off and grazed along her skin more often than not. She smiled, realizing she liked learning all these little pieces of him.

He tightened his grip and tugged across her middle so her rear fit nicely into his lap. A growing hardness pressed into her behind.

"Are you even awake?" she chuckled.

He made a throaty sound and kissed, or licked, the back of her neck, then tucked her in tight and rested his head back on the pillow. The sound of his soft breath evened out.

She remained content to spend her time tracing a finger up and down his forearm resting between her breasts and wondered what was going to happen next. Not knowing how her own future would unfold was an ever-increasing irritation. The bare hints she'd gleaned weren't enough. How was it fair that she could see into anyone else's future but hers?

Thaddeus hadn't come breaking down the door, so the curse must have worked to confuse him as to her presence. And then there was Bones. An involuntary shiver traveled through her. That man was despicable.

The glow of Rush's curse glanced off the furniture in the low lit room and amplified her anxiety. They'd have to get going to the Order after they had something to eat. A gnawing sensation of... something... tried to break through her reverie. Fear.

He'd said his curse was nearing its end. When it was done, he'd die. Just like that. Months. Maybe weeks were all he had left. She couldn't imagine a life without him. Since she couldn't see his future, she had to have faith that it was entwined with hers, but it didn't assuage her worry. His future may be with hers, but he could still die tomorrow... just with her at his side.

A knot formed in her belly. When she got to the Order, she would find a way to somehow trigger her psychic visions on demand. The way they just popped up was very inconvenient. Then she would learn how to lift the curse. If she couldn't work it out on her own, she didn't care if she used her abilities to exploit the people there. She'd done worse for greed. This was for Rush's benefit.

Wasn't it?

"You are fretting." His voice was still thick with sleep as he nuzzled into her hair.

"How can you tell?"

He took a deep breath and moved in a way that felt like a shrug. "Let me make you happy again."

He began a slow path down her front, hand splaying at her pelvis and holding her firm against his hips. She rolled to face him and found his gaze full of wicked intent.

"We didn't get much chance to talk last night," she said.

"We talked."

She frowned. "Okay, fine. Yes we did. But there's more. Remember that person I recognized at the barracks?"

He sat up. "The human?"

She hugged herself. "He was a very violent man. He tortured my friend to convince me to work for him."

"Then he is breathing his last. Tomorrow, I will—"

"No." Clarke touched his jaw gently, eyes soft. He hated not being able to protect her. She didn't want to remind him of his limitations, so steered the conversation. "We can't rush into anything. He could lead us to someone worse, and we're vastly unprepared. You were at Crystal City. Did you ever see him there?"

Rush threaded his fingers over his chest and stared at the ceiling. "When I visited, there was a new king. From what I gathered from the people, they were both equally awed and fearful of him. I never saw his face."

Clarke tugged on her hair. "I just think we need more information before doing anything. And hopefully we'll get some answers at the Order."

"I trust you and your visions. If you think this person is linked to a threat to Elphyne, then that's good enough for me."

Tension rode her body. She plucked a few strands out.

His hand covered hers, stopping the action. "You're fretting again."

"Maybe that's because I'm not sure if I can trust myself." She bit her lip and inhaled deeply. Here goes. "My mother abandoned me because of my visions. She thought I was demon spawn. My father ignored them. Bishop used them. I just... I don't know."

He kissed her on the shoulder. "I do."

"You shouldn't. I wasn't exactly a good person. I used to steal."

"I steal."

"But you do it out of necessity."

"Isn't that what you did?"

She lifted a shoulder. "Maybe."

"Then enough talking."

He lifted the blanket to cover his head and disappeared with a mischievous glint in his eye. The moving bulk of his body slid down the bed, and within moments, he pushed apart her knees. Another moment later she forgot her troubles.

"So," Clarke said, "to be clear, you want stew for breakfast, and some ale? But it's so early." She scrunched her nose as she tugged on her boot. "That's gross."

Being the only one others could see, ordering was Clarke's job. They'd made the decision to get dressed so they could head straight out after their meal. He'd conceded and was coming with her to the Order. It hadn't been hard to convince him when she said they could continue with his long list of fantasies the following night.

"The ale here is delicious," Rush replied. Now fully clothed, back in his worn Guardian jacket, he rustled through his rucksack with a mumbled, "I could have sworn I had more coin than this."

She made an awkward face. It was probably still in her pants from when she'd stolen it yesterday. She dug her fingers into the pocket and found not only the coins, but one of his little wolf carvings. She pulled both out.

"I think I have some," she said.

He tensed. "Where did you get that?"

"The wolf?" She bit her lip. "I took it from your bag."

A dark look flashed over his face. "It's not for you."

"Sorry. Here, have it back." She held it out.

"I... no, it is me who should apologize. I didn't mean to snap. I carved it for my son when he was younger." He picked it up and twirled it in his fingers. "I used to make them and drop them in his room. I hoped he'd see the resemblance and know his father was looking out for him."

He handed it back to her. "He's an adult now. I don't know why I brought it. You have it."

"I think it's beautiful. It reminds me of you."

He returned her smile and opened the door. "Head down to the bar. I'll finish packing and readying the portal stone."

Clarke made her way down to the tavern level of the inn. Already filling with patrons, the room had mainly fae she guessed were overnight guests. Some lone travelers. Some couples. None of the provocative females she'd seen were anywhere in sight. From the sounds she'd heard last night, they were probably all worn out. Bit like her.

She tested the position of the torn strip around her ears and couldn't help the smile that lifted her lips. There would never be a time she failed to think about Rush when she touched that piece of fabric. How things had changed since the last time she'd worn it.

Buoyed by her emotions, she walked up to the bar and found it empty. No servers around, but the smell of freshly cooked food wafted from the kitchen behind it. Some clanking noises clashed with a loud male curse. She walked along the length of the bar until she came to the spot where she could see through the kitchen door. Beyond was an old style scullery. It was still odd for her to see something so normally heavy with metal in her time, now so stripped bare of it. Instead of stainless steel counters, there was wood. Instead of iron stoves, a long stone hearth with ceramic pots bubbled away. A tall, but rotund, fae with wolfish ears muttered to himself as he briskly stirred a pot. He must have sensed her there, because he immediately lifted his head and paused. He had golden eyes, streaky short gray hair, and a crooked nose which he lifted her way as though he tried to scent her. His eyes narrowed and he put the pot down.

Wiping his hands on his apron, he came out of the kitchen. "You need something?"

"Hi." She put some coin on the bench. "I'd like to order some food and have it sent up to our room please."

The fae's gaze narrowed even more. Clarke thought he might tell her to go away, but instead, he gave a big belly shout. "Anise! You're needed."

Then he returned to the kitchen.

Strange.

Not long after, Anise emerged. She wore similar attire to the previous night and looked drained.

"Morning," Clarke said. "You been here all night?"

"Just got in." Anise's gaze dipped to Clarke's neck and then gave her a knowing smile. "You're looking mighty chirpy. Took advantage of the elixir, I see."

"Um." Clarke's hand went to Rush's mark, still visible on her neck. "Actually. We did fine without it. But thank you anyway."

"Right," Anise laugh. "Well, you smell like you've been drowning in its aftereffects. No wonder Angus wouldn't take your order."

Angus must be the cook. "What does that mean?"

"The wolf who claimed you did it good. Any male sniffing around you like this will be in for trouble when your mate comes around."

"But the cook was just going to take my order."

Anise shrugged. "You're not around wolves much, are you?"

"I guess not."

"We're a territorial lot. I'm surprised he didn't accompany you down here. I want to meet the guy."

"You know, I truly wish you could, but he's getting our things ready. We have to leave soon."

"What's he look like?" Anise waggled her brows. "With that sated look on your face, I'm imagining some big alpha type. Although, a real alpha wouldn't let his mate come down and collect the meal. You're making me very curious." She whined a little at Clarke's closed mouth. "Come on. Tell me. I've got nothing else to live for but endless work hours."

Clarke pinched her lips, but couldn't resist sharing. It was nice to have a girl to talk to. "He's tall. Longish silver hair. Beard. Total"—she couldn't come up with the right words to explain Rush's physique and flexed her hands in front of her shoulders—"he's like..."

"That good, huh?"

She laughed and nodded. He was everything.

"Maybe if I bring the food, I'll get a peek."

"I wish you could see him." Her mood dropped because

it was true. Wanting Rush to be visible and free of his curse was starting to dig a hole into her chest.

Nervous, she tucked hair behind her ear. It was such a habitual move that she'd not noticed she'd pushed aside the torn fabric keeping her ears hidden until Anise stiffened.

Alarm prickled through Clarke. Their eyes locked.

Neither knew what the other would do.

Anise made the first move.

"What are you doing?" She leaned over the counter and tugged the strap down. "Keep that hidden. If Thaddeus gets wind of your kind being here, you'll be gone before you can take a new breath."

"Sorry."

They went back to staring at the other, not knowing what to say.

"You're a Seer," Anise stated.

"Yes."

"But you're not an elf."

"No."

"And you're not fae." Anise lowered her voice.

Clarke shook her head cautiously. She waited for Anise to raise the alarm, or to look at her differently, but she only checked over her shoulder and then leaned over the bench to get closer to Clarke.

"Is there even a hot alpha in your room?"

"Definitely, that part is true."

"You know," Anise said, "I've always had a leaning

toward the psychic. It's why I waved you over in the first place. Now I see why. We'll meet again, Clarke. Mark my words." She eased her weight to one side. "Now, what would you like to eat?"

With a nod of appreciation, Clarke gave her order and headed back up to the room. She liked Anise, and now seeing that she wouldn't betray someone like her on sight, she liked her even more.

She arrived at the room and found the fire had been stoked back to life. Rush looked a little flushed. She first thought that perhaps it was the activity of restarting the fire, but then she caught the guilty gleam in his eyes. Her nerves jangled.

"What did you do?" she asked warily.

He scratched the back of his neck. "I got bored waiting."

"What the hell does that mean?"

"It means I left a little gift around the main streets. I marked my territory."

"Like a... wolf?"

Rush gave her a toothy grin and lifted his hands playfully. "It's in my nature."

A nervous tension crept up her spine. "I wish you waited until after we ate before you announced to all the town that you're here."

Rush prowled up to her, his playful grin still lighting up his face. "And where would the fun be in that?"

Clarke went over to the window and pulled the drape

to peer outside. Down in the street, life was beginning for the town's folk. Fae were bustling about. But no sign of his uncle. She let the drapes fall back into place.

"I thought you didn't want to rule this town."

"Doesn't mean I don't like fucking with his head."

She laughed. His finger hooked on her belt and tugged her close. The way he peered down at her, all mischief and joy, it was hard to stay angry. This was the side of him she'd seen when they'd first met. The same side that had attracted her to him in the first place. It was the real Rush. And she'd helped bring it out. How could she be cross with that?

"Just promise me we can get out of here on a moment's notice."

He nodded, dark lashes lowering as he closed the gap between their faces. "I have it all under control."

She sank into his kiss, running her hands around his waist, wishing that his Guardian jacket wasn't so thick.

A knock came at the door, interrupting them. Rush opened it with his goofy grin still stretching his lips. Neither of them expected Anise to see him, but as the door opened, and Anise came into view, her eyes widened to big saucers and her jaw dropped open. Her gaze ping-ponged between Clarke and Rush.

Holy shit. She could see him.

Anise clicked her jaw shut and gave Rush a cordial smile, then quickly entered the room and placed the tray on the small table near the hearth. On her way back to the door, she gave Clarke a secret flare of her eyes and whispered, "I see what you mean."

She shut the door on the way out, leaving both Clarke and Rush speechless.

He pointed at the door. "What just happened?"

"I don't know. I guess she saw you. Right?"

Rush strode to the door and stared at it. He rubbed his beard. "Did you speak to her downstairs?"

"Yes. She's the server who sold me the elixirs. We chatted a bit last night too. I like her."

He met her eyes. "Did you say anything about wanting her to see the truth?"

Clarke thought about it. "I guess I did mention something about wishing she could see what you look like."

He gave a grunt of understanding, mumbled something about her doing that with the White Woman.

Ushering her over to the table, he motioned for her to sit, and then proceeded to dish up her meal. He even tried to hand feed her again, but she took the spoon away from him, much to his displeasure.

"I think I can feed myself, big guy."

A scowl marred his face as he ate his own meal.

"You wolves are an interesting lot. Anise said something about being an alpha and wanting to provide for your mate. The cook down there also backed off once he smelled your special wolf cologne on me. Anise said he wouldn't go near a newly mated alpha's female."

Rush's jaw flexed. "It's not right that no one sees me by your side."

"Well," she squeezed his wrist, "perhaps soon that will change. I've done something already. First the bug-lady—"

"The White Woman."

"Yeah, that thing. Then Anise. Clearly I'm making something happen. Maybe the Order can help me the rest of the way."

As they ate their meal in silence, one unsaid thought hung over their heads. She could make someone see him, cut through the glamour that kept him hidden, but that had little to do with the rest of his curse.

Clarke was halfway through eating the last bit of fresh bread dipped in honey when a feeling of urgency rose swiftly and without mercy. Harsh buzzing exploded in her chest. The bread dropped on her plate.

"We have to go," she said.

He straightened. "Now?"

"Yes... something is—"

The door burst open, swinging on its hinges. Both Clarke and Rush jumped to their feet. He stood in front of her.

Standing in the doorway was a white wolf, snarling and baring its teeth. It took a step into the room, and then the air shimmered around it. Like a shifting mirage, the wolf became humanoid. It became Thaddeus, naked and pumped with fury. Behind him was a figure with a dark hooded cloak. And pushing through was Bones, also in a cloak. All three turned their heads her way.

None of them saw Rush, or the feral snarl curling his lips.

Thaddeus arched a brow and looked to Bones. "Is she the one?"

Bones' thin lips stretched into a smile as he took her in. "Yes. He will be pleased."

"I expect a bonus in the next shipment."

"Done." Bones' eyes never left Clarke, and a coldness settled into her stomach.

Who was the "He" Bones referenced? Someone who wanted her? Someone who knew her? The faceless Void loomed into her mind.

Bones dipped his finger into his jacket pocket and pulled out a red rose. He sniffed it, then tossed it into the room. It landed at her feet, rolled, and lost a petal. Clarke's heart stopped. The Void had always worn a red rose in the pocket of his suit.

Rush calmly slipped on his baldric and then secured his sword. No one noticed him.

That's what she thought.

The hooded figure behind Bones and Thaddeus faced Rush, and panic tightened Clarke's throat. He knew. He could either see Rush, or could sense him. Frozen, unable to move in case she alerted the rest of them to Rush's whereabouts, she didn't know what to do. Her gaze kept darting to Rush to check on his progress.

And then everything seemed to happen at once.

Thaddeus and Bones both caught her eyeing a seemingly empty corner of the room. They noticed the two cups on the table. Thaddeus sniffed the air and growled.

"He's here."

And then they were crowding into the room, Rush took hold of her arm, and a bright pop of light blinded them. She opened her eyes and wasn't in the room at the inn, but outdoors. Rush held her tightly. In his hand, a stone sizzled with smoke. He dropped it onto the grass.

"Well, that's spent," he muttered.

"What the hell happened?"

He nudged the stone. "I used the portal stone. We're at the Order."

# TWENTY-SIX

R ush held Clarke in his arms as she recovered from the effects of using the portal stone. The first time was never easy and the further you traveled, the greater the feeling of displacement. Her skin had taken on a greenish hue, and she clung to him. Any minute now, she might lose the contents of her stomach.

He helped her to her knees and pulled her hair back as she leaned forward.

"Take deep breaths," he instructed. "It will pass."

"Goddamned lack of cars." She made a gagging sound. "How come you don't feel sick?"

"Using portal stones is second nature for me. Some Mages and Guardians can create portals without the stones."

"Show-off." She retched again but covered her mouth.

Rush stayed with her while she crouched on the floor staring at the grass. It had been a risk to use the portal stone in close quarters. Many things could have happened. The energy rift in reality could have sliced through furniture and people too close. It was what he counted on. If Thaddeus and his men were smart, they would have jumped out of range to avoid being sliced in two by the rift. He'd closed the portal the instant he and Clarke were through. And if one of them tried to trace the portal, it would only lead them here.

To the Order.

His ears perked at the sounds of battle training coming from the distance. He squinted to scope their surroundings. As planned, the portal stone had brought them within walking distance of the Order grounds. Built like a fortress, a high stone wall and dense poisonous forest surrounded the grounds. Both kept the compound from prying eyes. Deep into the forest lay the ceremonial lake, an enormous turquoise body of water that fed into the Order academy buildings in small underground rivers. The lake seemed to have sprung from nowhere and was a source of power. There was no mountain range nearby, no sea, and they weren't particularly below sea level, but the water was aplenty and sacred. In all of Elphyne, it was where the connection to the Well was the greatest.

"Okay," Clarke grumbled. "I think I'm good. No puke. Winning, right?"

He helped her up but caught sight of a wolpertinger hopping cautiously toward Clarke. At first glance, the creature was benign, but the pest was known to turn on its victims. With the wings of a pheasant, the body of a rabbit, and the horns of a deer, the wolpertinger's blended traits from multiple species was the epitome of haphazard evolution in the new world. But if it came sniffing around, then it believed Clarke to be single, despite his scent on her. It was a sign that his curse still held, even in this magical territory where glamour was prohibited unless for training purposes.

He frowned. He'd have to make sure his scent was stronger next time. He wanted no one, even a little pesky fire-fae, thinking it had the right to Clarke.

Clarke saw the creature and cooed. "Oh, aren't you a cute little thing?"

"She's taken," Rush hissed and stomped his boot. "Begone."

Not understanding where the vibrations came from, the furry and feathered animal snarled, showed its fangs to Clarke, and then bounded off.

"Why did you do that? Surely you're not jealous of a little winged rabbit?"

"Wolpertingers target single females because they're the weakest. The easiest way to get rid of one is to let him know you're taken. Be careful what you deem cute, Clarke," Rush grumbled and offered his hand.

She took it and stood. "It had fangs."

"And a mean bite." He raised a brow. "It's also fire-fae."

"Meaning... it can shift?"

He nodded.

"Into what?"

"Into something that targets single females."

She shivered. "Are all animals to be feared here?"

"No." He glanced at the Order gate and unlinked their hands. "It's better you remain visible now."

Uncertain whether the bond leached his mana, he had to be cautious. Now that he had her, he wanted to make the little time he had left last. He wanted that timeline to be months, not weeks.

She scanned the area and the fortress. "In there?"

He nodded, then shrugged on the rucksack.

"So I just walk up to the gate?" Clarke asked.

"Chances are they know you're coming and they haven't deemed you a threat."

"Why do you say that?"

He shot her a sideways glance. "You're still alive."

Together they walked down the path of trodden sweet grass. A buzzing tingle hit his nose and then passed him as they crossed the magical protection wards set in place. If they didn't know Clarke was there before, they did now.

"HALT," shouted a Guardian from atop the gate tower. Made from reinforced leather, his helmet sat snuggly over

271

his head so it wasn't easy to determine what kind of fae he was. Rush liked knowing his opponents' strengths and weaknesses before heading in. The guard lifted the visor to see better, and all became clear.

The olive skin was a dead giveaway for vamp. That he worked the day shift must be either punishment or part of his rigorous conditioning. Probably a rookie. No matter what fae race, a Guardian had to be equally reliable in all conditions. Night fae had to be conditioned to function in the sun. Day fae had to get used to seeing in the dark. Nobody enjoyed working on their weaknesses, but the Well had chosen them, so they had no choice.

The vampires in the Guardian cadres could operate at any time of day.

Clarke darted a nervous glance at Rush. "I want to hold your hand," she whispered.

"You'll do fine. Tell them your name and that you're here to see the Prime."

With a lift of her chin, she repeated his words to the guard.

The vamp surveyed her, scrutinized her hair, and then nodded. "We've been expecting you."

Clarke relaxed.

But Rush didn't. This was the first time he'd been back to the place that had been his home for most of his life. When Thaddeus had called for Rush's punishment, the Prime failed to stand up for him. And Jasper, his partner, hadn't stepped in at all. He thought he knew Jasper better than that. That the more seasoned wolf wouldn't bow to the Prime's wishes if she decreed something so heinous. Rush had reasoned away Jasper's reluctance because he knew Jasper avoided any involvement with the Crown due to his heritage. But a part of Rush had always wondered. Maybe they weren't good friends after all. It had done more to deflate his courage than seeing his uncle call for his execution. Jasper's betrayal cut deeper than his thirst for vengeance against his uncle.

It was because the Cadre of Twelve were his family.

The Order was his home.

"Please step through the gate and wait immediately inside." The heavily perspiring guard tugged the collar of his blue coat. It wasn't snowing here, but it also wasn't hot. He was probably at his limits for daytime exposure. The rookie pulled a lever. "I'll be right down."

The arched wooden gate dwarfed them. At least thrice their size, it creaked open on stiff hinges.

Following Clarke through, Rush tried to keep his surreal emotions in check. He saw the campus as though for the first time. Stone buildings with deep red-tiled roofs and high arches were scattered around. Academy on the left, Mage dormitories to the academy's right. Straight ahead, the Guardian barracks housed the soldiers, and to the right, the armory and training fields bustled with activity. Majestically high at the back, lording over the entire campus, stood a moss-covered stone temple sparkling with glistening rivulets of water cascading down from the roof on rain chains.

Landscaped with lush green exotic plants and flowers, the campus was a beautiful sight. Rush could have happily stayed within the grounds most of his life. Many did, preferring the solitude of the library or engagement of the classrooms.

An almighty roar and gust of wind came from the training field. Instead of staying where she was told, as she should have, Clarke's eyes widened in awe and she trotted over to the lawn field surrounded by box hedges.

Two experienced Guardians were in the midst of sparring under the watchful gaze of a group of spectators near the infirmary. A semi-naked crow in angel form and a larger than normal white wolf circled each other. Rush's heart lodged in his throat. The wolf was his son, Thorne. Both had blood streaming down parts of their bodies. Rush narrowed his eyes. The dark-haired, tattooed crow-shifter had a wry smile on his face. One of Rush's old cadre. The wind gust had come from him, either from his wings beating behind his body, or a shot of mana induced air. He half-paced, half-flew around the unnaturally large wolf and twirled his dagger in his hand. Cloud wasn't known for honorable tactics, and the wolf seemed to like it.

Did he have a death wish?

The thought churned in Rush's gut. If Thorne fought Cloud, then he'd joined the ranks of the cadre. Perhaps he'd been promoted to replace the position Rush had left empty.

"Who are they?" Clarke asked, nodding at the couple fighting.

He cleared his throat and folded his arms. "The wolf is... my son."

"Wow."

"His opponent is the crow I told you about who was trapped in Crystal City for a decade in his youth."

"The thief?"

"Now the Order's best assassin."

"He's very..." She lifted her brows, assessing.

"Cruel. Reprobate. Deviant," was Rush's immediate response. Cloud had never done as he was told. He was the unit's nightmare. But he got the job done, and the Well had chosen him. They were stuck with him.

"I was going to say roguishly handsome, but okay, let's go with that. Rep-ro-bate." She made the word roll off her tongue.

A small rumble of possessiveness started in the base of Rush's throat. His inner wolf scratched at the surface of his control. He had been restless since the mating. Normally when a wolf mates another of his kind, the two spend not only days together privately, but time running in the wild. That primitive part of him still wanted out. It wanted to get to know its mate, feed her and play with her. Another rumble of dissent came out of him.

"Oh, settle down," Clarke chuckled softly. "I'm just observing."

"Observe me."

"Tonight." She gave him a placating pat on the arm.

Flexing his fists at his side, he forced his instincts to calm. He would have happily stayed within that room at the inn for days. They needed more time together and until they did, his restlessness wouldn't end.

Where was that damned Prime?

"That wolf is your son." She whistled through her teeth as though impressed. "He's certainly tenacious."

Rush shifted his gaze back to the battle. The wolf had his sharp teeth locked around a black feathered wing. As the wolf tore through it, a collective gasp rippled through the spectators. Black feathers scattered everywhere as though a pillow had burst. Red coated the wolf's jaw, and dribbled down his fur, but Cloud barely reacted. In one smooth motion, he twisted and shifted. For a blink, he wasn't a dark avenging angel, but a crow, flapping and cawing in the air, dagger in its claws.

The leather pants he'd been wearing drifted to the floor.

Rush snorted. "Show off."

"Why?" Clarke asked, eyes wide and fascinated.

"He's shifting without being connected to the land. He's showing the spectators, and his opponent, that his mana stores are high enough, he's confident he doesn't need to be connected to the land to shift back. Most fae need to be physically connected, but some of us Guardians can draw power from the Well from a few feet in the air. It seems the winged fae are best at this."

The crow circled around the wolf and then nose-dived. Just before hitting, the air shimmered around Cloud, and he elongated into fae form, and plunged the dagger into Thorne's white furry spine.

Clarke's hand flew to her mouth.

She soon found panic was not needed. Wolves were quick. Guardians were faster. Thorne had sensed the attack at his rear and rolled on the grassed floor, narrowly evading the blade as it embedded into the ground. Just like Cloud, Thorne shifted back to fae form and used the advantage of his hands to tackle and block his opponent. Both male bodies tumbled, grunted, and wrestled. Cloud could use his air-magic to blast Thorne off him, but he didn't. If memory served correct, Cloud was also adept with lightning. Perhaps he'd spent his cache of mana and hadn't replenished. Or he could be saving it for later. The battle was a display of strategy, of untamed strength and a struggle for domination. Naked and covered in dirt, grass and blood, neither fae gave a damn about spectators watching them in a state of undress. Shifters rarely cared about such human sensitivities.

"Oh my sweet Lord, if Laurel could see this now." Clarke whistled through her teeth. Then she tensed. Her eyes went white. "Rush," she whispered. "I see... I see my friend." She met Rush's stare, her eyes bleeding back to

277

blue. Then she darted a glance to the battlefield. "Laurel is destined for one of them."

"Another like you will come?"

"I think... yes. Not just one, but many more."

They both turned back to the sparring match. Thorne had inherited his parents' silver hair, but unlike them, he wore it buzzed at the sides and a few inches at the top. With the battle, and the recent shift, the leather cord that held the hair out of his eyes had fallen. This was something Cloud was planning on taking advantage of—Rush could see it in the way his dark eyes kept darting to the strands catching the wind. Cloud, who had short black curls barely long enough to grasp, wasn't beyond using dirty tactics to win.

Did Thorne see this intent in the crow?

A band constricted around Rush's chest. He'd missed so much. It was a regret that thickened his throat every time he thought about it. All he'd wanted over the past few years was to get here, to this point, where he had the means to talk to his son. And now that he was here... he didn't know what to say.

"Miss O'Leary." The gate guard came running up, his hand holding the too big helmet on his head as it drooped to one side. "I told you to wait at the gate."

She waved at the match. "There was something far better to do."

"Be that as it may, the Prime is expecting you."

"Can't I just watch for two more minutes? Please?"

While Clarke engaged in negotiation, Rush continued to scope the spectators. The team leader and a healer usually oversaw a sparring session this brutal. But then again, the Twelve had done whatever they wanted with training. In front of the infirmary, Leaf, the golden-haired and golden-skinned elf stood chatting with a tall, blue-robed male healer with underdeveloped goat's horns on his head.

So Leaf was still the team leader, Rush mused.

Continuing his search, he found another group watching from near the armory. And yet another group watched from near the forge on the opposite side of the field. The only of its kind in all of Elphyne, the forge produced the metal weapons the Guardians used to eliminate errant magical beasts. Among the watching fae, Rush recognized a good handful of his old cadre. The three Unseelie vampires, Shade, Haze and Indigo stood with their black leathery wings half out and their heads together. Knowing Indigo, he probably took bets on which Guardian would win the sparring match. Indi had only joined the Guardians because he thought it would be a grand adventure. Haze was the muscle of the group. With a shoulder span wider than brownies were tall, he'd joined the Order because he felt the incurable need to protect and he was quietly open with his mission. Obviously the Well had thought the same. Shade wanted power. Pure and simple. Rush was surprised Leaf hadn't fallen afoul of some training accident that relinquished him of his team leading duties. But vamps were good at lying in wait.

The hairs on the back of Rush's neck stood up, and every muscle in his body tensed in warning. A lack of sound came from the sparring match. The battle was done. He turned back to the field just in time to see Thorne lift his nose and scent the air in Rush's direction. No, the battle wasn't done, but interrupted. Thorne's sharp gaze snapped their way, but it wasn't Rush he locked his eyes onto. It was Clarke.

# TWENTY-SEVEN

Clarke only had time to register Rush's shout of warning when a large, white-haired and flesh toned *thing* collided with her, taking her to the ground. The wind knocked out of her lungs. Enormous snarling teeth snapped in her face and Clarke could smell the fresh blood on his breath. For the first time since arriving, true terror overwhelmed her.

The muscle-packed, heavy and very naked Viking lookalike pinned her down by the shoulders. Icy blue eyes glowed with adrenaline as he growled through clenched teeth, "Why do you smell like kin?"

But it wasn't the fury from Thorne that terrified Clarke, it was the reaction in Rush. She'd never seen him so close in appearance to his wolf. His eyes turned animalistic, his teeth elongated, and he reached toward Thorne with claw tipped fingers. The blue glyphs on Rush's face sparkled from the expense of his precious mana.

"Stop, Rush!" she shouted, tears in her eyes at what might happen. "You'll hurt yourself."

*Please, don't let him use up his reserves.* Not on her. Not like this.

"I'm okay. He's not hurting me. I'm okay." She held her palm out toward Rush.

Thorne jerked as though pulled, but it wasn't Rush who'd touched him. It was Clarke's words. Rush barely held onto his restraint.

"Who are you talking to, human?"

"It's him. It's Rush. Your father."

Surprise hit his eyes for a split-second, then he snapped at her and fisted the fabric at her chest. "My father is dead."

She squeezed her eyes shut and wished with all her might. *Please see Rush. Please see him.*

"You had better come up with an explanation, human, or you're—"

"Fuck me," someone said.

She opened her eyes. A group of powerful fae loomed over her, including the one who'd sparred with Thorne. He'd redressed in his leather breeches but stood back with unmistakable hatred in his eyes. The vampire guard looked green and panicked. A golden-haired fae skidded to a halt next to Clarke, wary eyes on Rush.

They could see him! Whatever she had done worked.

"Get off my mate," Rush snarled, eyes on Thorne.

*Shit.* This was not how Clarke had wanted this meeting to go. "Thorne," she said softly and patted his solid chest. "Please... this will all go much better if you get off me."

Thorne's wild gaze darted from Clarke to Rush, and then to the surrounding crowd. A collection of three winged fae in Guardian uniforms flew in on a dark cloud. Air gusted as they landed. All with similar toned skin and varying shades of dark hair, the trio circled around Rush, prowling for a fight.

As Thorne's grip eased off Clarke, she marked the similarities to his father. They were so alike it was uncanny. They both had a hard edge to their jaw, and a darkness to their eyes that told of untold heartache. But Thorne's eyes were blue, and Rush's were gold. Rush's beard was full, where Thorne's was trimmed close enough for her to see the dimples in his cheeks.

A lick of the unknown in the air had everyone looking to each other, and then at Rush with uncertainty.

"Ah," came a confident female voice from somewhere beyond the male heads. "There you are, Clarke O'Leary. I've been waiting for you. Do get off the lady, D'arn Thorne. She's our guest, and likely to stay for a while."

Thorne's face screwed up with malice. He shot Rush a dark look and then shoved off Clarke. It was hard not to see the clear anguish on Rush's face as he bent to help Clarke up. Choosing between a son and a mate wouldn't be fun.

Nor was holding in his instincts when he just wanted to fight.

"I'm sorry," he whispered. "I can't protect you."

"Because there was no need," she answered firmly. "I'm fine. And... they can see you."

Rush wouldn't accept her words as an excuse and ignored those surrounding him, as though he'd mentally shut them out. Every hard line of his body betrayed his struggle. Tension in his shoulders. Jaw pressed hard. Fingers flexing at his sides. Finally, he looked at the fae. God, this must be hard for him. She wanted to reach out to him but didn't want to make him look weak.

A brown-skinned woman with white feathered wings pushed through the circle of Guardians. Ringlets of never ending silver hair flowed around her shoulders. Her King-fisher blue dress draped from the empire line at her bust all the way to dust the ground as she walked with grace. The white, the brown, and blue came together in such a striking way that Clarke had to pick her jaw off the ground. The fae was beautiful, commanding, and regal all at once. Round face, dark plump lips, large eyes, and a long, slender nose. She gave the appearance of looking down at you without actually doing so.

"You—" Clarke pointed. "You have round ears too."

"Yes," she replied matter-of-factly. "Not all fae have ears like the elves. But most of us have other defining features that distinguish us apart from human. I'm sure you have many more questions about this time." She inclined her head. "We will endeavor to answer all of them." She then turned to Thorne. "You're dismissed. I'll leave it up to your team leader to allocate a suitable penalty for your reproachable behavior here today." She arched a brow at the golden-haired elf who had been watching, as stunned as the rest of them. His Guardian jacket was more embellished than the others in a way that gave him an altogether distinguished appearance. If it weren't for his formal attire, the golden tresses and tanned skin made him look like he belonged on a beach with a surfboard in his hands. "I meant you, D'arn Leaf," the female added. "And then be quick about the council meeting."

"Yes, Prime." He stared at Rush one last time and then gestured at Thorne. A gust of wind came from his hand and propelled Thorne back to the training field. *Magic*. Thorne stumbled, but tried to hold his position against the force of air. Leaf arched a brow. "I think you need to cool down first, Thorne," Leaf said and then nodded at Rush. "You can talk with him later."

From the look in Thorne's eyes, he didn't want to talk with either Rush nor Leaf. He turned and walked away.

The Prime snapped at the rest of them. "Show's over." She clicked her fingers at the rookie guard. "Get back to your post." Then she flapped her wings in irritation. "The rest of you, back to training. And you vampires, enough with the gambling on sparring matches."

The last of them trickled off. She laced her fingers and

met Clarke's curious stare. "Right. Let's get on with it then. Follow me."

As the Prime spun, her wings dragged a crescent shape in the sand and left sparkling dust. She strode onward, not looking back to see if Clarke followed or not.

Clarke turned to Rush. "She's not used to people saying no to her, is she?"

He shook his head.

"Do you think I should say no? Just to see what happens?"

She was trying to weasel a smile out of Rush, but he only flattened his lips.

"I wouldn't advise it. She may only be an owl-shifter, and a Seelie, but she didn't get to be Prime by falling there. Her talons are sharp."

# CHAPTER TWENTY-EIGHT

L eaving the training fields behind, Clarke followed the Prime through the campus. With Rush at her side, she attempted to regroup and went over everything she had just learned. So the Prime had been aware of Clarke... She'd even used Clarke's surname and mentioned they'd been waiting for her. Considering it wasn't out of the ordinary to be psychic here, Clarke wondered what these people knew of her shameful past.

Seeing her lover's full-grown son transform into an actual wolf also took some getting used to. Four paws, claws, snarling teeth with blood dripping down his front. An involuntary shudder moved through her. Thaddeus had also been a wolf. These fae were part animal. Even those fae with the black leathery wings. Vampires, but clearly a little different from human mythology.

Wringing her hands, she forced herself to emulate

Rush's ever watchful gaze, scanning for potential threats. But the architecture, gardens and citizens demanded attention. Small culverts of flowing turquoise water ran alongside every path. The trickling sound soothed her nerves like a spiritual retreat. Sizable buildings that reminded her of the Byzantine Cathedrals were to her left. Manicured lawns and fountains took up the space between smaller red-roofed buildings. Noticing the direction of her attention, Rush leaned over. "That's the academy and Mage classrooms. All those fae you see wandering the grounds in blue robes are Mages."

"Right." She nodded, then pointed to another set of close and cramped, one-story buildings. "And those?"

"The general barracks where the Guardians sleep. You'll recognize the Guardian uniform on most of those. The two big houses to the back are where the Cadres sleep. The Six are in the dark house. The Twelve are in the light— where the Guardians you saw today live." He cleared his throat. "Where I used to live."

"And where is she taking us?"

"Most likely to the temple for testing, or to her quarters nearby. It's only another few minutes walk. She said *we've* been waiting for you, so I believe other preceptors and council members will also arrive."

Clarke was all out of questions. Her intuition hadn't sparked in warning, so she kept following the Prime. It was a big campus, and the path wove in and out of outbuildings, a mess hall, and a library. The occasional blue-robed female or male walked by and stared oddly but said nothing.

A stone staircase rose up two levels from where Clarke stood at its base. At the top of the stairs, she saw a flat, red roof.

The Prime stopped and eyed Clarke's surroundings as though she were looking for something, or someone.

The Prime narrowed her white-tipped lashes on Clarke. "Has he gone, or is your hold on your mana slipping?"

"I don't understand. You mean Rush?" She glanced at him standing next to her. "He's right there. Can't you see him anymore?"

The Prime replied, "If he was visible earlier, but not now, your hold on your mana slipped. We can teach you to keep hold of the spell you wove to make Rush visible. First, you must prove to the others you are what we think you are."

"And what is that? You've told me nothing."

The Prime pinched the bridge of her nose and took a deep breath before responding.

"There have been Seers since the dawn of Elphyne who have predicted your arrival Clarke O'Leary. We have been waiting for you for a very long time. For some, too long, and they need a little convincing that you are who you say you are, and that the prophecies are real."

Prophecies?

"I'm sorry," Clarke said. "But—again—who, or what, do you think I am?"

"Both the destroyer and the savior. The darkness and the light. Chaos and order. You, my dear, are the first Well-blessed human to exist. Only you can lead us to more of your kind."

The shiver started slight. It began as an icy finger trailing up Clarke's spine, then a scrape, until it became a full drop in body temperature. Goosebumps broke out on her skin and she hugged herself.

"I..." She didn't know what to say. Hearing it laid out like that made it sound so important. So real. So dangerous. But what else had she been trying to do all this time? There was no going back. She came here to stop the Void from repeating what he did in her time.

"Look," she started, then paused, and tried to come up with a better way to say what she needed. But there was no sugar coating it. "Yes, I had an unfortunate hand in destroying the old world. I never intended it to happen. I admit to having a certain culpability. But I'm not a savior. I came here to tell you what I know about some bad people who may also have awoken from my time. I came to tell you, so you can help stop the evil man. I had a vision about him invading Elphyne for resources. Metals I know are used to make weapons. I'll help you fight him. Do you understand?"

The Prime stilled in a way that was more telling than if

291

she'd revealed some sort of expressional twist of the features.

"What I understand is that this is a lot for you to take in. You have been preserved in ice for a long time, yet the Well has deemed now is the time for your awakening. There is a reason you awoke. Events are in play. And we need your help. This world is vastly changed from yours, and you need training to understand your gifts."

"You don't know me."

"We know more than you think."

Clarke clenched her jaw. Helplessness was just a sliver away from her resolve. It was like her composure dangled at the base of a thin frayed thread, and one more tug would send her falling. She didn't want this woman to think she was weak. She wasn't. It was just... sometimes... she feared being taken advantage of. She needed to investigate these people, to assess them, and then to make an informed decision. They had done nothing to aid her at the moment.

"I want you to lift Rush's curse," Clarke stated.

The Prime's gaze turned downcast. "We cannot lift his curse, I'm afraid."

"What?" Clarke sputtered. "You can. *You* put the curse on him. It wasn't his fault."

"Clarke," Rush intoned and then shook his head.

But she wasn't giving up. "In what world does it make sense for a good man to be punished because of a moment of oversight?"

The Prime's white brows rose. "You tell me, Clarke.

What world do you know where a moment of oversight that causes devastating effects can go unpunished?"

The damned female knew exactly how that comment would cut deep. It wasn't Clarke who had paid the price. It was everyone else.

The Prime's poker face did nothing to convince Clarke of her integrity. She pointed at the Prime. "You're lying."

She held out her hand as an offering. "Take it and ask me again if you must."

Clarke strode closer, gripped the woman's warm, silken hand in hers and asked, "Tell me how to break Rush's curse."

"The only way to break it is for his Well-blessed union to snap into place."

Clarke looked into the Prime's large eyes and concentrated. Nothing came through her gift. The Prime spoke the truth. Clarke dropped her hand.

"I refuse to believe that you people, who made the curse, have no other way of breaking it."

"I regret you feel that way, Clarke."

Rush said nothing. He was probably used to more disappointment, but she wasn't. She would find a way, even if that meant scouring that extensive library she'd seen, talking to every single fae in this place, or forcing someone to tell her. She would see Rush freed.

"Now, if you don't mind." The Prime gestured up the steps. "The council have gathered and are waiting."

The Prime hiked her blue dress at the knees and

slipped off her sandals. Giving Clarke's boots a pointed look, she then added, "Please instruct your beau to do the same. I'm sure he hasn't been away so long he's forgotten proper temple etiquette."

Rush rolled his eyes and tugged his boots off. He laid them next to the Prime's sandals. The moment he let go of them, the Prime looked down.

"Ah. Now I can see them."

Clarke added her own shoes next to the pair. She was careful not to place it too close to the running water falling down the steps and disappearing into a grate.

She followed the owl-shifter up the steps and couldn't help the curl of her lip. She should feel better than this, but the knot of tension in her stomach wouldn't leave. She'd thought these fae would help Rush, but it was sounding more like they would use her. And the sheer lack of empathy really grated on her.

She glanced at Rush. Sometimes he acted as though he cared, other times she thought he acted without empathy —like when he'd brushed off the two fae stuck in the cages. Was it because he didn't want to get involved in politics so he had closed that part of himself off? Anise had accused Caraway of the same thing.

But maybe it had to do with years lived on this earth. Maybe the Prime was many years older than him. As usual, with the thought came the swell of rightness sitting in her chest. Yes, the Prime was old. Older than Rush.

It had been two thousand years since Clarke's time.

That was a long time to live. One could get emotionally weary from living that long.

They crested the top of the stairs and found a stone courtyard. Split into quadrants, each corner held a small colored pond with a pike coming out of the center. And in the middle of the courtyard was a larger pool, about two yards in diameter. The stone obelisk coming out of it had etchings similar in shape and size to Rush's blue glyphs.

Water dribbled down rain chains into the courtyard culverts, which then fed into the small ponds, which then fed into the streams running down the steps. It was all rather intricate, serene, and magical.

Six figures emerged from the temple doors. Three of the figures wore the blue robes of Mages, two female and one male. The other three were Guardians Clarke recognized. The golden one the Prime had called Leaf stood with his arms folded and a stiff posture. Next to him stood a vampire with black leathery wings. His short brown hair looked cover model ready and matched his soulful eyes. Sensual yet commanding. As if to prove status, he snapped his wings closed, and then they disappeared. His smug smile revealed short fangs.

The third Guardian was Cloud, the crow-shifter who had sparred with Thorne. The same jacket stretching across his shoulders looked extra wicked. Maybe it was because of the dark, oil slick tattoos gracing parts of his neck and hands, or maybe it was because the jacket was worn and cultivated, as though it had seen its fair share of torment, and dished out plenty. He stood leaning against the waist-high stone vase filled with pink blossoms, looking rather put out. She could almost feel his disgust roll onto her.

If this Guardian was treated poorly in the human city, then Clarke didn't blame him for having preconceived emotions towards her race. She may very well be the first human he'd associated with since.

"Clarke," the Prime started. "This is the Council of the Order of the Well."

"Try saying that five times real fast," Clarke joked.

It was the crow who snorted in amusement. The rest of them glared at Clarke.

"Sorry," she whispered. Temples weren't made for jokes, but religion had never been her strong suit. And she was nervous. "I guess, nice to meet you all. I'm Clarke O'Leary."

"Where is Jasper?" Rush asked suddenly. He went to the lip of the courtyard and looked down at the view of the grounds. Fae still swarmed about.

"Who's Jasper?" she asked him.

But one of the Mages answered. "Jasper has not been with us for a few years."

The Mage's robe was stained with green and brown bits. Twigs and leaves were stuck in his streaky long hair. His fae race was indeterminate, but he reminded Clarke of a wizard. He was the first fae she'd seen with some wrinkles around his eyes.

"He's missing," Leaf clarified.

Rush turned back sharply and locked eyes on Leaf. "For how long?"

"Wait. I'll translate in a minute." Clarke put up her finger to Rush. "Who is Jasper?"

Rush didn't answer. He began circling the room, scrutinizing the council members. They knew she'd spoken with him, but they couldn't see him, so stood awkwardly awaiting Clarke's signal that she'd received her answer. Rush began to poke and flick lint from their shoulders. He was clearly enjoying being invisible, so she didn't try to make him seen.

The Prime tugged on her ear lobe, irritated. "Enough. It's time to have you tested, Clarke."

"She must be initiated first." One of the female Mages stepped forward. Like the Prime, her skin was brown but her long curly hair was prismatic like a rainbow, as were her dormant dragonfly wings. Even her skin held a metallic sheen. "Anyone who steps into the sacred water must be initiated first."

"Dawn?" The Prime turned to the third and final fae Clarke hadn't heard speak. This one was not only quiet but seemed a world away. A jade butterfly clip held her short hair back from her eyes. Short, stocky, and with curling horns coming out of her head, she reminded Clarke of the same ilk as one of Thaddeus's hunters. Except where that one couldn't pronounce his name correctly, this female looked wise beyond her years. There was a reason the Prime asked for her opinion.

Dawn blinked and stared at the Prime. "Please repeat."

"Colt has suggested Clarke submit to the initiation ritual before she is tested. Your thoughts?"

Dawn's short fingers lifted to touch the butterfly clip and her eyes faded from blue to a glossy white. With a start, Clarke realized she was a Seer. The clip looked like a focusing tool.

"She's already been initiated." Dawn released the pin.

"Impossible."

"Can't be."

More dissent rumbled through the council. The Prime lifted a casual palm. "Please explain, Dawn."

"Her time underground has served as exposure to the Well. There is no point to initiate her in the lake. She's been in a permanent initiation ceremony for... millennia. You will see once we test her."

"Very well." The Prime motioned to the center pool with the obelisk. "You may enter now."

"Like, step into it?" She looked to Rush for clarification, but he was peeking inside the robe pocket of the male Mage.

Okay, then. She guessed she would just step into the pond. What was the worse that could happen?

She padded over barefoot to the pool. The icy water looked about a foot deep, so she rolled up the hem of her pants and then stepped in. Shock-waves of shivers wracked her body. She raised a brow and looked at the Prime.

"Now what?"

"Now touch the obelisk."

Clarke found the stone warm. Within seconds of touching, her will was ripped from her. A zing sizzled up her arm and held her in place. A bright light exploded, blinding Clarke and everyone nearby. It was white, hot and celestial. It felt alive. Light and heat invaded her body, getting to know her in a way that she had yet to give permission. It burned her nerves raw. A voice came from a distance, almost like a whisper.

"You can let go now."

She pulled away from the obelisk. The light dimmed. It took her a while for her eyes to adjust to the courtyard ambience. Even though swathed in daylight, the obelisk luminosity made the courtyard now seem dark.

"What did you say?" she asked.

Slowly her surroundings came into focus. Their expressions were no longer filled with disgust or thinly veiled wariness. Now they feared her.

"What's going on?"

"How long were you touching the obelisk, Clarke?" the Prime asked.

"A couple of seconds? Why?"

The Prime looked around. "It is late afternoon. If you didn't come out of your trance soon, your mate was readying to tear down the temple."

Clarke's eyes gravitated to Rush. Standing to her right, with one foot in the pool, he had dark circles under his eyes. "Are you okay?" she asked.

"I would ask you the same thing."

"He alludes to your extended period in stasis," the Prime added. "And yes, I can see him, although he appears to be fading. The illumination you cast upon touching the obelisk was the light of truth. I imagine that once you test yourself for elemental affinities, you'll be very heavily geared towards the spiritual energies. I dare say that one day you'll be able to use truth as a weapon."

"Lady, you're speaking in tongues to me." Clarke rubbed her eyes again. The weight of the event was dragging her down. How could she have been standing there for so long... hours it had seemed. "What was the point of touching that thing?"

She accepted Rush's hand and stepped out of the pond. For a brief moment, everyone lost sight of her and she considered running away with Rush. But then he let go, and his curse pulled away from her, casting her into the light.

"It proved what your capacity for holding mana is."

"And?"

"And if you weren't Well-blessed, you'd hardly trigger a glow."

"I made it go nuclear." The word left a bitter taste in her mouth. "Why was it so bright?"

"Because you are very strong in your gift. Perhaps the

strongest we have ever encountered, even among the fae. You may be able to go days at full strength without having to replenish. Weeks. Months."

"At full strength. So not like how Rush is using the minimum to stay alive."

"That's right. If you conserve your mana, you could perhaps last centuries."

"How is that fair?" Cloud snapped. No longer leaning against the stone vase, he was sitting reclined against it. "She's human. The Well doesn't reward greed. She must have stolen it."

"Just because you like the five-finger discount, Cloud, doesn't mean everyone else does," the vampire drawled.

"I don't steal mana, ass-face."

Ha! Clarke almost laughed out loud. It was good to see some things, like cursing out your friends, never went out of style. And it amused her to no end that, in a way, Cloud was right. She had spent most of her life as a petty thief. So, apparently, was he.

"It is not for us to decide who gains power from the Well." Leaf strode over and gestured at both vampire and crow. "We would have chosen better on more than one occasion."

Shade's and Cloud's wings snapped out and hovered. Tension vibrated in the air as all three Guardians faced off. It seemed a common occurrence. The Mages sighed, and the Prime pressed her lips. Rush stood with his arms folded, and a wistful smile, as if this were something he missed.

But Clarke was over it. Her muscles ached from standing in one position for too long. She rubbed her temples and turned to the Prime. "Are we finished here?"

The Prime glanced at the four other pools and a sinking feeling settled in Clarke. She thought she might have to do the same in all of them, but the Prime nodded.

"Tomorrow," the Prime said, "We will begin your training at first light and test for affinity to the elements. For tonight, D'arn Leaf will take you to your room. I'm sure D'arn Rush can take care of giving you a tour of the grounds and point out the mess hall for future meals. You are dismissed."

# TWENTY-NINE

Many thoughts coalesced as Rush followed Clarke to the Guardian barracks. From the moment the curse glyphs had covered half his body a few years ago, his mental state had shifted. No longer content to ride out his exile finding new adventures to occupy his time, he'd been consumed with thoughts of his legacy, and at that point, there had been nothing to be proud of. His curse had prevented him from teaching his son to be the best possible fae he could be, and it stopped him from so many other things. He'd always thought he'd be the kind of parent to make his own proud, but from the start, he never had the chance.

Clarke was the glaring symbol of a reward he didn't feel he deserved. What had he done to merit the little slice of happiness she'd given him?

Rush's top lip lifted at the thought of how the Prime

had reacted to meeting Clarke. Every protective instinct flared to life at the proprietary glint in the Prime's eyes. She had stared openly while they lost Clarke to the obelisk, and those big cynical eyes had seen everything. The future. The past. She calculated like a god. He knew it because he knew the Prime. She'd been the same when he was at the Order. It hadn't escaped his attention that she'd referred to Rush as D'arn, the same as she'd done with Leaf. It was their official Guardian title.

After all this time, why would she make the move to include him as one of the group? As though she'd never insisted he be cursed into exile. The female was up to something, and Clarke and he were in the middle of it. They were pawns in her game against the humans, or even potentially just within the realm. He intended to find out how far this plan of hers stretched, because he was under no illusion that if they weren't careful, neither Clarke nor Rush would come out of it intact.

Because he was lost in his thoughts, Rush failed to notice Leaf had bypassed the barracks and gone straight to the cadre house until they were upon the doorstep. The two-story behemoth had twelve private suites, a separate kitchen, and rooms for entertainment. The Twelve had earned their privacy through blood, sweat and kills.

Leaf took them inside and up the flight of stairs. He veered left down a red-carpeted corridor and stopped at the last door. Suspicion and disbelief coursed through him. This was his old quarters. He'd spent a century beyond that door. He put his palm to the wood and felt the memories: the proud day he'd arrived after being promoted at age forty-nine; the time Jasper had given him his first taste of mana-weed, and then the day after spent sleeping with a headache. As punishment for his tardiness, they had forced him to wash every window of the house. Jasper had laughed the entire time. But he'd also pitched in at the end.

"This is Rush's old room," Leaf said to Clarke. "I don't know if he's listening, but you can tell him we kept it untouched since he left." He paused, then added, "Upon orders of the Prime."

"Thank you," Clarke murmured.

Leaf pushed open the door. "There should be refreshments waiting for you. Someone will collect you at sunup."

"Am I a prisoner?" she asked.

"Not at all. But your tour will have to wait for another time, and exploring the grounds without a guide can be dangerous. You never know what concoctions the Mages have created." He scanned her up and down. "And if you come across any of the Six, run in the opposite direction."

"Who?"

"They're the cadre next door. All members are Sluagh and were part of the horde that led the Wild Hunt. Some say they still kidnap humans, so... stay away."

Leaf left and Rush followed Clarke inside. He shut the door behind them.

"He shouldn't scare you like that," Rush murmured.

"I can take it."

He smiled at her and then took in the room. Time reversed and his breath lodged in his throat with every memory his gaze landed on. *There* was Starcleaver's carved slice in the wall—an accident upon being gifted it for the first time. *There* was the stain on the carpet when he'd spilled mally-root wine. And *there* was the king-sized bed, made with its blue quilt and soft velvet pillows and most likely still complete with the squeak in the frame. Never in his wildest dreams had he imagined being back there, let-alone with a woman, a mate. It wasn't as though Guardians were forbidden to mate, it was just discouraged. They lived a dangerous life. Short dalliances were encouraged.

"I'm sorry about what the Prime said."

"What?"

"About your curse." Clarke frowned. "I wish I could have... I don't know, made her tell another truth. I wish what she said was different." Her face hardened. Rush had never seen such fire light up in her eyes. "I can promise you this, Rush. I will find a way. I'll stake my life on it. She might think she's my boss, but she's not."

The kiss he gave was everything he couldn't say. He wanted that to be true, but no one argued with fate. Fate was the tie that bound... and bound... and bound until it choked you in your own misery.

Her eyes had glazed and he let go of her, satisfied with the smile he'd left on her lips. He turned to inspect the room.

"Oh my sweet lord," Clarke murmured, and rushed over to a tray of food left near the settee on the opposite side of the room near the window. She began shoveling morsels into her mouth as though this was her last chance. A smile touched his lips. She ate with as much passion as she loved, making murmurs of appreciation with every taste.

"Hungry?"

She nodded and replied through a mouthful, "If I don't eat, I'm going to faint."

He left her devouring and paced around the sleeping chambers, getting reacquainted with the place. He ran his finger across the fireplace mantle. No dust. The bed had no residual scent, meaning no one had slept in it for a long time. He moved onto the bathing chambers. Clean and polished. A fresh bouquet of jasmine flowers was in a glass vase by the sink. The large tub and toilet were spotless and scentless. Maybe a hint of ginger and lemongrass beyond the jasmine. The house brownies still used the same products. Moving into the sitting room, he sat on the claw foot sofa and tested the cushion. The seat creaked, just like his bed.

He smiled.

Nothing had changed.

One last place in his suite to check. The storeroom. Before, it was filled with his clothes and weapons. He'd taken nothing into exile. Nothing except what he wore, including the Guardian jacket and Starcleaver. He pushed open the door and found everything was as he left it. No... not quite. He pushed aside the hanging jackets and found new female garments that smelled like lavender. Tension pulled across his shoulders. The clothes were like the style Clarke preferred to wear. No dresses. Just blouses and pants.

Gravity shifted. Horror dawned on him.

They knew Rush and Clarke would arrive back here one day. They knew what she would wear, and what perfume she preferred. The Prime had mentioned she'd been waiting for Clarke to arrive for a very long time. Perhaps even longer than Rush was cursed.

He slammed the jackets back into place and left the storeroom. Like a rising storm, every muscle and vein in his body filled with pressure. He couldn't see straight. His teeth hurt. And his fists sought something to punch.

He entered his room and found Clarke curled into a ball on the bed. He stopped still. The storm whisked away. Clarke. She was his calm. The very scent and sight of her so pure and vulnerable in his bed, heated his heart and filled it once more. She opened one eye and squinted at him. With a moan, she said, "I ate too fast and now I feel sick."

A rush of endorphins crashed through him. How could he tell this woman that since her arrival in this time she'd been a pawn in someone else's game? This fierce woman who insisted on doing things her way had been played, just like him. How much of their relationship was real? How much had been calculated and manipulated? Forcing himself to exhale and reveal nothing of his revelation, he strode to the bed. He brushed his knuckles across her cheekbones and then gently tugged the torn strap from her hair. "You won't need to hide your ears here."

She nodded and closed her eyes.

"Do you need anything, princess?" he asked.

She shook her head and then burrowed her face into the pillow. "It doesn't smell like you," she murmured.

"It's been a long time since I slept in this bed." He tugged down the duvet and shifted her so she was underneath. Then he covered her and tucked her in. Unable to resist, he brushed the hair from her face.

She caught his hand and tugged him down to her. "Sleep with me now."

His body moved before he'd allowed it, and he knew she'd always have this effect on him. He would do anything she asked. And that was dangerous.

He laid down behind her and flattened a hand against her stomach. She rolled to face him and lifted her nose to his neck. Inhaling deeply, she sighed on the exhale and then hugged him close. "Much better."

"Yes."

Much better. But only if he ignored the blue glow glancing off her face.

# CHAPTER THIRTY

While Rush laid next to his mate, feeling the soft push of breath on his face, he could only think of what he'd learned.

*Everything.*

The Prime's talons had been in *every* part of his life since birth. Scheming, shifting, rearranging. As Clarke softened and drifted to sleep, Rush's resolve hardened into an unbending desire for retribution. The Prime wouldn't get away with this. He'd dedicated his life to the preservation of the Well, to staying out of fae politics and to using his enhanced abilities for her prerogative only. This was the thanks he got.

He wasn't so expendable that they could throw him away. He would show her he was made of something more than trash. More than a second thought. More than a death sentence.

Rush waited until Clarke fell asleep and then left her in his bed.

Stalking down the hallway out of the house, he heard hushed voices in one of the entertaining rooms. Usually the cadre congregated at the end of a long day. They unwound with some ale, some wine, and the occasional misfit Mage in their lap.

He came up to the wooden doorframe of the games room and paused. It was cracked open. Obviously they weren't smart enough to keep it closed. If he wanted to, he could enter, and they'd forget they'd seen the door open, but he didn't want to risk the off chance that one of them remembered.

"I think if the Well chose her, then what more is there to say?" said a husky male voice he didn't recognize. Probably a new member of the Twelve since his time. Or one he'd forgotten.

"If the Well told you to jump off a cliff, would you do it?" This voice Rush knew well. Cloud.

"Now you're being overly dramatic." Shade's drawl was unmistakable. It surprised Rush that he wasn't out securing his meal. The vamps hunted at night, and like all living creatures, needed to feed daily.

"What do you think, Thorne," Leaf said. "You're the one closest to this."

Rush's ears perked up.

"How so?" came the gruff response. "The only link I

have to that wolf is my blood. There is nothing else that binds us."

Rush's ears went down and he fixated on a chip in the wooden doorframe.

"Blood is strong," said Shade. "And there is fate."

"Fuck fate," Thorne replied. "Fate tells us that Jasper's disappearance is part of some divine plan. It's not a coincidence he's missing. I say we find him. At least we'd be doing something."

Leaf grumbled. "No. We don't get involved. If Jasper is gone, it's the king's doing. We stay out of it."

A thump sounded as though something was hit. "How can you say that? He's one of us."

Silence, and then another whispered. "I can't say that seeing Rush today was an unwelcome sight."

Rush strained his ears and tried to place the voice. Someone he knew. But who? Indigo?

"That Well-damned bastard is still wearing a beard as though it makes him look tougher."

"Yeah. It was good to see him."

A few of them chuckled, but it was a warm laugh, not teasing. Rush rubbed his beard self-consciously. That's not why he grew it. It kept his jaw warm. The mountains were cold.

That familiar voice spoke again. "You may not be happy with your father, Thorne, but he is just the unfortunate victim of the same fate you hate so much. Dare I say he feels the same way."

It was Haze. The big vampire who'd been with Shade at the sparring match. Rush never expected him of all people to stick up for him. Haze was quiet, he kept to himself, and he rarely opened his mouth to voice an opinion. But in retrospect, it was always Haze who stepped in quietly to do the right thing. Perhaps the last fifty years had brought him out of his shell.

"Yeah, well, even unfortunate victims of fate can still take control."

"That's not exactly fair—" Leaf started, but Rush heard the stomp of booted feet approach the door. He jumped out of the way just in time to see Thorne storm off down the hall and disappear into his suites.

A coldness ran through Rush like a knife. Thorne had been right. Rush had been around. He wasn't dead. He'd seen it all go down. Thorne's mistreatment. Kyra being run out of the Hollow by Thaddeus. If Rush hadn't been so stuck in his self-pity, maybe he could have come up with a way to help keep Kyra in her home town. Maybe even put her up as the new alpha. She was strong enough.

He didn't need to hear anymore. It wasn't Thorne or anyone else who held his quarrel. It was the Prime.

THE EYRIE WAS cold and dark when Rush arrived. The Prime's house was grand, majestic and three levels high. It

313

also had a platform on the roof where she took flight, either in her owl form, or her preferred angel.

With Starcleaver unsheathed, Rush stepped up to the front stained-glass door and tested the knob. Unlocked. Was she so confident in her status that she believed she was untouchable? Rush knew one thing about winged fae. The higher they flew, the harder they fell.

He opened the door and went in, locking it behind.

He cared little for the ancient artifacts Cloud had procured for her. From the porcelain statues of little gnomes with red hats, to the glass picture frames holding a smiling old-world family inside. Once, the entrance foyer used to be awe-inspiring. Not anymore.

He failed to even give her a blink of respect. This female was about to have her comeuppance.

Sniffing her out, he followed the rose and ash scent to find her sitting in her office, in the dark, tapping her finger on a stack of papers.

The moment he stepped in the room, she lifted her head and stared right at him. "It's about time you came to see me."

# THIRTY-ONE

Clarke awoke the following morning with a start. She pushed her hand out of the sheets and found no warm body. And then she realized she'd dreamed, she knew Rush was not there. Sweeping the room with her gaze, she found him sitting on the settee, asleep but holding Starcleaver unsheathed and balanced on his lap as though he expected trouble.

A knock pounded at the door, and a male voice filtered through. "Rise and shine, human."

Her eyebrow lifted with a wry tug. She'd bet that was the crow.

"I'm up!" she shouted, in case he burst through the door and woke the sleeping wolf, not even understanding she'd just done the very same thing.

She slapped her palm on her face. It was too early to make decisions. Rush's eyes popped open.

"Sorry," she said. "Didn't mean to wake you."

"You have fifteen minutes and then you're expected for training," said the crow through the door.

"Got it!" She threw off the duvet and padded over to the tray with the food. God, she was hungry all the time since arriving at the Order.

Rush rubbed his eyes. Registering he held his sword, he casually sheathed it in the baldric he still wore, and then joined her at the table. Every nerve ending in her body pinged with his arrival, and her hormones were very aware of the hard, flat torso in the vicinity as he reached past her and plucked a grape from the half-eaten bunch. His brows puckered as he looked at the seemingly perfect grape.

"Is everything okay?" she asked.

The scowl on his face wasn't there when he'd woken.

The only way she could describe his expression was shell-shocked. "Rush? What's wrong?"

"Nothing. Sweet fuck all, in fact."

She laughed. "I swear hearing you say that word cracks me up. Some things never change."

"What do you mean?"

"The curse words."

"Same as in your time?"

"Shit. Fuck. Asshole. Most of the big ones are the same."

"Huh. I guess we like them." He popped the grape into his mouth and then lifted his arms and stretched grandiosely. She pretended to eat, but watched from beneath her lashes. She enjoyed seeing the way his skin played over the tendons in his neck, and the way his Adam's apple bobbed when he swallowed. He caught her looking at him on the down stretch, and a slow smile curved his lips.

"I'm hungry," she announced stupidly.

"I can see."

She blushed. "I mean... you know what I mean. Jeeze. Okay. I meant that too, and if I'm being honest, I don't care if you know it. I was too tired for round two last night, but just you wait, Wolfie. You wait for tonight."

He gathered her into his arms and looked down at her with amusement. "Tonight you will be even more tired. And the next night. And the next. Training is brutal, even for Mages."

"Is that what they want me to be?" She scrunched her nose. "They don't own me. I make my own rules."

Something flickered in his expression and the last of the ease with which he'd awoken dissipated. Gone was the sleeping wolf, and in its place, a hunter. The determined set of his jaw and distance in his eyes told her he kept secrets, but she didn't push him. They may be none of her business. If they were, they would come to her eventually, whether on their own, or from his mouth. She'd find out.

She had plenty to think about. Like, how to get information about the curse. Who did it? Who designed it? And who had the power to break it. Whatever the Prime had said, Clarke refused to believe. Something had been playing on her mind since her conversation with her the previous day. She'd said the Well had chosen Clarke. That because she had been kept in a frozen state, she was imbued with more magic than others in this time. Clarke knew other evil people who'd awoken from her time.

Did that mean the Well had chosen them too? Or was it all chaotic bullshit?

There were only two feasible explanations as far as she understood. One was that the Well was not the sentient deity or cosmic know-all they believed. It wasn't a God who picked. It was pure, simple, random shit. Perhaps it was even steeped in science, something the people in this time seemed to lack. For all she knew, the reason people were "Well-blessed" was because of some genetic anomaly.

If that were true, then how did she explain her own psychic abilities?

Taking a grape and eating, she thought of the second possibility for Bones to be awake in this time. Cheating. He and his boss, the Void—she shivered—had orchestrated their preservation from their time until now. Perhaps it was their plan all along. The world was too big back then for domination. Those mana stains on the dead satyr body outside Crescent Hollow came to mind. Rush had said it looked like mana had been wrenched from his body.

There were too many unanswered questions in her head, and she had to investigate. One thing was certain, she would not have her story written by someone else's pen. She'd done enough of that in her time.

"There are extra clothes for you in the storeroom." Rush moved to another room. He came back with an outfit on a wooden hanger.

Clarke smoothed her touch over the softness of the blue blouse and then stroked the navy linen pants. "Did you get this last night for me? Was that why you'd left the bed?"

He gave her a tight-lipped smile.

"You're so sweet." She kissed him on the cheek, and then took the outfit with her to the bathroom. Once dressed and relieved, she joined him in the main room to find he'd done the same. Gone was his worn and beaten Guardian jacket, in was a long-sleeved navy sweater that hugged his frame, and a pair of leather pants that did equal justice to his behind. More of his blue markings were visible. It didn't escape Clarke's notice that he'd discarded the old jacket in the hearth. But he said nothing about it as he slipped the baldric over his shoulder and strapped it to his torso.

"We'll find you more food downstairs," he said.

She was almost out the door when she remembered something forgotten on the nightstand next to the bed. Hurrying over, she collected the scrap of torn fabric she'd used as a headband. She wrapped it around her wrist. She may not need to cover her ears there, but she still liked to think of him every time she looked at it. Lastly, she took the sundial and tried to jimmy it into her pockets.

"I'll find a leather cord so you can wear that around your neck," Rush said.

"I'd love that." She signed her thanks.

He shot her an amused look and then guided her out the door.

In the kitchen, two shirtless Guardians ate breakfast at the center bench. Leaf, and a rather tall, dark and buff fae. As big in frame as Caraway, he would have made a good bodybuilder in her time. He could lift a car with those biceps and thick thighs. Buzzed hair. Tiny bone studs pierced the lobe of a pointed ear. Intricate tattoos down one side of his torso curved in and out of the line of his anatomy as though they were a part of him.

Irritation vibrated off Rush. His gaze darkened upon seeing their state of undress. Quickly, she nabbed a small round piece of fruit off the counter, and then bit into it. Juicy, sweet, and a little tart. Almost like water, but not. She chewed loudly and looked at the two fae, now staring at her with uneasy hesitation.

"If I had known the dress code was tits out, I would have worn something else," she said.

Rush rolled his eyes. But her joke had done the trick. It distracted him.

The large fae scratched his lower stomach in a way only a male could get away with. He studied her with curiosity. His deep baritone almost rattled her ribcage. "We've not met, human."

"It's Clarke. Not *human*. I'd appreciate it if you just called me that. Please."

He gave a grunt. "I'm Haze."

"Nice to meet you, Haze."

He bared his fangs in a way she supposed was a smile. "Long night. I'm off to bed."

Leaf nodded and then eyed Clarke. "Cloud will be back soon to escort you to the academy."

"Right," she said. "Training. And what exactly am I training for?"

The fae shrugged. "That's a question for the Prime."

"Okay. When will I see her? I have many questions."

Leaf grabbed another piece of fruit and shrugged. "No one has seen her since last night. She's probably out."

Rush made a sound that drew Clarke's attention, but by the time she looked his way, his face was expressionless.

"Out?" Clarke prompted.

"The Prime answers only to herself and the Well. I have known her to disappear for weeks on end, especially when she seeks answers and wants to consult the Well. With your arrival yesterday, I'm not surprised she's gone."

"Where does one go to consult the Well?" she asked.

"Ceremonial lake."

"Excuse me, coming through." A high-pitched feminine voice was the only warning before Clarke got jostled to the side by a waist high figure. Another holding a full tray of food was immediately behind her. Clarke bopped out of the way with a squeak.

Her eyes widened at the two... small fae. They looked like someone put little old ladies into an oven and shrink-wrapped them. Small, leathery and wrinkly, but with smile lines around their lips and eyes. Fuzzy hair grew on their skin in the most random places. Tufts out of their ears. Whiskers besides their noses. Their knuckles were big and their nails were long. Both wore a luxurious silk ribbon in their long braids. One was red, the other yellow.

Seeing her gaping maw, Rush explained, "House brownies."

"Almost done with the jobs," clipped the yellow-ribboned one, all business like, as she pushed the tray of food onto the center kitchen bench. The other paused and looked at Clarke with a scowl.

"What are you looking at, human?"

"I... um."

Leaf jumped in rather frantically. "She means no offense, Jocinda. She's never seen brownies as beautiful as you and your sister. I'm afraid you've left her rather speechless."

He gave Clarke a warning flair of his eyes.

"Um. Yes, I'm so sorry if I was rude. I love the ribbons in your hair. Stunning." She showed them the scrap around her wrist. "Mine's nowhere near as beautiful."

The brownie's hand fluttered to her braid, and she gave a grunt of approval, then finished busying herself with removing the old food and tidying the kitchen. Then the two of them left.

Leaf waited a full minute before turning to Clarke. "Don't offend the brownies unless you'd like to clean the house on your own. I find a well-timed compliment puts them at ease."

"Are they insecure?"

"It's common courtesy."

Then he nabbed a bread roll, filled it with some meat and then left.

Clarke found Rush eating and trying to hold in a laugh.

"What?" she said. "How was I supposed to know?"

"I could have warned you, but where's the fun in that?"

She threw her remaining fruit at him, which he dodged and then eyed the mess on the floor. "Don't let the brownies see you making a mess."

"Shut up." She cleaned it up and tossed the pip into the trash can by the stove when Cloud came in, dragging his feet.

Today he didn't have his wings out. He appeared to be a normal, every day fae. One with a dangerous glint in his eye and angry tattoos and scars on his hands.

They stared. And stared. But damn her if she blinked first.

"I suppose we should get this over with," he grumbled, and then walked away.

She trailed behind him down the hall and noticed his particular Guardian jacket wasn't the same as Rush's. At first glance, yes. But on closer inspection, the back panel was made of the same leather with Kingfisher blue piping. The panels weren't stitched together at the seams. Slots, she realized. Slots for his wings to push through if he deemed them necessary.

On their way out, they passed the darkened living room where another vampire—the model type from the council—sat on a couch, legs sprawled and hands on the hips of a top-naked female sitting on his lap as she necked him and grounded her hips against his. He leaned his head back on the couch and slid his lazy, hooded gaze to Clarke as she walked by. Parting his sensual lips, he licked an errant drop from his blood-stained fangs. His tongue was very pointy.

Desire was a heady bouquet in the air. It pulsed at Clarke from across the room, quickening her breath as though she'd walked straight into a sex dream. The Mage's moans of pleasure increased as she rocked against Shade. Still watching Clarke, the vampire lowered his lips to the Mage's neck. He lapped with erotic gratification at a wound Clarke barely noticed. His eyes twinkled as though he knew exactly what heated reaction his feeding triggered in Clarke.

Suddenly Clarke caught a face full of brooding snow-wolf shifter. Rush scowled down at her. His ears twitched in irritation. "It's rude to watch a vampire feed."

"Well he shouldn't do it in clear view, should he?" she

hissed and then jogged out the front door feeling as flustered as if she'd been the one on Shade's lap.

Shade's laughter echoed behind her.

HOT ON CLOUD'S TRAIL, Clarke followed the brisk pace he set as they crossed the dewy field in front of the Twelve's house. The sun peeked over the boundary wall, and the air was crisp. She rubbed her arms. *Should have brought a cape.* This field looked similar to the training field on the opposite side of the grounds, except perhaps more informal. She'd bet that the Guardians would mess about and rough-house there. She could almost see them playing the way college boys congregated and kicked the ball around in their free time.

Another big house stood next door. When she looked at it, shivers ran down her spine. Seeing as Cloud was doing his best to ignore her, she turned and asked Rush, "That's the other cadre house?"

"The Six. We don't talk to them."

"Why?"

"They don't play well with others."

Overhearing Clarke's half of the conversation, Cloud turned back and gestured at the house. "Horde. Blah blah. Kidnap humans. Blah blah. Don't go there."

Then he continued walking.

Now she was curious. Before she followed, Clarke tried

to spy any fae within, but branches draped over the windows with drawn black curtains.

Down from the cadre houses, they slotted through a thin alley which bordered on an enormous mess hall. The delicious scent of food wafted out. Clanks of productivity came from within. On her way past, a gaggle of novitiate Mages and rookie Guardians almost crashed into her as they burst out of the swinging glass doors. Upon seeing who she followed, they gave her a wide berth. But once they were five feet away, she heard the muttered "*Human*" from more than one mouth. Try as she might, she couldn't stop her shoulders from slumping.

She thought it wouldn't bother her, this name calling and segregation, but it did. It wore her down, even more so because they were right. She should be despised for the hand she'd played in the near oblivion of the entire planet. There were a lot of wrongs to right and it was all beginning to feel a little overwhelming, but she wouldn't give up. She could do this. Screw anyone who said otherwise.

"Don't worry about them," Rush mumbled. "Bunch of mewling litter box sniffers."

The novitiates followed her. It was cautious curiosity at first, but it gave way to hurled insults under their breath. Soon other things were thrown. A small piece of meat landed in her hair. She didn't flinch. She just pretended they weren't there, because if she turned around, she'd do something stupid and Rush would probably burst into protective beast mode. As it was, his hand rested on the pommel of the dagger clipped to his belt. Aware of her slowed pace, Cloud glanced over his shoulder. Catching sight of the group on her tail, his gaze darkened.

Black feathered wings snapped out and flared wide with a smacking whoosh. Air gusted in Clarke's face. Gone was the leather clad, brooding fae, and in his place was a dark avenging angel. Electricity and air whipped around his body, circling up his legs, torso, and crackling in his gaze.

That's all he did.

Stand. And stare. And electrify.

The group of novitiates evaporated. One minute they were there, and the next, scattered across the quad courtyard that separated the Mage buildings. One male Mage even backed into the three-tiered fountain at the center.

"I appreciate it," Clarke said to Cloud.

"Read nothing into it." He powered down and then resumed his stride across the quad.

"Next time," Rush growled. "You use your gift to show them I'm here. Understood?"

"So you can have a pissing contest with Cloud, or make yourself sick? No thanks."

His face screwed with fury, and he punched the glass window to the mess hall. The pane exploded as though a bullet had gone through it. Shattered slivers tinkled to the ground. The fae eating at a bench before the window all gaped. Rush shot Clarke a fiery gaze and then stormed off.

"Where are you going?" she shouted, but he didn't respond.

Cloud sighed dramatically. "What the fuck happened?"

"What do you think?" She threw her hands up.

It took Cloud a moment to blink the confusion of the curse away, then it dawned on him. "Rush did it. Lover's spat?"

"You don't think he's going after them, do you?"

"Who the fuck cares?" Cloud squinted the way the novitiates went and then shook his head. "He's not stupid."

At least there was that. "I guess we know where Thorne gets his temper from."

At the academy, Clarke couldn't help drawing the comparison with a fancy college. Made from a mix of wood, glass, and different types of stone, the architecture was old school Oxford mixed with a dash of Byzantine. Extensive mosaic decoration glittered on the outer walls, and a heightened limestone dome dominated in the middle. An overload of archways at every window or door made her feel a little inadequate.

Waiting for them at the base of the steps was the pixie who'd been part of the Council. While she was small in stature, she was large in attitude. With her dragonfly wings half fluttering, little swaths of prismatic light reflected against the cobbled walls and set to amplify her annoyance.

"You're late," she clipped.

"Whatever," Cloud grunted and gave Clarke a mock salute. "Colt will take it from here."

Colt did *not* want to take it from here. Clarke didn't need to be psychic to know that. The female looked sharply down her nose at Clarke, lifted her brows and sighed judgmentally. "It still makes no sense to me."

"Yeah, well, lady, I'm what you've got, so get used to it."

Colt's wings snapped shut and tucked in close to her body, but they didn't disappear like the shifters' did. Pixies must always be in winged form. It made sense.

She gestured at Clarke. "We'll visit the temple pools and find out what your elemental affinity is first. My guess is you're all spirit and chaos, no fire or ice. Then we'll work on your ability to draw on your mana. Then there's mana theory and uses with council member Barrow. Then Dawn will take you for specific training in Seeing. You won't get to the defensive and offensive arts until we're certain you can control your ridiculous abundance of mana. Crimson help us all that someone like you is the chosen one."

A surge of defiance stabbed through Clarke. "I'm not the only chosen one," she said. "More will come. More have already arrived."

Whether they were all set to be chosen, and for what remained to be seen.

"All the more reason for you to understand that I will not hold your hand through this. There are only a few preceptors around. Which leads me to another thing. You will address me as Preceptress Colt. You will address Barrow as Preceptor Barrow. Do you understand? Male teachers are Preceptor. Female are Preceptress."

"How ever will I know the difference?" The sarcasm dripped from Clarke's tongue.

Colt pursed her lips. "You're not one for respect, are you? Were they all like you in your time?"

She shrugged.

"Well. I guess we all have something to look forward to, don't we? Right. Another thing. Where the Guardians have a tear under their eye, we Mages have one on our bottom lip." She tapped her finger on the pillow of her lip. "If none are wearing uniform, then that's how you can tell us apart, even out and about in Elphyne."

Clarke narrowed her focus to see the tiny symbol etched there. The point of the teardrop started near the mouth and the heavy part of the drop ended where her lip joined her chin. "What does it mean?"

Colt straightened her spine. "With the Guardians, they shed a tear for each soul sent back to the Well. For the Mages, it symbolizes the Well is sustenance. We must be careful not to deplete our mana lest we become parched. We must remember to use restraint. Understood?"

Not really. "Okay. Got it."

"You don't. Mana can be like a drug, it can destroy. Or it can be like food and nourish."

"Like ingesting manabeeze."

Colt's lip twitched, and thoughts collided behind her

eyes. "Yes. Too much and you can go mad. Especially if you draw from the inky side of the Well."

Eventually Colt nodded and waved Clarke into the academy. Inside, more glass mosaics depicted many romanticized scenes Clarke could only imagine were the dawning of the understanding of magic. Robed in red, one figure moved from scene to scene in various states of repose, investigation, and spell casting.

"That is Jackson Crimson," Colt explained. "He is the first fae who discovered the link between the Well of life inherent in the world, and the mana we hold within ourselves. He founded the Order. I suggest you visit the library on your way home tonight and collect some books on our history. Since you will be living in this time, and defending this time, it's imperative you're all caught up."

Clarke bit her nail. "And where would I go to look up, oh, I don't know... let's say... how to cast and break curses?"

Colt whirled around, her robes, wings and curly prism hair swishing with her. "I beg your pardon?"

"Um. Curses? Where can I find out more about them."

"If you're referring to your mate's predicament, I believe the Prime has told you there's nothing more to be done about it. If I were you, I'd leave sleeping wolves lie."

"But you're not me," she replied. "And I won't ever stop trying to free him. So, you can either help me or you can hinder me."

"Why would I help you do something the Prime has directly forbidden?"

Clarke stopped. Stilled. And narrowed her eyes. "What did you say?"

Colt's eyes widened. "I meant that it's an impossible venture. If you want to waste time searching the archives, then knock yourself out."

That was the last word until they reached an empty classroom that housed about six desks and a chalkboard at the front. While Colt unlocked the room, Clarke's gaze wandered into the classroom on the opposite side of the hall. Set up like a laboratory, students sat at benches with scientific instruments. A Mage with pink hair leaned over the shoulder of another smaller fae, who in turn growled at her for spying. Glowing jars of buzzing balls of light were set up next to them. Each student experimented with individual recipes. Perhaps it was a test.

Barrow, who was at the head of the class, noticed her staring and walked over to the glass window and drew the drapes closed.

Yep. They were doing an exam. Goddamned college idiosyncrasies. Clarke rolled her eyes. "I'm too old for this shit."

"How old are you?" Colt asked.

"Twenty-nine."

A tinkling laugh burst out of Colt. "You're but a babe."

"And how old are you?"

Colt lifted a brow. "One never asks a pixie her age. But... fine. You're the all powerful Seer. You tell me. This can be your first lesson."

Okay. Clarke shook her hands at her side like a boxer. She could do this. Guess the lady's age. Got it. Squinting and scrutinizing, she looked for clues on her face. No lines beside her eyes like Barrow. No laugh lines next to her mouth. The skin on her neck was elastic. Going by Rush's age, and his appearance... damn. Who was she kidding? She had no clue.

"Stop looking with your eyes and start feeling with your gut." She tapped Clarke's stomach with her hand.

Clarke scratched beneath her ear and looked at Barrow's classroom window.

Fingers snapped in her face. "Pay attention."

"This is harder than it looks."

"Because you're untrained. It's like teaching a donkey how to fish."

"Oh-*kay*."

"I meant no offense. It's just the truth. I'm two-hundred-and fifty-nine years."

Clarke bit her cheek to stop herself saying something derogatory. Apart from the Prime, Colt was the oldest fae she'd come across. And she didn't look a day over thirty. She probably had a lot to teach.

Clarke followed Colt into the classroom. Set up exactly like one from her time, the familiarities set her at ease. It also disgusted her to be in a learning environment again. Her life had been about education on the fly. Street smarts, not book smarts. She'd earned her meal ticket every day. That was until Bishop got his hands on her. Then it was ignore the fact she felt the bad vibes in her gut because at least she didn't have to work so hard for a meal.

"Where did you go, just now?" the preceptress asked.

"Just thinking about some poor decisions I made, despite the bad vibes in my gut warning me."

"Bad vibes. Vibrations?" Colt tapped her finger on her lip. "They say the connection to the Well is like another brain thinking in your stomach."

"It can feel like a flutter for something good, or a bad buzzing for something bad."

"Good. I believe this is a solid foundation for your training."

This was going to be rough.

Through a long window on one side, students and Mages gathered around the quad courtyard and three-tier fountain. The one who'd fallen in when Cloud had frightened them stood to the side, wringing his robe. Another smaller female with blue hair tried to use some sort of magic to air-dry it. Steam curled into the air.

"Take a seat. There is a lot to go through, and Preceptress Dawn says you only have four weeks," Colt said and gestured to a wooden desk.

It was nice and smooth. Perfect surface for carving a "C" into. Huh. Maybe Clarke would enjoy this lesson, after all.

She took a seat and then jolted. "Four weeks? Why?"

"You'll have to ask her. Okay, so we'll start with recognizing the sensations of replenishing from the Well, how to compare it to drawing on your own internal stores, and then again how to distinguish it from the feelings you'll get when your gift is trying to warn you..." Colt droned on. Clarke knew she should pay attention, but she couldn't help the worry creeping up her spine.

It hadn't escaped her notice that Colt had let it slip the Prime had ordered everyone not to help her break Rush's curse. Looking out the window, she wondered where Rush had gone. And if he would come back.

# THIRTY-TWO

Cloud had escorted Clarke to the academy for eight days of training.

In those days, she'd been grilled, drilled and turned into a pumpkin. Well, that last one wasn't true, but she'd felt like it. Rush hadn't been wrong when he'd said she'd be exhausted after each day's lessons. She was the walking dead.

They kept her busy. Too busy. She'd not had time to research the curse.

On the ninth day, when the knock came at their door in the morning, Clarke and Rush were both surprised to hear the deep voice barking through, "Be ready in five."

Already half dressed, Clarke tugged on her boots and raised her brows at Rush.

Still in the bed, tangled gloriously in a sheet, he shrugged.

The voice had belonged to Thorne.

While Rush slipped on breeches, Clarke gathered the two books she'd borrowed from the library on elemental magic, and tucked them into a sling bag. She'd learned she had a small capacity for all the elements, but her strengths were in the spirit and chaos department... which was the psychic and the truth manipulation part of her magical canon. The teachers hypothesized she could one day learn to flip the truth on people, and make them think something was happening, when it wasn't. Like a mirage. But apparently that could take decades to learn.

And still, none of it revolved around breaking Rush's curse.

"Right," she said. "I'm ready."

Rush had been unusually quiet since their first day, and she put it down to the fact they'd not spoken to Thorne yet.

"I think today is the day," she said.

"For what?" He checked his appearance in a black mirror on the wall, and brushed his hair back.

"For telling Thorne whatever you needed to tell him."

He paused. And he slid her a look.

"Come on." She went up to him and hugged him from behind. With a sigh, she rested her cheek on his back. "It's been over a week. You wanted to speak to him so badly that you bargained with me, remember?"

The hard muscle under her face spasmed. "It seems like a long time ago."

Another rap at the door and Thorne shouted. "Let's go."

Clarke patted Rush's back and collected her bag.

Thorne waited in the hallway. At least he wasn't walking around naked today. The Guardian had on his uniform, and rested against the wall with his arms folded. He stared at her. The brooding animosity she'd felt on the first day was still there. Initially she had been offended, but then she came to see he was like that with everyone. The chip on his shoulder must be heavy.

"You know," she started, "I haven't had a chance to tell you that another Guardian told me to look you up. His name is Caraway. Do you know him?"

Thorne narrowed his eyes, but said nothing.

Okay, then. "Well, he said you're honorable. So... yeah."

He gave no sign that he cared.

What a tough crowd. She gestured down the hall. "After you."

Rush followed Clarke as they left the building. He never stayed with her at the academy, but he always joined the escort. It took her a few days to realize they weren't shadowing her because she was a prisoner, but because they were her bodyguards.

Passing the house of the Six, Clarke tried once again to spy inside the windows. She saw nothing but the twitch of a dark curtain. The Sluagh who lived inside were borderline evil, Rush had told her. Fallen angels, some said. Disgruntled fae spirits, others named them. During the Wild Hunt years ago, when the first war between human and the fae-folk happened, the Sluagh were sent by the Winter Queen to kidnap the humans. The Sluagh apparently developed a taste for them. They were rumored to fly to Crystal City and take humans into their horde. The humans were never seen again. But their cries were heard.

Rumors, Clarke decided. She'd make up her own mind. She just wanted one look inside the house. That was all.

These particular six Sluagh were Guardians, which meant the Well deemed them worthy of holding the extra power... they couldn't be that bad. Right?

Clarke shifted her gaze back to Thorne as he took brisk strides across the informal Guardian training ground. She glanced sideways at Rush, also taking brisk strides. They might not get another chance to speak and she was done waiting for their stubborn wills to concede. She stopped on the dewy lawn before the cadre houses.

"Wait."

Both Nightstalks stopped.

She fiddled with her bag. She swallowed.

"Rush. I think you want to say something to Thorne. Now's the time."

Thorne started walking again.

Clarke's irritation swiftly rose.

Rush gestured in the direction of the academy. "I still don't know what to say. Let's just go."

"No." She put her foot down. "Rush, you've been tying

yourself up in knots about this. It's the least he can do to hear you out. I'm not leaving this lawn until he does."

Thorne checked over his shoulder, cast a wary glance at the house of the Six and came back. "Fine. Hurry up."

*You're a jerk.* "Good."

She tugged on her gift, and felt the movement in her soul. The past eight days had only worked to help strengthen the skills she'd fumbled across all her life. The rest was a work in progress. She looked at Rush, then at Thorne. *"Let Thorne see the truth."*

She sent her intentions out to him. Energy rippled from her body with the wind. To Clarke, nothing else happened. But Thorne's gaze suddenly shifted to take in Rush standing to his right.

Neither of them spoke.

Silence.

The breeze blew.

She was sure she heard a cry coming from the house of the Six. She shivered. And then shook it off.

Five minutes later, the two wolves still stared. It was getting ridiculous.

And then Rush cleared his throat.

"I regret..." He cupped the back of his neck. "I regret the way things went down with your mother. And I'm sorry I didn't do more to help you and your aunt at the Hollow."

Thorne narrowed his gaze. "You just apologized."

"Yes."

"You're admitting to owing me a debt."

"Correct."

Thorne's harsh blue gaze whipped to Clarke. "You know he'll leave you."

"I'm working on the curse." She patted her bag. Tonight she would hit the library stacks again. Surely someone could point her in the direction of tomes on curses. She just needed to garner a little more information.

"He'll leave you before the curse," Thorne added. "It's what he does."

Something snapped within Clarke. "I don't think any of us expected you to welcome your father with open arms, but this attitude of yours just sucks. Shit happens, buddy. Grow up."

A low, defensive growl shot out of Thorne. Clarke stepped back at the wild animalistic flash in his eyes.

"You were right about Jasper," Rush blurted, stepping between them.

Thorne's gaze snapped to his. "What?"

"He's not on hiatus, despite what the Prime said. She's not to be trusted."

Thorne shuffled his feet. "Why?"

"How long has Jasper been missing?"

"About a decade."

Rush straightened his spine. "I may not be able to do much in this state, but I can watch. I can learn secrets. And I followed many of you around for years. Some time ago, I saw Jasper at the Summer Court, having a discussion with King Mithras."

"About?"

"I'm not sure what Jasper told you about his heritage, but he's the king's bastard. There's a prophecy that the king's son will dethrone him, so any descendent was killed. But since Jasper is a Guardian, the king couldn't touch him. It's a point Jasper always liked to rub in Mithras's face."

"He's a Guardian. He can't claim rights to the throne. The king shouldn't see Jasper as a threat," Thorne replied.

Rush shrugged. "I can only tell you that I saw them together and I agree with you. I think Jasper is in danger."

Thoughts clashed behind Thorne's eyes. Then looked back in the direction they came. Clarke tried to stay silent and invisible. This was the most the two had spoken. If they didn't notice she was there, maybe there would be more. But Thorne continued toward the academy.

When they arrived on the doorstep, he shot Rush a contemplative look, and then left.

"I suppose that went well," Clarke said.

"I don't know what else to do."

"Well, I don't know if this is worth anything, but from a person whose mother abandoned her, the best thing you can do is to keep showing up. He'll get the picture soon."

Rush's smile never reached his eyes. He gave Clarke a quick kiss on the cheek. "See you tonight."

And then he left too.

Clarke jogged inside the building and hurried to her class with apprehension. She was beginning to understand these lessons were a ruse to keep her distracted from discovering more about the curse. Learning the skills to harness her power could take decades, and since she apparently lived in harmony with the Well, she would live as many years as the fae. Since she'd learned the fact from Colt, Clarke did nothing but think about a possible long life spanning before her. A life without Rush.

When she arrived at Barrow's classroom, she stalled. Taking a peek inside, she saw students preparing their lab stations. She wanted nothing more than to walk the other way.

With a start, she realized that feeling was her intuition. *So walk the other way, Clarke.*

Ducking her head, she carried on down the hall and followed her gut feeling until she ended up at the library. Before heading in, she took a deep breath. If anyone said she wasn't meant to be there, she could just say she was returning the books in her bags.

She strode in with her chin held high. The smell of old books hit her nose and tension ebbed from her posture. Out of everywhere she'd been in Elphyne, this library reminded her most of her own time. And she wasn't even a studious person. It was that smell. And the familiar shape of the leather-bound books as they lined the walls of shelves. It was the hushed tones used when students whispered to each other. And it was the atmosphere of respect. Of ideas. Here, she felt anything was possible.

A senior Mage sat behind a reception desk made from a

dark cherry wood. His bushy brows lifted as his eyes met hers, and then he settled back to his work with obvious disinterest.

If the Prime had truly asked all the senior staff to avoid helping her with Rush's curse, she knew the senior Mage wouldn't reveal the answers she sought. Rush would probably know where to look, but he refused to come into the academy.

Scanning the floor, she let her gaze pass over each desk the students and scholars studied at. She let her intuition do the talking. There was definitely something here. She could feel it in her bones.

Her gaze landed on a table near the window. There was a tall, gangly Mage studying a large open book. He looked like a good place to start. Not too old. Not too new.

She shuffled along the carpeted floor and sat down next to him with a smile.

Completely taken with his book, he failed to look up. Now that she was closer, she took in more details of his body. The fae had a rather round head and golden skin with brown striations like a piece of french polished wood. A cow-lick of golden hair stuck up at the crown of his skull. He licked his long finger and turned the page, eyebrows lifting with avid fascination at whatever he was reading.

Clarke snuck a look at the text.

*Cultivating new growth from frigid landscapes using a combination of...*

Her eyes blurred with boredom. Yep. Not her thing.

"Hi," she said.

He craned his neck and blinked at her. Then his eyes went to her ears with a squeak. Little green leaves sprouted at his nose. His brown eyes went cross-eyed at the leaves and an incredible red blush hit his cheeks. When his gaze met hers, she caught genuine fear.

"I'm not here to hurt you," she whispered. "I promise."

"You're human." His voice broke like a teenager. "I... um."

"Yeah, I guess I get that a lot." She used her fist to make a circle over her chest. It was the sign for sorry. "I didn't mean to startle you."

"It's okay. It's just." He brushed his nose leaves away. They fluttered to the table. "I don't see many humans. Us Oak Men don't really get along... yeah. Humans kind of cut us down for wood. So we don't... yeah."

He shrunk away from Clarke.

Oak Men. Wow. And those leaves coming out of his nose. He was the first fae she had met who was blended from both human and plant. All others had some sort of animal or insect origin.

She offered another smile. "I can promise you I'm not here to cut you down."

"If you say so."

"Scout's honor." She crossed her chest. "Cross my heart and hope to die."

The Oak Man frowned. "Don't do that."

The senior Mage at the reception desk shushed Clarke.

She made the sorry sign again and lowered her voice to the Oak Man. "I'm Clarke."

He tapped his chest and whispered, "Frello."

Okay. They were getting somewhere.

"I'm hoping you could tell me if there are books on curses here," she asked.

He eyed her warily. "Why do you want those?"

"It's to help a friend."

His eyes widened. "Oh. The Wolf Guardian. Yes, I've heard about him." This knowledge seemed to relax him. He pointed down to the east end of the library. "They're next to the culinary section."

Elation lifted her clean off the seat.

And then she was forced back down when a hand clamped on her shoulder. She cranked her head to find Barrow's bushy wizard eyebrows scowling down at her.

Guess she would start her research tonight.

CHAPTER

# THIRTY-THREE

Three weeks later, on one of her nightly visits to the library, novitiates and scholars still filled the study area, and lined desks. Every so often, she heard the distinct sound of a page turning, and it drilled her insecurities in deeper.

She sat in the back, between two stacks of floor-to-ceiling shelves, surrounded by a collection of littered books. Some of them were ancient, glued together scraps of fabric, bark, or leather. Others were newer paper and wood. All were about curses, but none indicated how to perform one, or how to break one.

The Oak Man had pointed her in the right direction, but the books that existed here were more like a warning to those stupid enough to dabble in the forbidden art. None of them used the glyphs present on Rush's body. She was fast coming under the impression that the Prime had orchestrated the fact that nothing of actual use was available to the public, or there was a hidden section somewhere. A place where tomes on the inky side of the Well were kept. A place as dark as the depths of said Well.

She cleared her mind, crossed her legs and concentrated on her intuition. The idea was to nudge that gut feeling to look for something that didn't want to be found. The secret library must be here somewhere.

But thoughts of her failings kept coming to the forefront of her mind. She couldn't find this connection to the cosmic Well. She couldn't spark a flame. She couldn't create a breeze with her gift. It was hard to stay positive when they'd all said she was this powerful person. *Ooh, I'm the chosen one.*

Whatever.

There came a point where her teachers had stopped looking at her with a mix of trepidation and awe and looked at her as though she was a fraud.

Rush had also been busy and hard to nail down. With what? She couldn't say. Only that he crawled into bed with her each night and when morning came, she'd find him sitting on the settee, either awake or half-asleep, staring out the window with Starcleaver in his hands, expecting trouble.

It felt like he avoided her.

Something had happened that first night they'd arrived, and he refused to talk about it. Perhaps it was the fact that Thorne continued to keep his distance, even after their brief talk, or that the Prime was still absent and the Council was beginning to worry.

The ticking time bomb that was Rush's curse made her feel sick. She'd even asked Preceptress Dawn how to See into her own future, or to his, so she could help him. Dawn had only replied with, "Well-blessed mates can sense the other's emotions down the bond."

Clarke had snapped something back at Dawn which hadn't been polite. She was tired of hearing about this grand other union Rush could potentially have and how it could save him, while Clarke couldn't. Her. This great, strong, chosen one. But not strong enough. Not good enough.

Clarke had wrung one good piece of advice from Dawn. She'd said, "When looking for your own future, don't look to the stone falling into the pond, look to the ripples it creates."

All these thoughts and more crowded her mind and stopped her from being able to meditate properly.

"Okay, Clarke. You can do this," she murmured, and thought about the books surrounding her, and the books she wanted to find. "They're like that... but they'd feel... darker. More chaotic. More..."

The hairs on the back of her neck lifted as someone sat behind her. For anyone else, that sensation would trigger a warning, but now... it melted her. She smiled.

"I knew I'd find you here." Rush swept hair from her shoulders and brushed his lips across her neck.

He shifted so his legs sprawled on either side of her body. Two warm hands circled her stomach. Clarke melted a little more.

"But where have you been?" She tensed, waiting for an answer.

"Around."

She released a breath. Not even reactions to her prying these days held the spark of defiance from him. It was almost like he'd... her throat closed up, refusing to acknowledge the thought. Instead, she leaned forward and picked up a book. It was a cook book, but she'd noted similarities in recipes to some information Preceptor Barrow had relinquished about how rare ingredients were needed to make a curse. She picked up a second book. It listed ingredients from the oil-slick tattoos she'd seen on several Guardians. These, she'd confirmed, enhanced abilities. Cloud was covered in them.

Rush's knuckles grazed down her arms. His big fingers closed over hers on each book, and then he pried them away.

"It's late. Come to bed."

Normally, she'd jump at the chance, but since the moment she'd woken that morning, a knot of tension had been ever present in her gut. It had distracted her to no end.

She huffed. "I can't."

Time was running out.

"Baby," he breathed and nibbled her ear lobe. It sent

delicious shivers down her spine and heated her pleasantly. Hearing him use her own endearment was, well, endearing. He wanted to connect with her, to be closer. Because he'd been pulling away.

Unshed tears burned her eyes. She wasn't ready to let go of him.

She cleared her throat. "I have work to do."

"Forget about the curse," he said, voice all honey and spice. "You won't solve it by looking in the library."

"Where, then?"

She felt, more than heard, the sigh come out of him. "In dark places it's not safe to visit."

"I *knew* it."

"Of course you did."

"How do we get there?"

"We can't."

She craned her neck to look him in the eyes. Sadness pooled in the depths of his golden gaze.

"There's always a way."

"Not this time. You heard the Prime. Well-blessed mate only."

"Fuck your magical curse-breaking mate. *I'm* the one." She poked him in the chest. "I'm *your* one."

She knew it in the deepest parts of her soul.

His lips curved and he held her chin there as he sank into a kiss full of promises, need, and those wicked things she'd seen flashing in his eyes. A rumble of satisfaction rolled through him as she returned his heat, feeling every bit as beholden to his desires as her own.

"Let's go to bed," he insisted again, lips against hers.

"Rush…" She pulled away. "I can't even light a candle with my mana."

The truth hurt to say aloud. She knew all the theory to go with it, but still couldn't distinguish between the instinct that gave her vibes, and the sensation that supposedly connected her to the Well. It was all instinct to her, but it was something all fae inherently grew up with. She had a lifetime of bad habits to unpack.

"I've meditated so deep and long that I feel like I know every part of my body, but I still can't find the part that draws on the Well."

"It's not something you can find, Clarke. It finds you."

"Yeah, well how is that supposed to help me?"

She must have spoken louder than she realized because a hissed "Shhh" came from somewhere else in the library. She wanted to throw a book at them.

This was why she never went to college. It was filled with a bunch of pompous, stuffy do-gooders. Where were the party frat boys or sorority girls? Not here, that's for sure.

He sat back on his hands and considered her brooding face. She tried very hard not to think about the hard muscles slabbed beneath that deep burgundy sweater with the tantalizing V-neck he favored so much. The tailor or seamstress who made it didn't account for his broad shoulders and tapered waist. It was tight everywhere, except where it gathered with excess fabric around his abdomen. She tried to still her beating heart when he licked his lower lip. His beard had been trimmed short, making the angle of his jaw sharper than before. His silver hair had been brushed over as though he'd run fingers through it and shoved it to one side in agitation... or stifled passion. He still wore his weapons, even though it had become clear weeks ago that no other fae did within this compound unless specifically training. The Sluagh were overrated. She'd not seen a peep out of them. To everyone else, this was supposed to be a safe place.

Not for Rush.

He caught her frown and misconstrued it. "I can help you."

"What do you mean?"

Another shush filtered through the stacks and she shot the end of the aisle a disgruntled glare.

Rush's leather pants creaked as he stood and then strode down the aisle, disappearing around the corner. He came back with a lit half-melted candle stuck on a single pottery holder. He used a boot to irreverently shift her books aside and placed the candle down before her. Then he returned to sit behind her and spread his legs on either side. Two warm hands gripped her shoulders.

"Face the front. I will teach you how to blow it out with your power, and then how to light it."

She slid him a sideways stare. "I didn't know you could

manipulate elements."

"All Guardians can. For shifters, we prefer to use our mana for the shift, but sometimes we resort to the elements for help. Some elements are stronger than others."

"So... those who can't shift, like Leaf, he's—"

"Basically just a Mage who fights."

She huffed a laugh. "Don't tell him you said that."

"Oh, don't worry. We made it our business to tell the elves about their shortcomings every day."

The humor in his voice brought a welcome surge of joy to her heart. This part of him she wanted to see more. It was the part that still acted like he was a member of the family here, not the part that existed on the outskirts. It was the part that still held hope.

She focused on the flickering candle. "Okay," she said. "So... just access my mana and blow it out. No biggie. It's not like I've been trying to do this for weeks."

"Relax." Rush's thumbs pushed into sore spots on her shoulders and massaged in circles.

Her eyes rolled with pleasure, and her posture softened. A groan slipped out.

His lips touched her ear, breath hot on her neck. "The act of accessing the mana within your internal Well is something so intrinsic, it's like moving your legs. You've been trying to run before you can walk. Relax and let nature take over."

"I can access the mana that makes me psychic, but not

the other elements they tested me for. Easier said than done."

"I've done it."

"Shut up," she mumbled.

She felt his husky laugh down her spine. Every nerve in her body sang in his presence. She tried to think un-sexy thoughts, because if she didn't, fantasies about his clever fingers invaded her mind. Before her eyes rolled completely out of her head, she forced her lids to stay open and focused on the flickering candle flame.

"Air is breath." He blew gently on her ear.

She laughed. "You're so corny."

"Corny." He tested the word. "That's a new one." He massaged more, dug low on her back, knuckled down her spine, and just when she was about to fall back into him, he added, "Take a deep breath, hold it, feel it work in your lungs, and then let it go."

She shut her eyes, let the last of the tension out of her body and focused deeply.

"Breathe in," he murmured. "Breathe out."

For long moments, that was all she did. He stopped massaging, but she kept breathing. Air came into her lungs cold, filled her up, gave her life, and then left her lips in a warm rush.

"Good," Rush intoned. "Now open your eyes and push all that awareness to the candle."

Slowly her lashes lifted and, with a smooth exhale, she urged it onward with a sliver of her energy. She urged the flame to feel the wind enter cold, and then to fill it up. The flame flickered, guttered, and then died.

Silence. Dead silence. And then Clarke stifled a squeal. She twisted and climbed on Rush to plant a kiss on his face. He laughed, a deep chesty laugh, and then forced her off him.

"Don't get cocky," he warned. "You still have to light it up."

She waved. "No problem."

Then turned back to the candle, set herself up the same way and pushed that part of her conscience back to the wick, and urged it to light.

Nothing.

She cleared her throat and did it again.

Still nothing. Nothing but the echo of her stupid words coming back to haunt her. A frustrated growl tore out. She wanted to scream. Every day of her damned infernal training came back to tease her. For hours at a time Colt had forced her to do the same thing. No amount of meditating or lessons could give her the understanding. Her brain just couldn't click.

"I'm too human."

"Shh," Rush whispered. "You'll get it."

She mashed her lips together and took a deep breath. "It's not working. I'm doing the same thing as I did with the air."

"But is fire the same as air?" His hands moved down to

her hips and tugged her backward until she was flush against his chest. Warmth soaked into her back.

Clarke eyed the dead candle. "I guess not."

"So think about fire."

"Great. Sure. Said no one ever."

"Think about heat." His voice lowered with intention. The pad of his rough fingers traced along the join where her blouse met her waistband. He repeated the motion, teasing her.

Okay. She squirmed. This was different. He stroked over her clothes, sparking sensation. Her nipples contracted. A flood of heat gathered between her legs. She sucked in a breath.

"Wrong element," he chided, and tugged her blouse from the confines of her pants. "Heat. Think heat."

"Rush..." She darted a glance to the end of the aisle and heard someone sniffle, then a murmur.

"No one can see us now." He found skin. Lazy fingers circled her stomach, massaging gently until he sighed pleasantly and flattened his palm, tugging her closer. Tingles zipped everywhere, and a deep husky moan wrenched from her throat. He murmured, "Still wrong element."

How could she not focus on her quickening breath when his splayed hand flexed under her breasts, thumb touching the under-pillow, little finger dipping into her pants. Hot lips landed on her neck, on the mark he always gravitated toward. She glanced again down the aisle.

He clicked his tongue. "Don't think about being caught. Think about..."

The hand at her stomach lifted to band around her chest. His thumb grazed a bare nipple. She arched into him. Whimpered. His other hand ventured where his little finger had been, but kept going, over the fabric of her pants to rub along the seam. Her blood ignited and she ground into him with an almighty moan of submission.

He bit down on her shoulder when he found her damp through her clothes. She became a coalescence of sensation. The fingers down there. The ones up higher. The hardness at her back, pushing into her. The circles, the rubs, the *heat*. He owned her. Consumed her. Her heart thudded in her ears with each urgent stroke he made. Knowing she was safe against his chest, she threw her head back and pulled his hair in a desperate grip, sinking into the sensation of his tongue at her earlobe and his fingers on her body.

She didn't know what this would prove. But she hoped he wouldn't stop.

"Tell me how it feels," he snarled, breath ragged against her ear.

"It feels—"

His hand dipped into her pants. Fingers down the middle. On the point she'd silently begged for.

She gasped. Sparks crackled. *More*.

"Clarke." He swore. Swallowed. "Tell me."

She could only whimper and thrust into him.

His finger slid down her center and plunged into her core. He cursed at her readiness. Paused. Tensed. Another swallow behind her, as though he schooled himself to restrain his own desire. Impatiently, she worked herself on his hand. He muttered under his breath, but then resumed his game of exploration. In. Out. Around. Press down. Dip in. Slide. It was too much. She cried out and arched into him. He plumped her breast, rolling her nipple, reading her mind.

"Clarke," he growled low. "Tell me how it feels."

"Great. Amazing. Fucking... insan... hha... God, yes. Rush. Yes. There."

He increased the pace of his fingers between her legs. "Tight. So tight."

Her eyes fluttered. She lifted her hips to meet his hand. "Tight."

"Wet."

"Hot."

So hot. She was burning up. It was as though every stroke he made, every squeeze or twirl, was another drop of fuel to the flame. It all coiled tight, flamed brighter, burned darker until she simply combusted. A harsh cry of release tore from her lips. He brought her mouth to his in a punishing kiss. His long, guttural groan of satisfaction fed into her.

"Was it hot?" he asked, voice guttural, fingers still lazily circling, drawing out her pleasure.

"Mm-hm." So hot.

"Send it to the candle." He pressed his thumb on her sensitized bud, sending aftershocks rippling through her. "*Feel* the heat."

Her slumberous gaze locked onto the candle.

"Or do I need to start the demonstration again." His voice held a wicked, cruel lilt, and it was everything.

"I'm tempted."

He smiled against her skin at her neck. "It's now or never. Don't think about it. Don't analyze. Just do it."

She pushed the heat still simmering in her body toward the candle. Energy hummed and burned through the resistance of her skin. Power ripped out of her.

It wasn't the candle that set alight. It was the books. The wood. The carpet. Little flickering flames danced and skipped over every surface, rapidly spreading outward.

"Shit!" she shouted and shot forward, trying to smother the sparks with her hands and body.

"Clarke," he barked, and lifted her from the floor as though she weighed nothing.

He tugged her back to him and patted her smoldering front, smothering the flames. "Never do that to me again. You gave me a heart attack. Fire is... unpredictable."

A balding Mage in a blue robe came barreling into the aisle. His hand shot out, fingers splayed, and water doused them all. Covered from head to toe in a dripping waterfall that had conjured from nowhere, Clark gaped.

Not seeing Rush, the Mage had missed him entirely with the burst of water.

Rush roared with laughter.

"You practice your elemental fire elsewhere!" the Mage said. "What's gotten into you—and how did that candle get in here?" He grabbed his head and tugged what was left of his hair.

Clarke couldn't suppress the laugh. Guess she knew why he was going bald.

Rush took her hand, and the curse must have enveloped them, because the Mage began twirling in confusion, wondering what had just happened.

They ran all the way back across campus to the Guardian quarters. And when they got to their room, Rush made love to her in a way he'd never done before. At first, she thought it was the bright shine of hope burning through his passion, but as she drifted off to sleep and he crawled out of bed to sit on the settee, she knew in her gut that it was not hope.

*Forget about the curse.*

The memory of his words brought tears to her eyes.

He was different that night because this was good bye.

CHAPTER
# THIRTY-FOUR

**W**ithout Rush by her side, Clarke's sleep was fitful and full of nightmares. Dreams within dreams. Meanings turned inside and out.

She saw people frozen in the ice. She saw them thaw. She saw the darkness shroud them and the horror as they rejoined the living. And she saw them die. Every time it was a new person, a new life, a new death. From a stab in the back, to a slice across the throat, to a sword in the heat of battle. Fae. Human. Something in between. It was all order and then chaos until she landed in front of a shadowy figure she knew well. The Void.

Never had she seen his face. Never his skin nor eyes nor mouth, but always she knew it was him. There was a distinct feel to his soul. Because that's what she saw... the dark void of his soul. That's why he was a faceless black shadow. A black hole that devoured all life. He didn't care about the natural order.

And he was coming for them. For her.

Panicked, she wished herself away.

The dream suddenly shifted, and she was at the academy, watching Preceptor Barrow instruct his class as they poured some concoction of liquid into a bowl. With tweezers and goggles, they lowered a glowing ball of mana into the water, and then they added a dull stone. Ripples formed in the water.

Preceptress Dawn's voice floated into her head. *"Don't look for the stone dropping in the water, look for the ripples it creates."*

So Clarke shifted gears.

She took a step back from the nightmares and watched from the outskirts. To find the ripples affecting her life, she had to look to those she knew.

CLARKE DREAMED SHE WAS A BIRD.

Under a moonlit sky, she soared through the clouds above the rooftops of an unknown city. Coasting and taking her time, she circled above a particular house and landed on a branch near an open window. She hooted. Once. Twice.

A tall stately figure arrived at the open window. He was tall, golden haired and gorgeous. Square jaw, sensuous lips, and honey-colored eyes that echoed a cold entity inside. Clarke saw the opposite of a void. She saw the chaos of life as it sparked with electricity. Tightness contracted her lungs as he stared at her. His attention suffocated her. Then his lips stretched into a wicked smile, and he stepped back, allowing her entry.

Flapping her wings, she landed gracefully on the red-stained glass floor. The cool surface sent a shock as her talons changed to feet. The hands held before her face were brown-skinned, and so were her feet... and her naked body full of curves. She walked to the golden fae and stroked his unimpressed face. He took her breast in hand and squeezed.

"Prime," he said, voice smooth like silk.

"King," she replied, and took hold of his crotch through his pants.

He squeezed her flesh tighter. She wrenched her grip. Neither made a twitch of expression on their stony faces. Then he lowered his lips and slanted them over hers, letting her feel his wolven fangs on her lips.

She pushed him back and squeezed his jaw. "I want the bastard back."

Fire flashed in his darkening gaze. He cupped her between the legs. "Regret is not a pretty color on you, owl."

"It is not regret. It is a change of plans, wolf."

"We made a bargain. I keep the breeding law in place. You give me the bastard."

"We never said for how long."

He clicked his tongue with derision. "You made me wait *four* decades before you handed him over, and now you want him back after a measly one?" He scoffed. "You still owe me another three."

The king's jaw hardened and he shifted his hand intimately. He tried to kiss her again. Her talons grew until they pierced the brocade fabric of his pants. He sucked in a breath and studied her face, finally whispering, "You dare threaten me?"

"You are the one with your fingers where they don't belong."

He growled and let go. She held on for a second longer, then let go too.

"Where is he?" the Prime asked. "Where have you put Jasper?"

"I'll have no bastard of mine impede my plans."

"And I'll have no green king impede..."

The Prime's voice suddenly filtered away, and the sounds of a crowd became a deafening roar. She saw nothing but darkness. She was blind. Clarke couldn't understand where she was. It felt like the rhythmic beat of a stadium. Roars. Cheers. Shouts. Boos. Stomping on the stadium seating floor. It was the symphony of her broken life. In the never-ending darkness, the symphony was all that kept her company. That and pain.

*"Ripples... look for the ripples," Preceptress Dawn said.*

Clarke looked down again and her hands were no longer the talons of a bird, but human. At first she thought it was herself, but then she was being pushed into a cage. A tiny, cramped, ugly smelling and feeling cage she didn't recognize. She struggled against the bars, trying not to let them push her in, but the force at her back was too strong. It was like death in there, but it was worse outside. Choking on her panic, she tried to scream. She thrashed about.

The dream shifted again.

Clarke wasn't in the cage, but out of it. Two cages this time, one on either side of a familiar portcullis in Crescent Hollow. She looked further down the wall. Three cages. Four. Five. But who occupied the cages? The pixie? Her lover? No... it was... a tail swished in irritation from behind the body of a female and Clarke stepped closer... or her spectral body, or whatever she was.

"Water," Anise rasped.

The guard rapped on the wooden bars with his bow. "Not your time yet, she-wolf."

"It's been so long."

"That's what you get for harboring a human."

Clarke screamed awake.

"Anise!" she shouted into the darkness.

# THIRTY-FIVE

The room was gloomy when Clarke opened her eyes. She looked to the settee for Rush but found it empty. Unease dropped in her stomach like a stone. She'd always assumed he moved there after she fell asleep, but never considered he'd left the room altogether.

Throwing the covers off, she swung her legs over the side and fumbled with her feet until she found her slippers.

An inexplicable feeling of impending doom pulled her skin tight and quickened her pulse. *Where was he?* Scanning the room, it was clear he wasn't there.

She had to find him. Had to find *someone*. So many weird things she'd dreamed, but the one thing that wasn't murky or hard to decipher was Anise being in trouble. She'd been locked in one of those dastardly cages... all because she'd helped Clarke.

*"It's been so long..."*

Anise's voice was a puncture to Clarke's heart.

*"That's what you get for harboring a human."*

She'd probably been held captive for weeks.

Thaddeus must have needed to cast blame after he'd come bursting into the inn, narrowly missing Clarke and Rush as they went through the portal. She recalled him asking for more in the next shipment from the human, meaning Clarke had undercut some profit he'd hoped to make. She'd evaded him again. She—a despicable human. He would have assumed Anise knew, or even if she didn't, he wouldn't have cared. As long as someone remained locked and suspended in a cage, suffering for his humiliation, then the joke wasn't on him.

*Bastard.*

She blinked.

That was another word she recalled from her dream. The Prime had asked for the bastard. Jasper. At first, she'd thought the Prime didn't like Jasper, but it was more than that. Jasper was the king's illegitimate son.

God, there was so much of the dream to decipher.

Using her gift, Clarke sent heat to the oil lamps. Or she tried.

"Come on, damn you. Light." She forced the power welling in her body to spread out and touch the candle, but it wouldn't light. "No dice," she mumbled.

Damn it.

*"Feel the heat. Don't analyze. Just do it."* Rush's voice came to her like a dream.

She conjured the feelings he'd evoked and flames sprung to life in the sconces. She had but a moment to feel proud of herself before she busied herself with getting dressed, intuition taking her straight to the outdoor and weatherproof clothes. Leather pants, blouse, thick sweater, boots and a fur-lined cape. Rush's old strip of fabric went over her ears. He'd told her she might be able to disguise them with a glamor, but she hadn't gotten that far in her training. For now, she was going on a journey.

First, she needed help.

Clarke went to leave her room, but then noticed something on the table near the hearth. Two carved wooden figurines and her sundial, now with a leather cord attached. She put the sundial around her neck, and then picked up the wolf pup, turning it in her hands. She picked up the human female who had long hair, round ears and little dots over her nose. Freckles. It was unmistakably Clarke. So if that was her, then who was the wolf puppy? She picked it up again and stared hard, wishing she could get some kind of psychic imprint. But as usual, anything to do with Rush or her was empty.

But these carvings looked familiar. She went to the closet and rummaged in his rucksack until she found the wolf from the cabin. She placed it with the other two figurines. Her, Thorne, and a smaller pup. Her breath hitched and her hand went to her stomach.

When was the last time she'd had her period?

"Shit," she mumbled, and sat down. But the elixir

371

should have stopped any chance of her getting pregnant. How long had she been awake in this world for? A month? How long prior to waking had it been since... "Double shit."

All the symptoms had been there. She'd been hungrier than normal. Tired. Occasionally nauseous. She looked at the little carving. Rush knew, and he said nothing. He knew and—wait. Why wasn't Rush a part of the carved figurine family?

She swallowed.

And then she was up, ransacking the room, looking for evidence that he was still around, but everywhere she turned, she only found more signs that he was gone. The coin in his rucksack, gone. A brand new Guardian jacket from the closet, gone. His sword, gone.

Why don the Guardian jacket now, when he'd purposefully avoided it before?

A well of emotion sprung in her body, mixing and swirling with horror. The way he'd kissed her last night, the way he'd made love... she *knew* it had felt different. She thought it was because he'd given up, but it was more than that. Tears burned her eyes. He'd left her alone. Alone in this new world.

Why?

He loved her. He may not have said it, but she felt it in her heart. A little voice whispered in her ear, *"If you loved someone, you wouldn't leave them."*

Years of self-doubt pressed on her chest. A mother was

supposed to love her child, yet Clarke's had walked out of her life. All this time Clarke reasoned that her mother didn't love her, that she'd been disgusted with Clarke's abilities, or even afraid of them. Rush had accepted that part of her without question. She'd thought, yes, this is love. Unconditional. But maybe she'd had it all wrong. Maybe this was as good as it got, and she'd been too stubborn to accept it.

Forcing the tears away, she lifted the hem of her sweater and created a sling for the carvings to collect in.

The sun hadn't come up yet. Clenching her jaw, she left her quarters and gravitated toward a particular suite. She crossed the landing of the central grand staircase. Going up to the third door down the corridor, she raised her fist and knocked loudly. Within seconds, it opened.

A very naked Thorne glowered down at her from beneath a mess of white hair. *Did no one have decency here?* She could put up with the top half nudity, but the rest of it was just plain inconvenient. The past month had been a combination of her sorry hand-signs, and possessive growls and snaps from Rush every time she bumped into one of the half-nude buff residents, or worse, full-nude buff residents.

"What," Thorne grumbled.

"Rush is gone."

He lifted a brow, then tried to slam the door on her face. She stuck her boot in the gap. He made a frustrated sound and reopened it with a snap of his teeth.

*It's okay*, she thought. *He's not going to hurt me.* She forced the urge to run like prey. Sometimes she thought Thorne was closer to wolf than human. Sometimes he probably did too. His lip curled.

"Crescent Hollow has also been..." She couldn't even come up with a word for it. She looked at the ground as the vision of Anise almost dead in the cage swung into her mind. It wasn't only Anise, there were others feeling the wrath of Lord Thaddeus Nightstalk. Air rushed in and out of her lungs, gathering power along with her irritation. "I can't leave her like that. She was only nice to me."

"Crescent Hollow is none of my fucking business. Not anymore." He tried to close the door again, but she let the gathering storm of power go. She blasted the door open with a gush of air and threw a figurine at him. It glanced off his pec and toppled to the floor. He frowned down at it, then locked eyes with her, confused.

God, that felt good.

She threw another one, and then the last.

He snatched both out of the air with a superior look on his face. She couldn't stand it.

"You think you're so high and mighty with your sharp claws out all the time, but I got news for you. You're behaving the same way as Rush." She changed her tone to mocking. "Oh, we don't get involved in politics. We're all about protecting the Well. I'll give you a well. Well, fuck you all and your high horses. None of you are any better than the greedy assholes who lived in my time. Nothing has changed!"

His eyes glowed from the darkened recess of his room. His alpha fury licked across her skin and grew in power. He spoke through gritted teeth with a gravelly voice, no longer human. "You dare to come into my room, make demands, use offensive magic on me, and then you insult me. Damn straight I got sharp claws, and you're about to feel their wrath."

Claws sprung from the ends of his fingertips. Skin pulled tight over slabs of muscle and tendon. Every human instinct in Clarke was telling her to back the hell up, lay down and submit, but her newly honed instincts shouted for her to stay. Thorne was her only chance. He was the outlying ripple.

"Go on. Do your best," she taunted, and just when he stepped her way, she added, "I never pegged you for one to harm a pregnant woman."

He froze, face deadpanning. The claws retracted. "What?"

"Somehow Rush knew. And now he's left. So, in a way, you were right. Are you happy? He's gone."

Unable to accept the pity in Thorne's eyes, Clarke stared at the ground and waited while he put some pants on. She rubbed her forehead and forced herself to calm. It would do no one good right now if she caved to the panic growing in her body. It hurt to think of why Rush might have left. And then there were the other things.

"I had a premonition last night," she murmured. "Pre-monition, or vision... it was... I saw many wolves in cages. Some in fae form, some in wolf... I looked closer and recognized a female with a tail. Her name is Anise, and she worked in the bar at the Laughing Den. She's Caraway's friend. She was kind to me, and now Thaddeus is making her suffer for it." She paused, noticed Thorne had turned silent and watchful.

"Did Rush see the Prime before she left?"

She whirled to see Leaf standing in Thorne's doorway, hands dipped into the pockets of silk pajama pants. He lowered his brows, eyes laced with suspicion.

"Did he?" Leaf asked again.

"I don't know." She thought back. "He was different after that first night—the one she left."

"What do you think?" Leaf shared a look with Thorne. "Is he capable of hurting her?"

Thorne shrugged. "Whose sword other than his would leave such marks in her desk?"

"And on her windowsill."

"What's going on?" Clarke asked.

Thorne and Leaf shared a look over Clarke's shoulder. Damn it, these Guardians would never get involved in non-Order business. Not unless she forced them.

Her jaw lifted. "I know what happened to your missing Guardian."

She dropped the bomb and then pushed passed Leaf. Goddammit she was hungry all the time.

Thorne's footsteps came thudding after her. "Who?"

She hurried down the staircase. "You know very well who I'm talking about... but if you need me to prove I know too, then fine. His name is Jasper. He's the king's bastard."

Just as her feet hit the foyer floor, Thorne was there. He took hold of her wrist, stopping her before she entered the kitchen. "Rush told you that. It's nothing new. Don't lie to us, human. Don't play us."

Long, elegant fingers wrapped around Thorne's wrist. The air became thick, so stifling that it was hard to breathe, and then Thorne started gasping for air. From the concentration on Leaf's face, she knew he was behind the solidifying of air. Thorne's eyes watered, and he glared at Clarke as though he wanted to skewer her.

"Let the lady go," Leaf said through gritted teeth. "You of all people should understand her position."

Thorne's wild eyes darted to Clarke, down to her stomach, and then back to Leaf, who stood calmly through it all. Clarke's opinion of him went up a notch. She'd thought because of his sun-kissed looks and calm demeanor, he'd be a laid back pussy cat. But what she saw in the depths of that crystalline blue gaze was not calm. It was the tempest of an ocean. The waves that sucked you under. It was the reason he was the team leader, and no one else.

Thorne choked on the thickened air. His face went red. He shot Clarke one last look and then let go. He even hand-signed an apology. Oxygen came whooshing back, and he could breathe again.

She stalked to the kitchen and found it empty. The brownies hadn't been yet with new food, so she had to find some. She started by opening and closing every cupboard she could find, not caring if the loud bang of shutting doors woke the house.

The tension in the room shifted as others entered the room. Taking up residence beside the butcher block, Leaf flicked wrinkles from his pants. Thorne came in behind him.

"Now. Let's try this like civilized beings." Leaf gestured at Clarke. "What is it you know about Jasper?"

Her gaze darted between Thorne and him. He was right. She didn't know enough for them to go on, but they didn't know that. Every great con was steeped in truth.

"I know the Prime and the king had something to do with it," she said. "They conspired. That's all I'll tell you until you help me find Rush and rescue Anise."

With her hands locked on two different doorknobs, she bowed her head and took a deep breath. There. She'd said it. She wanted to find Rush. Even if the bastard had left her. She had to know why. She'd always thought that if it came to it, his curse would be the thing that took him away. Not his own... she swallowed the shameful words. Rush was *not* a coward. Not the Rush she knew. There must be something else going on.

Part of being a new person was not waiting for things to happen to her, she had to build the life she wanted. And she wanted Rush. There had to be a way. They might not have exchanged vows, but being mated was as good as being married in this time. They might not have said they loved each other, but Clarke knew she loved him. *This* was love. This aching longing squeezing every cell in her body. This *need* to chase him down until the ends of the earth just so she could wrap her arms around him one last time. Love was never giving up. Never quitting. Staying until the end.

Clarke opened another cupboard. Slammed it shut.

"What are you looking for?" Thorne asked.

"Food! I'm starving."

He came over, bent low and opened a base cupboard. Inside was a plate of bread, some sort of jam spread and the sweetest smell known to mankind. Coffee. Or something like it. While Thorne took out the bread and began slicing, Clarke opened the canister and sniffed. It was enough to make her relax and to feel like home. She didn't even need to drink it. But her father had. Those tears she'd held back leaked from her eyes. She missed him so much.

Thorne's eyes widened. "Don't cry."

"Shut up." She pointed the coffee canister at him. "It's hormones."

He held his palms up in defeat, but then cocked his head, listening to something near the door.

Was someone there?

Clarke narrowed her gaze through the other entrance of the kitchen where the dark hallway led to an entertaining area. A shadow moved. She almost choked when she noticed two others watching. The vampires. They blended so easily into the darkness that she'd not seen them. The moment she did, they knew, and came out of hiding.

The model, and the muscle, still dressed in their Guardian uniform.

Leather creaked as Shade folded his arms. He narrowed eyes in accusation at Leaf. "I *told* you."

Thorne pointed at Leaf in agreement. "Jasper's not on hiatus, or some secret mission. The king has him. Are we going to just let that slide?"

"We're Guardians," Leaf reminded them. "We don't get involved. Jasper knows this as much as anyone. The war we're fighting is very different to keeping everyday peace. If we don't draw the line, then our resources are expended."

"No," Clarke snapped. "Don't you dare hide behind your excuses. Staying isolated keeps your hearts hard. There's nothing wrong with getting involved to protect the ones you love. In fact, it separates us from the cold-hearted 'Untouched' humans you think are your enemy. Don't you see that?"

None of them argued with it. They knew it was true. They all used their position as Guardian to keep relationships at arm's length. But it was worth the pain. Being with someone you loved, even if it was fleeting, was the beautiful part of humanity she was fighting for.

"And what if the Prime is gone for good, too? What if staying out of politics got her killed?" Shade grumbled.

Clarke's hand went to her throat as she read between the lines. "You think Rush killed her."

"If it walks like the guilty and talks like a coward—"

Leaf silenced Thorne with his glare. "We don't know what happened. We don't know if she is dead. We don't know if the king has Jasper. We don't even know why Rush left. Let's be calm."

Hearing Leaf say it out loud made Clarke feel ashamed, for she was the first one who had lost faith in Rush. Her self-preservation reflex had been to revert to the defensive girl who'd run away from a man who'd used her. She owed it to Rush to give him the benefit of the doubt. She only wished he trusted her enough to tell her what was going on.

"There's something else you should know." Clarke swallowed. This would change all of their opinions. "The other half of the bargain your Prime made with the king was for him to keep the breeding law in place for another few years."

"What do you mean?" Thorne asked.

"I mean, the king was going to abolish it because Elphyne is flourishing. She made him keep it in place in return for handing him Jasper. Now why do you think she'd do that?"

Thorne stared at her long and hard while the pieces

clicked together. Then he shoved the plate of bread and jam to the floor. Leaf raised a brow at him. Shade rolled his eyes. And Haze... the big vampire was the only one whose gaze landed on Thorne with concern because if what Clarke had seen in the vision was true, then the Prime had orchestrated the death of Thorne's mother. Why else would she have wanted that law to stay in effect? Because she wanted to control Rush. Because she wanted him to bring the chosen one to her.

Clarke just couldn't figure out why the Prime had to take this exact path.

"My point is," Clarke added quickly, "that your Prime can't be trusted. I think Rush figured it out, and that's why she hasn't been back. She's hiding... or scheming."

"Or she's dead," Shade said.

"We'd know if she was dead," Leaf defended. "And she has a realm to protect. It's not easy being the Prime."

"But at what expense?" Haze added. "She's made us all stay out of the affairs of the kingdom, but she's in the thick of it."

"It's *because* she's in the thick of it," Clarke pointed out. Silence compounded until all she could hear was the beating of her heart.

"Very well," Leaf said to Thorne through a clenched jaw. "You will go with Clarke and help these people at Crescent Hollow." He then met Clarke's eyes. "When you get back, you will help us find Jasper in return."

"Agreed."

"Or we can just make her tell us." Cloud walked in,

cracking his knuckles. "Then we don't have to do anything but find Jasper."

"No," Thorne said with a sigh. "Clarke is right. Those are my people. I won't abandon them if they're in need. Jasper taught me better. I'm going."

"I don't answer to you," Cloud said.

"But you do to me." Leaf straightened.

"You lead the team, you don't make the rules."

"You don't have to join Clarke, but you won't force her to give up the information about Jasper until she's ready."

Cloud gave Leaf a derogatory stare and then left. When he was gone, Leaf turned to the rest of them. "Anyone going to Crescent Hollow, be ready and armed within the hour."

CHAPTER
# THIRTY-SIX

L ife had never gone Rush's way.

From the moment he'd come out feet first, his unnatural wants had always ended in tragedy or suffering. But the alpha, Lord of Crescent Hollow, was never who he was supposed to be. If only it wasn't those closest to him who paid for his desires.

His father.

His lover.

His son.

His sister, mother.

And now... Rush's throat closed.

Damn that Prime and her always prepared answers. He'd gone to her all those nights ago, ready to annihilate, so sure that he was the one who'd known it all. But he wasn't.

*"Did you ever consider that it wasn't fate doing these things*

384

to you? But yourself?" The Prime's smug voice was like honey clogging his throat.

Rush bared his teeth and planted Starcleaver's point in the female's desk. "You're the one who's doing these things, Prime. You. Not the divine Well. You've manipulated everything since... how long?"

She stared out the open window to the stars twinkling in the clear night sky. "Since before you were born."

"And after?"

"After too... but there is one thing I've never had a hand in —who the Well chooses." She glanced at Rush. "That has nothing to do with me. Not now, not ever. I just make the most of what I receive."

"Why?"

A laugh coughed out of her. "Why? You know why. So the Well doesn't dry up. So we have a bountiful land with plenty to grow. You may not remember the famine that plunged this planet into chaos, but I do. I was around when the last of our ancestors who'd fought tooth and nail to establish a stronghold on this land were still alive. And now because of the legacy they leave, it flourishes with beauty."

She was talking about the old ones. The ones who'd lived among Jackson Crimson's time, two thousand years ago. Was the Prime truly that old?

"You talk about legacy, but you have ripped mine from me."

She clicked her tongue, admonishing him. "That you have no legacy has nothing to do with me. All I did was put you in the right place at the right time. The rest was you."

*The anger Rush had fostered over the time of his curse flourished anew. It seethed like a rolling ocean. How could she think she had nothing to do with his plight?*

"Innocents have died because of your meddling," he ground out. "What about those?"

"No one is truly innocent. You know that."

*Rush stared at his sword. He stared at her.*

"I needed someone to bring her to us," the Prime conceded.

"Clarke?"

"Yes. We looked into many potential outcomes, and you were the only one who kept her from sinking to the inky depths of the Well. Has she told you what life she led in the old world? I'm not even sure if she told her friends at that time."

"If you're referring to her hand in the destruction of her world, then yes, I know. And I don't care."

"I'm not talking about that. I'm talking about the fact she used her gifts to steal from people. Cheat. Lie. Swindle. That was her motto."

*He shrugged. Who was he to judge?* "Perhaps. But the woman I know has honor."

*She'd saved his life when she could have walked away.*

"She has honor now," the Prime said. "Do you see?"

*Rush turned away and clenched his jaw. She was saying Clarke would be a bad person if it wasn't for him. But he wasn't pure himself.*

*The Prime continued,* "Because of your curse, you were the only one the Void could not See. And the only way to have you there, ready for her awakening, was to—"

*"I get it," he snapped. Nothing she said mattered anyway. Even if it was the truth, it was her truth. She'd played with his family, his life, as though they were all expendable pieces of a game. His fingers wrapped around the Starcleaver's hilt. Felt the familiar heavy weight in his hands.*

*She licked her lips. "I may have made it so you were cursed, but I had faith you would return. I made sure your quarters remained untouched. As far as I was concerned, you were always part of the Twelve."*

*He'd had enough of her excuses.*

*"Trust me, Rush."*

*"I'm done with trust."*

*"Don't," she warned, eyes on the sword. "You'll get sick. It will push you over the edge."*

*His upper lip curled as he tugged the sword from the desk. The heavy metal lowered to scratch the floor. He sauntered, etching a line in the ground as he made his way to her by the window.*

*"You forgot one thing when you cursed me," he said, looking at her from beneath his lashes. "A loophole, if you will." He lifted Starcleaver and inspected the special glyphs etched into the blade. They were useless. Metal was magic free. It repelled magic. It was why the Guardians used metal swords to fight magical monsters. It rendered the magic of monsters impotent. "You left me Starcleaver. That was your mistake. It blocks magic. It blocks the curse from affecting me when I use it as an extension of my arm. As long as no other part of my body touches another, the sickness won't affect me. Who do you think*

has been culling wayward humans in our territory all these years? Or the errant monsters cavorting in Seelie territory? I know you know about them."

A small confident curve of her lips. "It wasn't a mistake. I left you Starcleaver on purpose."

He shook his head. "I don't think so. I think it was an oversight. I can scent the lie on you."

"Ah, Rush. Have you been so isolated from your kind that you've forgotten the fae cannot lie?"

"You know what I mean. You deal in half truths and misdirection."

Her big brown eyes widened a fraction, and then she pursed her lips. "History is repeating. Do you understand?"

Another step closer.

"Rush—" she put her hand up. "Killing me isn't the answer."

"Then what is?" He drew his arm back, braced, and readied to parry.

"She is. And the child growing in her womb."

Time stopped.

There was no sense, no rhyme or reason. A child? Growing in Clarke?

Rush's surprise was the break she needed. She burst into a ball of white light. Energy slammed into him. Wind ruffled his hair. He turned blindly, arcing his blade in an almighty swing. It cleaved through something, caught on the windowsill and embedded. When he could see again, a white feather beneath his blade was all that remained.

*"If you want to save Clarke," she said, now suddenly behind him. "If you want to save your unborn child from suffering the same consequences as the first, then you have a choice to make."*

*He whirled to face her again. Drew back his sword. "You took my choice from me."*

*"This time, I'm giving it to you. A mouth for a mouth. Whose mouth will be the sacrifice for the new one coming into the world? Yours? Clarke's?"*

There had been no question.

Rush checked his surroundings to make sure he'd landed through the portal in the correct place. The stench in the air was the first clue that he had.

Cornucopia was a sometimes shanty trading town, sometimes luxe getaway, for those who wanted debauchery, anonymity, and indulgence. Half the city was a mess of clay and stone houses. The other half, glass and precious gems glittering in the sun. The problem was, it all mixed together. Walk down any street and you'd get a shanty next to a mansion. The rough next to the sweet. The rich next to the poor.

It was why people loved it there.

He chewed on some sweet grass and stared at the city with the morning sun peeking over the horizon of jigsaw building tops. Already the bustling sounds filtered down to him. Cornucopia never slept.

*The fact you have no legacy has nothing to do with me.*

Fuck the Prime.

*If you want to save your unborn child, then you will do exactly as I say.*

Ditching the spent portal stone into the bush beside a dirt track, Rush adjusted Starcleaver on his back and set out toward Cornucopia.

Clarke would forgive him for this. She had to. It was for the good of Thorne and the good of the unborn. The Prime may be a manipulative pain in his ass, but he believed her. She'd said the only way to save Clarke and the child was to end Thaddeus. And then put another Nightstalk in his place as leader of Crescent Hollow. His sister. He didn't have to like that the Prime used him again, but he would not leave this world without a legacy. It was exactly what that scheming owl had counted on.

A mishmash of Seelie and Unseelie poured in and out of the front gate. It wasn't really a gate, per-say, but an opening in the wall twenty feet wide. There were no guards and no soldiers manning the entrance. Enter at your own peril, the sign said. The line bottle necked, and he slowed behind a group of shifters, careful not to bump into them. He could smell the fire-taint on them but could distinguish no breed. They weren't wolf, that was all he knew.

Beggars held out their hands for food or coin, but as he walked past, their eyes glazed over and they shifted their outstretched arms to the fae behind him. A buzzing overhead alerted him to a harem of pixies flying. Four males and their queen heading the formation with pride from the front.

*Damned pixies and their wings, always skipping the line.*

Now he was just plain grumpy. He ground his teeth. He hated being here on the Prime's insistence. Especially since he'd regretted being her puppet for so long. It was like she'd beat him to this conclusion. He'd never know if he would have come here on his own. But he knew it was the right choice.

Just as he got to the delta, his impatience wore thin. A commotion had stopped the progress of entry. He spat out the masticated mess of sweet grass and withdrew his sword. He used the length to prod and poke fae folk out of the way so he could get to the front with minimal contact. For the rest of them, his curse worked to move people and leave them forgetful in his wake. He got near the front and stopped to see a young female fae with her wrist caught by a meaty looking orc covered in dirt. The satchel bag that had been over the orc's shoulder had spilled to the floor. The smell of sour mud, sweat and shit made Rush want to gag, but the scent hadn't come from the bag. Inside was exotic red fruit the orc had probably come to sell.

The girl had red stained fingertips and lips. She'd also pissed her pants because the moment they had caught her, she'd signed her warrant to be sent to the Ring. Unless she paid for the fruit, that was, but from the looks of the scrawny thing, she had no coin.

"Not magic, not my problem," was the first thought to enter Rush's mind. Guardians were there to deal in magical disputes, magical monsters, and the preservation of the well.

But that was the Prime's legacy. Not his.

He tightened his grip on Starcleaver and sized up the orc. How to deal with this?

The orc just wanted to make a living.

The girl just wanted to eat.

Was one more right than the other? Should either die?

He grunted. Fuck this meddling shit. He sheathed the sword and dug into his pocket to find some coin. He tossed it between them. The instant the coin left his hands, it became visible and glinted in the sun. Every fae in the vicinity caught sight of the red flashing glass and pandemonium broke loose. Bodies dived for the money. Big. Small. Winged. Furred. Fists went flying. Jaws got punched. Weapons were drawn.

And that's when a gap opened, big enough for him to slide through untouched. He entered the bustling metropolis unaffected. On a whim, he glanced over his shoulder and caught sight of the red-stained-lip girl escaping under the legs of greedy fae.

With a smile, he turned toward the Ring. It was the last known location of his sister, and hopefully where he would find her working today. What the Prime counted on was that Rush had kept some kind of relationship with his sister. And she was right. There had been little Rush's curse let him do. He'd tried to write letters, but every time he put pen to paper, the curse knew his intentions. He couldn't finish the words. But he'd found loopholes. He had managed to drop coin for Kyra every time he visited. He had managed to use Starcleaver to prod the odd overzealous patron at the Ring, stopping them from causing Kyra mischief as she provided security. And then he'd managed to stay out of her life when it became clear she'd sensed his presence and not being able to communicate had caused her grief.

A clean break always healed the quickest.

And now he was back.

In the past weeks, the Prime had written letters explaining the new situation. If Kyra had received them, and believed the content, then she would have finished up work and now be waiting for him. A small part of him hoped she believed the letters. The rest was convinced she would take one look, laugh hysterically, and then incinerate them.

And stay safe.

Kyra's life had been ruined too.

Rush arrived outside the giant colosseum and searched along the outskirts. If this were night, the inside would roar with bloodlust. This morning it was eerily quiet and emptied. The last battle it served had finished hours ago. He could scent the water being hosed to wash away the blood and eviscerated body parts left on the Ring's floor.

As Kyra worked the security at the doors, she most likely had worked all night. While the battle inside the Ring was to settle scores, occasionally the bloodlust spilled into the crowd. Especially if the two fae settling the score were representatives of a larger group.

He walked around the perimeter until a familiar scent hit his nose. Kin. He crested a corner to see his sister standing tall, tough, and proud against the buttress of an alcove. Long silver hair caught in a segmented ponytail dangled over a shoulder, almost hitting her ass. Folded arms. Set jaw. And a scrunched up letter in her hand.

She'd aged.

He wondered if she'd say the same for him. Humans believed the fae to be immortal. But they only aged in different, more subtle ways. The light in her eyes, the hard set to her shoulders, the way she favored one leg. It was all a sign of her times not within his orbit. He'd missed so much.

But she was there. Waiting.

Holding his breath, he stepped up to her and dropped his sword on the ground at her feet. The Prime had told him that all he needed to do to let her know he was there was to activate the portal stone, but he wanted to do more. He needed to show he was putting his faith in her, that he was there for her and that together they would take down their tyrannical uncle. The only way to do that was to lay down his prized weapon. A symbol of the organization that forbade him in the past from getting involved.

But this was his choice as much as the Prime's. It had been a long time coming.

Kyra blinked as Starcleaver came into being and then

her eyes hardened. She threw the letters on the ground. It took her a long time before she gathered the compunction to speak. "I don't hear from you for years, and then I get these? What am I supposed to do with this?"

He couldn't answer. Even if he did, she wouldn't hear.

She put her hands on her hips and paced a few feet of the colosseum wall. "I thought you were dead. You're a stranger to me. Your son—who is a Guardian—is more known to me. And now you want me to go back to the Hollow to fight an evil son-of-a-bitch for a title I don't want? That I never had?" She threw her hands up in the air. "I mean. You didn't want it either. Right? You're the one who told me to stay away."

She paused, crouched and squeezed the bridge of her nose. Taking deep breaths, she finally said, "I thought I'd put this all behind me." She steeled herself and stood up. "There is nothing left for me there. Why go back?"

Rush did the only thing he could think of. He picked up Starcleaver and fought the curse to scratch a word into the stone path. REVENGE.

# CHAPTER
# THIRTY-SEVEN

In the field outside the cadre houses, Leaf triggered a portal with his power, and sent the three winged Guardians through first. Then Thorne shifted into wolf as he went. Clarke was next.

Her stomach already churned at the thought of what would greet her on the other side. Bile hit the back of her throat and her hand flew to cover her mouth. She hadn't even traveled yet.

"You'll get used to it," Leaf said from beside her.

"When?"

He shoved her between the shoulder blades and pushed her through.

She landed in the field before Crescent Hollow and vomited. It took her a good few minutes before she could straighten, and when she did, there was no sign of life. No fee-lions flittering about. No soldiers manning the gate. Even the wind failed to blow.

Cages lined the walls as far as she could see. Each had a body inside. Each was dead silent. Including that of Anise, closest to the gate.

Fear gripped her heart and she started running. She got two feet before brawny hands slipped under her arms and lifted her clear off the ground. Kicking in a mad panic, she almost screamed as she lifted higher. Something had her.

"For a Seer, you're terrible at looking."

A shadow crossed her face as something blocked the sun, and the beat of wings gave her the final clue. Her gaze clashed with Shade's scowl. In angel form, his wings flapped from his back. He dipped and arced, turning them around in a deft maneuver, coasting to where Leaf closed the portal with some kind of hand signal and push of power. Rush had said the elves were better at using mana than any of them combined. She guessed that included creating natural portals without needing to imbue stones with a spell.

The moment her feet hit the ground, Clarke rounded on Shade. "Why did you stop me?"

"Are you mad? You never run into a hostile environment. Not without checking to see if it is safe."

She bit the inside of her cheek. He was right. Just because she could set books on fire and blast candle flames out, didn't mean she was a warrior. She had to calm down. Her strength lay in reading the future, and that was all about being calm enough to see the waves rocked by the boat. But... Anise. Still no movement in the cage.

"Are they dead?" she whispered.

Leaf's blue eyes narrowed with focus. "I don't think so, but Thorne's wolf ears will hear best." He looked at the big white wolf.

Thorne cocked his head, pricked his ears up and then dipped his head in what could be construed as a nod. Leaf turned to Cloud, Haze and Shade and pointed to the sky. He swirled his finger up.

All three took to the sky and spread out, flying in opposite directions. Two with the dark leathery wings of a bat, and the third with feathered wings as deep as the night sky. Soon, they disappeared against the backdrop of the azure and Clarke couldn't tell if it was because of their distance or if they'd used some kind of magical glamour to hide their appearance.

The sound of air ripped behind them. All three spun in time to see another portal burst into existence with blinding clarity.

Thorne's hackles raised. Leaf put his hand out, signaling for Thorne to stay. Clarke concentrated on her inner gift but felt no ill omens. Whoever was coming through wasn't the enemy.

A white-haired woman walked through holding a long curved bone scimitar in each hand. Tall, striking, and formidable, the female fae looked akin to a shield maiden stepping out of Viking lore. She was not someone Clarke wanted to get on the wrong side of. Her fur tipped ears flattened in a sign of aggression, but her eyes softened when they landed on Thorne. With that white hair, Clarke thought she must be a wolf, and perhaps related. Yes. Clarke knew who she was.

"You're Rush's sister," she said. "Kyra."

Kyra turned her way, narrowed her eyes, and then she said to Leaf, "Are you here to hinder us, or help us?"

Us?

Another figure came through the portal and paused, eyes wide and glued to her. *Rush.* Her stomach flipped. In the short time he'd left her, already her heart sang to see him again. Already she'd forgotten how terrible she'd felt when he simply disappeared. No goodbye. No explanation.

A yawning chasm of the unknown gaped between them. It could be closed with a simple few words, but the thoughts flitting behind his eyes were no sign he was ready to speak. No. He looked furious that she was there. Nostrils flared. Jaw clenched. Tendons at his neck taut.

His anger gave way to confusion as he caught sight of Thorne and Leaf. He closed the portal and then threw a mana-stone on the floor. It bounced and sizzled on the grass, spent.

"What are you doing here, Clarke?" He took a step her way with a growl of frustration. "You should be back at the Order, safe."

"And yet here you are."

"I'm a Guardian." Gold lightning flashed.

"Oh, cut the shit, Rush. I know a con when I see one. You're not here because of some duty to the Well. It's for Thaddeus and Crescent Hollow. Why won't you admit that?"

Why wasn't she good enough for the truth?

He stared at her.

She stared back. "What difference does it make if you tell me the truth? I'm here for the same reason. Why can't you speak plainly for once?"

"Clarke," he ground out. "Get Leaf to make a portal and send you home. Before it's too late."

"You know what?" she laughed. "Maybe if you had told me what you planned from the start, I'd still be there. Did you ever think that?"

To the rest of them, she must look like a crazy woman shouting at thin air, but they all knew who it was. She didn't need to make him visible. And she wasn't sure she was strong enough for them to hear her worst fears come into existence.

"It's not safe here," he said. "For you, or—"

"The baby?" She raised her brows. "Yes, I know. I also know that you conspired with the Prime to be here. But what I don't know is why you're doing it alone. I would have supported you in this. Why not tell me?"

And there it was on his face. The same look he'd given her in the library. The one that had said he'd given up. He didn't expect to come back.

Her face screwed up. Anger, denial, and pain lashed

out. "No! You don't get to do this! I was working on a solution, Goddammit."

She was going to track down that forbidden part of the library. She'd sensed it there. Just a few more days was all she needed. It was the next step. She was good at stealing things. They would never know.

"There is no solution for unsanctioned breeding. This is the second time for me. Véda took the brunt of the punishment before. A mouth for a mouth. That's the law. If I don't die, then you will have to. Do you understand? I may as well do it protecting this village."

"A mouth for a mouth? Is that what the Prime said to get you to do her bidding? She's using you!" she hissed low. "Did she tell you it's her fault the breeding law is still active? The king was going to end it, but she convinced him to keep it. She gave him Jasper as an incentive."

From the way he took the hit of news without a flinch, he already knew. Or he didn't care. He knew his life had been one big manipulation, but he was here anyway. Because it was the right thing to do.

"What did she tell you to get you here?" Clarke pushed.

"She said only one outcome predicted you stayed alive after the birth. I have to make a stand with Kyra and fight for Crescent Hollow."

"Make a stand and fight with Kyra," she repeated the words for the sake of those listening. "And why did that mean keeping secrets?"

"Because... you know why."

"Because you'll die. That's why."

"Clarke," he said, voice flat. "It was always going to end this way."

"Says you!"

"Says everyone." Rush unstrapped the dagger from his belt and held it out to her. "Take it."

"No." She stepped back, throat clogging. "Stay away from me."

But he wouldn't stop coming. The bastard knew she'd asked for his dagger once, and he didn't trust her enough to arm her. Now he was freely giving her one. Coward.

*She* was the coward. She pointed at him. "You're going to leave me."

He stepped closer.

She stepped back. "Without even saying goodbye. Who will hold me at night? Who will keep the nightmares at bay?"

Kyra came up to Clarke. She had something in her hands. Some papers. Or letters. She held them out to Clarke. "These will explain everything."

While her face was full of compassion, her eyes were full of painful understanding. It was a look of shared heartache. She knew what Clarke was going through. What she would go through. Clarke's gaze darted to Leaf and the wolf standing further back... even they looked at her like she was some poor victim.

She was never the victim. But she'd never been alone. First her father, then her girlfriends Laurel and Ada. It was clear to her that she needed to be surrounded by good people. She couldn't stop anything on her own, let alone face an omnipotent black void she couldn't even identify. And now... her hand fluttered to her belly. She had another little life growing inside, one that needed her to be strong.

She didn't want to be like her mother. But what if that was her destiny? All the fight left her, and then her eyes locked onto Rush. "I can't do it without you. I'm not a good person."

"Of course you are."

"I'm not!" She turned to Leaf and Thorne, tears now making her vision blur. "I lied to them to get them here! This whole time it's been you keeping me on the straight and narrow. Not because you're better than me, but because you make me want to be a better person. The moment you're gone... I don't know what I'll do."

"Clarke," he said, all matter of fact. "Everything you've done while I've known you is good. It was you who guided me."

"But you didn't know me in my past life. What if this new me *is* the con? Lying to yourself is the greatest con of all." She wiped her eyes. "Did you know that?"

"I know you." He made it to her side just as Kyra held out the letters. She had no idea her brother was approaching at the same time.

"Read them," Kyra said. "They'll explain a lot. The Prime has been very forthright in her letters."

But there was no chance to read. There was no chance

to blink. Another portal opened behind her, so fast and so bright that heat lanced along her spine. She only had enough time to register the wide, shocked looks on Kyra's and Rush's faces, and then she was pulled back into a vortex. A Void.

# THIRTY-EIGHT

Clarke tumbled to the ground, rolling across a hard and bumpy surface smelling like broken bracken and leaves. The wind knocked out of her. Half-blind from the portal flash, she couldn't see except to register the vague outline of trees, sky and shadows milling about. Ringing in her ears deafened her. The smell of ozone she associated with portals was rife in the air.

This wasn't Crescent Hollow.

She spat out dirt and breathed through the pain in her knees, hands, and side of her face. Nausea rolled in her stomach. She kept it down with a few gulps of air.

The ringing in her ears eased with every breath, but then shouts of battle in her periphery took over.

Horror locked her muscles. The cages at Crescent Hollow. It had been a trap. But who was the prey? Who

406

was the bait? She blinked a few times, and figures came into focus. Kyra. She must have come through the portal too. She had two scimitars out, slicing, parrying, stabbing, locking and twisting. She plowed through two attackers with the skill and force of any Guardian. But then someone who made her skin crawl turned up.

Thaddeus. His scar puckered as he scowled at Kyra from behind. That unadulterated contempt in his eyes. Too busy fighting, Kyra was oblivious to the long sharp bone sword dangling from his hand.

Clarke opened her mouth to warn Kyra, but a croak came out. She coughed and spat out more dirt.

"Behind you!" she shouted, threw her palm out and pushed air with her power. A gust of wind blew at Thaddeus. It tripped him, knocking him into a tree, but wasn't enough to do lasting damage.

Kyra's fierce gaze caught on Clarke. She paused. And then she shifted. Her face elongated. White fur sprouted over her body. But she wasn't fast enough. A stag horned fae—the same one she'd seen at the Laughing Den—hit Kyra over the head with a club. She went down and her shift reversed.

Thaddeus kicked her swords out of the way. "Put her in the cage." His scarred face turned to Clarke. "And put her in too."

Rough arms picked her up from behind. She hadn't noticed anyone behind her. But now she was coming to her senses, she saw her location clearly. They were in the woods. Unless there was another forest full of spindly spooky trees, and dark shadowy light, it was the Whispering Woods.

Trees had been lopped around them to make a clearing. There were tents. Fireplaces. Chairs. It was a camp. This was Thaddeus's hunting party headquarters, and it appeared as though they'd been there for a while. Perhaps months.

But if he had control of Crescent Hollow, why would he need the subterfuge of a camp in the woods? The obvious answer was to keep secrets. But why would he need to do that?

*"We're not allowed to play with the other humans we found, but you're not on the list. It means you're mine."* That's what Thaddeus had said to her the first time they'd met. Coupled with how he'd reacted upon seeing her at the barracks, and how he'd been meeting with Bones... it could mean only one thing. They were working with the humans to hunt humans. Ones Thaddeus was prohibited to play with. Humans who could be useful, like Clarke, frozen from her time only to wake in this time with powers.

If the Prime had schemed and plotted for decades to ensure Clarke was delivered to her, then what would someone else do for another?

The fae dragged her across the soil. Swaying in the wind, one solitary metal cage hung suspended from a tree branch, five feet from the ground.

Metal.

Not wood.

Metal would block her powers and cut her from accessing the Well. The terror of it dawned on her. Even the cages along the walls at Crescent Hollow were wood. They just raised you high enough to cut your access. But Rush had said those would never work on Guardians. Maybe these metal bars were thicker. Stronger.

Was this why Thaddeus had met with the Dark Mage and Bones? They wanted cages strong enough to control the most powerful fae in Elphyne.

She suddenly wished she'd taken that knife from Rush.

"Get off me." She kicked out behind her, but a sharp pain gripped her hair, causing her to cry out. She gritted her teeth and pushed fire backward.

A curse and the stench of smoke meant she'd made her mark, but once again, her power and skill with the elements just wasn't strong enough.

Within seconds, she was at the cage and being pushed through. Her head slammed into the metal bars as they shoved her in. Pain spiked at her temple and white spots danced in her vision. Then it was quickly move to the side or be squashed by the dead weight of Kyra's unconscious body as they shoved her in. Sticky red stained the back of her white hair. Alarmed, Clarke pushed her fingers into Kyra's carotid, but relaxed when she felt a pulse beating strong. She checked Kyra's wound. The bleeding had already stopped. Thank God.

The cage door slammed with a clang.

And... a feeling switched off in her body. As though an organ had been removed, she felt like she'd had something, and now it was gone. But this displacement was nothing compared to how Kyra faired. She moaned and clutched her head. Sweat broke out on her forehead as she started panting. This was more than the injury.

For someone born with the power of the Well, being cut from it was far worse. Kyra trembled, shaking all over.

"Hey," Clarke whispered and squeezed the female's arm. "It will be okay."

"Now, isn't that better?" Thaddeus gloated as he locked the gate with a padlock. He put the key in the pocket of his regal embroidered jacket. Much fancier than what he wore last time. He appeared like a high lord, or a member of the royal court. He must expect a visit from someone important. Where her air blast had knocked him into a tree, a small sliver of blood wiped onto his thumb. His face hardened. "Oh, I'm going to have fun with you."

He walked away and motioned for the fae who'd shoved her in to follow him. Left alone with Kyra, Clarke tried to comfort her, but she was now out cold. It was probably a blessing. Rush had once said being cut from the Well was like the worst hangover you'd ever experience. The square footage of the space wasn't big enough for two people. She had to hold her knees to her chest.

Clarke rested her head between her knees. How did she get into this position? By diving head first without caution. Her mind was awash with all sorts of panicking nonsense.

She took a deep, purposeful breath and exhaled. Then she looked up. Her eyes locked with Rush's.

He was there.

But lying prone on the ground, off to the side near a cluster of trees. Clarke pushed her forehead to the bars to see better.

At the time someone had pulled her through the portal, the rest of the Guardians were flying off scouting around Crescent Hollow, or had been standing too far away. But Rush had been right next to Kyra, and if she'd come through, then he must have done so by grabbing hold of her.

No, he wasn't injured. It was the contact sickness. His face glowed blue. She couldn't spot an inch of clean skin. Coming through the portal had cost him mana. Maybe all of it.

His eyes glittered with pain. Wincing, he reached over his back and unleashed Starcleaver. He held it in his hands as though it would ward off the agony.

"Hold on," he rasped. "Leaf knows... how to... trace portal."

And then he passed out.

# THIRTY-NINE

S he sensed him before she saw him. It was a shifting of the light composition in the woods. A shadow flitting over the sun. The temperature dropped along one side of her body. But he was neither God nor fae. He was a human in a tailored black business suit. Rose in the breast pocket. Standing by the trees, watching.

Gray at his temples sliced into the short black hair slicked from his forehead. Shrewd eyes looked out from an unremarkable middle-aged face.

Now that she'd seen him, and he knew, he moved toward her with a confident stride. Bones followed. No longer in a hooded robe, but wearing a SWAT like tactical outfit. Bulletproof vest. Black fatigues. Guns at her utility belt. Rifle in his hands. He looked like he did back in her time.

For a moment, Clarke needed to pinch herself. She had this surreal feeling that she'd stepped onto a movie set. They were so displaced. That maybe it was a dream. She rubbed her eyes. When she opened them, the Void stood before her cage, studying her. With the cage suspended, they were eye to eye.

"Clarke O'Leary," he said, voice like chills down her spine. "You've been a hard lady to find."

She said nothing and kept her eyes on him, not on Rush still recovering on the ground not far behind him.

"Well," he added with a wry smile. "To be fair, I didn't know I was looking for you until a few weeks ago. Somehow, you avoided the eyes of my Seer. I'm wondering if she didn't want the competition." He shrugged. "I killed her. So I suppose it doesn't matter now, does it? But now I have an opening for a new psychic."

She held her silence. He put his finger on Kyra's white hair and then cocked his head.

"Aren't they strange?" he murmured. "These animals? The more we learn about them, the more it seems to defy logic."

His tone suggested he spoke about a bug. Something he could squash beneath his feet or put under a microscope.

"You know," he said. "When I first awoke in this time and found this new evolution of homo sapiens, at first I was furious. I'd worked my entire life on a plan only to see it turn out differently. They weren't supposed to be here. It was meant to be the humans I'd prepared to live in a bunker, and I was supposed to be their king." He curled a strand of white hair around his finger. "These beasts were living on the land that should have been mine. They ate me out of house and home." He burst out laughing. Like a maniac. But when he came down, the humor had left his eyes. "I was their father. Their creator. If it weren't for me, none of this new evolution would exist. But just like children, there's always a use for the naughty ones."

He tugged on the hair and snapped it off Kyra's head. She cried out. Clarke reached out to soothe her.

And the Void watched it all with unbridled curiosity.

"You like these savages," he said. "You actually identify with them."

She lifted her chin. "From where I'm sitting, the savages are outside the cage."

Something flickered in his gaze, but then he stood back. "When I learned I had been gifted with some"—he looked at his hands—"abilities like these animals, I was pleasantly surprised. I was even happier to learn that this substance from their so-called magic Well of life kept me from aging. It also gave me incredible powers. On the outside, I looked the same, but inside was just as powerful as these immortal fae gods the new human settlement feared. It was so disappointing to see how regressed humans had become. Especially when I left such a detailed plan to keep them thriving." He sighed. "But, I'm a patient man. It was easy to spin a tale about being lost in the wilderness. It was even easier to convince them to install me as their leader and make them forget I didn't age, not like them. But the longer I stayed there, the more I learned of their fear for these beasts you so love. You know they'd tried to take Elphyne once and miserably failed." He shot Clarke a shark-like grin. "But they didn't have me. Or you."

"I'll never work for you."

He laughed. "Oh, we both know that's not true, don't we?"

He gestured to Bones, who left the campsite and came back with Thaddeus. He opened the cage and dragged Kyra out. And then Bones shut the gate, leaving Clarke still inside. She reached through the gaps in the bars.

The Void locked eyes with her. "You've always just needed the right motivation."

Tugging on the cuffs of his suit, he walked back a few steps to where Bones had retrieved him a chair. He sat down and waited.

For what?

Thaddeus pushed Kyra to her knees. She snarled and tried to shift. But the Void made a gesture in the air. Bones lifted his rifle, sighted, changed his mind and then pulled out a handgun from the holster on his hip. He pointed and then squeezed the trigger. A bullet ripped into Kyra's shoulder. She jerked, hit. Her shift halted mid-turn, leaving her face frozen in a state of flux. Half-wolf, half-fae. She was something between and howling in pain.

"You bastard!" Clarke shouted and rattled the cage. "Leave her alone."

415

"Oh, but it's so entertaining. Tell me what you see, Clarke." He gestured at Kyra. "Is that something you can identify with?"

"You're cruel. You're a cruel monster and you need to be exterminated."

"No. I'm a visionary." He tapped his temple. "They think they are ruled by some god of the earth, but we know better from our time, don't we? *We* are the gods. The fae existed once before in our time, but we got rid of them then. We can get rid of them now."

Kyra howled again, but Thaddeus pulled her head back by the segmented ponytail.

"How can you side with them?" Clarke shouted. "How can you do this to your own kind?"

Unguarded hatred and ego spilled out of Thaddeus's narrowed gaze. "My kind are stupid. They let the Order of the Well dictate how they live their life, but it's all been a lie. We need not follow their rules to be powerful. I make my own." He pushed his thumb on Kyra's wound. "No exit wound. The metal inside her prohibits the shift."

Clarke gasped. "That's why you're working with the humans. You want the weapons so you can take over Elphyne."

Thaddeus laughed, and the two humans smiled. The Void looked at Clarke. "Why bother with taking over Elphyne when you can let them destroy themselves?"

Attack themselves?

*The White Woman. The drained Satyr.* There were probably more.

"You're the one who's been making it look like Unseelie are attacking out of their territory."

Bones pulled a glass canister from his belt. It reminded Clarke of the one Rush had used to catch manabeeze. And when Bones walked toward Kyra, Clarke's heart stopped.

"No," she gasped. *Don't you dare.*

But he didn't slice her throat like a warada. He handed the canister to Thaddeus and pulled out a glass syringe, sloshing with metal in the tube. He depressed the needle, testing the pressure, and then jabbed Kyra in the neck.

Liquid metal injected into her veins and she screamed in agony.

"You see what's happening, Clarke?" the Void asked, fascinated. "With iron in her system, and the magic's aversion to the substance, the life force has to go somewhere. It's being forced out." He lifted his palms. "There's nothing special about it. Just science."

Little balls of light popped out of Kyra's chest. Thaddeus held the canister and trapped them as they escaped.

"Stop!" Clarke shouted. "I'll do whatever you want. Just let her go."

The Void nodded and Bones pulled the syringe out of Kyra's neck. The light stopped leaving her body, and Thaddeus screwed the cap on the glass canister. He handed it to the Void, who opened it and drank the contents. Light moved from inside his throat to his chest and then dispersed. Within moments, his pupils contracted. Every aspect of his body language projected bliss. It was like seeing a junkie take a hit. And then other changes happened. The color on his cheeks brightened, the lines on either side of his eyes lessened, and the gray in his hair disappeared altogether. He'd grown younger. He made a satisfied sound and patted his stomach. "Not purified, but I'm sure I'll manage a few memories of a measly female wolf."

"You will destroy the world," Clarke ground out. "I've seen it."

"No, Clarke. You must be mistaken. I will save it," he drawled.

She sat back in the cage and shook her head. He was deluded. Completely unaware that his actions would have devastating consequences. For him. The world. One day, there would be a painful reckoning for him. And she looked forward to being the one to show him the truth. The Prime's machinations made sense. She had told Clarke that truth could be a weapon and now Clarke was finally seeing the possibilities. One day it would come down to Clarke and the Void. Truth against delusion.

"Until then," the Void said, as though he'd read her mind. "I promised Thaddeus here that he could play with you." Then he turned to Thaddeus. "A psychic needs to keep use of her mouth, otherwise she can't speak the future. So just... you know, stay away from that area. Understood?"

Thaddeus nodded, evil eyes never leaving Clarke.

"Good. And when you're done, collect the last remaining mana from the she-wolf. She was tasty. There will be more people Clarke loves coming soon. More we can torture."

His sidekick helped him stumble away, wasted.

# CHAPTER FORTY

D rowning in agony, Rush could do nothing but lie on the dirt and watch as a bullet tore into his sister, and then they injected liquid metal into her system. Some blend of iron he could scent. Then that filthy rotten scum stole and drank her mana.

It was a violation of the highest order and they wouldn't get away with it. None of them. He would hunt them down and rip their innards out first. His inner wolf battered at Rush's restraint, wanting out. It wanted revenge. And he would give it to him.

The pain crippled him, but it gave him time to formulate a plan. He saw in perfect clarity how he would pick up Starcleaver and run them through. They wouldn't even know he was coming. Many long minutes later, Rush pushed onto his trembling hands and knees to breathe through the last remnants of pain. As his senses cleared, he zeroed in on the conversation.

"Until then," the human said. "I promised Thaddeus here that he could play with you." A pause. "A psychic needs to keep use of her mouth, otherwise she can't speak the future. So just... you know, stay away from that area. Understood?

Rush's head snapped up, and he locked eyes on Clarke in the cage. That's why the scum wanted her. For her gift. Control the future, control the world. A world he created. Wide-eyed and full of defiance, she ground her teeth and stared at the man in the black suit as though she could kill him with a look.

But he was too far gone on the mana he'd ingested. He swayed and then said to Thaddeus, "Good. And when you're done, collect the last remaining mana from the she-wolf. She was tasty. There will be more people Clarke loves coming soon. More we can torture."

A snarl ripped from Rush's lips. But he wasn't ready to attack. Not recovered. He had to be error free as he ran his enemies through. Any wrong movement and they'd touch him. He looked down at the bright blue lights twinkling over his hands and reflecting off Starcleaver's blade as it lay between. The weight of understanding settled in his heart. This was it. His last battle. He would make it count.

He lifted his gaze, but the humans were gone, and Thaddeus whispered animosity to Clarke.

"No." Rush pushed to his feet, every muscle and bone aching with each breath. "Stay away from her."

The pain forced him to rest his palms on his knees and catch his breath. But despite his weary body, the wolf inside was ready to go. It howled with indignation. It scratched at its cage. It filled Rush with adrenaline.

*Where were the Guardians?*

Leaf had to find them soon. He had been right there when the portal was opened. Rush just needed to keep Thaddeus at bay for long enough until the Guardians tracked the portal remnants and arrived. But when Thaddeus gave a shrill whistle, and two others from his hunting party returned to the camp, Rush's hope squashed. Three of them. How could he stop three? Kyra still lay on the floor, half shifted, but not dead. If he could get that bullet out of her shoulder, then finishing the shift might be enough to purge the remaining iron from her blood. Hopefully.

"Clarke," he croaked. "The cage isn't strong enough to keep all your power at bay."

Clarke's eyes darted to him, but then shifted back to an indeterminate spot. She didn't want to give him away. But she heard him. "Remember I said the metal cage couldn't hold me? That's why they used a curse?"

She gave a minute nod.

"So reach for your power. All I need is for you to feel enough to get Kyra to see me. Just her. Can you do that?"

Another quick nod, and then her brows drew together

423

in concentration. Rush checked Thaddeus's status. He barked orders at his hunters. They would turn on Clarke and Kyra any second.

*Come on Clarke.*

He couldn't wait any longer.

"Kyra," he croaked.

She moaned but didn't respond.

Gulping air, he tried again. "*Kyra.*"

Rolling to the side, her searching eyes landed on him. If she could get through this, he could too. "Get the bullet out," he said. "Dig into your wound with your claw and scoop it out. Do you understand?" He caught his breath. "It will allow you to shift and heal."

*Shift and heal.* The words stuck in his mind. If he shifted too, the last of the sickness would wash away... but it would also use the very last drop of his mana. Nothing would be left to hold the curse at bay. He'd age.

It might be enough.

"I think this will work better with you out of the cage," Thaddeus said to Clarke. "But we don't want you to cause any trouble."

"I will be nothing but trouble, asshole."

"Very well." Thaddeus paused with the key in the padlock and scanned the camp. "We need something metal to stick into her. It will prevent her from using magic. Bring me something."

The bastards discussed her torture as though ordering

something from the butcher at the markets. They disgusted him. Rush went to pick up his sword—

"Hey, Faddeus," the ram said, coming from the right. He picked up Starcleaver. "What's this?"

*Shit.*

Thaddeus glared at the ram, but when his eyes hit the sword, he froze. "That's my nephew's sword. He's here."

Like a switch being flipped, Rush burst into action. Willing strength into his legs, he launched at the ram. He covered the ram's hands on the hilt, twisted the sword tip to face the ram and then ran him through. To anyone else, it looked like the ram had stabbed himself. He went down to one knee, eyes wide in confusion, blood bubbling at his stomach. He wouldn't have known it was Rush.

"You idiot," Thaddeus snapped. "Find him!"

But the contact sickness doubled. Rush had touched the ram's hands. There had been no other way to control the sword. He collapsed on the ground while the other fae started looking around, stupid enough to check behind tents and chairs. Thaddeus went for the ram. He tugged the blade out of his stomach.

"I have to do everything myself." Thaddeus stood still and searched the clearing, but he didn't have to search far. His eyes landed on Rush and he laughed. "Oh, if you could see you now. All lit up like blue fireworks and crawling like a coward toward your mate."

*He can see me?*

But of course he could. Rush's mana was depleted. That last touch to the ram had tipped him over the edge. The curse was ending. Death waited for him on the other side of the veil. The wolf inside him howled—in fury, in pain, in longing. They could see Clarke. Just out of their reach but the weariness of time dragged him down, and he could barely breathe.

He was starting to age. But with the weakening curse, came access to the Well. He could feel the life of the planet in the ground beneath his touch. The connection wasn't as strong as a sacred place, but it was there. He just didn't have days to replenish his mana stores.

He had to get to Clarke. Whatever he gleaned from the source beneath his fingers, he'd give it to her. She'd broken through the metal cages restrictions enough to make him visible to Kyra. Maybe he could boost her somehow. At the very least, his mana would show her his memories, his feelings, his love. All the things he'd failed to say.

Clarke leaned back in the cage and kicked at the door, trying to get out. "Rush!"

"You're pathetic. Just like your father." Thaddeus stood between Clarke and Rush, a smile splitting his face as he watched Rush crawl to his mate. "You know he crawled too... at the end."

Rush choked and coughed. The blue glyphs moved on his skin as though they, too, heard the horrific confession. *Fuck him.* Rush wouldn't give Thaddeus his last moments. Pushing to his hands and knees, he tried once more to get to Clarke. The air moved in his raw lungs. His throat was sandpaper. His eyes were fire. He'd thought he could do this without her, to end Thaddeus and bring something right back to Crescent Hollow. To build a legacy. But now that he was here, in this moment, all he cared was that he couldn't leave this existence with things not right between them. She was everything.

His entire life had been one long winding path with her at the end.

"Clarke," he croaked. He was almost there.

Thaddeus booted him across the middle, sending him sprawling to the ground. He coughed into the dirt. He didn't have the energy to talk back.

"You didn't hear me." Thaddeus pointed the tip of the blade into Rush's arm and pushed.

White-hot agony lanced down his arm, and he roared in pain.

"I killed your father," Thaddeus clarified. "It wasn't you and your quest to join the Guardians. It was me and my men. I still can't believe how easy you were to fool."

Shock blanched Rush's face, draining the blood.

"Oh yes." Thaddeus grinned. The scar under his eye puckered. "Now you're listening. Well, let me tell you more secrets.... Your mother? I was in her ear every night, telling her to end it. Your lover? The mother of your child? Who do you think paid her to lie with you? Who do you think told her to keep the pregnancy a secret? And that magical monster that needed extermination on the exact day of her execution?" Thaddeus whispered into Rush's ear,

"*Who do you think asked the Order for you to do your Guardian duty?*"

Fury burned and churned in Rush. He'd thought it was all the Prime... but Thaddeus had orchestrated the worst parts of his life. His uncle. Rush couldn't see straight from the vitriolic rage coursing through his veins. The wolf crashed to the surface. Rush could feel his teeth elongating. He growled through fangs, catching Thaddeus in his sight, and he forced his claws to drag his useless, semi-shifting body. Closer. Closer. He pushed Thaddeus back to the cage.

The struggle to keep the wolf in check pushed Rush's control to the limit.

The pleased look on his uncle's face said it all. He thought he'd gotten away with it.

And then Clarke's pale hands poked between the bars of the cage. She swung her favorite strip of torn cloth around Thaddeus's neck, caught it in the other hand, and then yanked hard. It pulled tight across his neck, choking. She put her feet against the bars for purchase and pulled with her weight to garrote.

Seeing her like this, fighting for his honor, for their lives, it gave him the strength to push to his feet.

Taking a life left a stain on one's heart. He wouldn't let Clarke tarnish herself for this. So he did the only thing he could think of. He let the wolf out.

# FORTY-ONE

The grip Clarke had around the garrote slipped. She cried out. No no no. She had to hold on. Even though the pain in her palms felt like she was slicing right through her hands. She would not go down without a fight. This fae was the reason for all the pain in Rush's life.

This evil fae.

White hair pushed through the cage and she bit down, capturing a chunk in her mouth and pulling to keep his head against the bars. It was dirty street tactics. It was disgusting. But she was desperate. It took so much effort to will Kyra to see Rush, and that had been a part of her power she was more confident with. The fire and wind, less so. Nothing was easy behind the metal bars.

And then an unearthly howl pierced her ears. A flash of blue light.

She spat out the hair and looked around Thaddeus's head. What she found wasn't possible. Rush. Not Rush. His wolf. Beautiful. White. Large. Its head came up to Thaddeus's armpits. The wolf's golden eyes met Clarke's. She didn't know how, but she sensed his intention. His plan. As though deep underwater, a calm settled over her. Her breath bloomed. And then she let go.

Thaddeus threw up his hands. He faced Clarke, as though she could somehow help him.

"Please..." he rasped.

Clarke looked him straight in the eyes and said, "Oh yes, you'll beg. You'll beg right up until the end. Cowards always do."

And then the wolf attacked. She shut her eyes so she didn't have to watch. She blocked her ears so she didn't have to hear. And when she thought it was safe, she looked again.

Thaddeus was hidden from view, somewhere beneath the cage. And Rush... he was still in wolf form, head on the ground, tongue hanging out of his bloody jaws, panting.

"Rush," she cried and wrapped her fingers around the bars.

Somewhere behind them, another fight was happening. Kyra had managed a full shift. She was in the corner eating something... or someone.

"Hold on, Rush." She spotted Thaddeus's key, still in the lock. "I'm coming. Just hold on."

Tears burned her eyes as she fumbled with the key. And

when it dropped, the tears flowed over. She reached out, grasped air, but caught nothing. The key bounced on the dirt. Collapsing to the base of the cage, she dangled an arm through the bars, just like she remembered the pixie doing. The other hand, she placed over her womb.

"Rush..."

She squeezed her eyes shut. This couldn't be it. No. Please no.

"I love you," she whispered.

Now the tears were big, wracking sobs. Goddamn this world. Goddamn it for giving her everything and then taking it away. She wanted to scream. To hurl curses at the wind. But then a wet, warm pressure pushed into her palm. She looked down. It was the wolf's nose. He lifted his head, got to his paws, and touched her. One last time.

"I love you, you stupid fae." She cupped his muzzle. "You're so beautiful."

He whined.

A spark zipped from his body to hers. Power. Light. Life. Mana. It ripped into her body, wrapped around her heart, swirled around the life they'd created, and settled bone deep. Suddenly, she could feel him as though he were a part of her. She could sense his emotions. Knew he was there. A burning sensation itched along the part of her arm dangling out. It started small, like a tickle, and then built to an inferno in a way she'd never felt before. Blue light leaked from her pores in ripples of light. It enveloped the wolf. Sparked in his eyes. And then wrapped around both of them at once.

A bond snapped into place.

And through that bond, Clarke felt Rush's emptiness. He'd drained his mana stores, so she filled it up. She gave him energy. It wasn't much. The cage weakened her, but with her arm outside of the barrier and free, she sensed a sliver of the cosmic energy holding their planet together. The Well.

Rush had been right.

It wasn't something she could find. It had to find her. To find them. And it had been waiting.

Slowly Rush's wolf strengthened its touch at her hand. Tears spilling from Clarke's eyes turned joyful because the blue light that had leaked from her pores turned into a pattern along her forearm and hand. It reminded her of contour lines on a geographical map. The evidence was right there—the marking of a Well-blessed union.

The air around Rush shimmered, blistered, and then he shifted into his fae form. Naked as the day he was born, and with his own Well-blessed marking, he reached through the cage and pulled her lips to the gap. Mashed together between the bars, they kissed. Embarrassing sounds came out of Clarke as she cried and whimpered. He was okay. There were no curse marks on his body. He was young. Alive. This was it.

"I don't know if you heard me as a wolf, but I love you, Rush."

"I think I've loved you since the first time I carried you in my arms," he whispered, forehead on the bars.

"But that was so long ago."

"The heart wants what it wants."

She brushed his beard with her knuckles. "How? I mean, you said a Well-blessed union was instantaneous."

"I don't know. I think... I think because the curse cut me from the eternal Well, it couldn't approve of our union. It had to wait until the last of my mana was spent, and the end of the curse triggered. With nothing blocking that connection anymore, the last piece of the puzzle clicked into place when you said you loved me."

"The Prime. She knew. It's why she—"

Rush kissed her. "Doesn't matter. I used to think her manipulations mattered." His eyes softened, taking her in. "I don't need a blessed union to tell me I love you. I did that on my own."

"As did I."

He pulled away and picked up the fallen key. Two seconds later she was out and in his arms. They only had time for a small reunion, and then a portal ripped into being at the center of the camp. Bright light flashed, blinding them all. When it all came into perspective, the Guardians were there.

A white wolf. Three avenging winged fae. And a furious looking elf.

"You're late," Rush said.

# FORTY-TWO

From the moment Thorne stepped through the portal and found the bloody destruction waiting, he knew the battle wasn't over. The scent of fresh blood burned his sensitive wolf nose. Three bodies, two beyond comprehension. One still writhing from a sword wound in the shoulder. But the most arresting thing of all was seeing his father, curse free, and in a passionate embrace with his mate—no, *Well-blessed* mate.

It had been Clarke all along. A human.

The matching blue contours rippling up their arms proved it.

Seeing his father happy tied Thorne into all sorts of knots. A part of him saw how they loved each other, how the Well had approved, and something twisted inside. It wasn't hate. It wasn't jealousy. It was... an emptiness waiting to be named.

After arriving, the Guardians had spent the following hour canvasing the area, looking for further threats. Rush had mentioned there were humans who'd worked with Thaddeus. And the secrets he'd revealed were disturbing. Thorne had listened to it all from within the confines of his wolf form. Somehow, being on four paws made the truth easier to handle.

He couldn't see the Order staying out of it now. Not when the threat to the integrity of the Well was so glaringly obvious.

This was war.

And other secrets were revealed. About Thorne's mother. How she'd been paid by Thaddeus. It wasn't as though he'd thought his parents loved each other, but the truth had cast the situation into new light. How could he be angry at Rush for the part he played?

He couldn't.

But he *was* angry. That part hadn't changed. He just had no one to direct his rage at. So he would filter it into finding Jasper. He would find the missing wolf, and then fight this war he'd never asked to be part of.

Pacing by the campfire someone had set up, even though it was midday, Thorne decided he'd waited long enough. Someone had found a blanket and cast it over Rush's shoulders. He pulled a corner to cover both he and his mate. They spoke in low, hushed voices to each other while Leaf and the remaining crew who hadn't gone back to the Hollow were doing last sweeps of the area.

Thorne shifted from wolf to fae form, and then went over. Rush stiffened. Clarke made a point to stare at his face and not the naked half of him most females enjoyed.

"Rush. Clarke." He nodded.

She broke free and before Thorne knew it, she hugged him. Going tense all over, he looked to Rush with wide eyes. "What...?"

Rush smirked. "Let her have it."

The redhead lifted her gaze, eyes glistening with tears. Thorne frowned.

"Thank you," Clarke said.

Both Rush's and Thorne's eyebrows winged up. She didn't. Oh, yeah. She did.

"And before either of you rub in the fact I said thank you. I don't care. I'll say it again."

"Why?" Thorne asked.

Clarke stepped back to see him better. "Because in the end it was you who said you wanted to come to Crescent Hollow to help Anise. Leaf told me you were the first to get her, and the rest of them, down from the cages."

A weird feeling rolled in Thorne's chest. "I was just doing my job."

"Ah," Clarke laughed. "But you see, it wasn't doing your job. Anise is alive and recovering because of you. So thank you. This is me telling you that when you need something in return from me, I'll be here."

"Within reason." Rush held out his finger.

All three of them stared at each other, no more words coming to mind.

*Well, this is awkward.*

He turned to leave.

Clarke took hold of his wrist. "Wait."

She opened her mouth to speak, but no words came out. Her irises turned white and seemed to go somewhere else as the Seeing vision took her in its grip. With a gasp, she let go of Thorne and her eyes returned to normal.

"I lied," she said. "When I told you I could help you find Jasper at the Order."

"I know," he growled. "I heard your confession at Crescent Hollow."

"Well. The thing is... after touching you, just now, I saw something new."

Thorne tensed. "What did you see?"

"I saw the person who will lead you to Jasper." She bit her lip and slid a look to Rush.

"Whatever it is, you can tell me," Thorne said. "I promise I won't bite your head off."

Right now. Maybe later. If she lied again.

"Okay," Clarke replied. "It's just that... the person who will lead you to him is a human from my time. A woman."

Thorne folded his arms, chewing over the scenario in his mind. Okay. It wasn't so bad. Clarke had turned out... semi-bearable. And she was loyal. Strong-willed. A good mate for his father. He supposed.

"That's fine," he said. "Where do I find her?"

"She won't thaw for some time, but... there's more."

He growled, "And?"

"And," she flinched, "Never mind."

He narrowed his eyes at her. She was clearly hiding something. And it festered already in his mind. These humans, even the ones imbued with power, were tricky creatures. They lied as easy as breathing. It was enough to make him sick.

Rush must have seen the fire in his eyes, because his alpha energy swelled, brushing down Thorne's front in warning.

"Enough," Rush said to him. "When it's time, she will tell you."

"Jasper might not have time."

"He does. It's all he has." Clarke cuddled into Rush, her expression turning melancholy.

Thorne opened his mouth—

"Thorne." Rush's deep voice cut through the night. "I know you don't want to hear this, but I've always tried to be there for you. Being a Guardian was forced on you. If you want to leave, I will support your decision. When it comes time to go on the hunt, I will be right there next to you. Until you're ready to accept that, I need to be with my mate."

Rush lifted Clarke in his arms and carried her to where Leaf stood with Shade, discussing the containment of the area.

"Where are you going?" Thorne asked.

The only reply was something mumbled about a cabin. And when Leaf activated a portal, the two of them went through on their own.

Just before the portal closed, Clarke shouted to him, "We'll talk soon."

And then they were gone.

# FORTY-THREE

With the moon lighting the way, Clarke held Rush tightly as he carried her across the snowy shore of the lake near his cabin. Icy air nipped at her skin, but he shrugged the blanket from his shoulders and kept walking. Straight into the warm water. As the level hit his knees, he sank down. She gasped as they immersed in the heat. Steam curled between them. It was like a bath. A glorious bath. With deft, strong hands, he positioned her so she straddled his front, until it was just the two of them staring into each other's eyes.

She wiped silver hair from his furrowed brow. He was here. He was safe. He was alive. The emotion was too much for her fragile heart to contain and she felt it slide down their bond. She still marveled at how his injury healed when he shifted into a wolf. She'd seen Thaddeus stab him, but where the sword had entered his arm, only a pink scar remained. She lightly traced her finger around it, and then slid her hands over his shoulders to massage the hard knots on his back.

The long, guttural groan that came out of him rattled Clarke to the core, setting her pulse on fire.

"Feel better?" she purred.

Two eyes shuttered. His brows lifted in the middle as his body lost tension. Hands gripped her hips and pushed down, proving that not all parts of him had relaxed. He hardened beneath her and lifted his hips brazenly to prove it. A small moan slipped out of her.

"Yeah. Feels better," he muttered. "Mate. Mine."

She smiled. "Mate. I like that."

His eyes opened. Clashed. And he growled, "*Well-blessed* mate. The first in centuries. Us." Humor fled as his gaze turned smoldering. He lowered it to the luminescent blue markings twirling her arm. And then the mirror markings on his. Suddenly, Clarke couldn't breathe. His love fed down their bond, gushing like a tidal wave. Electricity rippled across the water. Wind buffeted their hair, tickling her skin. There was something in the air, in the water that... that was alive.

"Can you feel it?" she whispered, looking around in awe. Tree top shadows rustled against the gray sky. The wind whispered. The water swirled and eddied... and little sparks of bioluminescent blue swam about their bodies in a lazy dance. Her breath hitched. "What is it?"

"This lake is a source of power," he said, voice hoarse.

"It's welcoming us. Here we can replenish our mana faster than from the land. But it's not only the lake feeding me, refilling me. I feel your power through our bond, seeping into my body, making me whole. I feel your love. I feel..." He snarled and cupped her face with his hand, forcing her gaze back to his. Dark pupils dilated... almost helpless. "I feel..."

And then she saw it. It wasn't the world around them she was feeling. It was Rush. His power. His spark. Everything his curse had blocked was now coming back. At the academy, he'd mentioned he could control the elements as well as shift into wolf. When she'd first met him, she likened him to a storm. And now a storm raged around them. Swirling wind. Sparks skipping over his shoulders. Electricity in the air. Thunder crashing. All from him. And here he was, tense and full of energy, eyes and skin barely containing the tempest crackling within.

"This is you," she whispered. "The real you."

"This is what you do to me. This is us."

His lips crashed against hers. Tongue pushed into her mouth. He deepened the kiss with a shuddering groan. So much feeling bursting in her chest. Falling. Falling. She was drowning in his scent, his emotion, his heat.

Frenzy came over them. She couldn't get close enough, and he couldn't touch her enough. Her clothes? What clothes. They were gone. Only the sundial on the leather cord remained. The rest had simply burned off. Disintegrated. It had been him. His magic. She knew from his

443

wicked smile. His male satisfaction, and the possessive thrust of his cock into her now unimpeded entrance.

She gasped and fell back until her head landed on the water, eyes on the star filled sky. Reveling in the way he filled her completely, she yielded to his passion because it felt like her own. There was no way to tell where it ended or began. Strong hands braced her back and kept her afloat, while he slid into her from beneath. Hot lips trailed down her front. Fire skipped over her body, electrifying every nerve ending. He pulled her nipple into his mouth, growling around her flesh. "Mine, Clarke. You're mine."

She didn't need to speak, just feel, and he knew how much she loved him. The sensations hurtling through her body were almost too much. She felt his desire. He felt hers. They shared their very life-force. They were more than married. More than mates. They were one.

And they would be unstoppable.

SOMETIME LATER, Clarke cuddled Rush within his cabin. Lying on the bed, a fire crackling in the hearth, they couldn't let go of each other. The sprites were happy to see them, and danced in the flames.

But her stomach rumbled.

Rush pushed up onto his forearms. His laughing eyes landed on her stomach and then he pressed his ear to her womb.

"Is the little wolf hungry?" he asked.

She laughed and stroked his hair. "How do you know it will be a wolf? Maybe it will stay human."

He sat up, a serious look on his face. "Any babe this ravenous is surely a wolf."

"Yeah, okay. Whatever you say, Dad."

His expression turned somber, and he laid back to stare at the canopy of leaves branching across the cabin ceiling. She felt his guilt spear through their bond. With a gentle pat on his chest, she rolled to face him and rested on her elbow.

"Thorne will come around," she said.

He shrugged.

"He will," she insisted. "He has his own journey to go on first. Remember I mentioned my friend? The one who will lead him to Jasper? She's going to be his Well-blessed mate. I just didn't want to let him know. Somehow, I don't think he'll be receptive to a mating not of his choosing, and to be honest, she's not going to be happy either."

Rush turned to her, eyes hard. "There will be more unions like ours?"

She nodded. "I think many more. And for every one I find thawed from my time, there will be a Guardian as their mate. I think it's for a reason."

"Because you give me power. Power unlike any I've felt before." He rolled onto her, and crowded her with his strength. Muscles bulged. Tendons flexed. She had no doubt he would be lethal, dangerous, deadly. As if reading

LANA PECHERCZYK

her mind, he gave her a smile that displayed sharp wolf-like fangs. "With your mana replenishing mine through our bond, I feel invincible."

She bit her lip. It was like she was Rush's battery. His personal source of power. "Our ability to transfer power will come in handy when the war finally hits."

"Then we will be ready when it is time." He arched a hesitant brow. "When will that be?"

"Hopefully, if we keep fighting, it will never be time. But if you're referring to when will I need to go and find the next person from my time? Not for a few years."

He loosed a breath. "Good. I want to be alone with you first. Time without the pressure of fate scratching at our door."

A scratching came at the cabin door. Their eyes widened. And then a wolf whined outside.

Rush returned her grin. "Gray must be hungry too."

A lifetime of manipulation, machination, and sheer joy had brought Rush to this—sitting by his lake, watching a half nude woman wading in the shallows, hunting for pebbles. She was beautiful. Still. The same as the day he'd first laid eyes on her. And still, he leered like a horny teen.

He doubted he'd ever stop.

"What do you think," he mumbled to the cooing toddler wriggling on the blanket next to him. He tickled the child's stomach. "Does she look good enough to eat?"

She giggled and rolled on the blanket, trying to fight her way from Rush, but he caught her and dragged her back to him. Named aptly for the place of Rush's and Clarke's first kiss, Willow had redefined Rush's definition of life. Even though she was yet to shift into a wolf and prove her daddy proud, Willow had carved out new places in Rush's heart.

A yip came from Rush's right, and Gray came bursting out of the forest, followed by his own litter of new pups. Three little white and gray wolves chased him into the water, where they stayed, barking and yipping from the shore. Gray pranced around Clarke, splashing in the shallows. Rush hadn't thought the old wolf had it in him to rear another brood, but there he was, eyes lit up with new life.

In the past two years since Clarke had been in this time, the weather had warmed. The snow was gone from the mountains. For now. She said it would be back next year.

But Gray and his pack had stayed. The damned sprites had stayed. Even Thorne had begrudgingly visited a handful of times. Granted, each time had been to push for information on when they'd find Jasper, but he'd come. And each time the gap between them had closed just a little.

Kyra had established herself in Crescent Hollow as the new Lady Nightstalk. She was doing it on her own. No alpha mate to join her. But she had friends. Anise, Clarke's barmaid friend had also made a full recovery and supported Kyra's leadership, along with most of the town.

A trickle of unease traveled down their mating bond to Rush. Clarke patted Gray's old head. She pulled out the sundial on the cord around her neck, checked the time and then squinted his way. He knew that look.

Their blissful break was over. Things were about to change.

*The End.*

*Thank you for reading Clarke's and Rush's story. I hope you liked their journey. Please consider leaving a review online to share the love. Thorne's and Laurel's story is next.*

*Lana*

*xx*

# NEED TO TALK TO OTHER READERS?

## BOOKS ARE OUR LIFE!

Join Lana's Angels Facebook Group for fun chats, giveaways, and exclusive content. https://www.facebook. com/groups/lanasangels

# ABOUT THE AUTHOR

**OMG! How do you say my name?**

**Lana** (straight forward enough - Lah-nah) **Pecherczyk** (this is where it gets tricky - Pe-her-chick).

I've been called Lana Price-Check, Lana Pera-Chick-ywack, Lana Pressed-Chicken, Lana Pech...*that girl!* You name it, they said it. So if it's so hard to spell, why on earth would I use this name instead of an easy pen name?

To put it simply, it belonged to my mother. And she was my dream champion.

For most of my life, I've been good at one thing – art. The world around me saw my work, and said I should do more of it, so I did.

But, when at the age of eight, I said I wanted to write stories, and even though we were poor, my mother came home with a blank notebook and a pencil saying I should follow my dreams, no matter where they take me for they will make me happy. I wasn't very good at it, but it didn't matter because I had her support and I liked it.

She died when I was thirteen, and left her four daughters orphaned. Suddenly, I had lost my dream champion, I was split from my youngest two sisters and had no one to talk to about the challenge of life.

So, I wrote in secret. I poured my heart out daily to a diary and sometimes imagined that she would listen. At the end of the day, even if she couldn't hear, writing kept that dream alive.

Eventually, after having my own children (two fire-crackers in the guise of little boys) and ignoring my inner voice for too long, I decided to lead by example. How could I teach my children to follow their dreams if I wasn't? I became my own dream champion and the rest is history, here I am.

When I'm not writing the next great action-packed romantic novel, or wrangling the rug rats, or rescuing GI

Joe from the jaws of my Kelpie, I fight evil by moonlight, win love by daylight and never run from a real fight.

I live in Australia, but I'm up for a chat anytime online. Come and find me.

*Subscribe & Follow*
subscribe.lanapecherczyk.com
lp@lanapecherczyk.com

facebook.com/lanapecherczykauthor
instagram.com/lana_p_author
amazon.com/-/e/B00V2TP0HG
bookbub.com/profile/lana-pecherczyk
tiktok.com/@lanapauthor
goodreads.com/lana_p_author

# Also by Lana Pecherczyk

**The Deadly Seven**

*(Paranormal/Sci-Fi Romance)*

The Deadly Seven Box Set Books 1-3

Sinner

Envy

Greed

Wrath

Sloth

Gluttony

Lust

Pride

Despair

**Fae Guardians**

*(Fantasy/Paranormal Romance)*

*Season of the Wolf Trilogy*

The Longing of Lone Wolves

The Solace of Sharp Claws

Of Kisses & Wishes Novella (free for subscribers)

The Dreams of Broken Kings

*Season of the Vampire Trilogy*

The Secrets in Shadow and Blood

A Labyrinth of Fangs and Thorns

A Symphony of Savage Hearts

**Game of Gods**

*(Romantic Urban Fantasy )*

Soul Thing

The Devil Inside

Playing God

Game Over

Game of Gods Box Set